STILL YOU

ALSO BY CLAIRE ALLAN

Acknowledgements

This book has been a very personal journey for me – but it was one I could not have embarked on without the support of my family, who encouraged me to write a story which would shine a light on Alzheimer's. It was a big responsibility – and I can only hope that I have done our family proud.

In addition, I would like to very sincerely thank Michael McIvor, formerly of the Foyle Alzheimer's Society, who over the past number of years has invited me to speak with many families living with dementia and allowed me the very great privilege of telling their stories. The many insights I have received over the year, and the support of Michael in always being there at the end of the phone when I had a query, has been invaluable.

On an even more personal note, this book was written and edited during a particularly trying time for me health-wise and I cannot sufficiently thank those family and friends who supported me when I could not support myself. To Mammy and Daddy, my siblings, my friends, thank you for your endless support – practical, emotional and at times physical. Hopefully we are on the up now!

To my husband and children – I love you more than words can say. Thank you for allowing me the time to escape into an imaginary world and for teaching me about love.

A special word of thanks must go to my writing friends, including the Poolbeg girls, for their constant cheerleading from the corners, and to my long-term trusted friend Fionnuala Kearney. Fionnu, you know how challenging this last year has been but you have not allowed me to give up – and you always know the right thing to say to get me back at the keyboard. I am so delighted to see you get the recognition you so richly deserve.

Thanks to Paula Campbell for putting her faith in yet another Claire Allan title and to Gaye Shortland for services to editing which went above and beyond the call of duty!

As always, thanks to my agent Ger Nichol – who never allows me to stop believing in myself, even for one moment.

And to you, lovely reader. You are never, ever taken for granted. Thank you sincerely for reading and allowing me to share these stories with you. It is a huge honour.

For my grandmother, Anna Davidson, for the love we will always remember

&

For those who care for her with such compassion, in particular my Auntie Lorraine – who I love and respect with all my heart

Prologue

Charlotte says I always have my head in the clouds. She calls me 'Dolly Daydream' – says "Áine, you never pay attention to what is going on around you".

She says I must live in some pretty fanciful worlds in my head – I imagine she thinks I spend my days dreaming of movie stars and a big house in Hollywood or something really glamorous. She says I would do well to get my nose out of books and into newspapers – see what is really going on in the world. See what is out there – what I can have if I want it.

But I don't want to. I don't daydream about things I know I'll never have and, if I'm honest, I don't want. For sisters we are like chalk and cheese. Charlotte has the wanderlust and I'm a home bird. I always have been – and I don't see it changing. When I disappear into my daydreams I think about the life I will lead – right here. Of the men I'll kiss. The man I'll marry. The children we will have and what we will call them. I dream of knitting a soft white Christening shawl, lacing the edges with ribbon and wrapping our baby in it.

I dream of days at the beach with my family at my feet –

1

long, hot, stuffy train rides out of the town, followed by sandwiches wrapped in brown paper on an itchy blanket by the sea. If I close my eyes for long enough – and if Charlotte gives me peace for long enough – I can almost feel the warm breeze wash over me and I can almost hear the gentle crashing of the waves.

Maybe I'm silly. My ambitions aren't grand. I just want a husband, a family, to push a pram, to run my house. Charlotte wants to travel the world. She says women don't need a man to make them happy. She will only get married if a man looks like Rock Hudson and sweeps her off her feet and has the same wanderlust she has. It makes me feel sad sometimes – that she wants to leave. I can't imagine this house without her in it – but she'll never stay, just as I'll never go. And that's okay.

When I Grow Up
By Georgina Wright, Aged 9 and 2/3rds
Summer 1985

When I grow up I will work two jobs. I will be a nurse during the week and at weekends an air hostess so I can see the world. I will always wear pink nail polish and my hair will be yellow. I will wear high heels which clip and clop when I walk. I will get married to a man called Chris or Steve and live in a house with a big garden and a swimming pool. I will have three babies – two girls and a boy – and I will have my ears pierced.

Chapter 1

"Did you ever see that picture on Facebook? One of those e-card things – the funny ones. It says '*I miss being the age where I thought I would have all my shit together by now*'?"

Sinéad snorted and sipped from her wineglass. "I don't think I have – but I like it."

"Well, that," I said, "is pretty much how I feel now. I really, truly thought that by the time thirty-nine reared its head I would have it all in place. You know, like that article I wrote for the primary-school magazine?"

"Where you wanted to be a nurse during the week and travel the world at the weekends?"

"Yes . . . that one. I pretty much thought I would be there by now."

"You do wear shoes that clip *and* clop when you walk," Sinéad said with a smile. "And your ears are pierced . . ."

"But I'm not jet-setting, am I? My weekends are spent doing the grocery-shopping and cleaning the house. Not to mention the occasional bout of weeping with loneliness." I pulled a face which I hoped conveyed the message that, while

I wanted her to feel sorry for me, I did not want to appear to be a miserable cow who felt sorry for herself. I wanted to pretend to be one of those women who laughs at her own misfortune – all 'look at me, I can cope even when it's all going south'.

"You have a lovely home. You have two lovely, if occasionally challenging, teenage daughters and you have wine," Sinéad offered, shaking a bottle of white in my direction in the universal sign language for 'want a top-up?'.

I shook my head and put my hand over the top of my glass. "I'm fine," I said. "I suppose I'm just feeling old. You know, I saw Louise from our class in school in town today."

"Ah, did you?" Sinéad asked, topping her own glass up.

"She's great, I think. But she looks . . . she looks grown up. You know, like a proper adult. Like a mammy. We don't look like proper grown-ups, do we? In my head we're still twenty-five – or early thirties at the very most. We don't look grown up."

Sinéad laughed. "I think we look amazing. Of course we don't look thirty-nine!"

I smiled back. "I bet Louise has it all together. I bet she wears pink nail polish and travels at the weekends."

"I bet she sits around in her pyjamas binge-watching *Real Housewives* like the rest of us."

"Sinéad, you have never sat around and binge-watched anything. Two episodes in a row is not proper binge-watching. You have to watch the seasons change without shifting off the sofa to properly qualify. You know, I shouldn't really be having this conversation with you – you are the 'have-it-all friend' that I would hate if I didn't love you so much."

"Have it all?" she grinned.

"You have a bespoke kitchen," I offered weakly. "One you ordered yourself and which didn't just come with your house. Your dinner sets match – not like the mismatched collection you get in my house. For the love of God, the twins are almost sixteen and we're still eating off melamine plates! Your bed sheets are Egyptian cotton and not Primark's finest and you drive a car which can be described much more favourably than my 'skip on wheels'." I laughed again, but I was sure there was a more hollow tone to it.

"You're in a bad place tonight, aren't you?" Sinéad said. "What prompted this? The silly Facebook card? Seeing Louise from school? Because she always looked freakishly old anyway. Remember, we used to send her to the off-licence for us? Everyone did."

I took a deep breath and said the words I hadn't wanted to say out loud until now because saying them out loud made them real and I was definitely not sure I could handle them being real.

"Matthew is seeing someone," I said, not meeting her eye and reaching across the table to grab the bottle of wine I had previously shunned, to top my glass up.

"No!" she exclaimed. "You're not serious?"

"Well ... I think so. I don't have conclusive proof but the girls were at his house at the weekend. When they came home they were quiet – which as you know is not like my girls at all. Eventually I was able to break Sorcha's silence and she told me they had found a pink bra amongst their father's laundry when they were helping him to tidy up."

"And they're sure it's not one of theirs?" Sinéad asked, parroting what I had asked Sorcha myself.

Sorcha had raised one perfectly drawn-on eyebrow at me and told me she was sure she would know if she owned a lurid, pink, lacy bra with strategically placed holes in the cups.

When I relayed this to Sinéad, she got up, turned her back to me and I watched her head disappear into her drinks cupboard.

"Before we go any further," I heard, "it has to be said that we need a bigger boat ..." She turned around and sat a bottle of tequila on the island. She quickly produced two shot glasses, salt and started to slice a lemon. "So … shit … a lacy pink bra? I'm assuming they didn't ask him about it? What did they say to you? Did they really mention strategically placed holes?"

She grimaced as she asked – and I grimaced as I heard the words again. It all seemed so very sordid. Matthew was my husband – or ex-husband, or maybe-ex-husband – and the thought of him getting up close and personal with anyone wearing lurid underwear made me feel nauseous.

I took a deep breath, and eyed the tequila suspiciously. Tequila and I were not traditionally good bedfellows. "No, they didn't ask him. They just told me what they found. And they were mortified, absolutely mortified, about the bra – and to their credit they blushed a lot. I can't really ask him about it, can I? Is it my business? I mean, we are separated. Although when he suggested a trial separation I didn't think that meant he would want to try different things – things which didn't include me …"

Sinéad pushed the glass towards me over the kitchen island and took a deep breath.

I knew she felt conflicted. She wasn't a member of the Matthew Casey fan club and was never likely to be – but for me she had maintained a respectful silence over the years. Even when we had separated – at his suggestion, it has to be said – on the premise that it would allow us to see how we felt apart. Because, he said, we *had* been together since we were sixteen and he was worried he might have missed out on life. It was probably just a mid-life crisis of sorts, he had laughed. A small one. Nothing serious. Just the chance for a bit of space. Sure we didn't have much time for each other these days anyway and wasn't it better – before we entered our mid to late years together – to know we really, really still loved each other and weren't just together out of habit?

I had been stunned by the conversation – but Matthew had a way of talking, a Jedi mind-trick kind of skill, which had me nodding in agreement as he spoke even though there was a tiny voice, buried deep inside, screaming for a celestial pause-and-rewind button.

But he had left – and I had, for a while, really believed he would come back in a matter of a few weeks telling me he realised how good he had it.

Sinéad had tried to prepare me for what might happen, but of course I had pushed her concerns away and she hadn't pushed me harder to pay attention. She knew that the one way to put me offside was to launch an all-guns-blazing attack on my husband. She had done that once, when the twins were small and he was being a feckless eejit, and I had gone on the defensive and our friendship had been severely dented for a few months.

"Well, if he's leaving items like that around for the girls to see, you could ask him that way?" Sinéad finally said. "Play the concerned mother? I mean, it isn't the most appropriate thing he could be doing. But you have to ask yourself if you are ready for the answer."

I threw back the shot of tequila, the warm amber liquid burning the back of my throat. It hit me just how much I hated the taste of tequila and I reached for my glass of wine to wash it down before spluttering as I tried to catch my breath. Sinéad, who had followed my lead, was expertly sucking on her slice of lemon like a pro without a hint of a splutter or cough. I *knew* she had it all together.

"I think I know the answer," I told her when I composed myself. "But I think I can live without having it confirmed just yet."

I supposed I needed to get my head around what I wanted from him. I never thought we would break up. I thought we would be one of those smug couples who sit holding hands on their fiftieth wedding anniversary, nodding and saying they have been together since they were sixteen. That their marriage worked because they made it work *blah blah blah* and young ones today give up too easy.

Also there was that huge, massive, all-encompassing fear of being single and being out there again. Being the kind of woman who looked like a proper grown-up – like Louise from school – but who had to bother herself with buying pink bras which were sexy and exceptionally uncomfortable. My poor nipples shuddered at the thought.

"More tequila?" Sinéad offered.

I shook my head, my stomach turning. "You know, I should probably head on. I have a new client tomorrow and I want to be in top form for her. Mrs Brightly says she's some big name – or her family is or something – and they're high maintenance, so I'd better put my best foot forward and not smell of intoxicating liquor."

"You know how much I admire you," Sinéad said. "I'm not sure I could do what you do – looking after the elderly and infirm."

"It has its moments. Not as glam a life as the editor of a magazine, I'm sure," I said with a smile. "But rewarding in its own way." I glanced at the clock – it was past nine o'clock and I knew the following day would be a busy one. Maybe I *was* getting old – after all, there was a time when I could manage on a few hours' drunken sleep and still function relatively well the next day with the assistance of caffeine, a Mars Bar and a couple of Nurofen. But now I knew my limits.

"Right, pet, I'd better make the long walk down the street," I winked. "Tomorrow waits for no woman."

In the hall I slipped my coat on and opened the door to a cool spring evening. When I turned to hug Sinéad, she pulled me close and gave me a tight squeeze.

"You know, I don't think anyone ever feels like they have it all together – and I know this sounds all Oprah or Dr Phil – but you are a strong woman and you *will* get through whatever happens. Chin up – if nothing else, it makes your wrinkles look smaller."

I hadn't always worked. I was never what you would call a career woman. Matthew and I had married young – at twenty-one – thinking we knew all there was to know about love. I had worked a series of jobs while Matthew had gone to university, qualified as a teacher and worked his way up the career ladder. He was now the very respectable principal of a local primary school while I had only returned to the workforce two years ago. At that stage the girls had been older, well settled into secondary school, and no longer keen on school pick-ups from their mother at the end of each day – they would much rather travel home in an overcrowded bus where they could gossip with their friends and they didn't like me cramping their style when they got in. That wasn't to say they were horrible teens who cringed every time they were forced to be in my company – they were good girls. I just hadn't factored in their social scene and as they grew they craved my company less – so I had decided to take on a job, something part-time which got me out of the house. Matthew had told me I didn't need to – but the truth was, I wanted to. I was thirty-seven – still young (on paper anyway) and it was dawning on me that the girls wouldn't be around forever and, when they were gone and Matthew was still working, I would have little to amuse me bar repeats of *Homes Under the Hammer* and housework. And I wasn't the biggest fan of housework (hence my mismatched dinnerware and my decidedly unorganised kitchen). I was never the kind of woman who could be a lady who lunches – who could swap the school run for Pilates in the health centre and mornings lost over a half-fat latte in Starbucks talking bikini-waxes, tiger-parenting and being a surrendered wife or whatever fad was doing the rounds. I never really fitted in with the school-gate crowd. The 'yummy mummies' tended to be older, swathed in pashminas, expensive make-up and wearing designer boots, while I was always rushing in last minute in a pair of battered trainers without a scrap of make-up on my face – often looking more like the girls' scruffy older sister than the wife of the local school principal. I didn't have fashion tips to share with them and I wasn't interested in listening to PTA gossip, so more often than not I slipped away as quickly as I could before they could ambush me.

So when I applied for, and got, a job as a care assistant for Brightly Care Ltd I was delighted, if nervous. Matthew had shown the appropriate pleased-for-me response – and had even complimented my uniform – which was going above and beyond the call of all marital duty, There was little to compliment in the elasticated-waist trousers and flat, non-slip shoes which lacked grace and made my feet look clown-like. He even packed me a small lunch on my first day, even though, at first, the job was just for four hours a day and there was no need for lunch.

When he had left – when that break had happened with an unexpected thud of pain on what had started as an ordinary Wednesday evening – I had been grateful for my job. I clung onto it, increased my hours and revelled in the relationships I built with my clients. They appreciated me. They needed me and, if I was as honest as I could be, I needed them too. Matthew still provided for us financially and, while I didn't let it take a fizz out of me when he handed over money for the girls' expenses, there was no way I could bring myself to dip in our hitherto joint resources for anything for myself. So my job became even more of a lifeline – the downside being that I had never fully realised just how exhausting it could be raising teenage twins, working full time and keeping our house in order.

I pushed open the front door of our suburban semi – eight doors down from Sinéad's altogether more elegant affair and hung my coat at the bottom of the bannister. I could hear the familiar thump of bass notes from the girls' bedrooms, confirming they were in and listening to music as they normally did on weeknights, so I climbed the stairs, peeked into both their rooms to let them know I was back and then ran myself a deep, bubble-filled bath.

Sinking into the water, I closed my eyes and pushed aside thoughts of Matthew getting it on with someone who wasn't me. Instead I focused on the good things in my life. The girls were healthy and happy. I was … well … okay, even if I was older than I wanted to be, and I had a new client to meet the following afternoon. I had a roof over my head and a good friend in Sinéad and that was worth a lot. I exhaled and promised myself I would be asleep before ten and that my need for sleep wasn't a sign of premature aging.

Chapter 2

"Right, Georgina, here she is," Cecilia Brightly said, her back to me as she riffled through a raft of papers on the table behind her desk. She turned around and handed me a thin client file in one of her trademark glossy yellow folders. "Her name is Áine Quigley. You might know her? Taught at St Claire's for years? Her nephew is Jonathan Hegarty – the businessman? Owns a couple of hotels, a few bars, an office block or two. I think he owns one of those big houses near the beach at Buncrana too. A real-life Monopoly champion. If we'd had a power station and a train station to sell, I'm sure he'd have bought them too." She snorted at her own weak joke.

I was vaguely aware of Jonathan Hegarty in the way everyone in Derry was vaguely aware of Jonathan Hegarty. I had a hazy memory of meeting him at a fundraiser for Matthew's school. He might even have been on the Board of Governors – but I couldn't really remember. I knew Matthew had made a point of getting a few high-profile local business people on board after his appointment.

It wasn't surprising that Cecilia wanted to make sure to

keep him on side – especially as his aunt was a private client and private clients were worth their weight in gold.

"Ms Quigley will get ninety minutes of your care a day. It will be fairly basic stuff – she doesn't need any lifting or intense personal care."

I opened the folder and looked at the scant details for her. My heart sank a little when I saw her primary diagnosis was of Alzheimer's Disease. I had never worked with a dementia patient and I'm ashamed to say the thought of it filled me with a certain sense of dread. My apprehension must have been written all over my face and, just in case it wasn't, I made sure to voice my worries.

"Cecilia, are you sure I'm the best person for the job? Surely some of the more experienced carers would be better suited? You know, someone with more experience of dementia care? I've none and if she's a high-profile client you won't want to take a risk."

Cecilia sighed and sat down, gesturing at me to take a seat opposite her. "Here's the thing," she said. "The girls who are more experienced with dementia patients are completely tied up dealing with the more advanced cases. I need them where they are. I'll be honest with you, this is more a touch of baby-sitting than anything else. Her nephew assures me – and her medical notes do back this up – that she's lucid *most* of the time. She's at the early stages of the illness, her diagnosis is fairly recent. I'd go as far as to say she's not at a stage where most people would normally look for external care but Mr Hegarty was insistent – and insistent on the ninety minutes a day. He wants to make sure she has something decent to eat, her night things laid out and a bit of company. I had to balance our current demands with staff availability. You were the only one of our more senior carers with a suitable window in their schedule – and I knew you would be able to cope."

I wasn't so sure. I wasn't sure I would cope but I knew that once Cecilia made up her mind there was no point in trying to change it and it would be foolish of me to continue down a road of telling her how inexperienced I was or how I feared a challenge.

"I thought you would be delighted," she continued. "No diving between appointments like a madwoman – a quiet end to your afternoons in a nice house with someone who needs minimal care?"

I wanted to tell her I actually thought spending ninety minutes with one client was grossly unfair. That I wished I could divvy up my time better – spend more time with the clients who needed me more – instead of the twenty minutes we were allotted to them by the local Health Trust but again I didn't think that would be wise. Cecilia Brightly may have been my boss, but she didn't make the rules.

"Look, I know it's a bit strange but we aren't in a position to turn away money and I'm sure Miss Quigley is a lovely woman," she said. "And we need everyone here to be a team player."

I nodded, plastered a smile on my face and said it wouldn't be a problem, before looking at the file in front of me again as Cecilia left the room. It didn't list much – a few medications, some basic contact information for her next of kin – who appeared to be, solely, Mr Hegarty.

I recognised her address immediately – I had coveted the exclusive development of beautiful old houses at Temple Muse since I was a child and my father had taken me walking through the private park they surrounded. To my little outsider eyes it had the look of *The Secret Garden* about it – mature trees, winding pathways and tall imposing houses peeking out over the tops of the hedges. I had told my daddy that one day I'd love to live there and he had smiled, hoisted me onto his shoulders to see a little more and told me to work very hard, and be very good and I'd never know what would happen. Of course I hadn't thought of Temple Muse for a long time – I'd been more than happy with the house I'd bought with Matthew – even if we didn't have our own private park. But now, if I was honest, there was a part of me that felt as excited as the young girl I once was at the thought of getting a proper nosy inside those hallowed halls. I had always imagined them to be bursting with character – old in an elegant way with sweeping staircases and kitchens the whole family could live in if they wanted, a cosy range burning through the day into the night and a pot of soup bubbling constantly on the hob. I imagined the mature gardens – trees with rope swings tethered from their branches and pebbled paths which crunched underfoot.

I slipped on my Brightly Care Ltd fleece jacket, picked up my files and set out for the day, but not before dropping a quick text to Matthew asking to meet after work. No matter how uncomfortable the conversation would be, we needed to talk about whether or not he was seeing someone and discuss appropriate behaviour in front of our daughters. To keep matters light – because I wanted to appear cool with whatever sexual activity he may have been up to – I added a quick line that Jonathan Hegarty was my new boss and asked if Matthew knew whether or not the wealthiest man in town was single and looking for a middle-aged mum of two to be his companion?

By the time I reached Temple Muse I was focusing on the positives of having an easier end to my day. Each day as a carer was different. Some days I visited my clients and we shared a good laugh and a nice chat while I got on with my work. Today, however, there seemed to be a general darker mood in the air. My clients had been in bad form, or in pain, or both, and I had been frustrated at my lack of ability to make everything all better for them. Despite the promise of spring all around, it was a dark and damp evening and I had a dull headache which I blamed on the two glasses of wine and one horrible shot of tequila I had shared with Sinéad the night before. Matthew had also sent a reply to my text, saying he was busy for the next few nights and he had no idea if

Jonathan Hegarty was single but I'd do well to remember to act professionally at all times.

It was always hard to read the tone of text messages but I got the impression Matthew was both a) avoiding me and b) not impressed with my inquiries about Mr Hegarty. I stuck my tongue out at my phone in what I will admit was a very childish manner and slipped the phone into my pocket before taking two paracetamol washed down with some lukewarm water from the bottle I kept in the car.

I took a few deep breaths to compose myself and set off up the gravelled path to Áine Quigley's house, hoping that the day would at least end on a better note. I knocked on the perfectly maintained green front door and peeked through the glass panels on either side to see a small woman with grey, bobbed hair, pulled to one side with a clip, scurry down the hall towards me, a look of relief spread across her face.

When she pulled the door open I couldn't help but notice that the woman, who I had to assume was Áine Quigley herself, looked as though she had been crying and that she was twisting a worn corner of her cardigan through her fingers.

"I thought you weren't coming," she said before I could speak, turning and starting to walk away down a long hall – parquet flooring, pictures of smiling loved ones on the walls, a Tiffany lamp casting a soft glow. "Come to the kitchen," she said. "We'll have tea."

I followed her because it seemed the only thing to do. I hadn't yet introduced myself although I supposed the brightly coloured logo on my fleece jacket and the file in my hand might have done all the introducing I needed. As I followed her towards the back of the house I glanced around at the dark mahogany doors which closed off four rooms, all of which I was dying to get a nosy in. An imposing staircase dissected the hall. It was the kind of staircase I dreamed of having – perfect for photos on special days, or for flouncing Scarlett O'Hara-like to my bedchamber.

16

The house was silent bar the ticking of a large grandfather clock which stood as if on guard duty at the end of the hall and the mutterings of the woman who had now made her way into a large, old-fashioned kitchen which while spotless had clearly not been updated since the fifties or sixties. Painted cream-and-green cabinets, a large Belfast sink, the expected range in the corner. It looked just how I had imagined it would look when I was small and longing to get a peek inside. The small woman with the grey bob had made her way to the range and was rattling an old-fashioned kettle before placing it back on the hob.

A large kitchen table sat in the middle of the room, surrounded by six chairs, as old as the cupboards by the looks of them – and of various styles. Resting on the table were two cups and saucers, a teapot, sugar bowl, milk jug, silver spoons and a plate of sandwiches covered in cling film.

"Sit down, sit down," the woman fussed in a tone I didn't feel like refusing.

It was clear this was the famous Miss Quigley – or at least she certainly had the demeanour of a school teacher and I felt intimidated. So I did as I was told, sat down and watched as she opened cupboard after cupboard, muttered a little more under her breath and twisted her cardigan a little tighter.

"I hope you don't mind me asking," I offered, trying to speak as clearly and politely as I could in my best impress-the-teacher voice, "but are you okay?"

"Fine," the woman sing-songed, her back still to the table as the kettle started to rumble and boil. "I just, well, I was worried. I didn't know if you were coming."

"I'm sorry if I worried you, Miss Quigley," I apologised, even though by my watch I was right on time. "If you want to tell me what I need to do, I can get on with it."

The woman turned and looked at me, a smile breaking across her face as she crossed to the table and picked up the teapot. "You are silly, Charlotte," she said. "Miss Quigley?

You always did like to tease me. Honestly! Miss Quigley! Áine will do nicely, just like it always has."

She giggled and carried the teapot over to the counter. There she warmed it, added tea leaves from a canister, and poured boiling water from the kettle into it. Then she stirred the tea with a spoon before replacing the lid and carrying the teapot back to the table.

Sitting down, she looked at me again.

"Silly Charlie – now be a good girl and pour the tea, would you? I've not eaten since lunch and I'm starving."

I looked at the woman before me – her face open with trust and, if I wasn't mistaken, love. Not five minutes before she had looked grief-stricken but now her face was positively glowing. She looked delighted – which was infinitely preferable to looking sad and worried. I didn't know how to proceed. Should I tell her I wasn't Charlotte – whoever Charlotte was? Would it be wise to risk upsetting the woman in front of me when she was now sipping her tea from her fine bone-china cup contentedly.

"Are you not eating? I made cucumber sandwiches because I know you like them."

If the truth was told, I hated cucumber sandwiches. I hated anything cucumber-related – but Áine was looking at me with such expectation that I lifted a sandwich and nibbled it, washing it down with a swig of strong tea.

I felt out of my depth. Baby-sitting? This was not 'baby-sitting' and I was hopelessly ill-prepared for it. I took a deep breath, swallowed down another miniature-sized bite of cucumber sandwich and tried to think rationally about the best course of action. I didn't want to risk upsetting this woman, but it was awkward to be here under false pretences – to act the role of some unknown figure. Charlotte? Her previous carer? A friend? A pupil? The file Cecilia had given me had only listed Jonathan as family. The title of 'Miss' implied she wasn't married and most likely did not have children. I cursed myself for not pushing Cecilia for more information or telling her I needed some sort of insight into caring for someone with dementia. But that would do me no good now. I was well and truly scuppered.

Five minutes – I would indulge Miss Quigley for five minutes and then I would try and get on with my duties – whatever they might be. I would very calmly ask her what help she needed, try and find out where she kept her medication and if she needed anything taken care of around the house. But from the gleam off the work surfaces and the carefully prepared food in front of us, it didn't look as if Áine Quigley needed anything done around the house. What she seemed to need, simply, was some company – from someone called Charlotte, whoever she was.

"Are you here on your own?" I asked when I had eaten my way through two cucumber sandwiches and some shortbread.

Miss Quigley nodded, stirring an extra sugar into her second cup of tea. "Everyone else is out. Thinking about it, they have been away a while. Maybe they should be back now? There was someone here earlier. She made the sandwiches and told me I wasn't to eat them till later – not even if I wanted to. She was silly. I didn't like her." She winked and laughed, bringing me into her confidence but it struck me that I could be anyone.

Anyone could have knocked at the door of this grand house in Temple Muse, filled as it was with trinkets and a doddery old woman, and they might well have been mistaken for Charlotte and invited in for tea as well. I shuddered at the thought. Miss Quigley clearly didn't have the wherewithal to ask for ID or check who was calling at her door. I resolved to get away when I could – just for a minute – to call in to the office and let them know she was more unsettled than we'd expected. Maybe I would contact the famous Mr Hegarty if need be. I couldn't let this go on much longer.

"Can I help you at all?" I asked again. "Surely you need a

little help? Can I wash up or help you get your night things together? Maybe make you something warm to eat for later?"

"No, no, you are on your holidays!" she said, clapping her hands together. "Oh, I have missed you so much! Just you sit and drink your tea, my darling Charlotte, and tell me about your adventures."

I swallowed hard. I couldn't exactly make up adventures. "How about you tell me about your day?" I said.

Áine put a half-eaten sandwich back on her plate, stood up and walked to the sink where I noticed her start to twist the cardigan again with her wiry fingers as she stared out the window to the garden. She didn't turn back towards me when she replied. "Nothing. There was nothing. I don't remember … you know … same old …"

I tried to plaster a smile on my face, to try and force a sense of calmness. She turned to look at me again, and her happy demeanour was gone. She looked scared. Like she had suddenly realised that something wasn't ticking over the way it should be.

She looked at me quizzically, as if my face was coming into focus for the first time and it didn't make sense any more. She started to shake, her face coloured.

"I … I'm. Where's Charlotte? What did you do with Charlotte?" Her voice was quiet – but her fear was palpable.

"Miss Quigley, I'm Georgina. I'm here to help you. Jonathan sent me."

"No," she said.

"I can show you some ID," I offered but I wasn't sure she was lucid enough to take in what I was saying. Still, I didn't know what to do or how to handle this, so I stood up and reached for my ID and showed it to her anyway, but by now she was backing off from me, frightened, and I felt wretched. I also swore that if I got out of this without some form of post-traumatic stress for either me or Miss Quigley I would tell Cecilia Brightly that I didn't care about her staffing issues and she simply had to get someone else to take over.

She made a pitiful sight in front of me – almost cowering, as if nothing made sense and I was the big, bad bogeyman. Baby-sitting, my foot!

I was never as glad in my life as I was at that moment when I heard the turn of a key in a door and the sound of footsteps on the parquet floor coming towards the kitchen.

The man – a tall, tanned man in his fifties – was dressed in what was clearly an expensive suit in a charcoal grey which highlighted his salt-and-pepper hair perfectly. Initially I pegged him as handsome.

His face creased with genuine concern for the woman cowering away from me.

"Áine," he said and she looked at him.

It was the strangest thing – seeing her expression change. It was as if her world, as it was, had come slowly back into focus. Her demeanour changed and, while she was still upset, she reached towards him and pulled him into a hug.

"Jonathan!" she said. "I didn't know if you were coming. I was scared."

But any notion I had of his handsomeness quickly passed when he scowled at me – very clearly unhappy that his aunt had been so distressed. I felt rotten, really rotten because I knew I had let her down – or Brightly Care had. She should not have been so distressed. Or if she had become distressed I should have had the skills to deal with it. I had flapped around eating sodding cucumber sandwiches and, as it now seemed, making the situation much worse.

I felt the sandwiches turn a little in my stomach as I reached my hand out towards Mr Hegarty, to introduce myself and try and salvage what I could of the situation. It would be bad news for both Brightly Care and me, if I blew this gig.

He ignored my outstretched hand though – and barely allowed me the chance to let the words start to form before he turned again to his aunt and pulled her close.

"I'm sorry," he said. "I'm really sorry."

"This woman said she was Charlotte, but she's not Charlotte, is she? I don't like her," Miss Quigley said, and I felt whatever shred of hope I had that this situation could be saved extinguish.

"I'm Georgina, from Brightly Care," I said with much more confidence than I felt. "Your aunt invited me in. She called me Charlotte . . . I didn't know what to do . . ."

"Do they not train you people any more?" Mr Hegarty's voice was calm and measured but the intention of his words was unmistakeable. He was angry and it was only a matter of time before his anger was communicated down the phone to my boss. And people like him – in designer suits with their sharp haircuts and menacing voices, who lived in big houses – tended to have the power to get people fired.

"I'm sorry," I replied weakly – not sure if it was the right or wrong thing for me to do. Something inside screamed that you should never apologise. Apologising was an admission of culpability – a highway to a P45 and an appointment at the local dole office. The last thing I needed, with Matthew gone and seemingly moving on with his life, was to find myself out of work. I felt like crying myself, making Miss Quigley and her muddled ways look positively calm and collected in comparison.

"I was told that your aunt was very much lucid. I'm sorry I was a little blindsided. I didn't expect her to be so confused and I didn't want to confuse her further. I was just trying to calm her down enough to be able to talk some more. She seemed so together. She had sandwiches, and made tea ... but then she became more confused ..."

Jonathan glared at me again before turning back to Áine and continuing with his attempts to soothe her. She seemed to respond to his touch and his soft tones.

"It's okay, Auntie Áine, I'm here. And this lady was just being friendly. She *was* friendly, wasn't she?"

Áine nodded, blinking back tears. "But I . . ." she started but trailed off, the conversation losing its way somewhere in her mind. "I want my tea," she said. "Will I make a fresh pot?"

"That would be lovely," he said softly and I watched as she repeated her routine of earlier – shaking the kettle and filling it with fresh water before setting it on the range and setting out cups, saucers and side plates.

Still Jonathan didn't speak to me – he didn't acknowledge me at all. Instead he lifted my file – the pathetically thin file in which I didn't have a chance to fill in any observations or records – and opened it.

"What's this?" he asked – finally speaking to me.

"This is the information we hold on your aunt."

"But I gave more information than this! What does it amount to? A paragraph? 'Minimal care needed'? Do you think I would pay out the money you lot charge for 'minimal care'? Do you think I would only want 'minimal care' for this woman – who raised me almost as her own?"

I felt what little remained of my resolve crumple and I forced myself to take a deep breath, determined I would not be reduced to tears even if, in glorious hindsight, I should have pushed for more information. I had known the file was flimsy in comparison to our usual information.

I watched as he threw the file on the table, turned on his designer heel and stormed from the room and, perhaps because I was clearly developing masochistic tendencies, I felt compelled by some strange force to follow him. If I'm honest I no longer wanted to be in the same room with Miss Quigley, who was happily making tea and whistling to herself, lest any of my actions be misinterpreted further.

In the hall I watched Jonathan take his iPhone from his pocket and punch in a number as if the device in his hands needed more than just the gentlest of touches to access its database of contacts.

He lifted the phone to his ear and turned to glare at me again, which rocketed my body directly into fight or flight mode – very much veering towards the flight side of things.

"Cecelia Brightly," he started, "Jonathan Hegarty. I've just called in to visit my aunt, who is in an extremely distressed state. One of your so-called care workers is here – and seems to have no clue of what she is doing – not a notion of how to calm her down. I had done everything to make her first day as easy as possible. I made sure she didn't even have too much to do – had our cleaner prepare some sandwiches and shortbread for a light tea. All so she could take today to get to know my aunt as well as possible but, instead, she has upset my aunt and shown me a half-baked effort at a care file she was supplied with and I have to say to you that I'm less than happy. And, when I say less than happy, you can take that as a massive understatement."

I felt a little part of me wither and die right there and then. It shrivelled up as I heard Cecilia try and make what excuses she could. Occasionally Jonathan glanced at me, his glare making me feel increasingly uncomfortable. In fact, as the conversation between the two people who held my employment future in their hands continued, I decided it was time to call it quits and beat as hasty a retreat as possible. If I could just retrieve my files from the kitchen and my fleece which had been hung over the back of a chair, I could be out of there in a matter of seconds. I would just have to go in, in as swooping a movement as possible, and get the hell out.

Miss Quigley looked at me as I walked in, her face composed in a smile as, sitting at the table, she poured tea. "Are you the girl Jonathan has asked to come and sit with me?" she asked. "I'm Áine. You must call me Áine. What's your name?"

I was shocked by how she had calmed down so quickly. How things suddenly seemed so normal at this big kitchen table.

"I'm Georgina," I offered.

"Well, Georgina, you may as well sit down and have a cup of tea and you can tell me all about yourself. Is Jonathan here? I'm sure I heard his voice."

"He's just in the hall. He's making a phone call." I sat down opposite her.

"He's always busy – that one. Always on the phone." She laughed, all traces of the scared woman she had been earlier gone. She was back to being the happy woman she had been when she'd answered the door to me. "I like you." She reached across the table and took my hands in hers. "Maybe you could talk to him about working a little less? Do you know something? You remind me of my sister Charlotte. Isn't that the strangest thing?"

I bit back a semi-hysterical laugh and nodded.

"Have we met before?" she asked, her hands moving to the corner of her cardigan again.

"No, Áine, I am sure we haven't," I replied softly. It wasn't her fault that things had gone so terribly wrong, so terribly quickly.

"Well, I am very happy to meet you," she said. "I don't get a lot of company these days. I've not been well. Jonathan, he comes to visit me. He's a good boy. Comes most days when he can – but he's very busy. Did I say that? Always on his phone."

She poured milk into the three cups before standing up and reaching into her kitchen cupboard. She poured some biscuits onto a plate and brought it back to the table. "I'm sure he won't be long – and we can talk about what we will get up to, now that you're going to be my new companion." She sat down and pushed the plate of biscuits towards me. "He had our cleaner Maria make those sandwiches there earlier – wouldn't fill a gap in your back tooth!" She laughed. "He tries. Bless him. Maybe when he's gone, I'll put a wee pot of potatoes on – you could help me. He gets nervous about my cooking – just because I left a pot on once. Set the alarms off. There was such a commotion – such a fuss. I was fine."

She smiled as she took a sip of tea – and I got a glimpse of the woman she used to be. Young and beautiful – she had definitely been beautiful, I could see that much. I felt sad for the woman she used to be and I felt my heart sink yet again. I wished I wasn't so soft-hearted – but I knew that I would have to face whatever Jonathan threw at me if I was to keep this scared old woman happy for just that little bit longer.

Chapter 3

I pushed open the front door to the smell of lasagne wafting from the kitchen. Eve called to me that she was just making a salad and that dinner would be ready whenever I was, if I wanted to jump in the shower first.

I offered a silent prayer of thanks to whatever deity was up there who had granted me a teenage daughter in Eve who was not grumpy and who did not appear to hate the very sight of her mother. In fact, since her father had left, Eve had come into her own as my own personal cheerleader and, despite the fact she was in her GCSE year at school and weighed down with homework, she frequently made the dinner for us. Which was a good thing – as my cooking skills left a lot to be desired. Eve, however, was passionate about all things culinary and was never afraid to try something new. Perhaps I was taking advantage of her enthusiasm for cooking by allowing her such free rein in the kitchen – but it saved on awkward silences followed by the pitiful sound of my uneaten efforts being scraped into the bin before the girls made toast "for supper".

"You are a saint," I called to her, as I started to climb the stairs and dream of the shower I was about to take. A little voice deep inside wondered would it be going too far to ask her to pour me a large glass of wine and bring it up to the bedroom. But, as I stripped off and glanced at my tired face in the mirror (another wrinkle, I was sure, and an extra grey hair which I would very firmly blame on Jonathan Hegarty), I decided that self-medicating with alcohol was not the answer. So I self-medicated with Flying Fox shower gel from Lush, which promised to ward off PMS and stress and make me feel sensual and relaxed. Sensual? I almost laughed.

I was wrapping my hair in a towel and slathering on some moisturiser when my phone rang and I saw that Sinéad, obviously keen on a report on my new client, was calling.

"Well?" she said as I answered.

"Well," I replied, "remember that time when we were at school – and we had to take those enrichment classes with the boys from St Columb's College. And I walked into the room with my skirt tucked into my knickers and they all laughed and I was so mortified I started to cry which made me even more mortified so that I had to leave the room in case I threw up with the shame of it all?"

"I promise you I will never, ever forget that day," Sinéad said, "but I'm worried about where this is going ..."

"Well, if I had a choice between reliving that day again, on a bigger scale – say on national TV – or reliving the last two hours of my life, I would be tucking that skirt as far into my knickers as I possibly could right now."

"Oh dear," Sinéad said, her voice grave.

"Indeed," I replied and launched into my tale of woe, which in the retelling perhaps sounded even worse. There I was, essentially pretending to be the sister of this poor woman who hadn't a notion what was going on and then, to top it all off, the most influential businessman in town walked in and made me feel like a complete moron. Although by the time I

28

reached the point where I told her of his facial expression as he walked back into the room and saw me taking tea with his aunt – who by now was happy as Larry and delighted to have a new friend to talk to – I found I was smiling. A bit. Not much, to be fair, but a bit.

"What did he do?" Sinéad asked.

"He looked at me strangely – which seems to be his standard look – and then he sat down and drank his tea and had a very pleasant conversation with his aunt about the changing of the season. She told him it was great to see a stretch in the evenings – he agreed. Then she thanked him for getting her a visitor to come in each day – and asked him did he not think I looked like his mother?"

"And his response?"

I could tell Sinéad was enrapt. I could visualise her, sitting on her cream sofa in her stylish living room sipping a glass of wine from one of her fancy glasses, taking in my every word. At least I could tell a story.

"I didn't quite have to perform the Heimlich Manoeuvre on him but he did choke a bit all the same. Anyway, the upshot is that he told his aunt he wasn't sure I'd be back because I was very busy and she told him that was a huge shame – because she liked me. I left soon after – and had a text from Cecilia asking me to call into her office first thing tomorrow. Something tells me she doesn't want to present me with an employee of the month award."

"Oh, George," Sinéad said, using my pet name, one only she and Matthew ever used, "I'm sure it won't be that bad."

"Oh, it probably will – he was really angry, you know. But sure I've become quite adept at rolling with the punches these days. I will just have to deal with it. Listen, pet, Eve has dinner ready for me and as I've only had a few rotten cucumber sandwiches today I'm starving."

"Can you send me a doggy bag down? Or better still clone that girl and send her down?"

I laughed. "I'm afraid not. You'd have to take a Sorcha clone as well and she's not as even-tempered or as handy in the kitchen. But, if you are stuck, I can get Eve to bring you down some dinner later?"

"It's okay," Sinéad said. "I have the dinner in the oven here already. The benefits of meal-planning."

Meal-planning. Another reason Sinéad was a proper grown-up and I was still scrambling around – getting my children to take care of me.

"I must try it sometime," I said, signing off and pulling on my distinctly unpink and unlacy underwear and some fresh pyjamas before following the enchanting smells downstairs to where my dinner was waiting for me.

When Matthew first left, he called me or called in or texted every day. At the time, of course, I thought this added further fuel to my belief that he was simply having a male moment and would be back shortly, having missed us all terribly. I plastered a smile on my face – even on the days when I found it hard to breathe let alone look presentable. I welcomed him into our home and invited him for dinner (cooked by Eve, of course). When he texted me I would spend too much time on composing witty responses – ones which would show him what he was missing. But I never put an "x" on the end. I didn't want him to think I was crowding him. I wanted him to think I was still the carefree person he had fallen in love with all those years ago – when we had nothing to worry about except Double Maths and whether or not our pocket money would get docked if we didn't clean our rooms well enough.

Of course, as the weeks passed, contact become more infrequent. Visits were almost unheard-of, speaking to each other on the phone was saved for very serious situations only and texts became our primary – and occasional – form of communication. Until the pink-bra revelation I had still been trying to convince myself that this was part of the process – that perhaps it was too painful for him to talk to me knowing that he would then be going home, alone, to his flat to eat tinned soup or a microwaved meal for one rather than sitting at his own dinner table in our lovely home eating some freshly prepared feast.

It was only after the aforementioned pink-bra revelation that I realised that probably wasn't the case. He was probably skipping home and eating his dinner off some nubile young thing and his lack of texts were further evidence he was removing himself from his life. In a fit of pique I had scanned through my phone and noted that I had instigated fourteen out of the last fifteen text chats – which were no longer witty exchanges and instead revolved around bills, childcare arrangements and letting him know if he had any important-looking post.

So I was surprised as I sat on the sofa watching some godawful documentary about the benefits culture when my phone pinged to life with a message from Matthew – which was unrelated to practical matters.

"Well, how was your hot date with Mr Big Shot Hegarty?"

Was he jealous? Was he being sarcastic? Was he mocking me? I used the time I would have spent trying to be flirty and witty to compose a message telling him I wasn't at all sure what he meant. I had been at work. Of course, I did know what he meant – and he *knew* that I *knew* what he meant. But still … I emitted a long, loud sigh which prompted Sorcha to lift her head from her tablet and look in my direction.

"*What?*" she barked. It was as large an attempt at being a caring teen as I was likely to get.

"Nothing, pet," I answered – not wanting to fall into the trap of giving out about her darling daddy and she grunted a response while I sat back, staring at my phone, wondering just what kind of game Matthew was playing.

He didn't respond, of course. Leaving me angry and

confused – which, on top of my fear about what the morning might hold – did not bode well for a good night's sleep.

"It will be okay," I told myself as I lay in bed that night. "I'm healthy and have a roof over my head. The girls are healthy and happy. Or at least not totally miserable. Eve's lasagne was the best yet. I have Sinéad to laugh with. And I didn't tuck my knickers into my skirt at all today. Not even once."

I plumped the pillows, tried to get comfortable and promised myself that I would keep my cool if Matthew texted me again and that I would keep my cool when Cecilia and I had our meeting in the morning.

"It will be okay," I whispered at about three thirty in the morning, shortly before I finally fell asleep.

Chapter 4

The first thing I noticed when I walked into Cecilia Brightly's office the following morning was that she had done her hair in a particularly bouffant-y style. She was also wearing make-up and, instead of her usual work uniform, she wore a black skirt-suit with a crisp white blouse which was, to my mind, not buttoned up far enough to be decent. Her office was heavily scented with a musky perfume as well and she seemed particularly on edge.

"You wanted to see me?" I said. "Look, I know yesterday was a disaster but none of us were expecting Mrs Quigley – Áine – to be so confused. It caught me off guard."

Cecilia was one of those women who could wriggle out of every awkward situation and didn't have a moral objection to selling anyone down the river if it saved her own skin. I was expecting that, despite my voicing my concerns to her, she would already have prepared a speech about how I had made a huge error with an important client. The best I could expect, I reckoned, was an official warning. The worst? Well, I was under no illusions that my job wasn't at risk – especially if

Jonathan Hegarty remained as angry as he had been the day before.

But, if I wasn't mistaken, Cecilia had a smile on her face and had taken on an almost girlish glow. She didn't look ready to launch into one of her trademark dressing-downs.

Just as she opened her mouth to reply, her phone rang, and raising one finger she gestured to me to wait.

"Yes," I heard her say. "Could you bring Mr Hegarty through to my office?"

She hung up and asked me to take one of the two seats in front of her desk. "Georgina, don't worry. I'll sort this out. I'm used to sweet-talking high-maintenance clients."

At that moment her door opened and Jonathan was shown in. I stood, nervously, before Cecilia directed me to sit down again and bustled out from behind her desk, her smile dazzlingly bright, as she launched a full-on charm offensive.

"Ah, Jonathan, lovely to see you! Please, take a seat and I'm sure we can sort all this out. As I said to you yesterday, we fully admit we didn't get the first visit with your aunt just right. We were unprepared – but you know that things were a little different to what Georgina here expected."

"I would have thought you would have assigned someone with more experience of dementia care," Jonathan began without so much as glancing in my direction. "And that is something for which the responsibility rests entirely here with you, Cecilia."

Cecilia's flirtatious blush very quickly drained from her face.

"But I'm not here to go over old ground," he went on. "This is very much about fixing things. If it were solely down to me I would have no hesitation in cancelling our contract with no notice and making it my mission to tell as many people as possible about this disaster. To send someone in with minimal, if any, experience with working with dementia patients? To send an incomplete file? It's simply unacceptable.

However, it just so happens that my aunt is quite taken with Georgina."

He looked at me then, for the first time since entering the room. There was a vague look of something which differed from disgust on his face that made me feel a little strange. I nodded – a quick gesture of acknowledgement of his aunt's good taste – and looked back to Cecilia who seemed to be struggling to regain her composure after hearing just how close she had come to having her professional reputation trashed by one of the most influential businessmen in town.

"I'm also willing to accept," he said, "that things yesterday didn't go as I thought they would." He coughed and took a deep breath before continuing. "Áine has never been so confused before. It was a shock to me, and if I had known she would be in such a state then I might have approached things differently. I've since discovered she had missed a day or two's medication. I found her tablets in the bathroom cabinet upstairs, sitting in a row. It's a part of her condition." All traces of any earlier bravado and bolshiness were gone.

I actually found myself feeling a little sorry for him – even if he was an insufferable arse the day before.

"Yesterday brought things into a sharper focus for me," he continued. "And I spoke with my sister last night – we've agreed that we need more care for her. I can't be there myself – and I can't trust her with just anyone. We thought a home help – someone to make sure her personal-care needs were met once a day would be enough – but it isn't, obviously."

"I understand," I said. "I would feel the same if it were my aunt. You have to do what is right for her."

"Well, I'm glad we're in agreement here, Georgina. Because what I think is right is that you come on board for more than the agreed ninety minutes a day."

I glanced at Cecilia who looked like a woman just saved from the gallows and I looked at Jonathan Hegarty who seemed back to his assured self. Clearly he was used to getting what he wanted – and there was no way Cecilia was going to disagree.

"It's going to be a bit fluid for a while. I'm going to spend more time myself with Áine at the weekends – I will take care of her needs then, but during the week I need to work. Our cleaner, Maria, will continue to take care of her each morning and make her breakfast but we need someone – you, Georgina – each day from one to six who will make lunch, care for her, make dinner, make sure her clothes are left out for the following day, and try and help her cope with the changes in her life. I will visit each evening. It might not be enough, but we'll try it and see how we get along."

I had to speak up, because, as much as I felt sorry for Áine and her predicament, I had felt so deeply uncomfortable the day before, not knowing what to expect or how she might react. It was scary – and I was scared.

"As much as I would love to," I began, ignoring the death stares from Cecilia, "I have a number of other clients here who really do rely on me. And, as you have said yourself, I've no experience of dementia care. I'm sure there would be someone much more suitable."

I dropped my gaze to the floor as quickly as I could.

"Well, we clearly have a problem then," Jonathan said. "Because my aunt is taken with you. You remind her of her sister, Charlotte. She made me promise that I would bring you back and my aunt has never asked much of me."

Internally I was screaming that I was not someone who could be bought – a commodity who could be ordered wherever Jonathan Hegarty wanted me to go but I knew, just knew, I was fighting a losing battle.

"We can reassign your clients, Georgina," Cecilia said, confidently. "If Mr Hegarty here wants you to work for him for longer hours we can arrange that, without any fuss. We always put our clients first."

Yes, I thought, we do. Especially if they have a lot of money.

"I'm sure you could learn more about dementia – you're a smart girl, Georgina," Cecilia said and I couldn't help but feel her words were loaded.

Yes, I was a smart girl who would stop putting up barriers to more private money coming into the coffers of Brightly Care Ltd.

"It would mean a lot to me," Jonathan said. "My aunt is a very special woman. Having more company, having someone to look after her would make a huge difference to our family. Unfortunately she never had children of her own – my sister and I have been taking care of her – but my sister lives in England with her family and I'm quite busy, as you can imagine."

"There's no question here, is there?" Cecilia asked me. "You'll do it, Georgina."

It was a statement, not a question. And yes, even though I had very, very deep misgivings, I would do it. I didn't have a choice.

My new duties would start the following day. Today I just had to call in on Áine in the late afternoon. Cecilia at least gave me time to visit my existing clients and explain to them what was happening and that they would have a lovely new care assistant with them from the following day. It was not a fun day. And when I say "not fun", I mean that I left almost every house fighting back tears and feeling as if I had been torn away from a family who had come to know and trust me. Such trust was not to be underestimated when you had a sick or infirm relative – the people I visited felt vulnerable. Change was not good and I felt awful as I said my goodbyes although I was sure they would be cared for really well by my colleagues.

By the time it came to late afternoon, and I was due to visit Áine again, I felt so emotionally wrung out that I wanted to curl up into a tiny ball in the backseat of my car and mainline chocolate until it all felt a little better.

But, as was my duty, I put my best smile on my face – planned to stop at the shop on the way home to buy one of those really big Dairy Milks – and headed to Temple Muse to once again spend some time with Áine.

I opened the imposing front door with the key Jonathan had given me and, in stark contrast to the silence the day before, I was greeted by the sound of a too-loud TV playing what sounded very like *Deal or No Deal*.

I called out for Áine and heard no reply – but then again there was a chance no one living or dead would have been able to hear a thing over the sound of that television and Noel Edmunds' dulcet tones.

"Áine!" I called again, making my way down the hall where some of the dark mahogany doors which had been closed yesterday were now open. Following the sound of the TV, I turned into a room on the right and found Áine sitting on a Parker Knoll armchair, glued to the television with her hands over her eyes.

"I can't bear to watch," Áine said. "She should have taken the offer from the banker, but now … I know that box has nothing in it and she's going to go home with nothing. It's such a shame."

I watched as Áine dropped her hands slowly, and Noel Edmunds intoned that this could be very bad news indeed.

"Hi, Áine," I said.

"Shhh," she replied. "We can talk after this."

I was fairly sure Áine hadn't even registered who was there – and she clearly didn't much care at that moment. I wondered did Jonathan know just how his aunt could welcome anyone into her home. Surely he had to be concerned someone could take advantage of her – I decided I would have to mention it to him. But then again, perhaps I should wait a little while. Even a few days. Let a little water run under the bridge. Or I'd end up living in this big house in Temple Muse 24/7 keeping an eye on Áine and watching *Deal or No Deal*.

"I told you!"

I watched as she sprang to her feet in as sprightly a fashion as a woman half her age. "You should have listened to me," she scolded the TV. "You'd have gone home with some money in your pocket!" She walked across the room, switched the TV off and turned to look at me – where I was still standing in the doorway afraid to speak until spoken to.

"Right, well, I would say that it's time for tea then?" Áine said.

There was no twisting of her hands, no look of uncertainty. No obvious confusion. Perhaps this would be a good day?

I nodded. "That would be lovely, and then you can tell me how you've been today?"

"Ach, sure I have no stories to tell. I've not even been outside the door. But if it keeps my nephew happy I will sit and chat with you for the time you are here."

There was no doubt Áine was like a different woman from the person I had left the day before. She seemed confident, sure of herself.

"I can tell you all about *Deal or No Deal* or *Homes Under the Hammer* – I'm an expert at daytime TV," she said as I followed her through to the kitchen. "Jonathan even had a TV installed for me in the kitchen so I can watch the cookery programmes."

As on the day before, a plate of cellophane-wrapped sandwiches sat on the table along with the teapot, sugar bowl, milk jug, cups, saucers and cutlery. I took it as some sort of gesture of conciliation from Jonathan. Sandwiches again. Save me making anything for tea. Give me time to get to know Áine properly again.

"Do you want me to put the kettle on?" I asked.

"I'm actually quite capable of making tea," Áine said defensively. "I'm even capable of cooking. I used to love to cook. I've been cooking hot dinners since long before you were born. Probably before your mother was born – and yet," she glanced at the table, "it makes Jonathan feel better to send me a nursemaid. And to have sandwiches made for me. I am sick of the sight of sandwiches. He's been having Maria make them for me for a week now. For the love of God, who could eat sandwiches every day without losing their mind?" She laughed at this. Not a bitter laugh – it was almost girlish and it faded off as she became aware of what she was saying.

I watched her – watched her expression falter and change – and wondered what it must be like knowing that your mind was slipping away. I watched as she lifted the kettle, filled it and put it on the range as she had the day before – an automatic process. And I watched as she stopped in her tracks in front of the range as if trying to catch up with her own thought processes, turned to look at the sandwiches and then looked back at the kettle.

"Tea," she said and went to get the teapot.

"We can cook something more substantial if you like?" I offered. "See you through till morning properly? Some potatoes, or pasta – what would you like?"

Áine was warming the china teapot. "Sometimes," she said softly, "I don't remember what I like any more. Isn't that silly? You must think me silly. Imagine not remembering what you like any more?"

"Can I let you in on a secret, Áine?" I asked, unwrapping the sandwiches. "Sometimes I'm not quite sure what I like any more either. So we'll make a deal – we'll have these blasted sandwiches tonight and then maybe we'll have a look through a couple of those cookery books I see over there and, if anything takes your fancy, we can make some of that tomorrow? Does that sound okay?"

Áine smiled thinly, her shaking hands carrying the teapot to the table. She sat down. "That sounds perfectly lovely, Charlotte," she said before a shadow passed over her face. "No, not Charlotte. Sorry. Your name …"

"Georgina."

"Georgina, that sounds lovely. I met you yesterday, I know that. Jonathan arranged for you to come here."

"Yes," I said. "He cares about you a lot."

We ate together and I made sure to give Áine her medication. We maintained a relatively calm patter of small talk. The weather. Then Áine switched on the TV that sat on one of the kitchen counters and I located *Come Dine with Me* for her. She immediately became absorbed in it and I began the washing up.

As I put the last cup onto the drainer we heard the front door open and close.

"That'll be Jonathan," Áine said absently, still focused on the TV. "He always calls at this time. Since the pot incident, he's been making me some dinner. God love him, he's not much of a cook, but he tries. I tell him I'm okay, it was only once. I can still cook – he doesn't need to come here and try and make something but he still calls. He still tries. He's an awful fusspot."

"I'm sure he's just concerned about you," I said, even though I was sure in fact that he was more worried about me and what I might or might not be doing, and whether or not Brightly Care was pulling its proverbial socks up.

And, sure enough, he walked into the kitchen and gave a cursory glance at his aunt before meeting my gaze. Despite feeling totally ambushed by the events of the day I was, admittedly, hugely relieved that the scene that was greeting him was one of calm and contentment and that Áine seemed more than happy with the new face in her house.

"Auntie Áine," he said, turning his gaze from me again, "how are you?"

"Well, I'm just fine. Not overly impressed with cucumber sandwiches two nights in a row – but Georgina here has promised we'll have something decent tomorrow night. Look at what these boyos are cooking up on the TV. I'd like that."

"We'll have something special tomorrow, Áine," I

interjected. "Pasta maybe – lasagne?"

"My aunt is a plain eater," Jonathan spoke.

"Says who?" Áine demanded. "You don't know me as well as you think you do, Jonathan. Just because you were fussy as a child and I had to cater to your whims, don't write me off! You should know full well that I'm fond of Italian food." She smiled and looked at me. "It's himself that's a plain eater. Making me spuds and beans every night this past week – not that I mind spuds and beans … but every night?"

I stifled a smile as Jonathan blushed. I went back to putting away the crockery.

"We've had something to eat. I've made sure your aunt has had her medication. We've had a lovely chat about Noel Edmunds and I have tidied up – and we've made a few plans about what we are going to try next. Including some nice dinners."

Jonathan bristled. "Routine is very important to people with … people like Áine."

"I'm a grown up, not a child," Áine snapped. "You can say it, you know. The word. Alzheimer's."

"We'll still maintain a routine," I said. "Áine and I talked over tea earlier and we thought we'd just try a few things. Easy recipes. Just basic home cooking. She has told me about the incident with the pot being left on the range too long, but I can assure you I will be here the whole time. If it gets too much for either of us, I'll just bring over some leftovers from home. My daughter is a great cook."

Even as the words were out of my mouth I wondered if Jonathan, with his urge to judge me on every occasion, would think I was giving his aunt less than top service with my mention of basic cooking and leftovers.

"Maybe we'll do some soups and the like for lunch too, Áine? Something nice and warm and filling."

"Will your daughter make the soup too? I'm sure Maria will be delighted to know her food is being pushed aside for leftovers." Jonathan smirked in a sly way which made me want to hit him squarely around the head with the plate I was drying.

"Maria has more than enough to do, without having to worry about making me lunch or baby-sitting me," Áine said.

"She's paid well enough to do it," Jonathan said, his condescending tone doing nothing to warm me to him. "She's our cleaner," he added.

I nodded. "I know. You said."

"Yes, but she is more than that. She's like one of the family."

One of the family who is reduced, in conversation, to just someone paid handsomely to make sandwiches, I thought.

"She has been doing a lot for us. She helps Áine to get dressed, cleans and makes her lunch and these last few days she has helped by making this tea for you both."

"She sounds like a gem," I said.

"She is," Jonathan said.

"But she is the cleaner, Jonathan, as well you know," said Áine. "And she has other clients – who she has been sorely neglecting since the unfortunate incident in the kitchen. She can't lose her clients – and she's not paid that handsomely. She's paid well, for a housekeeper and cleaner, but she needs to be elsewhere ..."

Jonathan looked suitably chastised and I couldn't help but smile inwardly at how his aunt could put him in his place.

He blinked, puffed himself up and opted for a complete change of subject, knowing that Áine had won this round. "Anyway, Georgina, I thought, while I was here, if you have time, I could show you around the house a bit," he said.

"Very well," I said, hanging up the tea towel.

He led the way out of the room, leaving Áine to the company of the TV. In the hall, he stopped and turned to me.

"I'd like to let you know a bit more about Auntie Áine's routine," he said. "Not every day is as good as today. Not every conversation is as coherent, as you learned yesterday. And the truth is more days are going to become like the day she had yesterday, over time, so I don't want you lulled into a false sense of security."

"Mr Hegarty, I can imagine how difficult all of this is for you and I know how this disease can be very cruel."

"Yes," he said. "It is very cruel. You didn't know the woman she was – and we know, she knows, that is starting to slip away. She's a very intelligent woman – a very proud and independent woman …"

He looked as if he would go on but he stopped himself and I saw the shutters come down. I could sense that this conversation was difficult for him, that he was a proud man who didn't often show any emotion.

I thought of Áine the day before. Lost. Childlike. Not sure of where she was or who she was talking to – and while I had found it deeply unsettling, I could only imagine how Jonathan found it. For all his considerable faults as a condescending, bossy man who didn't know how to exist outside of getting his own way, he did seem to genuinely care about his aunt.

"I can see that," I said. "She seems to be a lady who is a force to be reckoned with. I'm here to try and understand more so let's talk routine."

Jonathan nodded, took a deep breath as if to settle himself, and gestured to me to follow him. He pointed to the room Áine had been in earlier. "This is the sitting room where my aunt likes to watch TV, although you have probably already figured out that she likes to spend as much time as possible in the kitchen. It has always been her favourite place."

He proceeded down the corridor and stopped, opening a door to the left to show me a grand dining room, its heavy mahogany furniture and dark-green wallpaper making it look foreboding against the fading evening light. It looked like the kind of room where people used perfect manners, where conversations were clipped, where children were seen and not heard. I thought of our dining room at home. Our dining table was currently holding a week's worth of clean washing which had yet to be ironed and put away. One corner of the table had become a nail station for the girls, where they would invite their friends over and make their best attempts at gel art. Twinkling lights swirled around some grand willow branches, pictures of my family filled the walls, along with some framed pictures the girls had drawn when they were smaller. The French doors let natural light flood in and the walls were painted in a light duck-egg blue. It was a far cry from the staid room of Áine's house. It was a room that buzzed with the busyness of family life. This room looked unlived in, unloved. But then again, I supposed it didn't get much use. I couldn't imagine there were many dinner parties held there now.

"We don't use the other rooms any more," he said, pointing to the closed doors in front of him. "A formal sitting room – where my grandmother would entertain guests," he said, nodding to the right, and then pointed to one on the left. "We used that room as playroom and study when we were younger – not much need for it now there are no children in the house." He turned and walked back up the hall to the staircase, gesturing for me to follow him.

We reached the top. Light glinted in through a stained-glass window at the end of the landing but the rows of closed doors along the corridor gave the whole house a gloomy feel.

"We keep most of these rooms locked," Jonathan said.

I raised an eyebrow. To say it seemed unusual was an understatement.

"We don't want to confuse Auntie Áine," he said. "We figured if we kept things simple, she would have less chance of getting confused. These rooms – they hold a lot of memories, they could send her into a spin."

I nodded, even if I didn't really understand the logic. I may have been relatively clueless about dementia care but I was pretty sure memory-work was a pretty big thing in those circles these days.

"And we want to limit the damage she can do to herself. It might sound strange but the fewer choices she has, the less chance she has of hurting herself."

He walked to the end of the corridor, gestured towards a bathroom and then opened the door to a bedroom which looked almost as stark as the dining room downstairs.

A metal-frame bed, covered with a patchwork eiderdown, stood against the wall. Beside it sat a side table holding a lamp, complete with a faded pink silk lampshade and a glass of water.

Across from the bed stood a fifties-style chest of drawers and beside it a dressing table. I wasn't sure what I had been expecting but this didn't look like the room of a woman who had lived here most of her years. The number of personal items were limited. A bottle of face cream and a bristle hairbrush were all that sat on the dressing table. Just two photos rested on top of the chest of drawers – one black-and-white, two young girls grinning widely at the camera, standing on the shore of some unknown beach as the white foam of the waves hit the back of their legs. Curls, wild and frizzy, were pulled back in identical ribbons.

Beside that photo an older woman, with traces of Áine's familiar face, stood in seventies faded colours holding the hands of two older children. All three were grinning at the camera, their faces so utterly bright that I wondered for a second who they were smiling at. Whoever it was, I thought, they loved that person with every part of them. It was the most precious thing I had seen in that big, imposing house since I got there.

Chapter 5

Charlotte laughed, throwing her head back as she watched her children, Jonathan who was just five and eight-year-old Emma, run through the vineyard close to their villa on the edge of Lake Garda. Her face was sun-kissed. Her golden curls were bleached by the sun and by a month in Italy. Charlotte thrived in the sun.

Her husband, Jack, called it "work" – this life in the sun. And sure, he worked. He had meetings and made deals and talked yield and profit and import taxes and blends and Charlotte had heard those snippets as she walked through the terracotta-tiled dining room, the breeze blowing through the open doors – warm and comforting as it caressed her bare legs under her chiffon kaftan. She wasn't there to work – she was there to live, to breathe in the sun. To play with the children – to watch their bodies tan and glow and to listen to the gorgeous tinkle of their laughter as they splashed in and out of the pool.

She lit her cigarette, lay back on her lounger, slipped off her kaftan and let the sun caress her bare skin. If the children weren't there, she would have slipped off her bikini too, she thought. Oh, the scandal it would cause if people back home even knew she was contemplating it. Maybe she would later. Maybe, when the work was done and her two little sun-kissed babies were asleep, she would slip off her bikini and entice her husband into the pool. Skinny-dipping. Then drinking wine, letting the warm evening air caress their naked bodies. Laughing, smoking, making love until dawn.

There was nothing that could beat it – that freedom. That was what life was about – embracing every moment. Not caring. Just living it to the full. She paused amid her thoughts of decadent living – the kind of living that would make the old women of Temple Muse rearrange their cardigans, cross their arms and purse their lips in judgement. Jealous, she figured. They were all just jealous. They could do with a week in the sun – all of them. And good wine. And good sex. She smiled, listened to the children squeal with delight and drifted off as the sun warmed her skin.

Later, when she was warmed through to the bone and the children were tired from running around in the sun they – along with her husband's business partners – sat around a long wooden table in a cool dining room where the cook served huge steaming bowls of pasta, with breads and oils, and wine like she had never tasted before. Each taste, each bite, each delicious morsel made Charlotte feel even more alive. For a moment she wished Áine and their mother were there – that Áine wasn't playing it always so safe with her stubborn determination to stay close to home and play the good girl. And their mother – through no fault of her own except her desire to remain attached always to the home her beloved husband had bought for them – she was only too happy to allow her younger daughter to stay with her. She would never encourage her to leave the nest – to experience the world in the way Charlotte had. Charlotte wished she would – wished Áine would find her courage and move on.

Áine loved cooking – she would have adored this, adored exploring these new flavours, enjoyed the easy chatter around the table. Then again, she might find it all too relaxed – she might struggle to fit in. She definitely wouldn't be sunbathing topless by the pool anyway. Charlotte loved her little sister – so much – but she wished she would just live a little. If she could get her to try new things, to visit new places she was sure she would be happier.

"You can't wait for life to happen," Charlotte once told her. "You have to go out there and grab it by the balls."

Áine had blushed furiously and walked away. She didn't use that kind of language. She didn't appreciate it. She was the very definition of a goody two-shoes, but she had such a kind heart. She would do anything for her family, Charlotte knew that. And even if their mother had encouraged her out into the world, she had the notion Áine would do everything she could to stay closer to home. She sighed as she took another forkful of pasta. Maybe if Mohammed wouldn't go to the mountain … She resolved to ask the cook for a few recipes and when she got home she would land at that big old, oppressive house and she would slosh olive oil in one of the heavy copper-bottomed pots and she would crush garlic, chop herbs, and the whole place would sizzle and steam with the smells of Italy. And even if it was cold and rainy outside, and even if Áine was still wearing that awful powder-blue cardigan she insisted on wearing and had her hair pulled back in that ridiculously unflattering manner, she would do it.

⟶ Present Day ⟵

Eve had played a blinder with a delicious beef hotpot for dinner. The smell of it had my mouth watering as soon as I walked through the door. I kissed her cheek and told her I loved the very bones of her while she dished out a large plate before pouring me a glass of milk to wash it down with.

Even Sorcha couldn't help but voice her approval for her sister's latest creation and, much as I tried not to dwell on the day that had passed, I had a brief moment of being exceptionally grateful to have my two girls and for the fact that we tended to rub along quite nicely together.

They had adapted relatively well to their dad moving out. Sorcha had been more sullen for a few weeks and Eve had cried but said she would support us – but there had been no mad histrionics. They were incredibly mature about it and, sitting in our kitchen now, talking together, laughing over dinner and thinking of the messiness that was both our home and our family life I, despite everything, felt incredibly blessed. I knew – just knew – my girls would always be there for me. We would always be close. I would not have to worry about being alone in my later years. I hoped, one day – in the very distant future, to have grandchildren run through these rooms. That my walls would be covered in pictures of smiling faces all that little bit similar to my own – our family together. Whatever happened with Matthew.

"Girls," I said, as I mopped the last of the gravy from the plate with a hunk of crusty bread and devoured it, "I love you both very, very much and I'm proud of how you have coped with everything. You are remarkable young women."

Eve reached over and squeezed my hand, while Sorcha rolled her eyes and said: "Are you sure that's just milk you're drinking, Mum? Are you sure you didn't drop a wee something extra in there? A drop of vodka?"

"Vodka and milk?" I laughed. "No. I just love you."

"We love you too, Mum," Eve said, starting to clear the table. "Don't we, Sorcha?" She eyeballed her sister.

"Yes. Duh!" Sorcha intoned, but I noticed she helped clear the table as well, instead of sloping off to her room like she normally did.

Later I sat talking with Sinéad, who had walked down the

street to my house. She was curled on my comfy (codeword for 'battered') sofa, cradling a cup of tea and munching on chocolate biscuits with abandon. She didn't keep chocolate biscuits at home – it would tempt her too much, she said.

Although Sinéad was perhaps one of the most streetwise people I knew, she was floored by the events of the day. "I know Jonathan Hegarty likes his own way – but taking you away from all your clients?"

"I know!" I intoned in my very best 'Monica from Friends' voice. "And then he went on to be mean to me – and then nice to me – and then mean to me again. I don't think I like him."

"I must ask my ad reps what he's like to do business with. See if he runs hot and cold with them." She dunked a chocolate finger into her tea and slurped at it with gusto.

"It's an odd set-up," I said. I knew it was against the rules to talk about clients – but I had known Sinéad since my school days and I knew I could trust her with my very life. I would tell her things that I never could have dreamed of telling Matthew. "He showed me round the big house today."

"Oh, you must spill! Is it just gorgeous? All elegant and oozing wealth and stature?"

I shook my head, then shrugged my shoulders. "Not really. The kitchen is lovely – stuck in the fifties but cool in a retro way. The rest of the house is kind of typical old-woman style. He keeps most of the doors locked upstairs so that Áine won't get confused."

Sinéad's eyes mirrored the disbelief I had felt when I had learned about the closed doors.

"And when he showed me her room . . . it just felt strange. It didn't feel like the room of a woman who had lived her whole life there. It felt a bit cell-like – bleak – just a couple of pictures."

Sinéad curled up a little more. "God, very odd. I mean I know people are strange and all that – but that just seems weird. Even if he does say it's for her own good – keeping her house locked up. I wonder what is behind all those doors? All the family jewels, perhaps? Or is he making sure 'the help' doesn't 'help' herself?" she added with a wink.

I stuck my tongue out. "You are a cheeky one!" I laughed. "But whatever his reason, I'm stuck with him – and I need to find a way to work through this. I need to hit the books about dementia."

"Rather you than me," Sinéad said. "I've said it before and I'll say it again – I don't know how you do it. I'd find it all just horribly, horribly depressing."

"Well, that's my job. It is hard at times – and depressing at times – but it has its own rewards. And I don't think 'Oh no, that made me sad' would wash with his nibs if things went wrong again."

"Your place in heaven is assured," Sinéad said.

"Nope," I laughed. "I blew that with the sex before marriage, the swearing and the impending divorce."

"Oh, sweetheart, I'm not sure if divorce is still a sin," Sinéad said, lifting another biscuit.

"Give it here and I'll look for you," Sorcha said, trying to grab her laptop back from my knees. She clearly wasn't all that impressed with my lack of technical prowess – but, to be fair to me, I'd never really had a need to know too much about computers. I used Facebook on my phone and sent a few emails but that was it. The world of Google searches was a minefield. One word wrong or phrased badly and you never knew what shockers you might stumble upon.

I had started to question just how much of a free run my children had over the internet and its dodgy ways, as I shook my head at some very questionable pictures of some old people doing some very strange things, when Sorcha's patience ran out.

"Mum, look, tell me what you want and I will find it for you."

"Erm," I said, trying to make sure my wording was spot on this time, "best practice for dementia patients. Or Alzheimer's – type in Alzheimer's – and early onset. And perhaps memory work."

"Hang on, hang on," she said, her fingers flying over the keyboard and her eyes scanning the screen. "There," she said, turning the computer towards me. "There are some articles there – on decent sites, reputable sites. And there's a link to the Alzheimer's Society – seems like they could give you some advice."

I looked at the articles she had found and kissed her on the forehead. To my delight she didn't grunt or shrug. Instead she got up from where she had been sitting on the sofa beside me and told me she was going to bed.

"Just leave my laptop here when you're done," she said. "I'll get it in the morning."

If I hadn't been so busy I might have wondered why my normally truculent teen was being so accommodating. Instead I focused on the pages in front of me and started reading.

Chapter 6

"You're back again," Áine said, smiling as she opened the door.

"I am indeed. And I bring food – some hotpot my daughter made," I said, nodding towards the casserole dish I was carrying. "As I said, she's quite the cook."

"That's nice of you," Áine said, "but I've just had lunch."

"It's for dinner. Remember I told you I would be here a little longer from now on?"

She looked blank for a moment and then nodded. "Of course. Silly me."

I wasn't convinced that she had remembered but I wasn't going to panic that today would be a bad day. It was important to keep things as calm, as normal, as possible – for me as well as for her.

"Not silly at all," I said. "Things have changed quite quickly – it's hard to keep up with everything."

"Yes," she said.

She led the way to the kitchen and showed me where to put the dish before she went to the range and lifted her trusty

54

kettle. I should have known that every afternoon would begin with a cup of tea.

"Well," she said, "you might as well sit down and I'll make the tea."

"Áine, why don't you sit down and I'll do it? After all, I'm supposed to be here for you."

"I've done enough sitting down for one day already – and I'll have plenty of sitting down to do once you go again. And soon enough, I imagine, I'll be spending my time laid out in a pine box, so I might as well make myself useful while I still can."

It was hard to argue with her logic but still I felt awkward sitting down and waiting to be served a cup of tea in a nice china cup.

"And I imagine a young thing like yourself has been on her feet long enough today already," she said.

I was starting to really warm to her – considering me a young thing. I smiled as she busied herself making the tea. When she eventually sat down, she smiled at me.

"Well then," she said, "if we are going to be spending some time together, I suppose we might as well figure out what we're going to do with our time. Tell me, Georgina – it is Georgina, isn't it? – what do you normally do with your clients?"

"Well," I told her, "I normally only have twenty minutes with them so it can be pretty rushed. I make sure their personal-care needs are met – washing, changing, making sure they have their medication – that kind of thing. And then perhaps making them a cup of tea, giving them a listening ear, if I have the time."

Áine exhaled slowly. "Well, if you don't mind, I don't need help with washing, changing or anything of a personal-care nature. And, as you can see, I make a nice cup of tea myself."

"I can see that – all of those things. But your nephew was quite insistent that I spoil you and do as much for you as I can." I winked at her – trying to reassure her that I still considered her a fairly capable woman.

She nodded. "He can be insistent all right. I told him that I didn't think a carer was needed – but when Jonathan makes up his mind that is it and nothing can change it. He's like his mother in that regard. She was one very determined lady."

"He clearly cares for you very much," I said softly.

She smiled. "Oh, I have no doubt about that. My nephew may come across as quite gruff at times but he does have a good heart. I know he worries. I'd like to say he has no cause to, but I know things aren't right. I don't think I need a baby-sitter every afternoon – but I know – I know what is happening to me."

"It must be a worry," I said softly.

She smiled – a weak smile that didn't reach her eyes. "No point worrying about what you can't change. It will become easier for me – in a while I won't even realise – won't remember, I imagine. But, you know, that's all awfully depressing – and maybe we should talk about something else."

She lifted her cup of tea to her mouth and drank slowly.

"So," I said, breaking the silence, "what would you like to do? Is there anything I can help you with?"

"You know, just having someone here is nice. This house used to be so busy once. You wouldn't think it now – with just me rattling around in it. But at one time it was a busy home – with children running up and down the stairs, and my mother busy in the kitchen. So having someone here – believe me – that helps."

"Well," I said, "why don't you just tell me about those days then? And maybe top up these teacups again?"

"Sounds lovely," Áine said – and her smile was genuine this time.

∞ 1964 ∞

"You look lovely," Áine said, embracing her sister who kissed her on each cheek in a manner she thought very cosmopolitan.

She couldn't deny it, Charlotte was positively glowing. And Jonathan and Emma looked so alive too – like two little brown berries, sun-kissed, with their hair highlighted by the bright Italian sun. The two had scampered into the house, running straight at their aunt and squeezing her tight. They shouted "*Ciao!*" and "*Bella!*" and ran on through to the kitchen to find their grandmother while Áine waited for Charlotte to follow. Her sister brought a whole new colour to the house at Temple Muse. She brought life to the muted tones and dark wallpaper and she brought noise to the hallway which was more often silent but for the rhythmic ticking of the grandfather clock by the kitchen door.

"My lovely little sister," Charlotte breathed, and Áine could smell her Chanel No. 5 mixed with her favourite cigarettes.

"Charlotte, it's wonderful to see you."

Áine felt a little dowdy – more than a little wallflowerish beside this glamorous bombshell beside her. She felt conscious of her flat shoes, her A-line skirt and her buttoned-up blouse. Charlotte had arrived wearing a sundress and espadrilles, a loose crocheted wrap around her shoulders. Her nails were painted a deep red and eyes slicked with liner. Áine had never even tried to put on eyeliner – a bit of blush was enough for her on the (very) occasional night she went out. But she always loved to see her sister arrive back from her travels and bring the house to life.

Charlotte linked her sister's arm and the pair walked together towards the kitchen where the children were already delving into the large cookie jar Áine had stocked with her freshly baked goods that morning.

"I'll put the kettle on," Áine said, as Charlotte hugged their mother, who had been encouraging her beloved grandchildren to take at least two cookies to make up for "the foreign stuff your mother feeds you".

"Mum," Charlotte said softly, hugging the smaller woman,

"they have cookies in Italy too!"

"Oh, I know, but nothing like the biscuits our Áine bakes. Surely you know that? And if I can't indulge the children I see so little of, then there is something wrong with the world. My, how they have grown! Has it really only been a few months?"

"Three, yes. And of course we have missed you as well. Both of you. You look well yourself. Not as well as you might look if you gave in and decided to come with us on one of these trips – away from the smoky air here. Away from the mizzling rain."

"It hasn't rained in five days," Rosaleen Quigley said, sitting back down on the armchair which nestled in the corner of the big sitting room. "And there is nothing like being back home in Derry, on the banks of the Foyle. Sure haven't they written songs about it?"

"They've written songs about a lot of things – war, death, all sorts of horrible things!" Charlotte said, laughing.

"Charlotte Anne Rose, you know full well what I meant. Now I've not seen you in three months so let's not fall out within three minutes. You know we have agreed to disagree on such matters."

"Sorry," Charlotte said, dipping her hand into the cookie jar herself and then taking a giant bite from a cookie before swigging a mouthful of milk straight from the bottle which was sitting on worktop, much to her mother's chagrin.

"You would think you were dragged up not raised by a decent family," Rosaleen huffed.

"I was raised by the best mother in the world," Charlotte said, taking a glass from the cupboard and pouring herself a good helping of milk. "You know I just like to keep you on your toes."

"On my toes and on my nerves," Rosaleen said.

The daughter who lived for the moment – who didn't care about saving or planning for the future or keeping her children close enough to home to enjoy a good, solid, Irish education – was the cause of many sleepless nights for Rosaleen Quigley. While she said she enjoyed having her family around her, it was clear that the flamboyant nature of her eldest child left her feeling uneasy. And if Rosaleen Quigley was uneasy, Áine felt it. In a way it was easier when they were in Italy. Áine imagined her mother was able to shut the door on her worries for a while when they weren't there, staring her in the face. When they were away she could imagine them in the next room – living a sensible life. The kind of life Áine lived. The kind of life that Rosaleen had worked so hard to give her daughters. But when they were actually in the next room and under her nose, she could see just how bohemian their lives were becoming and, while she did her best to hide it, she couldn't help but let her concerns shine through. She tried to smile and laugh and enjoy the brief time she had with them, but Áine was aware of the way her mother pulled concerned faces when the children didn't talk about school so much, or when they mentioned the grand dinner parties at the Italian villa which ended after midnight. She would try not to show any disdain when Charlotte retold a story about Jack's contacts, their work practices or how she thought there was no better education than seeing the world rather than simply learning about it.

"It's lovely to be home," Charlotte said, cutting through Áine's thoughts. "Cold, but lovely. The weather in Italy was just divine."

"Yes, well, it's less divine here so maybe you might want to wear something a bit warmer. Áine, why don't you get your sister a cardigan?"

Charlotte laughed it off. "I don't need a cardigan," she said. "I'm fine right here beside the stove. And isn't our Áine making a lovely cup of tea. That'll warm me up!"

Áine set out some cups, and poured some milk for the children, cherishing their gap-toothed smiles as they said thank you.

Worry aside, she reckoned, life was definitely more colourful when her sister was home and she was already looking forward to that evening when their mother would go to bed, the children would be asleep and they could sneak a swig of wine, a cigarette or two, and she could lose herself in her sister's glamorous lifestyle.

"These biscuits are the best," Jonathan grinned. "Thank you, Auntie Áine."

"You're welcome, sweet pea," Áine said, ruffling the hair on his head. "It's so nice to have you both home for a little bit. I can't wait to hear all about your latest adventures."

"We brought you presents," Emma chirped. "Mummy said you would like them. I helped her choose them in the market."

"Well, I can't wait to see them," Áine said.

"It's not much," Charlotte said, "but if you refuse to come with us on one of these trips ..."

"It's not that easy," Áine said, trying not to glance over at her mother who relied on her to keep the house running and take care of her now that arthritis had left her in daily pain. The last thing she wanted was for Rosaleen to worry that she would disappear for months at a time travelling the world too.

"We'll not get into that now," Charlotte said. "But one day, my lovely sister."

Áine nodded. Maybe one day. But, if the truth was told, she had no great ambitions to travel the world. She wanted some of what her sister had – of course she did – but she'd be happy baking cookies in her own oven, in her own house, for her own children. That's what she wanted more than anything in the world.

∽ Present Day ∾

It was strange going home that evening. The day had not felt as hectic as my days normally did, largely consisting of eating biscuits, drinking tea, doing a little light housework and talking with Áine about her life. She was a strange one, I thought, as I showered and changed into a fitted T and jeans. In some ways she was so open, so willing to welcome me into her house, to be a daily part of her life – but also guarded. I didn't want to push her too far or too hard – I had asked her a few things about her life and, while she had answered me, the answers were short – as if she wanted to keep the information to herself. Then again perhaps she didn't remember all the details. I'd have to find ways to tease the memories out, I thought as I towel-dried my hair.

I was just making my way downstairs to the kitchen, where Eve had prepared a delicious pasta sauce, when my phone beeped in my pocket. I took it out and saw a message from Matthew. **"Call round tomorrow at 7. We can talk then."** It was an order more than a request – and I found myself glaring at it. Did he care if it suited me to call round? I know I had said we needed to chat but it would have been nice to have been consulted on the when's and where's. I typed back a quick **'OK'** and put my phone back in my pocket – trying to shake the feeling that my world was that little bit off balance. That I no longer understood the person I had been sure I was going to grow very old with. But, not wanting to let the girls know something had rankled me, I pasted on a smile and walked into the kitchen making all the right appreciative noises.

"Eve, you really do put me to shame," I said, as she ladled out bowls of steaming pasta before pouring her home-made Arrabbiata sauce over it.

She had outdone herself again – the parmesan cheese was grated in a bowl and there was garlic bread and salad prepared.

"Mum, you know I like to cook. It's a hobby. I wouldn't do it if I didn't want to."

Sorcha sniffed and mumbled something that sounded like "goody-two-shoes lick-arse" but when I looked at her she was smiling. Normally I would be concerned about Sorcha being in good form two days in a row, it being very uncharacteristic of her, but I decided to push that worry away, just like I pushed my anger at Matthew away. Perhaps she was just maturing and was finally coming out of the teen-horror years, I thought. I shouldn't look a gift horse in the mouth by questioning. That would make me kind of insane. So I smiled back at her, reached out and squeezed my two girls' hands before we started to eat. And once again I was grateful to have company in my home and to be able to share a meal with my children.

"I love you both, so very, very much," I told my girls between mouthfuls of pasta. "You know that, don't you?"

They nodded, gave each other a strange look and continued eating.

Later as I poured some of the leftover sauce into a Tupperware container to take to Áine's the following day, I thought about how none of us ever really know how life is going to turn out. I wondered if Áine had ever thought she would end up with dementia? None of us knew what was ahead of us. I suppose the best we could do was run with it and see where it took us – even if the thought of it taking me to Matthew's new digs the following night filled me with a certain sense of dread.

Cross that bridge when you come to it, Georgina, I told myself as I put the Tupperware in the fridge and switched on the dishwasher. There would be enough time for worrying about how to address the mystery lingerie in my husband's house tomorrow.

Chapter 7

ᴄᴏ 1964 ᴏ

Charlotte was sitting on the back step, smoking a cigarette. Áine watched the smoke swirl and rise, blowing away on the breeze.

"It's like another world," Charlotte said. "The heat, the brightness of the sun. It makes here look just so positively dreary."

Áine looked around the garden from where she knelt, weeding a flowerbed. It was a bright day. The garden was in bloom. There was a haziness, a comfortable relaxing atmosphere that she revelled in. She couldn't imagine anywhere in the world less dreary than this garden filled with bright flowers, the smell of the herbs, the sweet scent of lavender filling the air and the sound of only a distant lawnmower.

"I know you think this house is the centre of the universe," Charlotte said. "But's it not. This town is not the be-all and end-all. Oh Áine, you should hear how they talk. It sounds like singing. Sexy singing."

Áine blushed at her sister's description.

"Better than the harsh tones of the men around here who wouldn't know how to compliment a woman if their life depended on it. These men – the Italians – they could simply be asking for the time and it sounds like they're trying to seduce you."

"But you don't want to be seduced," Áine said, the word 'seduced' feeling coarse in her mouth. "You're married."

"Yes, I'm married, not dead!" Charlotte laughed, tilting her head to the sun and batting away a butterfly which had landed close to her. "And besides, Jack doesn't mind. It makes him feel like the king of the forest to have all the men pining over his wife. He says my boobs have helped him secure at least three export deals."

Áine blushed furiously and patted the soil from her gardening gloves – aware that her boobs (God, to even call them that! She preferred not to refer to her bosom at all if possible – she barely even registered she had one) had never secured anyone a deal – nor could she imagine they ever would.

"You are awful," she teased her sister.

"Not a bit. I just live life to the full," Charlotte said, reaching her arms out as wide as she could as if trying to grasp the whole world. "There's a big world out there, dear sister, and I want to see it. If only you knew how much of a life there is outside of this house, this town, this dreary country of ours. I know you would love it. I know you would come to life – step out of your comfort zone, live a little."

Áine bristled. She knew her sister cared for her deeply – she always had – but she just couldn't accept that Áine was happy with her lot. At least, she thought she was happy with her lot. In a way. She wanted to fall in love and get married. Of course. She wanted to start her own family, decorate her own home, plant her own garden. That was enough for her. Charlotte could never understand. She considered her boring. Áine knew her sister didn't understand her quiet lifestyle, that she wanted her to see the world – but Áine didn't want that and every now and again she wanted to scream at her sister to let her make her own choices and to stop trying to persuade her to be a person she never could be.

"I do live a little," she replied tersely.

"Well, maybe you should live a lot then," Charlotte said, stubbing her cigarette out on the concrete step and standing up to put her butt into the bin by the ivy-covered wall. "Do you not feel like a prisoner here? Living your life caring for Mum, keeping house, going to work. What do you do for fun?"

"I have fun!" Áine said. "This is fun –" She gestured around her garden – the garden she had nurtured to life. "Cooking is fun. Teaching is fun. I go to the dances, sometimes."

Charlotte crossed the garden and hugged her sister. "I just worry about you," she said, almost whispering.

"I would tell you if there was something to worry about. I'm not the one living on the other side of the world, flirting with handsome Italians when I'm already married – waving my … my … boobs at them."

Charlotte never took offence. She never got cross. She just laughed off her sister's comments. "My darling sister," she said softly, "I can assure you that you have nothing to worry about with me either. Let's not fight." She hugged Áine. "I'm only here for a short time before we have to go to Italy again – I think we should have as much fun as possible. Let's not ruin it with cross words? I'm sorry if you think I'm judging. I'm not judging you – I just want to share the world with you."

Áine lay her head gently on her sister's shoulder and breathed her in. She could never quite pinpoint Charlotte's scent. Her own was Pear's Soap. But Charlotte, she smelled of expensive perfume, her skin always glowing with the effects of the sun. Her skin always felt so warm that Áine was transported in that moment back to the nights when she would have woken from a bad dream and climbed into the bed beside her sister who would have moved over and allowed her in, even though the bed was narrow and Áine liked to hog the covers. It was Charlotte who comforted Áine back to sleep, who hushed her and hugged and reassured her that the world was a good place and that monsters were not even one bit real and that the sun would always come up in the morning.

"I miss you when you go," Áine whispered. "You and the children. The house feels so much warmer when you're all here."

"And noisier, I bet," Charlotte said, kissing her little sister on the top of her head. "Those children of mine are going to give Mother Dearest a heart attack if they don't keep it down!"

Áine laughed. There was no doubt this grand house – which had been the envy of all their friends growing up – was noisier and brighter when Jonathan and Emma were about. It would have been impossible for it to be quieter than it was in their absence in fairness. Apart from the tinkle of the piano keys as she played for her mother or the occasional tinny rattle from the wireless on the kitchen counter as she prepared dinner or watched her mother measure out the flour and yeast for baking bread, the house was often in total silence. After her mother went to bed she would creep back downstairs to the kitchen where she could feel the warmth from the Aga, switch on the light and the radio and listen to songs of love and longing while she planned her lessons for the next day. Occasionally, and only when she could hear the snores of her mother echo down the wooden stairs, she would allow herself to sing along – and to close her eyes and imagine the songs were about her own life.

"Jack is going to take the children to see his parents for a day or two," Charlotte said, lighting another cigarette and taking a deep drag on it.

Áine watched as her sister exhaled and the smoke rose, twirling into the sky, like clouds rising to meet more clouds.

"Mother will be happy," said Charlotte.

Áine nodded. "You know she loves the children. But she is getting older. She is set in her ways."

"She's only in her fifties for God's sake! The way she goes on you would think she had one foot in the grave."

"Charlotte, she loves us all very much but she likes her routine. She likes things the way they were. She had to struggle for long enough – she doesn't 'do worry' well now. Don't judge her harshly for it."

Charlotte took a deep breath and exhaled just as slowly. "I'm not judging. But the pair of you … stuck in this house. Like Miss Havisham and that … God … that girl she had with her …"

"Estella …"

"Estella, that's it."

"We're nothing like them," Áine said, her hackles rising slightly. "We're just different to you. Mother says you got Daddy's genes. That he had the wanderlust and she was always happiest at home."

Charlotte sighed, inhaled deeply on her cigarette. Áine knew her sister didn't like to talk about their father. Perhaps it was easier for Áine because she didn't remember him. She missed him, of course. It was something she wondered about from time to time – how she could miss someone she never really knew. But she did – yet when she tried to talk of him she could see a deep pain and sorrow in the eyes of her sister and her mother that made her back off – not wanting to cause them further pain. She had seen his picture of course – images of a bear of man looking stern and formal – standing tall beside her mother. Neither were smiling, despite the fact they were clearly both wearing wedding clothes and this was the happiest day of their lives. Charlotte told her once that he had a lovely smile. That Áine's smile mirrored his. She had stood that night in front of the mirror and pulled a hundred different smiles, wondering which one she got from him.

"So anyway," Charlotte said, deftly changing the subject from one which obviously made her deeply uncomfortable, "with the children away, I thought us girls could go out to a dance. I know you say you are happy – but I know you love music. I know you love dancing. Áine, you always loved to dance – and you were good at it as well. Not like me and my size-seven left feet."

She removed her shoes from her feet and waved them at her. They had always laughed at how dainty Charlotte had less than dainty feet. When she was pregnant they had swollen to a size eight and she had spent the latter stages of her pregnancy wearing house slippers as they were the only thing that would fit.

"So we'll go," said Charlotte. "I'll lend you one of my dresses if you feel you have nothing appropriate. Hopefully you will have a pair of shoes suitable for outside of the classroom or gardening and we can do each other's hair and make-up and I will even sneak in a little Babycham for us before we go out. Mother will never know. You can retain your Perfect Daughter crown! We'll get Auntie Sheila to come over and sit with her. You won't have to worry about her for a night."

Áine shrugged her shoulders. She couldn't deny it – the thought of a night out sounded appealing. Especially if Charlotte would lend her a dress to wear. Charlotte had the most beautiful dress – lilac flowers, a full skirt – it was like something out of *Vogue* magazine. She wondered if Charlotte would loan her that dress? She had the perfect pair of cream shoes she had bought to wear to a wedding the year before which would go with it perfectly. But she was nervous. She hadn't been out in a while.

"Don't shrug your shoulders," Charlotte said. "I'll be gone soon and you won't go out and we won't have the chance to dance around and be silly and flirt with men and smoke and laugh and have a little drink. Say you will, my lovely, lovely sister? If I can't persuade you to come to Italy with me ..."

"You know I can't leave Mammy and make a trip like that."

"Bring her. Get her away from here. From the ghosts of the life she could have had."

"Charlie, you know she would never leave here. He's here for her. She couldn't be anywhere else. And I, even if I wanted to, couldn't leave her ... not after everything ..."

"But you can leave her for a night? You can come dancing. Actually, I refuse to take no for an answer. You will come with me. I have seen you eye the lilac dress – you can wear it. In fact I insist you wear it. You can keep it even if you just agree to come out. Please, please, please!"

Áine laughed. When Charlotte turned on the pleading, the big doe eyes, the cheeky smile, Áine could sometimes forget who was the big sister and who was the little sister.

"Okay," she said.

"Yay!" Charlotte said, kissing her and clapping her hands with joy.

Chapter 8

"Just the right amount of basil," Áine said as she forked a mouthful of Eve's pasta into her mouth.

I couldn't help but smile with pride that once again my daughter's cooking was going down a treat. The poor old woman wouldn't have been quite so complimentary if she was eating one of my creations.

"Some people overdo the basil – but I prefer more oregano. And a splash of balsamic vinegar. And you know the secret to a good sauce? Just a square of dark chocolate."

Áine seemed more enthused, more alive than I had seen her yet.

"You remember that, don't you?" she said. "You taught me that, Charlie. When you came back from Italy? When Mother was shocked you didn't want potatoes for dinner …" Áine stopped, taking another mouthful of her meal, and looked back at Georgina, her face falling a little, the realisation kicking in that she had drifted off again just a little. "You know what I mean … when my sister came back from her travels …"

"Of course, Áine," I nodded, playing it cool as if nothing untoward had happened. "Chocolate? I'd never have thought of that. Does it really work?"

"You must try it ... I could help," Áine said, her voice lifting again, her face wide with expectation.

"That sounds lovely," I said. "I'm sure you could teach me a thing or two. I could bring some ingredients over."

"I used to have a larder full of fresh herbs and spices. In fact I used to grow them in the garden."

I glanced out the window to see a large garden that was clearly once loved very much. Now it had fallen into an awful state. Overgrown flowerbeds, flattened weeds, raised beds which looked sad and unloved dotted the garden, and the pathways which had clearly once been covered in gravel looked messy, tall brown weeds sprouting up like stubble.

"Jonathan has plans to get it all covered over – a nice lawn laid. Says it will be easier to manage," Áine said. "I know it makes sense – but my garden was my pride and joy for so long. I just can't keep it now."

One of my biggest problems in life is that I often open my mouth before engaging my brain. It has got me into trouble more times than I care to think about, so it was no surprise that it was leading me almost directly back into trouble as I started with a "Well, maybe we could talk to Jonathan about saving even a little bit of the garden? We could work on it together."

Áine's face lit up at the prospect, which gave me a nice warm glow that lasted all of about three seconds before I realised this meant I would have to talk to Jonathan – and ask him for stuff. Gardening stuff. It simultaneously dawned on me that I knew as much about gardening as I did about cooking – and that I was voicing ideas and making promises that I might not be able to live up to.

"Oh, do you think so?" Áine said. "I would love it. I can't bear the thought of a summer not being out there getting my hands dirty in the soil. I know some people don't get gardening, but it's just one of those things I love …"

I couldn't go back then, I thought. And sure, from what I had read, if it was something that Áine always did it could well help with our memory work. I'd sell it to Jonathan like that. I was sure he would understand – after all, he did say he would do all he could to help his aunt.

"Well, that's two plans we have then," I smiled. "Cooking and gardening. You just let me know what else you like and we'll try and do it. Sure we have the time and we might as well make the most of it."

"Before I lose my mind altogether?" Áine said.

She was smiling – but it didn't reach her eyes. She was a smart woman. I imagined she would have been quite the wit in her day. We could skirt around her need for a carer but she knew what was happening to her – and while she tried to joke about it now, it was clear it weighed heavy on her mind.

"You have to try not to worry about that, Áine. You've years ahead of you yet – and more adventures to have. Gardening sounds like an adventure to me. I've never so much as managed to keep a houseplant alive in the past. My girls used to come home from school with sunflowers each summer and I never once saw one bloom. I would nip out and buy some from the garden centre so the girls wouldn't get upset."

Áine laughed – and I couldn't help but notice there was something so girlish about her when she giggled. "You are very like her in a lot of ways, you know. You're like Charlotte. She did what she wanted to. She was fearless. No one held her back. And she was absolutely atrocious at gardening too!"

She looked wistful and I wondered what layers I could peel back. I wished I had known her years ago – but then again I supposed I had time to find out more. We were going to be spending a lot of time together.

Jonathan arrived just before six – just as I was getting ready to say goodbye to Áine. The house was tidy. The dishes were done and put away. Áine's night things were laid out and a small fire was burning in the hearth. It would be enough to keep the slight chill in the air out of the house – and of course it made the place feel so much cosier.

Áine seemed content – well fed and a head full of ideas about the garden – and now it was up to me to bring up the matter with Jonathan.

While he had a very broad smile for his aunt, he looked at me with a slightly more wearisome look on his face. His shirtsleeves were rolled up, his top button undone, and he looked as if it had been a tough day at the office. I was well used to that look when Matthew would walk in from a hard day at school and find himself good for nothing for the rest of the evening. Funny, in hindsight, that no matter what the working day had thrown at me I still managed to find the energy to look after the house and make sure the girls were okay.

I felt awkward. I wasn't quite sure how to address him. It seemed to be crossing the line to say "Tough day at the office?" but then again would I seem completely dense not to acknowledge that he looked stressed out and just land him with more requests in relation to his aunt? I decided to play it safe and make a comment about the weather – how it was a little colder despite the arrival of spring – and he nodded, grunting an affirmative response.

I could have walked away, I supposed – and left the matter for another day but I had seen how Áine's face had lit up at the thought of even a small plot of her beloved garden being saved – and I knew I had to bite the bullet.

"Jonathan," I said, "could I have a quick word before I leave?"

"Fire away," he said, rubbing his temples as if to ease a headache.

"Can I get you a glass of water or something first?" I asked.

He looked at me strangely, but then he nodded again. "Yes, actually. I would love a glass of cold water. I have a headache coming on." He grimaced.

"I have some paracetamol in my bag if that helps?"

He looked at me again – quizzically – as if he wasn't expecting that I would even dream of helping him, and thanked me for the tablets before he sat down at the kitchen table.

"Right, now, what is it you wanted to talk about?"

I sat down and started to tell him how I wanted to help his aunt as much as possible – and I told him about some of the articles I had read and how I thought saving a little of the garden would be of benefit to Áine. It could go either way, I thought as he looked at me, nodding and taking in what I was saying. He could tell me the plans were made, that I was overstepping the mark and that I was getting on his nerves. He looked like the kind of man whose nerves were "got on" easily.

"I thought giving her less to do would make it easier," he said eventually – looking at me with a kind of defeated look on his face.

It was not the response I was expecting – and once again I found myself feeling sorry for him.

"I'm sure you're only learning about this – I have only starting reading up on it myself. It's natural to want to wrap someone in cotton wool," I said.

"But from what you're saying, I've been in danger of smothering her in cotton wool?"

Unexpectedly, without thinking, I found myself reaching across the table and rubbing his arm as if to comfort him. All I could think was that this must be so hard on him – hard on any family – to watch someone they love start to slip away.

My face blazed as he pulled his arm away as if I had pinched it. He stood up and coughed, turned his back to me and then turned to face me again.

"You tell me what you need, Georgina. Come to me with something more concrete – and tell me what I can do. I'll do it. She deserves it. Now, it's past your finishing time and I'd love to spend some time alone with my aunt so you may as well get going."

I felt the heat from my face creep down my neck – I had, again, made an eejit of myself. Reaching out to comfort this man had been one move too far and he clearly wasn't impressed. In fact if the look on his face was anything to go by, he looked absolutely horrified that I had touched him.

"Right," I muttered, lifting my bag and my files, "I'll be off then. I'll come back to you soon about the garden."

"Yes. Yes, do that. Whatever we need to buy, to get, we'll get it."

He didn't say thanks. He didn't say goodbye. He just stood in the kitchen as I walked down the hall, poked my head through the door to say my farewells to Áine, and left – my face still blazing.

It was only when I got to the car that I allowed myself to let out a string of expletives. And when I remembered that I had planned to go and see Matthew – to discuss Pink Bra-gate amongst a number of other things – I let out a second string of expletives.

I fished my phone out of my bag and texted Sinéad, asking her to put some wine in the fridge and to have the tequila ready – just in case.

Normally I would have made an effort. Since we had split up I had tried my very best to always look like the best possible version of me when I saw my husband. I wanted to show him what he was missing – so before any scheduled visit I would brush my hair, touch up my make-up, wear something figure-flattering and spray on some perfume. I would plaster a big old smile on my face, even when I wanted to cry or shout, and I would adopt the nonchalant approach of a woman trying to show her husband that she was absolutely okay with him "finding himself".

But of course that was when I thought "finding himself" would also involve finding me again – remembering the woman he had fallen in love with and realising that even though we were older, and perhaps not wiser, we were still the perfect match we totally thought we were when we were teenagers.

It was becoming increasingly clear to me however that Matthew was finding a whole different side of himself – one which preferred women in lacy lingerie. It hadn't been like that with us. It didn't need to be. I don't mean that we never made an effort with each other – of course we did. I had my share of silky, skimpy and uncomfortable underwear stashed in my bottom drawer for weekends away. But ordinarily we didn't need to make an extra effort to want each other. That side of our relationship had never been a problem. Or so I thought. When he cleared off (and I played the part of the supportive wife, fully believing that if you loved someone you let them go and they would come back to you if it was meant to be) I started to question things about our relationship that I never had before. Had we become complacent? Too comfortable? Too routine-led? I mean it was hard to be spontaneous with two teenage girls in the house. I had beaten myself up about that since he left – and decided that it was time to try and make more of an effort.

But sitting outside his house now, straight from work and still burning from what had happened with Jonathan, and knowing what I was going to discuss, I didn't have the mental energy to think too much about how I looked. I pulled down my sun visor and gave myself a cursory glance in the mirror. My make-up was a little blotchy – but decent enough. My hair was a little frizzy, and the neat ponytail I had put in that morning had come loose. I looked tired – but then again I felt tired. What could Matthew expect though? Doing it all – on

my own – wasn't easy. Feeling cranky, I thought perhaps it
was time he saw just what his leaving was doing to me.

I got out of the car, walked to his door and rang the
doorbell. Yes, it was strange to wait for my own husband to
let me in. I saw his familiar shadow move down the hall and
it dawned on me that I had no idea how to broach what I
needed to with him. Did I just jump right in there with a quick
"So, a pink bra, eh?" or did I start with some social niceties?
God, this was enough to drive me insane. This was a man I
had known for more than twenty years – who I had grown
into adulthood with – and now I didn't even know how to
talk to him any more.

In fact, as he opened the door and said hello I felt a wave
of emotion wash over me. Awkwardness mixed with
embarrassment mixed with betrayal.

"Can I come in?" I managed to stutter and he laughed.

"Of course you can. God, you're my wife. I'm not going to
leave you standing on the doorstep. Come in, come in, have a
coffee. I may even have some biscuits. It's amazing how long
they last without the girls eating them."

I put on a fake smile – biting back what I wanted to say –
which was that of course I wouldn't know what it was like
not to have the girls around. The girls were with me. There
was never any question but that they would be with me.
Matthew had never once hinted that he wanted them with
him and, while that suited me, the part of me that was waking
up to all that had happened over the last few months thought
that it was incredibly selfish that he never even considered
asking the girls to go with him.

Watching him move around his kitchen with an ease he
never seemed to display in our kitchen, my ire only grew
stronger. He had bought a coffee machine – one of those fancy
yokes you put the pods in and it made lattes and cappuccinos
and the like. It was a far stretch from the instant we drank at
home. He even had one of those little shakers to add a little

sprinkle of chocolate to the top. I was half expecting him to present some home-baked biscotti – and I was glad when he brought some chocolate digestives. I might have had to kill him otherwise.

"So," he said, as he took a seat at his kitchen table opposite me. "I'm assuming this is more than just a social call?"

I looked at him – really looked at him. He had showered and changed into jeans and a T-shirt with a slight V-neck. I could see the smallest tuft of hair poke out from the top of his T-shirt and I wanted, though I was angry with him, to reach out and touch it. To draw some comfort from the familiarity of the feel of him. But I couldn't. Just as it was inappropriate for me to reach out and comfort Jonathan earlier – it was inappropriate for me to reach out and touch my husband. My own husband. Fighting the urge to burst into tears, I decided instead to stuff a chocolate digestive into my mouth – feeding my emotions with sweet biscuit-y goodness.

Of course, answering Matthew while my mouth was stuffed with chocolate biscuit was not one bit easy and I had to chew and swallow as fast I could, which, in keeping with the evening I was having, led to a mild choking fit. I managed to abate same with a sip of the fancy coffee Matthew had made for me, which just brought back my sense of raw anger.

"Pink bra!" I blurted when I could catch my breath.

His face coloured (a colour similar to a pink bra, as it happened), and he glanced down at his coffee. Slowly he lifted his teaspoon, stirred his drink and sucked the foam off the spoon before putting it down. I'm sure it only took a matter of seconds, but it felt like forever.

"I'm not sure I know what you mean," he said – but he couldn't hold eye contact.

"I mean," I said, taking a deep breath, "a pink bra. The girls, they found one, when they were here. They were helping with laundry."

"It's probably just one of theirs. You know, if they leave

stuff here I wash it and have it ready for them." Still no eye contact.

"I think, Matthew, they would recognise their own underwear," I said slowly. "And besides, from what they tell me, it's not the kind of underwear a teenage girl would wear. It was – more – adult in nature."

His face coloured deeper. I could almost hear the cogs whir in his head as he tried to think of something to say. I could feel my own face colouring.

"Look, Matthew, if you're seeing someone, well, then you're seeing someone. I can't pretend I'm comfortable with it," I said, my voice shaking. I begged myself not to cry. "But it's your life. I suppose. I just don't want the girls exposed to it."

"Georgie," he began but the sound of him calling me by my pet name was enough to send me over the edge.

My eyes filled with tears and the knot of tension that had been sitting in my stomach since I had met with Jonathan shifted.

"Please don't call me that!" I blurted.

"Georgina, I never meant to hurt you in all of this. I just wanted to find myself."

I nodded, like a grotesque water feature – each downward movement sending forth a flurry of fresh tears. I had well and truly completely arsed up my entire 'play it cool' persona.

"I didn't think," I managed, "when you said you wanted some time out that you really wanted someone else."

"I didn't think I did – I don't know what I want," he said, his eye contact still sketchy. "It was just this thing – a fling. I'm not sure it means anything. But it was nice to feel desired …"

I wanted to scream at him to stop talking. To tell him he was making it worse. To tell him that when you're in a hole, you stop digging – or you at least have the decency to hand me the shovel so that I can brain you with it.

"I desired you," I squeaked, in perhaps the least 'I desire you' voice known to mankind.

"Did you?" he asked. "It didn't feel like it."

He was looking at me now and I stared back at him – directly at him. Had we been living in alternative worlds? We had still had sex. I hadn't dreamt it. We were still together. Okay, it was a bit more functional that it had been, but what did you want after twenty-two years? Swinging from the chandeliers? Fifty Shades of Debauchery? It was supposed to be comfortable and comforting now, wasn't it?

"Of course I did." The tuft of hair was still taunting me. Although now I was in some weird twilight zone between wanting to touch it, to caress it and to prove to him that I desired him and always had, or to pull it, hard, until his eyes watered and he begged for mercy.

"I'm sorry," he offered.

"Then don't do it," I countered. "Not until we know where we are going. I mean –"

"Oh Georgie!"

"Don't. Call. Me. That!"

"Right, look, I'm sorry. But don't you think we are past this now? I thought things were settling down? I thought we had reached some sort of acceptance?"

His words hit me. Like body-blows on top of the body-blows he had already loaded on me when he left. He seemed to think a lot for me. He seemed to make all the decisions in the world for us. And he seemed to find a way to come to terms with tearing the world we knew apart without ever feeling the need to tell me about it. Sure we were reaching some sort of acceptance?

I looked at him again – it was almost as if his features transformed in front of my face. The face I had known and loved – that I had seen get older, more weathered, more handsome, more mine over the years, blurred. I didn't think I knew him at all.

It's hard to know how to react when someone turns your reality on its head. I wanted to shout again, to challenge him, but then again a part of me worried that I was the one who had been living in my own world all these years. Had I been so blind?

I tried to steady myself – which was no mean feat as my legs were like jelly – and I stood up, leaving my fancy coffee where it sat on his table in his fancy coffee cup.

"Try to watch what you expose the girls to," I managed before I turned on my heel and walked to the door.

As I walked I wanted him to call me – to stop me. I wanted him to make some grand big romantic gesture and run and block the door, tell me he was sorry and he had just been scared by the strength of his emotions for me. I wanted him to say he had worded it all badly and of course he loved me. That he wanted me. I wanted him to kiss me and for that kiss to fix everything that was broken.

But I knew, with each step I took, that wasn't going to happen. It was – I realised once and for all and with a searing pain in the very pit of my stomach – over. Totally over. He didn't stop me. He didn't even call half-heartedly after me. He didn't watch from the window as I drove off. He didn't text to say he was sorry and he hoped I was okay.

He didn't care, I realised – and we were never going to get that happy ending I dreamt of.

Chapter 9

◌ 1964 ◌

Áine had to take several deep breaths before she followed her sister into the Corinthian ballroom. She had felt nervous and sick to her stomach even when she was getting ready to go out. Maybe Charlotte was right – she was much too sheltered. She didn't go dancing – not really. Not unless she felt she simply had to avoid being labelled a hermit. So when she went out, she felt her stomach tighten with nerves.

"It's excitement," Charlotte had said. "It's a good thing."

But it didn't feel like excitement or a good thing. And, as Áine had applied her blusher and sprayed some perfume on her wrists, she had contemplated not going at all. It was only when her mother had knocked gently on her bedroom door, and had pressed a few coins into her hand to help with her night out, that she had felt there was no turning back. Even her mother was trying to get her to go out a bit more.

"You know I love you, Áine, and I will always be grateful for all you have done for me," Rosaleen had said. "But you can't spend your entire life in this house with me. What kind of company am I for a young thing like yourself? You're only twenty-seven. You should be building a life for yourself. Like your sister."

Áine had taken her mother's hands in hers, conscious of how her fingers were starting to bend and twist with the force of the disease which was ravaging her body.

"I will be here for you, Mother, always. I'm happy with my lot. I swear to you. Charlotte does enough living for the both of us – I'm happy being set in my ways."

Rosaleen had responded with a weak, watery smile and Áine felt herself relax. She could not bear the thought of Rosaleen being hurt – not when she had already been through so much – and she was for the most part happy with her life. A little lonely at times, perhaps – when Rosaleen had gone to bed, or sometimes when she saw the look Jack would give Charlotte and the way her sister exhaled and closed her eyes in perfect bliss when her husband embraced her.

She tried to relax as she walked into the dancehall but there was no denying she felt a little out of her depth as she was surrounded by a fug of smoke, a strong smell of perfume and music from the band on stage in full swing.

"Cheer up!" Charlotte turned and nudged her. "It's supposed to be fun. You look like you're on your way to the firing squad."

Áine plastered on her biggest fake smile and told her sister she would be fine. She just hadn't been out in a while and it felt a little strange.

"A gin and tonic will help with that," Charlotte said, weaving her way to the bar to order before Áine could decline the offer and say she was fine with water.

Áine put her hand to the fine gold chain which she always wore around her neck and played with the charm – a set of angel wings – on the end of it. It was a nervous habit, she knew, but it gave her comfort.

She was thinking of how she would break it to her sister that she didn't even like gin when she saw one of her colleagues from the school wave across the room to her and begin to move in her direction.

Lorcan O'Hara taught the Primary 7 class – and it was thought he had his sights set on becoming headmaster one of these days. Áine always felt awkward around him – although she wasn't quite sure if that was awkward bad or awkward good. She just knew she always felt tongue-tied in his company and on most occasions she tended to avoid conversation with him to avoid making an eejit of herself. She most certainly had not been expecting to see him out at the dance – she supposed she hadn't given much consideration at all to who she might bump into.

"Well, Áine Quigley – out and about on the town! You're looking well," he said, smiling brightly at her.

She dropped her hand from the chain around her neck and crossed her arms awkwardly, wishing she had worn something less colourful – something that would allow her to fade into the background in a way that made her feel infinitely more comfortable. He looked less stern, and more handsome out of the school environment. That realisation did nothing to ease her nerves.

"Thank you," she mumbled, struggling to think of another word to say.

"It's not often you're seen out."

"I'm here with my sister," she said. "She's back from her travels."

"Ah! You did mention that, didn't you? Can I buy you – the both of you – a drink?"

"I think we're fine," Áine said, wishing he would just leave before the blush that was rising from her chest rose any further. She couldn't think of how she could make this situation any better – when it came to members of the opposite sex she had no social skills and felt acutely aware of her shortcomings. Not to mention it would be nice if he was gone before Charlotte returned. Áine knew how this would pan out if Charlotte saw the two of them talking and realised that Lorcan wasn't wearing a wedding ring.

"Well, maybe a dance later?" he asked, his deep blue eyes hopeful.

"Maybe," she said, casting her eyes downwards, hoping he would take the hint – and sure enough he did, saying a quick – and awkward – goodbye. She suddenly craved the gin and tonic that Charlotte had said she would bring her and when her sister handed her the glass she had to stop herself from downing it in one, the bitter taste of the gin catching in her throat.

"Whoa, little sister, go easy," Charlotte said, laughing.

Áine coughed, searched through her bag for a handkerchief and dabbed her mouth. "Sorry," she muttered, her face red, feeling increasingly uncomfortable as the music and cigarette smoke swirled around her.

"Let's get a seat," Charlotte said. "You need to relax a bit, Áine, honestly. You're like a coiled spring."

Áine forced a smile on her face. "I'm fine, honest. I'm just not used to being out and about."

"Well, we'll have to do our best to rectify that, dear sister," Charlotte said, sitting and rifling in her bag for her cigarettes. "We'll have to get you out into the world. And if not into the world, into this town at least. And not just when I come and force your hand. Do your friends from school never ask you out with them? Who was that you were talking to while I was at the bar? You know, the tall handsome kind you didn't think I saw you with?"

"It's just someone I work with," Áine answered. "No one for you to be concerned about."

"Single?"

"I – I'm not sure," Áine lied.

"Of course you know!" Charlotte laughed. "You want me to believe you never checked out if he was wearing a wedding ring or not? You're shy, not dead."

"Okay. He's single. He teaches the older boys."

"And did he offer to buy you a drink?" Charlotte raised an eyebrow.

"He offered to buy us both a drink," Áine said. "He's a gentleman."

"A single gentleman with the means to buy us drinks," Charlotte said, smiling. "And so where are our drinks?"

"I told him we were fine."

"You may be fine," Charlotte said, downing her drink, taking a drag of her cigarette and squeezing out from behind the table, "but I'm thirsty."

She looked around and Áine reached out and touched her arm. "I'll buy you another drink, Charlotte."

"As I said, my lovely sister, if you won't go out into the world, then the world will just have to come and find you." She shrugged Áine's hand from her arm and set off across the room in search of Lorcan O'Hara and his offer of a drink.

In that moment, as Áine took a long, hard drink of her gin and tonic. she didn't know whether she wanted to kill or hug her sister. There was no way Charlotte was letting her get away with anything. She tried to convince herself, as she sat there, that it might be no bad thing. Perhaps having someone else who took the first steps would be positive and lovely and make her feel better about everything.

Then again, she thought, as she saw Lorcan walk back towards her table with a grinning Charlotte by his side, both carrying drinks, maybe there was still time to run for the door.

"You didn't tell me your sister was such a charmer," Lorcan said.

Áine blushed, taking "your sister is such a charmer" to be code for 'I love your sister and haven't twigged yet that she is married and not even slightly available'.

"She is that," Áine replied, casting her eyes downwards.

"Must be in the genes," he said. "Just like her sister."

His smile was gentle, modest – shy even. There was an honesty in his expression which took her breath away. How had she not noticed before just how handsome he really was? Then again she tended to keep her head down in the staffroom. A quick cup of tea, her head in the books for five minutes, and then she would scuttle back to her classroom.

"Oh no," Charlotte interjected. "Áine here is nothing at all like me. Not at all. She's the better of the pair. Charm is the least of her many, many attributes. She's quite the dancer too. You should show him, Áine," she said, jabbing Áine in the ribs. "There's a lovely song playing now. Why don't the pair of you take a turn around the floor? I'll keep an eye on the drinks. I don't mind playing gooseberry – from a safe distance. What else is a boring old married woman like me to do anyway?"

She shuffled onto the bench where Áine was sitting, nudging her along the length of the seat so that she risked falling flat onto the floor if she didn't get up and move towards where Lorcan was standing expectantly.

Warmed by the gin, and by Lorcan's kind smile, and perhaps even a little by her sister's kind words, she took a deep breath and held out her hand to feel the warmth of his as he led her to the dance floor. Now all she had to do was to try not to be her usual clumsy self and show him that she could no more dance than she could whistle 'Dixie'. The cream-coloured shoes, which were already pinching her toes, would have to give her a certain grace she had never possessed before – or at least she hoped that the gin would give her some Dutch courage to be able to hold her own on the dance floor.

"I hope you know what you're doing," he said, smiling at her. "I never was one for dancing much."

She smiled back. "It will be the blind leading the blind perhaps," she said. "My sister may have oversold my dancing skills."

"Well, I know she hasn't oversold everything else, and I'm sure as long as we keep moving and don't step on too many toes no-one will be any the wiser."

She felt herself exhale.

Chapter 10

∽ *Present Day* ∾

"I have to work tomorrow," I blurted to Sinéad as she opened the door to the horror story that was me post meeting with Matthew.

Any trace of make-up was gone. My eyes were red. My throat was croaky from even more swearing in the car and I was shaking like a leaf.

Sinéad looked at me for a moment, trying to take in the sight in front of her and, I suppose, think of an appropriate response. For the first time since I had I known her, she was speechless.

"I have to work tomorrow, and I need to get very drunk," I added, as she stood back and watched me walk through to her kitchen.

Her husband, Peter, who was sitting at the kitchen island reading the paper and drinking a coffee had the good sense – on seeing my face – to very quickly announce he was going to leave us alone for a while.

Sinéad's house was one of those places where I felt so comfortable that I could, without feeling strange, reach into

88

her fridge, lift out the bottle of wine she had been cooling on my instruction, and open it as she took two glasses from her perfectly neat kitchen cupboards.

"I know this is a stupid question," she said, "but are you okay?"

I filled my glass as high as I could and took a long drink, feeling the bitter hit of the wine turn my stomach. And yet I drank more before setting the glass down and looking at my friend.

"It's over, Sinéad. I know you probably knew that. I know that you have probably been trying to tell me that for a long time but it's over."

I could see the pity on her face when she looked at me.

"You talked to him?" she asked.

I took another drink from my glass. "We've reached an acceptance that it's over, apparently," I said. The words – the whole concept of what had happened – sounded so strange. It still made no sense. None of this made sense. "He has slept with someone else. He doesn't know if he wants her or not. But he doesn't want me. But he didn't mean to hurt me, so that's okay."

The tears started to slide down my face once again – I could hardly believe I had any tears left to shed.

Sinéad put her untouched glass down, crossed the room and pulled me into a big hug, and I allowed myself to sob on her shoulder.

"I know I shouldn't say it," she said, "but you were too good for him anyway. Much too good for him."

"How will I tell the girls?" I sobbed.

"Oh, pet," Sinéad soothed, "I think you should give the girls more credit. I think they probably already know it's over."

"So it's just me that's been hanging on like an eejit then?"

She pulled me a little closer. Which was brave of her in hindsight. My nose was now running like a tap and her hug only managed to force me to use her beige cashmere as a tissue.

"No, not an eejit. You just weren't ready."

"I'm not sure I'm ready now, but I've no choice," I sniffed.

She stroked my hair and shushed me as my sobs subsided, and then when I had managed to get my breathing back under control she gently pushed me back.

"Listen to me, Georgina. You are my best friend. You are an amazing mother. You are probably the most caring person I know. This will not break you. You will come through this. I promise."

I nodded with a confidence I didn't feel.

"And when you feel stronger we can plot suitable revenge strategies," she smiled. "You know, prawns in the curtains, cress seeds on his deep pile, potatoes up his exhaust pipe ... that kind of thing."

I managed a snort which was more a laugh than a sob and then I reached for my wineglass again.

Sinéad reached out and took my wrist. "My darling, you know I love a drink as much, if not more, than the next person, but go easy. You don't want the girls seeing you fall apart and you don't want to deal with work with a killer hangover and a broken heart. Those are not happy bedfellows."

I let go of my glass. "You're right, of course you're right," I said. "Besides I think Jonathan Hegarty worries enough about me without me arriving smelling of drink."

"Oh dear," Sinéad said as she filled her kettle to make a pot of tea. "What happened now?"

By the time I had regaled her with the story of Jonathan, the garden, his headache and his swift move away from me as if I had leprosy, I had calmed down. I had even managed to laugh.

"I think he thinks I might want his body," I laughed, eating and actually enjoying a chocolate biscuit this time.

"And do you?" Sinéad asked, her eyebrow raised. "From what I know of Jonathan Hegarty, his body could merit a bit of wanting all right."

I grimaced. No. No, I did not want his body. I liked his aunt. I occasionally felt sorry for him – but if I could avoid spending any time in his company at all I would. Each meeting seemed to end awkwardly, or with me doing something I didn't want to. And not in a fun 'try anything once or twice if I like it' way.

"Ah no. I don't think so. Besides, I imagine the likes of him goes in for the trophy wife type. You know, fat lips, skinny arse, fake boobs and no brain? My lips are thin, my arse on the wide side, my boobs all too real thanks to breastfeeding twins and I like to think I have a brain. Although my stupidity around Matthew and the disastrous state of my marriage may indicate otherwise."

Sinéad shrugged. "Don't be too hard on yourself."

"Force of habit," I smiled. "But all that aside – no. Even if I was interested in a relationship with anyone it wouldn't be Jonathan Hegarty."

I didn't add, because I knew Sinéad wouldn't understand, that the only person I still wanted a relationship with was my husband. But then again – I guessed from our earlier conversation the chances of me having a romantic relationship again with Matthew were about on a par with my chances of having a romantic relationship with Mr Hegarty.

Eve and Sorcha had treated themselves to pizza while I'd been out so I found myself in the awkward position of having no leftovers to bring over to Áine. I didn't want to revert to sandwiches so I thought of a quick and easy recipe even I couldn't mess up. I stopped off at the supermarket in my lunch break and picked up some vegetables, herbs and a couple of chicken breasts with the intention of making a fresh soup with Áine. It would be the first step towards helping her regain a little independence – and regain her passion for cooking.

I felt quite positive about it and, after a relatively sleepless night thinking about the painful state of my personal life, I was embracing every sense of positivity I could. I had even spent some time in the wee small hours Googling 'gardening for dummies' and the like – and had put together a short list of basics that would help get us started. I would leave a note for Jonathan – figuring it was better if we avoided each other as much as possible.

The day was still cold – an unseasonal cold snap leaving a light frost that refused to shift even by lunchtime – but the sun was bright and I tried to focus on the positives as I walked up the path to the big house at Temple Muse and opened the door with my key.

But there was something about the quietness of the house which immediately made me feel uneasy. I was already well aware that Áine was a creature of comfort and routine so the silence, apart from the ticking of the clock, alarmed me. I was alarmed all the more when I called out but received no response, then looked into the sitting room where the TV stood, switched off, and where the armchair in which Áine usually sat was empty. Its cushions looked freshly plumped – and it didn't look as if anyone had sat in it any time recently. The room felt as lifeless as it looked without the presence of Áine leading a battle with the banker while watching *Deal or No Deal*. Next stop was the kitchen where again I found an empty scene awaiting me. The sandwiches, presumably lovingly prepared by Maria that morning, sat untouched. The TV was off and the room was cold. It all felt very wrong and I had to steady myself before I investigated further. I checked my phone – just in case Jonathan or Cecilia had left me a message and there was a perfectly understandable excuse for Áine's disappearance.

Perhaps her nephew had taken her out for the afternoon and had just forgotten to pass the message on. Or, thinking on it, my signal often dropped out when in some clients' houses – the more remote ones which sat on the Donegal border. Perhaps Cecilia had been trying to get in touch with me and couldn't? Perhaps Áine was at the doctor's or something similar? Something innocent.

I walked back up the hall, deciding to check the strange, impersonal bedroom at the top of the stairs before I would allow any real panic to kick in. And it was as I started to walk past the dining room that I heard a sigh of frustration echo around the dark walls. Gingerly I popped my head around the door – and saw Áine – sitting at an old piano, her hands poised as if ready to play. Her eyes were focused – straining at the sheet music propped in front of her.

She sighed again, turning her hands over and looking at them as if they were betraying her in some way. She sat there for a minute, just staring, before turning them back and poising herself to play again. I waited again, not sure what to do, and when Áine hit the keys the noise made me jump. The notes clashed, ricocheting around the room, and Áine sat back, slamming the lid of the piano down and cursing loudly at her own incompetence, before dropping her head to her hands and crying.

The sight was pitiful but I knew I had to be careful. I moved towards her slowly.

"Áine," I said gently, but she could not hear me over the sound of her own crying. "Áine, it's Georgina. Are you okay?"

"I can't do it any more. I don't understand. I'm sure I used to play. I know I used to play. Without even looking at the music. I played all the time but maybe it's this piano. I can't make it sound like it should. I've been trying and trying and I can't …"

I sat down, slowly, on the stool beside Áine and, at a loss

for any comforting words which could make this situation any less cruel, I simply took one of her hands in mine.

But she broke the hold and sat staring at her hands again. "You should ask Jonathan. He will tell you. He loves it when I play. He's going to learn one day. When he's older. His mother will be so proud …"

I nodded and listened, trying to place just where Áine was in her mind – and how I could get her back in touch with her life as it was.

"Charlotte?"

"A free bird," she nodded. "Beautiful. Not like me. But she can't play piano." She stifled a laugh between her tears. "She's awful at it. Tuneless. You can't have it all."

"No," I said. "I suppose not."

"Do you want me to play for you?" she asked. "I could." She lifted the lid of the piano as if the past minute was lost somewhere in time and poised her fingers again over the keys.

I rested my hands on hers. "I would love you to play for me but I wondered could we make soup? I've heard you're a great cook?"

"Did Charlotte tell you that?" Áine said, her face lit with excitement.

Thinking of how her face had crumpled just minutes before when her fingers could no longer find the right keys to make the music she had so loved, I nodded again. "Yes, yes, Charlotte said you were a fantastic cook."

I stood up and Áine shuffled out from behind the piano and followed me out of the room. And I vowed that I would not try and think about how long Áine may have been sitting in that room playing over moments of her life while trying to play a tune on the piano. There was a sadness to the situation that was almost tangible and in that moment I almost decided to give up on the notion of making the soup from scratch. Maybe it would be too much? I could have maybe found a tin of soup in the cupboard and supervised Áine while she heated it. But it was important to hold on to what we could. Even simply adding some vegetables to a pot and seasoning them. The time would come, I realised, when Áine would spend more time lost somewhere else so while it scared her, and while I felt sad, I knew that the best way to lift us both out of our reverie was to get on with things.

"Accept, move on, and never let the bastards get you down," I whispered to myself – it was the mantra Sinéad repeated over and over when things were particularly tough. And it suited this situation too.

If Áine's hands had let her down at the piano they certainly seemed to know what they were doing in the kitchen. I watched as she expertly chopped, sliced and diced the veg and shredded the chicken breast before simmering her stock.

"Of course if we had been better prepared we would have used the bones of the chicken from the Sunday roast and boiled up a nice broth," she said. "Nothing tastes as nice – none of your shop-bought stocks or cubes do. If my garden were in better condition I'd be out there lifting herbs, chopping them, adding them. Oh and my home-grown carrots. Jonathan was raised on those carrots. I wondered if his hair would turn orange he ate so many of them. When other children were stealing biscuits – sneaking snacks when their mothers weren't looking – you could always find Jonathan hidden in the garden, munching a carrot. I couldn't ever be cross with him. Not even when he ate so many he got a stomach ache and was sick in the grounds of the chapel before Mass."

She laughed at the memory and I realised the room she was standing in already felt a little warmer. And I couldn't deny it – I loved the story of Jonathan as a carrot-munching mayhem-maker. It was so at odds with his stiff-upper-lip persona that I enjoyed any hint of a chink in his armour.

By the time the soup had simmered I had ensured Áine – who was thankfully less confused now – had her medication and I had made sure her nightgown and slippers were laid out for her. I lit a fire in the sitting room to fend off the cold. I served the soup in large, heavy Denby bowls at the rugged kitchen table. Áine sat down and savoured the smell and texture of the meal in front of her.

"There is nothing so satisfying as enjoying a meal you have prepared yourself," I said, not that I would really know. But the soup did taste good.

"My mother used to say that."

"Was it your mother who taught you how to cook?"

"In a way," Áine said, softly. "In a way. And it was Charlotte too – the more adventurous stuff, mind. Charlotte always said you had to have the skill for it yourself – a nose for what worked with what. She said I was like a doctor – mixing potions which made you feel better."

"Charlotte sounds like she knew what she was talking about."

"She sure did," Áine said, sipping on a glass of milk. "The only problem is, I think I realised it too late."

"Hindsight is a wonderful thing," I said, thinking of all the things I had realised too late.

"It's nice to look back sometimes," she said. "I know, you know. That I'm losing my marbles. Doting. As they would say. My mother – she was doting. Young and all as she was. She lost her marbles too. I remember trying to make sense of it. And when I got older than her, and it didn't happen, I thought I was in the clear. But I know I'm not. I can't control it – but I know what I take those tablets for. Jonathan liked to tell me at first they were vitamins – like I was already gone. Silly boy. I know why – I know how scary it is – both inside and outside. I know I'm a silly old woman sometimes. But I'll do what he wants to make him happy – so I play along, you know. Because it makes him feel better. I let him send his carers and keep this house simple so I don't get confused. Because I do get confused. It's like I can almost see it – I can almost reach it but something doesn't work. And then it's like I black out. Maybe I do black out. And then I'm back ... but another part of me is gone."

"I can't imagine ..."

"No. No, it's hard to describe. And I'm scared. I know we should expect such things as we grow older. I thought when I got to this age I'd be able to look forward to my twilight years. I've everything in order – these were supposed to be the good times. I was supposed to be able to look forward to falling asleep in my own bed, very peacefully and very contentedly, and just slipping away – not knowing what had hit me. When I first took ill – when I first started getting scatty – I told myself it was because I was tired or just old. It wasn't anything serious, I told myself. I'm just doting, I told myself. But this isn't just doting, and my wee plan to just slip away in the night some time is running away from me – along with my mind." She looked into the bowl of soup as if it contained the answers to all the world's tough questions.

I didn't know what to say – what could be said? I had been prepared for a lot. I had been prepared for ill patients, for patients who needed their medical needs tended to – who couldn't dress themselves, or feed themselves, who needed all aspects of their personal care tended to as well. I hadn't really prepared myself for someone who knew what was ahead. I hadn't really thought about that part at all. I hadn't thought of how a person came to terms with that – how they accepted such a diagnosis. I guess I just assumed that once a person's mind started to wander, it continued to wander until it lost itself altogether. And I assumed that was the point where I entered the picture.

I looked into my own soup bowl, wondering if I could find the answers myself, and we sat, two women lost in quiet contemplation over the soup we had created together, as the grandfather clock tolled out the turning of the hour.

"What would you like to do?" I said, conscious of the fact

that for the here and now I had Áine with me – the Áine who knew who she was and what was going on – not the woman who couldn't remember the tunes she had played so beautifully on the piano and who confused me with Charlotte.

"Eat more soup," Áine replied, shrugging her shoulders. "I might just serve another wee half bowl."

"I mean, generally," I said. "What would you like to do? While you can? Instead of just waiting? Instead of being scared? We can do the garden and we can cook more – but what else? There must be something?"

Áine put her spoon down into her bowl and sat straighter in her chair. "I'm not sure what's real any more," she said. "But I'd like to go to the seaside. I'd like to feel the sand between my toes and know it's sand, and feel the chill of the water and eat chips out of paper at the shorefront after. " Her smile was bright – as if a trip to the seaside and a walk along the beach was as good as it could get. "I know Jonathan would take me if I asked him – but he's so busy, Georgina. And now he is wearing himself out coming here every evening and every weekend – and I don't like to take him away from his work too much. Even at weekends he seems so snowed under."

"Then," I said, "we'll go to the beach tomorrow."

"And get chips?"

"And a sausage too if you want."

"That sounds just perfect. Absolutely perfect."

The decision to go for a drive to the beach the following day made me feel that I would have to put my awkwardness aside and stay a little later to face Jonathan. I knew he was due to call after six. I would keep calm, cool and professional – tell him what Áine wanted, give him my list for the garden and leave without any inappropriate touching or embarrassing moments.

I was all done with making a fool of myself – so I steeled myself when I heard his key turn in the door. Áine and I were in the sitting room, in front of the TV, when he popped his head through the door and said hello. He had the good grace to blush when he saw me – which made me feel better about blushing at seeing him.

"Jonathan," Áine said, "Georgina here is going to take me to the beach tomorrow. Do you remember how we loved the beach?"

He looked at me, I nodded, and he looked back at his aunt. "I do, Auntie Áine, of course I do. We had some good times, but you know I could take you if you wanted?"

"Áine said you would, of course, but that you are very busy at work," I said. "I don't mind taking her – it will do us both good to get some fresh air. Áine wants to get out for a bit. I thought it would help."

"Well, you are full of ideas, aren't you?" he said.

I wasn't sure of his tone. Was he being rude, or complimentary, or indifferent?

"Just a few," I answered, trying not to read anything untoward into what he had said. "And on that subject, you wanted a list of ideas for the garden, things we might need?" I handed him the envelope.

"Right," he said, immediately putting it into his back pocket. "Well, you are on the ball."

Again I didn't know how to read him, so I nodded. "I suppose so."

"Well, leave it with me," he said. "And be careful tomorrow if you do take Áine out."

"I wouldn't be anything but," I answered, trying to mimic his own unreadable tone. "But, look, I'd better be off."

It was his turn to nod and I said goodbye to Áine and told her to make sure to dress warmly for the following day. He didn't bid me goodbye as I left and I didn't try to say goodbye to him.

He was an odd creature and I already had an odd enough creature in my life in the shape of a husband to be coping with. Besides I was paid to look after Áine – not baby-sit some gruff, charmless businessman.

Chapter 11

Present Day

When I arrived at Temple Muse the following day, I found Áine waiting in her overcoat, scarf, hat and gloves in the sitting room.

"I've been ready a while," she said. "I know, it's silly of me. But I have been so looking forward to this. And I asked Maria to lay everything out this morning so it would be easy to find. No fooling this old mind." Her smile was as bright as I had ever seen it.

I sat down on the sofa opposite her, took her hands in mine and I felt myself choke with an unexpected wave of emotion. "Of course there's no fooling you, Áine. I'm impressed by your organisation."

"I'll not feel the benefit of this coat when I go outside. My mother used to warn me of that. And I've been wearing this coat for a while now … but I don't mind. I even had Maria help me pack up some sandwiches for us. If you don't mind taking a packed lunch with us?"

"I don't mind at all. Sure I have a flask in my car and a wee pint of milk and all – and there may just be a scone with

101

strawberry jam."

"Home-made?" Áine asked.

"Neither the scone nor the jam are home-made. I don't get much time and I have even less talent! I wouldn't know how to bake a scone if my life depended on it."

"I'll find the time to teach you. That can be our next lesson," she said, walking from the room and leaving me to follow her through to the kitchen where she was, gloves still on her hands, hat still perched on her head, taking flour from the cupboard and muttering about heating the oven and having enough buttermilk.

"Áine," I said softly and she turned to me, the mention of her name pulling her out of her reverie and leaving her standing, staring at the flour on the worktop – the packet opened, a small dusting of white powder having tumbled onto the granite.

She looked at me and back at the flour, her face colouring. "I've been silly," she said, her voice breaking.

"We're all silly sometimes," I said, trying to reassure her and seeing the tears brimming in her eyes. "I found my phone in the fridge this morning. No harm done – none at all. And I will hold you to the scone lesson. I've never been able to bake. My home economics teachers used to despair of me. I told you before – it's my daughter who is the cook in our house."

"You should bring her too," Áine said, her face brightening. "It's a long time since there were young ones about this house. When Jonathan and Emma were young we were always bustling about this kitchen – always into something. Emma would stand there – right there were you are standing – and ask to help and Jonathan ..." she laughed, "he was keen to help with the tasting. A greedy guts!" Her laugh was girlish, the upset of just seconds earlier forgotten. She stood there, the tears still in her eyes but her face bright now, alive with some memory that obviously meant so much to her. In her hat and her coat and her gloves, in the quiet and cavernous kitchen of the big house on Temple Muse, before we set off on our journey to the beach where we would drink tea and chat some more.

Even though the wind was just about starting to pick up and there was a definite chill in the air, Áine and I had taken a long walk across the beach front at Buncrana and now we stood side by side staring out over Lough Foyle, watching it open out into the Atlantic Ocean.

"I suppose it's too cold for paddling," Áine said, glancing down at the soft waves which crept closer and closer to our feet as the tide made its way in.

"I would say so," I laughed. "I wouldn't want to have to explain frostbite to Jonathan."

"He used to love the beach," Áine said. "I'm sure he probably still does but when he was a boy he was never happier than when he was in water. It was his time in warmer climes, I suppose. But even here, even on the days we came down here in Lorcan's car in the winter, he would be the one who'd tear off his coat as soon as he got out of the car." She started to laugh, and clutched at her stomach as if trying to hold in the memory. "I remember Lorcan chasing him the full length of the beach – and there he was leaving a trail of clothes behind him saying he was going for a swim. By the time they were both back with me, Lorcan's face was red and Jonathan's was blue. I'll never forget it ..." She paused, and held her tummy tighter before glancing at me.

I saw it in that second – the fear in her eyes again at the memories she might lose and I reached out – in a way I knew I would for however long I could – and took her hand and rubbed it as we stared out over the rushing waves and listened to the wind whistle around our ears.

"We'll do our best, Áine. We'll do our best to make sure you hold onto those memories for as long as you can. Tell me more. Tell me all you can remember. Who's Lorcan? Was he Jonathan's father?"

103

Aine looked into my eyes and blinked, shaking her head. "No … no, Lorcan was … he was the person I should have … no … he wasn't Jonathan's father. Jonathan's father was Jack." She wiped a tear away and I wondered if some memories were too painful to remember even if you were scared to let go of them.

⌒ 1964 ⌒

The windows were wide open – the smell of the lavender plants on the sill permeating the kitchen while the range heated and Áine set about kneading the dough to make the bread for the next few days. The sounds of summer were all around – the buzzing of the bees in the garden, the tinny sound of the wireless from where Charlotte had been sunbathing on the lawn. The sound of the children playing had just quietened as Emma had come in, declared herself exhausted, and said she was going to read for a while in her room. Jonathan had wandered in just after and begged a glass of home-made lemonade from his grandmother who was now sitting dozing in her armchair. The heat didn't agree with her, she had grumbled before leaving Áine to bake the bread alone. In the stifling heat of the kitchen beads of sweat were forming on Aine's brow and still she loved kneading the bread – she found it therapeutic and rewarding. At the end of her labours she would have something that the family would enjoy with their dinner – a salad she had planned along with a few slices of home-roasted ham. Hopefully the heat inside the kitchen would have dissipated enough so that they could all eat together without anyone getting hot and bothered. It would be pleasant – and she imagined the children laughing and chatting, Jack telling his tall tales and Charlotte drinking it all in and complimenting her on her cooking. She was lost in her reverie when her sister walked into the kitchen.

"Dolly Daydream," Charlotte said, laughing, "You off in your own little world again? Is it a world with Lorcan in it?"

Áine tried to stop the smile from forming on her lips but she couldn't. It had been most unexpected. When she thought of how she almost hadn't gone out to the dance and how she had originally told Lorcan she was fine and didn't need a drink from him, she thanked her lucky stars that Charlotte had been around to turn things about. If her sister hadn't been there – and if she hadn't insisted that she dance with Lorcan – well, she would have missed the feeling of being held his arms and the comfortable way in which her head rested on his chest as they moved around the dance floor at the end of the evening, their feet sore but their hearts light.

She had felt giddy when the lights came up and she gathered her things.

"I'll walk you home – both of you," Lorcan had offered and Charlotte had stepped in quickly to accept the invitation.

"But don't mind me," she said. "I'll walk ten steps ahead the whole time and I'll not look back even once. I'll not eavesdrop – unless it gets really juicy and then, to be honest, I'll not be able to stop myself. I always have been terribly nosy. But I don't tell stories, not beyond Jack anyway … and he doesn't listen most of the time."

Lorcan looked at Áine quizzically and back at Charlotte and back again at Áine who was more than used to her sister's mannerisms.

"She's good for her word," she said, emboldened by the few drinks she had taken and the warmth of the look on Lorcan's face as he took her hand.

"Well then, lovely ladies, I would be more than happy to escort you back – one of you at a safe distance – to your home. Although as a very respectable man there may not be too much juicy to report back. Not on a first date anyway."

"He's calling it a 'date'," Charlotte said, nudging Áine who was flushed with a combination of embarrassment and excitement.

A date. He had definitely said 'a date' – even if it hadn't started that way. And it certainly felt like a date. A pretty perfect date – starting off a little awkwardly perhaps but soon transforming into something altogether more memorable. As they'd danced they had chatted, about work of course – and the perils of the classroom, not to mention the perils of the staffroom – but they had spoken of much more. Their shared love of the cinema, of good books, of good music. He loved to potter around his garden as much as she loved to potter around hers. The conversation was free and easy and neither seemed to mind when the other stepped on their toes or moved just that few seconds out of time with the music.

As they walked back to Temple Muse the warm night air washed over them. Lorcan took her hand and she felt secure, warmed by his touch. Yes, she felt shy. She still felt like the wallflower she undoubtedly was – but perhaps just a little less like an outsider in her own life. It was a feeling that she revelled in – even if nothing else would come of it. Even if it was just the gin and tonic talking. Even if it was just Charlotte's meddling and determination to play Cupid gifting her with her very own pair of rose-tinted glasses. She was out, and she felt a little tipsy and light-headed and the man who was holding her hand – standing a full head above her, occasionally glancing down and smiling at her, his face creased, his stubble forming, his suit smelling of cologne and cigarettes – was telling her he was sorry she didn't live further away as he wasn't quite ready for the walk home to end just yet.

They reached the path, the gravel crunching a little too loudly now that they were getting ready to say goodbye. Then again her heart was thumping pretty loudly too. It had been a long time since she had stood this close to a man, since she had felt a man's breath on her cheek, felt the touch of his hand on her face as he moved it up towards his. She tried to look at him – to stay cool, to stop herself from trembling like the inexperienced eejit she felt herself to be. She could almost imagine she heard Charlotte telling her to calm down and relax enough to enjoy the moment. So she did, as he kissed her. And she did as he told her he had a wonderful evening, and that thanks to her he was very much looking forward to the summer holidays being done and dusted and going back to work. But he wondered could he see her, again, and soon?

Standing now, in the kitchen kneading the bread, planning for dinner and thinking of the following day, when Lorcan had promised he would pick her up and take her for a drive to the beach, Áine couldn't help but smile again – even if it did annoy her when Charlotte called her Dolly Daydream. Sure there was nothing wrong at all with losing yourself in a memory or in thinking about what is yet to come.

"Are you thinking about Lorcan?" Charlotte asked. "You've blushed a little."

"Don't be so nosey," Áine smiled, turning back to her work but soon finding herself lost in her memories again – and blushing at them too.

Charlotte of course took the pause to confirm that Áine had indeed been thinking about Lorcan and she walked across the room and wrapped her arms around her sister, squeezing her tight.

Áine shrugged her off, pinching some flour from the sack and throwing it at her sister.

"You're an awful tease," Charlotte said to her. "Not spilling all the gossip about Lorcan right away."

"Sure what if I am? I'm a woman of mystery now, with a life of her own and secrets. Wasn't that your plan all along?"

Charlotte rubbed the flour from her cheeks and laughed. "Well, maybe not all along. You know, my original plan was that you would finally agree to come and see the world with us but you have steadfastly refused ..."

"You know I can't –"

"I know you won't," Charlotte replied pointedly, "but that's by the by. Let's not argue. Anyway as you won't come and see the world with us – as you refuse to believe that wine really tastes so much better under the Tuscan sun, or that the gardens in Italy can be more sumptuous than anything you can have imagined here, or that there is more to life than baking bread and walking to school to teach in the rain … the next best thing I could ever wish for you is that my lovely little Dolly Daydream sister has something real and lovely and wonderful to daydream about. It's because I love you, so utterly, so very much that I worry so. You do understand that?"

Charlotte's eyes were wide and her voice was choked and, for a second, just the briefest of moments, Áine wondered if Charlotte – she who so rarely showed any emotion – might just cry.

"Of course I understand, Charlie. Of course I do. I love you, my lovely sister, and I love that you watch out for me so."

"It's just us, you know," Charlotte sniffed.

Áine took a deep breath. She knew where this conversation was going – and it always ended in tears. With the death of their daddy they had leaned heavily on each other. Charlotte had vowed that she would always be there for her little sister and yet she had fought all her life between that need to take care of Áine and her need to spread her own wings and get away from a house which contained the one great sad memory she could never escape. She had torn herself to pieces with guilt when she had first fallen for Jack and decided to travel Europe with him. There wasn't a moment she wasn't aware that she had left her sister back at home taking care of their mother who had withered with age and was becoming more and more reliant on a young woman who should be in the prime of her life.

Every time Charlotte came home, they had this conversation – in one way or another. Charlotte would tell Áine how she would always be there for her and she would say she knew and they would make mention of their sometimes difficult past. Áine loved her sister so very dearly but she felt uncomfortable with this conversation. She wanted Charlotte to accept she was no longer the scared little girl who had climbed into bed with her when she had bad dreams, nor was she the teenager who, despite being happy for her sister at finding a man who loved her as much as Jack did, cried at her wedding day. She was okay and she could find her own way.

"Let's just enjoy tonight," Áine said. "I'm making a salad to go with this bread. Why don't you help me by washing that lettuce and chopping some tomatoes? I was hoping you might make up some of your famous potato salad as well."

Charlotte wiped away a tear. "Good change of topic, Áine."

"Yes, well, we don't need to keep going over old ground. Believe me, I know you love me. I know you are there for me and I know all you want is happiness for me. And that's all I want for you as well. And yes, I'm going out with Lorcan again so you can be pleased that your scheming has worked – but let's just be happy. All of us. Mother too."

Charlotte nodded. "Okay," she said, lifting the lettuce and beginning to run it under the tap. "But you know, don't you?"

"I know," Áine said, nudging her sister gently. "I always know."

∽ *Present Day* ∾

Áine was quiet on the drive back to Temple Muse. I presumed she was tired, as I had stifled a yawn or two myself since our walk along the shorefront and our chat in the car while we enjoyed our makeshift picnic.

"We'll come back in the summer, get those chips then. And

we'll drown them in salt and vinegar," I had said as we sipped our tea, Áine having said she didn't feel up to them just then.

"And ice-cold milk. My mother used to wrap the bottles in wet newspaper. She swore it kept them cool," Áine had replied, staring out across the lough, watching the sunlight twinkling off the rippling tide.

"I must try that trick," I said, "if ever I can persuade my girls to come out for the day with me. They don't think it's too cool to spend time with their mum any more. Not for daytrips anyway. It's all about going into town with their friends and spending a mini-fortune in Primark."

I watched as she sipped again from her tea.

"I suppose we all go through a bit of that," she said. "Not wanting to spend time with our parents. And then, when we can't, we would give anything for another day out. I still miss my mother. It sounds silly, doesn't it? I'm an old lady. I never thought old people still missed their parents. But I miss my mother. She was as tough as old boots. But she had her moments. She could make it better, when she wanted it to. She tried her hardest ... and I miss her."

Áine's words trailed off and again I tried to think of a way to comfort her, but what could I say? Áine was right. I had never really thought of old people grieving for their parents. I had imagined by your senior years you would have made peace with whatever life had dealt you. So, lost for words, I simply reached out and held the older woman's hand and gave it a gentle squeeze.

"Wouldn't it be brilliant," Áine said, "if this disease worked in my favour? If I could choose what I get to forget? And choose what I never will? I'd make that list. I'd know what I would forget – and what I would hang on to forever."

"I could do with that deal myself," I said, softly. "I'd like to erase parts of life – whole swathes of it. But I suppose we don't get that chance so we just have to make the best of what we have."

"And enjoy the moments at the beach."

"And the hot cups of tea."

"And a warm car to get back into," Áine said.

"And a warm bed to sleep in," I said.

"At the end of the day, it's the small things that matter. Thank you, Georgina. Thank you for taking me out today and for the scones. Although promise me you will bring the girls of yours round for a baking lesson? I know I could teach you to do a much better job than those shop-bought efforts."

Áine smiled and I smiled too before switching on the engine and heading back to Temple Muse.

Chapter 12

☙ *Present Day* ❧

"You don't have to work tomorrow!" Sinéad cheered, shaking a bottle of wine in my direction when I opened the door that evening. She had also bought a box of Maltesers and a family-sized bag of Tayto Cheese and Onion.

I welcomed her in, and she followed me to the kitchen and we set about taking a few glasses and some bowls out of the cupboards.

"Well, my dear," she said as we curled up on my sofa and sipped from our glasses, "how did the trip to the seaside go? And, more to the point, how is grumpy Hegarty and his grumpy but probably misunderstood ways?"

"The trip to the beach was lovely. Strange, in a way. I could tell Áine was lost in her own memories. It's very sad, you know – watching someone look back on their life and try to hold onto it."

"I can imagine," Sinéad said solemnly.

"But she's a lovely woman. I don't want to be all doom and gloom about it. She has a wicked sense of humour when she wants to."

"And a handsome and eligible nephew?" Sinéad winked.

"Would you ever stop about that man?" I laughed. "Honestly, he's insufferable. But thankfully today I didn't have the pleasure of his company."

"Doth the lady protest too much?"

"Sinéad!" I chided her. "Don't push it. When it comes to Jonathan Hegarty, there is no way I could protest too much. It's hard to see how he and his aunt could be so close. They seem to be polar opposites."

"Okay, okay!" she said, raising her hand. "I hear you. I just want you to be happy. You know what they say, pet, the best way to get over a man is to get under another one."

I shuddered at the thought of Jonathan Hegarty, and his reserved snobbery, in the nip trying to be passionate. Then again I shuddered at the thought of myself, and my inexperienced, baby-battered, middle-aged body in the nip trying to be passionate as well. I'd only ever been passionate with one man in my life – and I didn't want to be passionate with anyone else. I wanted the last few months to disappear and for everything to be how it was when I thought everything was ticking over just fine in my marriage.

Sinéad must have seen the look on my face because she continued: "I don't want to be insensitive. You know me. I just like to fix things. Throw solutions at problems. It works well in the magazine – perhaps it doesn't work so well in friendships. I know you still have issues with Matthew."

Issues. Him not loving me any more was simply 'an issue'?

Unexpectedly tears pricked my eyes again.

"Are the girls with him this weekend?"

I nodded, and took a deep breath to settle myself. "They weren't keen to go. I think last week rattled them – knowing for definite their daddy was moving on. Eve wanted to stay with me – but I don't want to risk him telling me that I have turned them against him."

"He could do with a bit of you turning them against him,"

she said, before looking at me. "Look, I'm sorry. I'll stop it. I know that you still have feelings for him. I know that I shouldn't speak ill of him. I'm just angry on your behalf."

"I'm angry too," I admitted. "He just walked away and is getting on with his life. I'm picking up the pieces."

"Well, I've big hands and don't mind helping you lift a few pieces whenever you need me to."

"I know, pet. And I love you for it. I really do."

"You had better. After all, who else would bring you such fine snacks as Maltesers and Tayto on a Friday night?"

"Indeed. I am spoiled rotten."

"And don't you forget it. Look, pet, you know I love you to the moon and back. You will come through this and be happy again. I know it. I feel it in my bones and my bones are never wrong."

I smiled a watery smile back at her. At least I had Sinéad. She was like the sister I never had and I knew she would never let me down.

☜ 1964 ☞

Jack Hegarty was, in every sense, larger than life. Áine supposed he had to be to convince her sister to settle down. Áine couldn't have imagined anyone else ever convincing her sister to marry and have children. She had always vowed to travel the world and to never have to worry about lugging children with her. But Jack made her feel and think differently. There was something about his over-confidence – his way of making everything seem infinitely doable – that made Charlotte feel she could take on the world, even with children by her side. And, to her surprise, she thrived at being a mother. Sure, her idea of parenting was far from conventional. She didn't believe for one second that children should be seen and not heard and it was always obvious when the Hegarty family were in residence by the noise they created

114

– the singing, the laughter, the shouting and constant, unending chatter. Áine revelled in the confidence that poured from every nerve of her niece and nephew. She loved watching the caring mother her sister was. The children had Jack's confidence and Charlotte's sense of fun – but they were raised well. They knew their limits. The lack of conventional schooling had not deprived them of a wealth of knowledge they loved to share and Áine was seldom happier than when sitting at the table at mealtimes with her family around her, talking about all the things her niece and nephew had seen and experienced. And she loved watching Charlotte positively glow with pride as her children spoke. She loved the way Jack would reach across the table and stroke her sister's hand and how the four of them seemed to have their own way of communicating – their shared jokes, the secret smiles. She would have been jealous if she didn't love them so much and if, of course, they didn't have a way of making her feel that she belonged when she was in their company.

They sat down to tea that evening, her freshly baked bread sliced and set in the middle of the table, surrounded by cold cuts of ham and corned beef, salad, boiled eggs and cheese. Jonathan perched on her knee making a sandwich while Emma, with all the authority of an eight-year-old, regaled them with stories of their trip to the Leaning Tower of Pisa.

Jack was pouring generous measures of wine into glasses for himself and his wife and was even allowing Emma a small taste. "On the continent lots of children have wine with their dinner – they say it stops them developing too much of a fondness for it in later life."

Emma winced as she sipped from the glass before asking for a cold glass of milk instead which Áine was only too happy to pour for her while Charlotte, Jack and Jonathan laughed. Rosaleen, at the other end of the table, pretended to be horrified but was unable to keep the smirk from her face. It was one of those moments Áine wanted to bottle and keep forever – that she willed to stay in the back of her mind so that she'd be able to recall it whenever the world seemed a little gloomier. All that was missing, she realised with a faint smile, was Lorcan to join them. He would love an occasion such as this – would love chatting to Emma and Jonathan and telling them all about Pisa and whatever nuggets of history he could. It was his favourite subject bar none.

"Grandma, Grandma," Jonathan said, "have you ever been to Italy?"

"I've no call to go to Italy," Rosaleen answered. "I'm happy with what the good Lord has given me. I have no need to go gallivanting."

"What's gallivanting?" Jonathan asked. "Have we ever been gallivanting, Mamma?"

Charlotte laughed. "Gallivanting is travelling – seeing the world around us – and we sure have done a lovely amount of it and I hope to do much more. It's not such a bad thing. Perhaps Grandma should think about trying it sometime."

Áine felt her stomach twist and hoped this conversation was not heading in the direction she feared.

"Well," Rosaleen said, forcing a smile on her face, "maybe I will someday, Jonathan. Scare you all and just decide to run mad around the world. Your mamma might have second thoughts about all her bullying then."

"I'd never bully you, Mother," Charlotte interjected. "I just want you to live your life. I love you with every fibre of my being, so I am saying this from a place of love – sitting here in this big house forever is never going to bring Daddy back and that's what it all comes down to, isn't it?"

The children fell silent and Rosaleen looked as though she had been struck across the face.

"You've grieved enough," Charlotte said. "We've all grieved enough. Can we not just be happy together? Can we not just move on?"

Rosaleen stood up, slowly, placing her knife and fork in the centre of her plate, indicating she was finished with her meal. She pushed her chair back into the table and headed towards the door, stopping as she reached it to turn and speak.

"I only pray, my darling daughter, that you never find yourself having to 'move on'. You may see it differently then. I don't judge you, my darling, even though you live your life so differently to how I have lived mine – and you raise your children in a way so alien to how you were raised. Please, all I ask is that you don't judge me either."

Áine watched her leave and then looked at Charlotte who only shrugged her shoulders. Jonathan slipped off her knee and walked back to his seat. They listened in silence to the slow creak of the stairs as Rosaleen made her way up to her bedroom.

"We're going on Wednesday," Jack said. "Maybe it's not a bad thing. Always go before you are asked to leave."

He rubbed his wife's hand then and returned to asking Emma about the history of the Tower of Pisa.

Áine simply sat and watched them – the spell broken. She didn't care any more if she never remembered this day again.

She was quiet that night as she climbed into the passenger seat of Lorcan's car and pulled the door closed.

"You look lovely," he said as he reached across to kiss her cheek.

She revelled in the soft touch of his lips and allowed herself a moment or two just to breathe in and absorb the uncomplicated moment she was in. She had quickly learned that with Lorcan there were no games. He was upfront about everything – from how he felt about her, to what he hoped for the future. More than that, she realised she didn't have to pretend to be anyone she wasn't, with him. Even Charlotte was always pushing her to change, while her mother resisted any tiny change she tried to make. With Lorcan she could be as settled or as flighty as she wanted to be.

117

When she blew her fringe from her face in exasperation, despite the softness of his kiss, he guessed that once again tensions between Charlotte and Rosaleen had flared.

"I can take you away from it for a few hours at least?" he offered.

"Could you, please?"

He smiled. "You're too good to them both, Áine."

"And maybe one day they will acknowledge that," she said, stretching to relieve the tension in her body. "Ach, never mind me. They are both so different – I don't think they will ever agree. But if they could just learn to live in peace with each other's choices we would be on to something."

"Do you think they ever will?"

"I'm not sure," she said, shaking her head. "But Charlotte and Jack are leaving again on Wednesday so, if nothing else, peace will be restored for another while."

"You'll miss them though, and the children?"

"Of course I will," she said. "I always do. But it will be nice for Mother and me to get back into our routine again."

"Ah good," he said. "Because I hope one day to be brought home to meet her and I would prefer to meet the not-grumpy version."

Áine blushed. She knew things were going well between them but still she was delighted to hear he was thinking as far ahead as coming home to meet her mother. Although she was wise enough to know that would cause issues of its own. Her mother was a frightened woman who wanted to cling on to whatever she knew as tight as she could. However, she had also said, many times, that she wanted Áine to be happy – and Áine, for the first time in her life, had a glimpse of what happiness could really mean. This time it wasn't happiness for other people – it wasn't any kind of vicarious happiness. It was her own. The time she spent with Lorcan was like her own little bubble of joy. The way he looked at her, with his deep, dark-blue eyes, made her feel like she was the only woman in the world. She sometimes felt as if she would have to pinch herself to make sure it was real. She felt like she was living every romantic cliché in the book and she didn't even care if people thought the way that they looked at each other sickening.

They'd have to be careful, of course, when the holidays were over and they went back to school. She looked forward to sneaking the odd coy smile across the staffroom but she knew they would have to play it cool. The headmaster might not approve – and sure it was still early days. She couldn't quite believe that it had only been a matter of weeks, the course of Charlotte's summer holidays back in Derry, and she had already felt the balance of her life shift.

She tried to focus on that – on those beautiful positive feelings as they took a drive out to the seaside – instead of thinking of the tension which was building at home and which would no doubt come to a head when Charlotte packed the children up and they left. There would be the usual tears and hugs and promises that they would stay safe. Jack would try to encourage Charlotte to leave, telling her they were messing up their travel plans and they needed to be on the road. Charlotte would fall on their mother and weep. It was the one time Charlotte showed her vulnerability. The bravado always disappeared with those goodbyes. Rosaleen would crumple and so would Charlotte which would inevitably set the children off. Áine would be the stoic one – the one who held it together – the calm amid the storm. And she would be the one to pick up the pieces after, when Rosaleen took to her room for a week to recover from the annual loss of her daughter.

When Lorcan told her, as they walked along the beach that night that she seemed distracted, she willed herself into the now. "I've a lot on my mind," she admitted, "I'm sorry I'm not the best company."

"You're fine company," he said, putting his arm around

her shoulders to reassure her. "I just worry about you, Áine. You take on too much. You've too kind a heart and people take advantage of it."

"I don't mind – not most of the time. They are my family. I love them."

"But you spend so much time looking after other people, Áine Quigley," he said, turning her towards him – staring into her eyes as the sinking sun sent shards of pink and gold across the ripples of Lough Neagh. "What you need is someone to look after you. Doesn't that sound lovely? Someone whose primary concern is to make sure you are okay at the end of every day?"

There was something in his eyes which made her want to fall into his arms, there and then, and beg him to be that person. Then again she knew she wouldn't have to beg – not with Lorcan – and the soft way in which his lips brushed hers just seconds later assured her of that fact.

Chapter 13

It was strange how quickly Áine and I fell into a routine of sorts. We found our pace and I started to look forward to my afternoons with her. Even Jonathan seemed to be warming to me – not calling over to check up each afternoon – saving his visits for shortly before I was due to go home. It made my life so much easier not having to deal with the sense he was judging every move I made.

He did his duty by his aunt though.

Midway through my fourth week with her, I had arrived at Temple Muse to find her gloriously excited.

"Wait until you see what Jonathan has done," she chirped as I walked in.

She was positively animated with joy and I couldn't help but smile as I followed her down the long hall to the kitchen.

"It's more than I could have hoped for," she said as she walked through to the green back door which led to the overgrown garden.

I followed her out to find two men working at the rear of the garden. Stacked against the side of the house were a host

121

of gardening supplies. Compost, trowels, seeds, watering cans. All ready to go.

"The men are landscaping the back of the garden," Áine enthused. "And they are going to build some raised flowerbeds for us. I'm going to get my garden, or at least some of it back."

The joy on her face was infectious and I couldn't help but reach out and hug her. Perhaps that was crossing some line too – but I didn't care in that moment. It was as if the simple act of having a little piece of greenery back to call her own had given her a renewed joy in life. It was uplifting to watch and, as I felt her hug me back and whisper "Thank you" in my ear, I started to think of the conversation I'd had with Sinéad the week before about being happy again. Okay, so it hadn't come in the form of the husband who had decided I wasn't enough for him, but from making a real difference for someone who would care.

When I finished with Áine that night I scribbled a quick note to Jonathan. I thanked him for arranging the gardeners, and for supplying what we needed for the garden. I told him how elated his aunt had seemed and told him she had a great day – with no memory lapses.

The following day when I arrived for work there was a short note from Jonathan – just two words – "No problem" – and that was it.

It was as much communication as I would have wanted with him and I think it suited us both fine.

Now, with our occasional cooking, our garden to look forward to and a weekly run out in the car to get some fresh air, Áine and I found ourselves increasingly comfortable in each other's company. She gave me a positive focus that I clung to – after all, my personal life was still very much in the doldrums.

Matthew's contact with me was limited to the occasional text about the girls. Sorcha appeared more sullen than usual and even Eve seemed a little down. Two weeks after Matthew had dropped his "we've reached an acceptance" bombshell on me, the two girls traipsed into the living room where I was sitting catching up with the latest episode of *The Good Wife* and sat down opposite me expectantly.

"Are you two okay?" I asked.

"Can we talk, Mum?" Eve asked, her young face lined with worry.

Even Sorcha, Queen of the Death Stare, couldn't look me in the face.

"What is it, girls? You have me worried now." I put the cup of tea I had been drinking on the floor and sat up straight.

"We don't want you to be angry," Sorcha said.

"Or upset," Eve added.

"But Dad wants us to meet his new girlfriend."

They looked terrified. I didn't blame them. Somewhere in my brain I was sure there was a stroke just that little bit closer to rendering me seriously ill. His girlfriend? The girl with the pink bra? The girl who didn't mean anything? The girl? (Not a woman?) My stomach lurched and I thought there was an ulcer taking shape to join the imminent stroke. I tried to compose my face. It wasn't the girls' fault. They were clearly horrified at the thought and even more horrified at telling me.

"Okay," I muttered, breaking the silence. I supposed this wasn't my call to make. "And how do you two feel about this?"

"I don't want to," Sorcha said petulantly. "This wasn't meant to happen, was it, Mum?"

I didn't know what to say. I didn't want to turn the girls against their father.

Eve broke in. "It would hurt you, wouldn't it, Mum?" She looked more torn than her sister – but she always had been a daddy's girl.

"Does this mean it is definitely over between you two?" Sorcha asked, her voice wobbling slightly. This was serious.

Sorcha may have been one to shout and huff and slam doors but she rarely showed her vulnerability.

I shook my head and willed it to stop hurting and instead think of an appropriate answer.

"Look, girls, this isn't easy for any of us. You know your father wanted some space – well, it turns out he likes his space. But you two, you don't have to do anything you don't want to. If you want to meet this woman, then meet her. Don't worry about me. But if you don't want to, that's okay as well. I'm sure your father will understand."

"How do you feel about it, Mum?" Eve said. "Are you okay with him seeing someone else?"

"I don't think I could ever be okay with your daddy seeing someone else," I said. "But I can't make him stay where he doesn't want to either. And if he has made the decision to see someone else, I can't stop him. But look, I don't want you to think less of him. None of this changes how he feels about you, or how we both feel about you."

"Ah Jesus, Mum. That's the most clichéd line in the book!" Sorcha said, but she was crying now.

"I'm sorry, girls. I don't know what to say. I'm not used to this any more than you are and I'm sure I'm messing it up royally."

I watched as my daughters got up from their seats and came and sat on each side of me, hugging me while the three of us had a good cry.

"I hate him," Sorcha said while Eve stayed silent.

"Try not to be too angry," I said, even though I was starting to hate him a little too – especially as I saw how upset our beautiful girls were.

The following night the girls went to see their dad overnight. They had told him they didn't want to meet his new girlfriend just yet and he had sent me a fairly passive-aggressive text message hinting that I might have had something to do with that decision. I didn't dignify it with a response – as he was unlikely to believe me no matter what I said. And there was also the possibility I would just actually completely lose the run of myself and let all my pent-up feelings come pouring out – and I wanted to have some measure of control when they did. Just then I didn't think I could control myself – so I buried my emotions as deeply as I could.

I considered calling Sinéad and inviting her up – but she had been there for me so much over the last few weeks I didn't want to impose. Besides, I wasn't actually sure I was in the mood for company. I quite fancied having an evening to myself – of finding some way on my own to pick up the pieces. I had cried the full night after my conversation with the girls and it hadn't changed anything except to leave my eyes puffy and red-ringed and my head sore. I decided to pamper myself for the evening instead of allowing myself to wallow further. I filled my bath, loading it with bubbles. I lit candles. I poured a glass of wine. I clipped my hair up on top of my head and slipped into the warm water and lay back. I closed my eyes and tried to find a sense of peace in the quiet ambience of my bathroom. What a change it made to be able to slip into the suds knowing that there was no chance of a teenager demanding to be let in, or wanting to sit on the toilet and talk over their day's woes with me.

The house was quiet around me – maybe a bit too quiet so I started to hum to myself. What started as some random notes turned into a full on chorus of 'I Will Survive' before I climbed out of the bath, switched on Sorcha's laptop and loaded Spotify to find the song itself. I shimmied into some fancy underwear of my own (a tasteful set, in simple leafy green and cream from M&S) and slathered rich moisturiser on my legs. I grabbed my hairbrush and started singing loudly and dancing around my bedroom. Once 'I Will Survive' was done, I moved to Adele's 'Rolling in the Deep' and then on to Beyoncé's 'Irreplaceable'. It didn't matter to me that I couldn't really hold a tune and I ignored the rather disturbing reflection I glimpsed every now and again of me, mummy-tummy and all, dancing in my underwear. The more I sang, the more wine I drank but I refused to fall into melancholy. Instead I allowed myself to sing, to feel and to be angry when I wanted to be and to lift myself up again.

I feel asleep, eventually, in my fancy underwear on what used to be Matthew's side of the bed. It no longer smelled like him, I realised. I no longer felt the indentation of where his body used to lie. My heart was still aching – when I let it. I was still angry. But in my gloriously tipsy state I started to convince myself that this was something I could get over.

It might take a little time – but I could. And if I couldn't, I thought with a drunken smile, I could always hire a hitman.

"A pint of milk to line your stomach and a banana," Áine said. "I know a hangover when I see one."

She was sharp, I had to admit. For one supposed to be losing her faculties nothing got past her. Of course I shouldn't have been seeing her that day. I had planned to sleep the hangover off from my pity party in front of a roaring fire and a Doris Day movie or three while the girls were still with their father. But the peace and quiet I had been hoping for was thrown out the window when Cecilia Brightly phoned just as Calamity Jane was singing about her secret love.

"Georgina, sorry to call you on a weekend but Jonathan has just called us and something has cropped up at work. He can't go to his aunt's until much later and he really, really doesn't want her left on her own. I know it's a huge ask – but we would pay the usual overtime rates. You know it would be bad for her if we sent in a new face and we know how fond you are of her – and she of you."

Cecilia had simpering down to a fine art, I thought. While it might have been true that we were fond of each other, in that moment I knew that it wouldn't have mattered one iota to Cecilia if the pair of us were sworn enemies as long as she didn't have to let down one of her private clients. One of her clients who hadn't had the manners to call me himself and tell me how valued I was, even though I knew he had my number.

"I wouldn't ask if I wasn't desperate," Cecilia said. "You have to agree, it wouldn't be good to leave Áine on her own. You have said yourself how routine is important …"

Cecilia, it seemed, was almost as adept at emotional blackmail as she was at simpering. And, as the full force of the emotional turmoil that comes with a hangover had just about fully hit, I was unable to refuse. "Yes, of course I will," I found myself saying, even as my body screamed at me that it was perfectly comfortable where it was, prostrate on the sofa, warmed by the glow of the fire. I couldn't leave Áine on her own, not for such a long time. The guilt would have eaten me alive – and my emotions were battered anyway.

So I pulled on a T-shirt and jeans, clipped my hair back off my face, took two paracetamol downed with an ice-cold glass of Diet Coke and grabbed a packet of cheese-and-onion crisps to try and settle my stomach.

But it was no use. By the time I reached Áine's I was feeling worse than I had first thing that morning when I had woken to a thumping headache and a dry mouth.

"I'm sorry," I said to Áine.

"Strange, isn't it?" she said with a laugh as she poured me a glass of milk. "I can remember this, but I don't remember my own name half the time."

"A bad day today?" I asked.

"Not as bad as you're having," Áine answered, handing me a banana. "Just quiet. I'm used to Jonathan being here at the weekends. Even if he is working here, I'm used to him being about the house. It's comforting. Too many echoes around this place and I'm not always sure which of them are real."

I reached out and took her hand – there was a slight tremor to it. "I'm sorry. If I had known you were all alone all day I would have come earlier. And I definitely wouldn't have had so much to drink last night. You have to know, it's not like me at all. I can't remember the last time I had a hangover and I hope this will be the last for a long time."

"I thought of calling you," Áine said, "but I didn't want to impose. Jonathan said I'm not to cross the lines."

I sat for a moment, thinking of Áine rattling around the big house feeling alone, and I felt a wave of sadness wash over me again. Damn drink and damn horrors.

"You're to call me any time," I said. "Now, how about we make some lunch?"

I checked the fridge, found some pork chops and green beans and then set about peeling some potatoes.

"Well, we'll have a nice big lunch just now and a bit of a chat," I said, "and I'll help make sure you have everything you need. It's not much but …"

"I'm sorry for being such a Negative Nelly," she said. "Charlotte used to tell me I was too serious. I'm fine honestly. I've been keeping myself busy. I tidied my room."

I thought of her room, almost like a cell, and couldn't think there was much tidying to do. "Look," I said, "I'm here for the afternoon now. So how about we watch a movie together? Or just chat?"

"I couldn't ask you to stay here, not on your day off. I hope that care crowd are paying you well at least?"

"I honestly don't mind being here. I've nowhere else to be. Anyway, didn't you promise me before that you were going to tell me all about Charlotte and your family? It must have been amazing growing up in this big house – with those lovely gardens. We can plan some more about what we can do there. You know I'm not blessed with green thumbs, but I will give it a good try."

"I loved the garden," Áine said. "Especially our vegetable patch. Grew all our own stuff – well, a lot of stuff. Potatoes, carrots, those … those … green things … the green things.

You know … the things …"

"Cabbage?" I offered.

"No … no … the things – the long, and green. Damn it … the green things …"

I could see Áine was getting flustered. "It's okay," I offered. "It'll come to you. Cucumbers?"

"No! Not blasted cucumbers!" Áine said, her mood changing and something that looked like anger flashing across her face. "Green … damn it … damn it …" She began to open all her cupboards as if looking for inspiration. Slamming them closed, she seemed to get even more in a panic.

"Áine," I said softly, although I wasn't sure if I was doing the right thing or even if I should be doing anything at all. "Please …"

She opened the fridge and pulled out whatever she could. I doubted she even knew what she was looking for any more. I walked to her and called her name again, taking her shoulders and gently trying to pull her to face me.

Áine shrugged me off. "Don't!" she shouted. "Don't touch me. I'm not going to let it beat me!" Tears began to fall from her eyes. "This is stupid!" She hit the side of her head repeatedly, with a force I was surprised she was capable of, as if trying to dislodge the word she was struggling to find.

I fought the fear that was rising inside of me, feeling more than a little out of my depth. I reached for Áine again, and took her wrists as gently as I could, shushing her and trying to calm her.

"It's okay Áine, it's okay," I said, the fear I was feeling echoed in her eyes. "It's okay," I soothed again, and again, until the fight had gone from Áine and she slumped into my arms as the pot of potatoes on the stove bubbled over.

Áine was quiet as she ate her dinner. She had repeatedly apologised for her behaviour and I had repeatedly told her it was okay and that I understood.

"I don't know," Áine had said as she sipped from a glass of water after pushing her dinner around the plate for a while. "I don't know anything about this. How quick? What will it end like?"

"You have to try not to think about it too much."

She offered a watery smile. "That's part of the problem, isn't it? Not thinking about things. But I have to accept it, don't I? And learn not get so angry when words escape me, when memories escape me."

"I know it's scary," I said, remembering the look of fear on Áine's face as she tried to find that one missing word.

"I'm not scared of dying," Áine said, sitting back. "I'm scared of forgetting them – forgetting Charlotte, forgetting my mother, forgetting Lorcan, forgetting Jack."

"Then tell me," I said. "Tell me about Charlotte. Tell me about the kind of person she was – the kind of things she did."

"She was the most beautiful person I ever knew," Áine said. "Flighty and free and she let me believe I could be anything. She was my best friend. I have missed her every day since she left. Every day."

∽ 1964 ∾

The days before Charlotte left were strange. They always were. It was always the same – the same cramming in of happy memories, knowing that they wouldn't see each other again for a long time. There was a falseness to it all, of course. Almost every situation was played out with extra niceness and extra kindness and a saccharine tang of family bliss that, even though everyone knew it was not strictly real, they revelled in all the same.

And the sun shone for those few days. The flowers bloomed. The birds sang. The house felt warm from the very inside out and Áine reminded herself to take a few moments every day to consign these moments to her memory. The house would be quiet soon enough. The rooms empty. The stairs, which now rattled and thudded with the sound of the children's footsteps, would fall silent soon enough. Even Rosaleen had freely admitted she would miss it – that she would miss how Jonathan watched as she moved around the kitchen or how Emma would read to her in the early evenings. Her eyes were often too tired now to read herself so she would sit in her armchair, Jonathan on her knee, and she would listen to his sister's soft voice retell the stories of Narnia. She was nearly as excited as the children to hear the stories – to revel in the excitement in Emma's voice as she delved further and further through the wardrobe doors into a world so different from that which they knew. She had convinced them both that the tall mahogany wardrobe in her own room had magical powers – when the moon was full and frost lay on the ground and Jonathan asked her could he please come home during winter to try it for himself.

When the afternoon sun was highest, they would sit together in the garden. The children would dip in and out of the old tin tub Áine usually kept for scrubbing the clothes and, while it was no match for their swimming pool in Italy, it seemed to give them almost as much pleasure.

They talked, of course, of going to the park. They talked of the beach. They talked of many things – but Áine felt that in the safe bubble of the garden at Temple Muse they did not have the need to go any further. The house was big enough to offer enough adventure – enough places for their games of hide and seek, sanctuary when they needed a few minutes' rest but room enough in each space for them all to sit together.

And what she found most remarkable – most magical of all – was that she felt a bond in the house in those few days that she didn't think anything could break.

Charlotte would creep into her room at night and crawl into her bed. They would cuddle together like they did as children and talk as they watched the moon and the stars through the window.

"Do you really like him?" Charlotte asked one night, her voice soft.

Áine nodded. She felt shy – embarrassed even – but she could not deny that she liked him.

"And does he like you?" Charlotte asked.

"I think so," Áine replied. "He says he does. He kisses me as if he likes me."

Charlotte smiled. "Can you make me one promise, my sister – because I do believe that the next time I see you, you will be on your way to being a married woman? Can you promise me that before you say yes to any proposal –"

Áine nudged her, blushing. "You're getting ahead of yourself."

"Now, now, stranger things have happened. Just please … if he asks you to marry him, before you say yes make sure to consider everything I told you. You don't have to settle for anything less than magic. Consider whether or not you really like him and whether or not he really, really likes you. Only ever say yes to a marriage proposal when you know, without a shadow of a doubt, that he loves you like he has never loved anyone else before."

"And Jack, Jack really, really loves you back? He loves you like he has never loved anyone before?" Áine asked, rolling onto her side and looking at her sister.

Charlotte smiled. "He does. Sometimes I think maybe he loves me too much – that he relies on me too much for his happiness – but yes, when I ask myself that question I know that he does. I know I am lucky. I want you to be that lucky. I want you to live a full and wonderful life full of wonderful memories, great children, amazing sex."

Áine poked her sister again. "Charlotte! You are bold!"

Charlotte grinned. "Don't underestimate the importance of good sex. It's not as important as true love but it's important enough. Don't marry a man who cannot kiss – a man who cannot kiss cannot make love."

"Charlotte, you are incorrigible!"

"You love me for it. Who else could speak to you so freely? Mother won't. That's not to say she wasn't loved or that she doesn't know love. She and Daddy were hopelessly in love – so hopelessly in love that they couldn't cope without each other. There's a romance in her never moving on, don't you think?"

"I have never thought of it like that," Áine said. "I never knew him – so I never really thought too much about them – not as a couple. Not really."

"They were hopelessly in love," Charlotte said. "Just like Jack and me – and just as I hope you and Lorcan will be in love."

Áine blushed again – a different kind of a blush – one which came with the hope that she would indeed fall in love, properly in love – the kind of love which lasted – with Lorcan.

Rosaleen's fingers were sore and swollen. She muttered under her breath as she threaded the needle and set back to work.

"I can help you with that, Mother," Áine said, taking a seat close to her.

"You can help by staying out of my light," Rosaleen said with a smile, a smile which hid her frustration as the thread slipped from the needle again.

"You've done a great job. Why don't you just let me sew the buttons on?"

"I can do it," Rosaleen said, with a firmness which let Áine know there was no point in continuing to badger her.

The dress had been a labour of love for Rosaleen since Charlotte had announced they were to leave. It was fairly simple – not with the frills and flounces that she would have sewn into her own daughters' dresses when they were little – but it was still beautiful. And it had taken a great deal of strength and willpower for Rosaleen to complete it – her hands no longer able to deftly work a sewing needle in the way they once did.

"Alright, Mother," Áine said, proud of the determination in her mother's eyes. She wasn't going to let anything stop her.

"Do you think Emma will like it? I know she is used to her fancy Italian clothes. This might not match up."

Áine smiled. "Oh Mammy! Do you not know how special this will be to her? Of all the dresses I had as a child, the dresses you made for me were my favourites. I got so many admiring glances as we went to Mass and when I went to play with my friends. I'm sure Emma will just love it. It's beautiful – perfect for a gorgeous little girl dancing in the Italian sunshine!"

"It's not too old-fashioned?" Rosaleen looked genuinely worried as she snipped the cotton thread and set about sewing the last button into the simple cotton dress, decorated with delicate blue forget-me-nots. She had found the perfect pearlised buttons to match.

"Not at all! What eight-year-old girl wouldn't love this? And I know she has a lovely white cardigan which she could wear with it when it gets chilly in the evenings."

"I don't think it ever gets chilly in Italy," Rosaleen said.

"Oh yes, it does. I'm sure the dress will be perfect. She will love it."

"I'll miss her, you know – Emma. She's growing so fast. Jonathan too. When they come back it's like we have to spend so much time getting to know them again and, just when we settle into a lovely routine, they leave again."

Emma and Rosaleen had become close in the last few weeks. Emma loved cuddling up with her granny – the two of them reading to each other, sharing cuddles and sneaking cookies together from the jar in the pantry. They had been caught on more than one occasion with milk moustaches and guilty smiles. All Áine and Charlotte could do was laugh –

and sneak off themselves for cookies and milk while they talked about how much younger Rosaleen seemed when the children were around her.

Jonathan, despite his younger years, was the quieter of the pair – but he and Áine had become close – as they always did when he visited the big house at Temple Muse. He would spend his time with his aunt in the garden, intrigued by the flowers and plants, not to mention the bugs and worms which he spotted. In the evenings he would sit beside her at the piano, his small, chubby fingers matching her notes – delighted to make it through 'Chopsticks' perfectly. And then he would beg her for a bedtime story – his own finger following the words she read, trying to sound them out.

Áine and Rosaleen looked at each other sadly – the house would be different when they were gone. While they enjoyed their peace and quiet, every year after Charlotte and her family left their routine felt meaningless, the peace and quiet unsettling rather than reassuring, and when they sat side by side in the evening they could feel the physical loss of the children who would have sat beside them and offered them hugs and would have fallen asleep before needing to be carried up the stairs to bed.

"There is no doubt we'll miss them," Áine said.

"And Charlotte too," Rosaleen said.

"And Charlotte too."

Chapter 14

⸎ Present Day ⸎

I woke early the following morning and padded downstairs. I took two paracetamol from the cupboard beside the cooker and washed them down with a glass of orange juice and then I switched on the kettle to make a cup of coffee. The twins were still with Matthew and the house was silent. I should have been enjoying a well-deserved and luxurious lie-in but for the last fifteen minutes I had been lying in the half-light thinking about the day before and the stories Áine had told me of Charlotte. I'll admit it was a nice distraction from thinking about my own woes.

I made my coffee and slipped two slices of bread into the toaster, waited for them to pop up and then spread them thickly with butter before switching on Sorcha's laptop, opening a new Word document and starting typing – pouring out the memories Áine had shared with me. It wasn't well written. It was little more than bullet points but it was the framework of my charge's life. It was a rough family tree – a basic spider-web of connections between people who had been mentioned. Jonathan of course, and his sister – and

Charlotte and her husband Jack. Lorcan too, I supposed, though I couldn't quite work him out – how had their story ended? And Rosaleen, her mother, a woman who seemed to have experienced her own share of pain.

I imagined the rooms of the house – those that were locked away from us and I vowed that I would talk to Jonathan about it the next time I saw him.

I saved the notes I made into a new folder on Sorcha's cluttered desktop and searched out more information on reminiscence work with dementia patients. I could do so much, I realised as I read, if only I had the key to Áine's past. Where she worked, everything about these people who meant so much to her, what music she listened to. Áine could fill in the blanks – now before it was too late – and I could remind her of those memories when things were tougher.

I stretched and poured a second cup of coffee before glancing at my watch and seeing that it was past nine. There was no time like the present, I assured myself, so I took my mobile from my handbag and searched out Jonathan's number. I typed out a quick message, deleting and rewriting a few time so as not to cause him any alarm. "Jonathan, would like to meet to discuss your aunt. Nothing to worry about, just a few ideas. Let me know when suits." I read over the message once more, deciding it set the right tone – professional but also chatty. I wanted to come across as approachable. I realised above all else I needed to get Jonathan – the man who seemed to have taken against me from our first meeting – on board if I was to even try to do what I intended. Hopefully he wouldn't think I was snooping. God, what if he did think I was snooping? That I was only interested in unlocking any secrets the big house might hold? But I couldn't live my life based on what-ifs – and I realised I would never forgive myself if I didn't at least try and help Áine more. The realisation hit me in the pit of my stomach. Yes, Áine was more than a client. More than a dementia patient. More than a charge. She was my friend and I wanted to help her.

I took a deep breath and pressed send and then wandered out into my own pitifully suburban and boring garden where I had never in my life planted a flowerbed, where I had never created an almost magical playground for my daughters.

∽ 1964 ∾

Áine woke as the early morning sun began to stream through the windows at the front of the house. Her mother had offered before, many times, to get heavier curtains for the room but Áine liked being woken by the sunrise – even in summer when it seemed as if the sun never really set in the first place.

She would lie there in her bed and breathe in the sights, sounds and smells of the old house. There was a haziness to these summer mornings. The old house held the heat from the day before and the room was warm despite the fact Áine had left the sash window open just a fraction. She could hear the birds break into their morning song, the soft whistle of the breeze through the leafy trees whose branches brushed against the windows. Áine breathed in and out again, slowly, and turned to look at the clock on her bedside locker. It was just before seven. It wouldn't be long until the house woke up around her. Bit by bit the sound of the ticking grandfather clock in the hall, and the whistle of the breeze in the leaves would be replaced by the squeaking of the hinges on bedroom doors, by the gentle thudding of footsteps on the wooden floorboards, the shouts – friendly and not so friendly – between the two children vying for the bathroom. Rosaleen would call that she was making breakfast. Charlotte would sing as she walked downstairs, and Jack would whistle – his own tunes that no one else ever seemed to know. The kettle would whistle on the stove. The knife would scrape over the toast. The cups and plates would clatter and the bacon would sizzle and the house would buzz into existence.

There were mornings the seemingly quick transformation from her restful sleep to a house buzzing with people would make her want to stuff her head under her pillow to drown out the noise but she promised herself that today she wouldn't take a second of it for granted. Charlotte, Jack and the children were due to leave before lunchtime. This was their final morning to cram as much in as they could. Everything was packed – including the beautiful new dress and a few books she knew Jonathan would love practising his reading with. The children had a small satchel each and she had made them cookies which she had wrapped in brown paper for the journey. She had put a colouring book in each of their bags and some crayons and she had made some little books in which they could draw. She had bought them each a bag of marbles. Charlotte had gently scolded her and told her the children had plenty and there was no need to spoil them. Rosaleen had butted in, of course, saying that the children would always be spoiled in Derry and that when they came home again at Christmas Charlotte could expect more of the same.

"Lord knows, we don't see half enough of them and, when they are here, we want to do everything and get everything for them," Rosaleen had said, ruffling Jonathan's hair. Turning to Áine, she added: "Imagine it, Áine – all together in this house at Christmas again! We'll have to get a big tree and make paper chains. Will we buy some new baubles – ours are getting a bit tired?"

Áine couldn't remember the last time she saw her mother look so alive – but she had to admit she was excited herself. She was already planning to sew some new Christmas stockings for the children and she had seen a few jigsaws which she would love to wrap and put under the tree. She was sure she could find a simple pattern and some lovely fabric for her mother to make a Christmas dress for Emma. She would have to remind herself that Charlotte and Jack would have a say in the festivities as well – but she knew her sister well enough to know that, despite her protestations that the children should not be spoiled, she would go along with whatever Áine and Rosaleen planned. She was one of life's travellers – she went with the flow.

But before Christmas could come they would have to say goodbye for four months. Áine allowed herself to lie in her bed for a moment longer before she sat up. Four months was not long. And sure school would be starting again soon – and once she was in the whirl of the classroom and piano lessons the weeks would fly by. Lorcan had also promised to provide his share of distractions as well. She smiled at the thought – of all the distracting he could do, all those soft touches and gentle kisses and not so gentle kisses.

Four months was not a long time and then they would enjoy a truly unforgettable Christmas. Perhaps Lorcan would even join them for dinner. He would look quite fetching in a paper hat, she thought smiling, and it would be lovely to kiss him under the mistletoe after the children had gone to bed.

"Think of the good times still to come," she whispered to herself as she slipped her feet into her slippers and pulled on her dressing gown. She tied her hair up in a ribbon and opened her bedroom door as quietly as she could, padding her way downstairs to where Charlotte sat nursing a cup of tea and smoking a cigarette.

"You're up early," Áine said, allowing her sister to pour her some tea from the pot before adding her own milk and one sugar.

"Lots to do," Charlotte said with a smile. "It's not easy transporting all of us across a continent. It takes a lot of planning. Or least a lot of tea to get me through the day."

"Admit it," Áine said, "the tea is just not as nice in Italy as it is here at home."

Charlotte laughed. "I cannot tell a lie. And I have a box of finest Irish tea leaves in my case to prove it – but, even at that, it doesn't feel the same drinking it in the Italian sunshine."

"My heart bleeds," Áine said with a smile.

"I'm sure it does, dear sister. I am sure it does."

"You'll be back soon," Áine said softly. "I'll make you as many cups of tea as you want at Christmas. Consider it your present."

"And I couldn't ask fo r a better one," Charlotte said, taking her sister's hand. "It has been a lovely few weeks, hasn't it? I mean once Mother and I stopped going for each other's throats at every opportunity."

"She worries about you."

"And I about her – and about you. That's what families are all about, isn't it? Worry. They say it's love but the two are linked together – you can't love someone or something fiercely without worrying about it just as strongly."

"I suppose," Áine said. "If we didn't worry about each other we would be angry at ourselves. It wouldn't feel right."

"Precisely. So I promise, dear little sister with a big romance on the horizon, to always worry about you and you can promise always to worry about me."

"I will," Áine said softly. "I will worry about you with all my heart."

"Good girl," Charlotte said, topping up their teacups. "Now, some more of this fine Irish tea before the brood wakes."

Áine did her best to keep a stiff upper lip as Charlotte and Jack climbed into the car and the children waved at them from the back seat. Rosaleen wasn't quite as reserved and she allowed the tears to flow freely, even if she had a strange smile – for the benefit of the children – plastered on her face at the same time.

"Be good, I love you! Take care and we'll see you soon! Don't forget us!" Rosaleen called after the car.

Áine put her hand gently on her mother's arm, partly

because she wanted a little bit of comfort herself and partly because she had a small but perfectly formed fear that her mother might just take off running down the driveway after the car and her newly departed family.

Rosaleen took a deep breath, a shaky breath which ended in the smallest whisper of a sob, and straightened herself, adjusting her pale-blue cardigan and smoothing down her blouse.

"That's that then," she said, in a voice not as strong as the sentiment she was sharing. "Best get on with things, my dear."

She turned without meeting her daughter's gaze and walked back into the house – which was already colder for the loss of the four voices that had rattled around it over the previous few weeks.

Áine took a moment to watch the car leave the estate, to get the last glimpse of a small hand – Jonathan's she was sure – waving back at her before they went out of sight and then she walked back into the house and to the kitchen where she filled the kettle and placed it on the range.

"A cup of tea will make it all feel a little less sad," she said to her mother.

Rosaleen nodded, but she was somewhere else in her mind. "You know, pet, I think I'm getting one of my headaches and my hands are aching a little. I might just go for a little lie-down. I know it's terribly lazy of me, but I do feel tired. All that running around with the little ones, I imagine." Still she didn't meet Áine's gaze.

Áine wanted to reach out to her, to say it was okay to feel a little bereft, but she knew that her mother just needed some time to adjust, just those few hours to be still and quiet and lick her wounds a bit. Besides, Lorcan had promised to take her for a drive to take her mind off her sister's departure. She would feel easier leaving the house knowing her mother was sleeping. So she just nodded and agreed that a little sleep might do her a power of good. "Nothing as healing as a good sleep," she said and she promised to wake her mother later in time for tea. "I've everything ready for a nice salad," she added. "I even got some of that tinned salmon in that you like and that bread is still nice and fresh."

"That sounds lovely," Rosaleen said. "I'll look forward to that."

"It will feel easier after a sleep," Áine said.

"I know, pet," Rosaleen answered. "I know."

With that she shuffled off up the stairs and Áine wondered if it was possible that someone could look five or ten or fifteen years older just because they no longer had children around them keeping them young.

She lifted the kettle off the range – no longer in the mood for a cup of tea. Instead she poured herself a glass of cool lemonade and made her way to the sanctuary of her garden where she would wait for the beep of the horn from Lorcan's car as he arrived.

The beach was busy – families set out in little camps on itchy woollen blankets, baskets overflowing with sandwiches, mothers pouring tea – milk and all – out of flasks into enamel mugs. Children screamed as the waves crashed against their legs, Lough Swilly never quite warming up enough to take away the shock of the chill.

Áine felt the sand between her toes – warm and soft as she walked along observing all life in front of her. Lorcan took her hand and she turned to smile at him. He looked strange – in his trousers, shirt and tie – his bare feet being his only concession to their surroundings, but he also looked so very handsome against the backdrop of the hills of Donegal, the sun shining on his face.

"Nothing clears the head like it," he said. "You just can't beat a walk along the beach."

"A paddle in the sea could beat it," she teased but she had already tried to persuade him to dip his toes in the water to no avail.

143

"I really don't think so," he smiled. "I never was one for the water. Fierce fear of jellyfish!"

"I think you might just be afraid I would splash you," she said. "And I don't blame you. It brings out the child in me – a wee paddle in the water. Sure what's the point of it if you can't splash the person you're with?"

"And you see, Miss Quigley, this is why you will never tempt me down to the hard sand and the surf. I'll take my chances up here on the soft, warm and dry sand." He squeezed her hand and led her on. "I don't even mind a little wander among the rocks, somewhere more secluded. Somewhere we won't get watched if we share a kiss."

Áine blushed, her stomach tightening delightfully at the thought of his lips on hers. She wanted so much to nod, to drag him towards the sheltered cove at the end of the beach where less families had set out their pitches for the day – where they could sit on the sand and enjoy a quiet cuddle together. It would all be okay, she realised. Missing Charlotte would pass. Missing the children would be tough but not as tough as it had been before, because this time she had someone all of her own to help her while away the lonelier times. That someone was handsome, she thought as she walked hand in hand with him in the sunshine, imagining that just as she was envying the families enjoying their picnics there were people among the crowds envying her and the tall, dark-haired man she walked with.

She leaned towards him, resting her head briefly against his arm and momentarily let herself close her eyes, feeling the warmth of the sun on her skin as she walked. She felt him pull her a little closer, winding his arm around her shoulders and kissing her forehead gently. When she opened her eyes she looked out at the sun glinting off the ripples of the water, the hills rising out of the horizon, and she listened to the soft sounds of familiar accents around her and felt a wave of contentment wash over her.

Chapter 15

∽ *Present Day* ∾

By the time Matthew sent me a text to tell me the girls were staying with him for the rest of the day so that they could go out for a late Sunday lunch together, I had managed to get myself into a bit of a funk. Feeling lonely, I decided to make the most of the beautiful spring day which had graced us with its presence and head over to see Áine. Perhaps I was crossing a line, again, but it seemed like a perfect day for working the garden. I'd just spend a few hours there – maybe have a spot of lunch – and then be on my way.

I was sure Áine wouldn't mind – and she had told me that she normally spent Sunday mornings on her own before Jonathan would call over. It would also allow me the opportunity to make sure she was okay after the upset of the day before. It was a win-win situation. And no, it wasn't at all sad, I convinced myself, that I didn't want to be on my own on my day off.

I dressed in some linen trousers and a light T-shirt and set off, stopping on my way to stock up on some delicious salad goodies and some fresh-baked crusty bread.

Áine's smile was bright when she saw me which in turn made me happy – then as I walked through to the kitchen she faltered slightly.

"I know I'm doting," she said, "but it's not Monday already, is it? It's Sunday? And you're here?"

I blushed – ashamed I hadn't realised that the upset in routine could cause her confusion. "Oh sorry, Áine! It is Sunday! It's just that my girls are with their daddy today so I was only sitting around the house like a sad soul anyway – and I fancied some company."

"Aren't you kind?" she smiled. "It's lovely to see you – but only if you're sure your family don't need you?"

I stifled a laugh (again doing the being-positive-in-the-face-of-life-being-rubbish thing). My daughters were happy with their daddy and their daddy was more than happy doing his own thing.

"I won't pry," she said, looking at me quizzically, taking in the wedding band I still hadn't brought myself to remove. "I know it's one of the biggest clichés in the world, but it doesn't make it any less true. Everything happens for a reason – and things work out if they are meant to."

"I do believe that," I told her, unloading my shopping into the fridge. "I just have some trouble coming to terms with what is meant to be."

"Don't we all, pet," she said, reaching out and rubbing my arm gently. "Now, I always found one of the best ways to take my mind off things that were bothering me was to lose myself in the garden for a bit."

"Well, it sounds like a plan to me," I smiled. "It's a great day to make a start."

Áine opened a wardrobe and pulled out two, rather battered, wide-brimmed straw hats. "Best put one of these on," she said to me. "No point in the two of us getting a little sick in the head."

She smiled brightly and I was glad that I had come over – and as I followed her into the garden I was excited about actually getting started on our project together.

Áine was a natural as she moved about, setting things up for our first two raised flowerbeds.

"This was where the vegetable garden was," she said. "We didn't always get a good crop, but when we did it felt brilliant to have grown the food ourselves. I didn't bother so much after mother died – seemed pointless growing for one and I suppose my heart went out of it a bit. Besides I had other things on my mind then …"

"Life always has a habit of running away on us, doesn't it?" I asked, as I set about turning over the fresh soil with a trowel, to ready it for planting.

"It sure does. But you know people say we have to stop and take time to smell the roses more but no one does. Not until you are like me anyway, and the roses are past their best. Life gets busy."

"That's for sure," I said. "Seems like only yesterday my girls were toddlers, starting out in the world, and now they're studying for their GCSEs, looking grown-up and thinking about leaving home to go and study."

"You don't look old enough to have teenage daughters," Áine said.

"I was a child bride," I laughed. "I married my childhood sweetheart. We had the girls young. We thought we knew it all."

"The young always think they know it all," Áine said. "And so it should be – none of us are guaranteed the luxury of growing old."

Her face clouded and I knew not to push further – not today anyway. Today we would have a good day.

We worked companionably together for a few hours, Áine animated as she explained to me exactly what to do. She was a natural teacher – and was in her comfort zone. I relaxed in her company too and knew that I had done the right thing by coming over. It was a definite improvement on sitting around the house moping.

Shortly after noon, we heard a male voice call out from the house. It was Jonathan.

Áine smiled brightly at the sound of his voice and chirped, "My boy has come to visit!"

He looked strange – dressed casually – as he walked into the garden. There was no sign of the tailored suit, the super-shined shoes, the close shave. He wore a pair of loose chinos, a smart checked shirt over a white T-shirt and a pair of Converse. He had a trace of salt-and-pepper stubble on his face.

He smiled broadly at his aunt. It was a rare unguarded moment – that is, until he spotted me, leaning over the flowerbed, trowel in my hand. I offered a brief hello, and he raised his eyebrow in return.

I wondered if he was concerned I was billing him for this – so I spoke quickly. "It was such a nice day and I found myself at a loose end, so I thought we could get started on the garden. Don't worry, I won't get in the way."

He looked at Áine, as if looking for some confirmation of what I had said.

She smiled at him and said, "Isn't she lovely? We've had the nicest morning. We were just about to have lunch so your timing is perfect!"

"Well, I had made us some reservations for a Sunday carvery," Jonathan said. "Georgina, you can head on now if you want."

"Oh no," Áine said. "It's not a day for some stuffy restaurant. Georgina brought some nice salad. We should enjoy that while the weather stays nice."

"Don't feel obligated on my behalf," I told her. "I can always take it home for the girls."

"No, no, my mouth has been watering at the very

thought," she said, smiling. "Jonathan doesn't mind. Do you, Jonathan? You love a nice salad?"

He seemed lost for words so I stood up and began to make my way towards the house. "I'll get started on it then, shall I, and let you two have a bit of time together? I have some baked ham and crusty bread to go with it."

Jonathan smiled (actually smiled) and looked at me. "Well, that sounds good," he said. "And if Auntie Áine would prefer a lighter lunch who am I to argue?"

"Exactly," Áine said. "Remember your place, young man."

They both laughed and I could see, for the first time, a family resemblance between the pair.

As I rinsed the lettuce and tomatoes in the sink I glanced out the window and watched Áine and Jonathan as they talked. They had moved over from the flowerbeds and were sitting on the wrought-iron garden chairs to the right of the garden. They talked easily and it was lovely to see how they interacted. Jonathan seemed so much softer when he didn't realise he was being watched – and Áine seemed to light up in his company in a way I hadn't seen before. It warmed my heart to be honest – to see how they obviously cared for each other and in those few moments I re-evaluated just a little how I felt about Jonathan. Maybe he wasn't the completely obnoxious creature I had him pegged as.

I busied myself chopping the vegetables, slicing the ham and bread, and curling the butter onto a saucer ready for spreading. If I said so myself, it looked absolutely delicious and, with a nice pot of tea to wash it all down, I was sure it would hit the spot. Pleased with how I had laid the table I walked to the back door to call Jonathan and Áine in – but, as I caught sight of them again, I realised something had changed. They were clutching hands over the small wrought-iron table and Áine's face was serious and stern. Jonathan was shaking his head – and while I couldn't see the expression on his face his whole body had tensed up. I watched as Áine reached out and placed her hand softly on his cheek – and I watched as she started to cry, but then settled herself and offered him a weak smile. Suddenly I felt as though I was intruding on something I shouldn't be a party to, so I quickly turned my back, took my place at the large kitchen table in front of the lovely lunch I had prepared and told myself I would give them at least five minutes before I peeked out again and called them in for something to eat.

It felt awkward – and I felt for both of them, but I was simply an outsider in their lives, someone who had known them a matter of weeks and it wasn't my place to ask too many questions and stick my nose in too far. God knows I was pushing my luck as it was. I poured myself a cup of tea, buttered an end piece of the crusty baguette and sat back and waited.

When I looked out the door again, they were talking more companionably so I called them in for lunch. If their smiles were a bit too bright, I pretended to notice nothing and we sat down and began to eat together.

"This is lovely," Jonathan said, smiling.

"Thank you," I replied, feeling myself blush.

"I told you it would be nicer than dinner out in some stuffy restaurant," Áine said, slathering some butter onto her bread. "Don't you remember when we all used to sit round this table and eat lunches like this when you were little?"

"In those lovely warm summers?" Jonathan said.

"Yes," Áine laughed, loading her bread with thick-cut ham. "We had some good times."

"There are good times still waiting, Auntie," Jonathan said, with a smaller smile this time – but Áine just laughed again – a smaller laugh.

After lunch Áine couldn't stop herself stifling a yawn or four. I set her up on her favourite chair, with a soft blanket over her knees and an old black-and-white movie on the television but it wasn't long before she had dozed off.

I made my way to the kitchen with the intention of cleaning up before leaving – but there was Jonathan, his arms in the sink, washing the dishes, the rest of the kitchen already gleaming.

He looked around at me and smiled. "I'm not averse to washing up sometimes," he said.

"Feel free!" I laughed. "Look, I'll leave you to it. Sorry for gate-crashing your Sunday with your aunt."

"Did you not want to talk to me? I got your text. Or are you in a rush to get off?"

"No, not at all," I said, glancing at the clock on the wall. "My girls won't be home for a few hours yet – but it's not that important, really." Seeing how he had interacted with Áine, how they had shared their memories over lunch, I wondered if I was being a bit gung-ho about things.

"If it's about my aunt, it's important," he said, drying his hands and turning to face me, crossing his arms.

"I've been researching 'reminiscence work'," I started. "Have you noticed Áine seems to light up when talking about the past?"

"Well, of course I have," he said brusquely. His tone had turned once again to awkward.

"Sorry," I offered, "of course you must have. It's obvious you are close. It's just the more memory work we do with Áine, the more we can help slow the progress of her illness. It mightn't be much – but it's something. And it would give her a certain sense of confidence."

"I'm sorry too," he offered. "For my tone. I just – you know – find it hard sometimes, knowing what to do for the best. Give me a business deal and I know just what to do. Give me this … this awful illness … and I feel as if I'm just flapping around."

"You seem to be doing a good enough job," I offered.

"Áine is content."

"Not content enough," he replied, staring downwards. "But anyway – what can I do to help?"

"Do you have any photo albums? Memories. Things she used to like? I've been able to tease a certain amount out of her – but with your help I think we could do much more."

He took a deep breath. "Of course," he said. "Anything that will help."

"Great," I smiled. "It can't do any harm."

"Georgina," Jonathan said, looking straight at me, "thank you. Thank you for caring enough to go above and beyond."

"I do care for her," I said, finding to my shock that a lump had formed in my throat. "I mightn't always get it right – but I do try."

"Which of us always gets it right?" he said with a smile.

I found myself feeling flustered by his gaze. Perhaps, hat or not, I had caught too much sun.

"I'll dig some pictures out," he said. "We'll talk through it."

I nodded, finding myself unable to speak, and I lifted my bag. Smiled and gave a little wave.

Only as I left the kitchen did I find my voice coming back to me. "That would be great. Look, I have to run. Take care, bye now. Bye bye."

Chapter 16

∽ 1964 ∽

The first day of term held a different meaning for Áine that year. She always felt a certain excitement returning to the classroom – to the unique smell of the newly varnished floorboards, the fresh chalk, the clean duster. She loved the smell of the jotters – white and clean, not yet muddied by tiny hands trying to find the correct way to hold their pencils and crayons and form their words on the sheets.

She loved the blank canvas of the classroom walls – wondering what this year's offering of pupils would bring, what pictures they would paint, how they would adorn the walls. She had made sure the pencil pots were filled, that everything was good to go. But she couldn't control the extra nervousness she felt, knowing that this year everything had changed. Lorcan would be there as he always was – but in previous years she didn't know what it felt like to kiss him. She hadn't known what it felt like to walk hand in hand with him or how he could make her laugh. She had never gone back into her workplace as a woman with a boyfriend before. The summer had changed her – in so many ways – that she was sure her colleagues would be able to see the confidence beam from her as she walked the corridors of the old school building.

She had even invested in a new skirt and blouse for the first day back and had bought a pair of shoes with the slightest of heels which made her feel feminine. She had taken extra time to fix her hair and had dabbed her face with pressed powder and a little blush. Her mother had commented on her appearance as she had prepared to leave the house.

"My goodness, dear, you have a lovely glow about you. You should hope not to see too much of your young man during the day because you will be sure to distract him from his work."

"He teaches at the other end of the school, Mother," Áine said, blushing at how easily her mother had seen through her attempts to doll herself up.

"But I'm sure you will see each other in the staffroom. Don't be making a show of yourself."

"I'm hardly going to French-kiss him over the Rich Teas, Mother," Áine said and laughed as her mother's face paled.

"I should hope not. You were raised better than that."

"I really was, Mother. Please don't worry. I promise I will do nothing to embarrass you. I just wanted to put my best foot forward. But I really like him, Mother. I really do."

Rosaleen smiled and took her daughter's hand in her own. Áine couldn't help but notice how gnarled her mother's hands were becoming – how they were losing the softness she had cherished as a child. "All I want, my darling, is for you to be happy."

"I know, Mother, and I am happy. I really am."

"That's great, pet," Rosaleen said, taking up her seat by the range.

Áine had done what she could to make sure her mother's day would be as easy as possible. She had left a pot of soup ready to be reheated and the bread for lunch had been sliced and was ready to be buttered. The fire in the sitting room was set – a quick strike of a match and it would be lit.

"You will be fine, won't you, Mother?"

"Don't you worry about me," Rosaleen said. "I have my book here and you have me ruined. After a summer with the lot of you around my feet it will be blissful having the house to myself."

"As long as you are sure," Áine said, aware there was touch of emotion in her mother's voice.

"I'm sure. You're a great teacher, Miss Quigley, and you have a class of youngsters waiting to be educated – not to mention your young man waiting to see you looking so pretty. You'd better hurry or you'll be late."

"I love you," Áine said, pulling on her overcoat and picking up her satchel. "I won't be late and I have a lovely piece of chicken for our dinner."

"Take your time, pet, and sure why don't you invite that young man of yours over some night for tea? Isn't it about time I met him?"

Áine smiled as she walked the short distance to the school, meeting parents bringing their charges to school for the first day of term – girls in pigtails and pony-tails, boys with their cowlicks slicked down. The air was fresh, the breeze still had a hint of warmth to it and everything felt right with the world.

℘ *Present Day* ℘

By the time I arrived at Áine's the following day I had convinced myself that my feeling flustered the day before was indeed down to the warmth of the spring day, the morning spent in the garden and an inordinate amount of heat directed right at my head. Sunstroke, I had heard, could make you a little delusional. Jonathan Hegarty had not, I told myself, made me feel a little bit wobbly at the knees. Yes, he had shown a gentler side of himself and I always was a sucker for a vulnerable man. Matthew used to be able to wrap me about his little finger with a doe-eyed look and a downturned smile. But, I was not to forget that Jonathan Hegarty had shown me on more than one occasion that he could also be insufferably arrogant. And, with Matthew in my life, I already had one too many insufferably arrogant men to be coping with.

I dusted myself off and walked up the drive to Temple Muse, hoping against hope that I wouldn't see him that day – not while it was still warm and I was probably still suffering from sunstroke. Because, as much as I tried, I couldn't help but have the image of his smiling face enter my mind on an uncomfortably regular basis.

Things were not helped by Áine greeting me with a bright smile. "Jonathan's here. Wait until you see what he has with him."

If it was at all possible, my heart leapt and sank at the same time – which made me feel a little nauseous. Of course, I put that down to the sunstroke. Nothing else.

"This is my mother, on Charlotte's wedding day," Áine said, handing the photo to me.

"She was a very handsome woman," I told her. "She looks so glamorous here."

We were sitting at the kitchen table, pictures that Jonathan had brought scattered all around us.

Jonathan, who had simply said hello when I arrived, was making a cup of tea and had poured some chocolate biscuits onto a plate.

Áine stroked the picture as I held it in my hands. "I remember the row they had over what she should wear. They never did agree on anything. But, of course, Mother gave in – she always did when it came to Charlotte."

Jonathan carried two mugs of tea to the table. "Her bark was always worse than her bite," he said softly. "She liked to pretend she was fierce as old boots, but she was as soft as they came."

Áine took the photo and held it to her chest. All I could do was watch – I saw how she closed her eyes, how her grip on the photo became tighter as if the act of physically holding onto the grainy image would help her keep the memories of the woman before her alive in her mind.

"I miss her," Áine said, a tear rolling down her cheek. "I really miss her."

Momentarily Jonathan looked panicked and he looked at me, as if wanting me to provide some sort of anchor for this moment.

I took a deep breath and took Áine's hand. "It's okay to miss her," I said. "If you miss her, it means you remember her. And that's a good thing."

"She was a good woman," Jonathan said. "I think she had a tough life – she had a lot of loss in her life."

"She always had a soft spot for you and Emma. She would turn into a different person when you two were around," Áine said. "She loved being a grandmother. She might have had a bark on her at times but she was proud of you and your sister – more than anything else in the world."

"Oh, I think she was proud of you too, Auntie Áine. You did so much for her."

Áine looked at the picture again, showing it once more to me. Rosaleen looked back at me, a small, formal smile tight on her lips. She stood in a fitted suit in a pale golden colour which came to just below the knee, clutching a small white handbag in her white-gloved hand. A pillar-box hat sat on top of her head, her curls beautifully styled. Once again I saw the resemblance between mother and daughter and I smiled.

"You are like her," I said. "Two very attractive women. It must be in the genes."

"I always wondered would she find love again but she never got over my father's death," Áine said. "I never really knew him, you know. He died when I was a baby. I have vague memories – probably what people told me about him when I think about it. My mother should have tried to find happiness again."

"She had happiness in her own way," Jonathan said. "With you, and my mother … and us."

Áine nodded, and she looked back at the pictures in front of her. "Thank you for bringing these over today," she said. "I haven't seen these photos in such a long time."

"I shouldn't have taken them out of the house in the first place," Jonathan said. "It was very selfish of me. To take all these pictures – I did mean to scan them and bring them back. I just never got round to it. I wanted my own collection, you know?"

"And you're entitled to them too – all these pictures, your parents' wedding day, your grandmother – of course you should have them."

"I'll bring my laptop and a scanner over here," he said. "I'll scan them here."

"That's a good idea," I told him as I saw Aine lift another picture – the happy couple – and stare at it intently.

"They made a beautiful couple," she said softly. "A very happy couple too."

Jonathan nodded and reached out and held her hand. "Happiness comes in different forms," he said.

Later I settled Áine in her room, helping her into her night clothes and dressing gown. I couldn't help but notice she was looking utterly worn out even though it wasn't long after seven.

"It was nice to see that picture again," she whispered. She rested back on her pillow.

"Your mother?" I asked.

Áine nodded. "There are so few pictures of her. Fewer still when she was all dolled up – looking so happy. That was a happy day – a really happy day. It was just so nice to see that again – to see her at her best." She sniffed and I could see she was starting to get emotional.

"You mustn't get yourself upset," I soothed, rubbing her hand.

"I'm starting to forget her a little. Just little things – details. It's just fading a bit."

"It's happens to all of us, regardless of this hateful disease. We have so much to remember – things get hazy."

"But everything is fading a little bit. It's all gone a little fuzzy around the edges."

I wanted to reassure her – to tell her that it would okay but I supposed it wouldn't. Not entirely, Things would get fuzzier. Things would get scarier. I couldn't imagine how I would feel if it was me who was sitting watching pieces of my life slip away bit by bit – knowing perhaps that something was there but just a little out of reach.

"I'll be here," I said. "No matter what."

"I know," Áine said. "Thank you."

"That was a good thing you did for your aunt today," I said. "Bringing over those photos."

Jonathan was sitting at the kitchen table looking every bit as lost as his aunt had done in her room.

"She seemed upset."

"She misses people. She's scared of losing her memories."

"I never thought to bring them over before. They were just in my house – waiting to be scanned. If I had known, if I had thought, I would have brought them over much earlier."

"You can't beat yourself up about it. You didn't purposely keep them from her," I said. "She enjoyed looking at those pictures. Of course it was going to be bittersweet. Don't we have memories which cause us as much pleasure as they do pain?" I was thinking of the wedding pictures sitting on my own mantelpiece. "Your aunt is doing remarkably well," I added and she was – Áine was still able to spend large swathes of time in the house on her own. She could hold a conversation. To people who didn't know her – who spent brief interludes of time with her – she could, on a good day, come across as perfectly fine. "But she wants to remember. She has spent so much time talking about her life. About you as a child, and your sister, and your mother. But they were fading. They are fading. She is fading. It probably won't be quick. And please God she will stay well for a long time – but to help keep those memories she needs prompts. I can't prompt her about stuff I don't know."

Jonathan still looked lost. He looked tired and he rubbed his temples as if warding off a headache.

"I can't pretend to know how hard it is," I said, resisting the urge to reach out and touch his arm. "I don't have personal experience of dementia. I know that no matter how fond I am of your aunt, I'm always going to be one step removed from where you are."

"She is more than just my aunt," he said. "She was my second mother. I don't think I would be half the person I am without her. My sister the same. In fact I'm pretty sure that almost everyone who ever came through this house owes something to her."

"Can I ask a personal question?" I asked.

He smiled a soft smile. "Well, it seems you are getting to the heart of this family's secrets one way or the other, so fire away."

"Why did your aunt never marry? She has told me of a man called Lorcan – but not what happened there."

Jonathan coloured slightly and sat back in his seat. "I don't really remember Lorcan all that much. I don't think they saw each other for very long – and then things changed. We moved back when I was eight and Áine took on caring for us."

"And your mother, Charlotte?" I asked, wondering where this wonderful mother Áine had spoken of had gone.

"No, she never came home," Jonathan said. "Did Áine not tell you? My mother died when I was eight. She drowned at our villa in Italy. She's buried there. Everything changed that day. As I said, not all our memories are happy ones."

I could hardly take it in. Each time Aine spoke of Charlotte, she seemed so alive – so vibrant. She never mentioned her death – and those children, those poor children. I felt shocked to my very core.

Chapter 17

∽ 1964 ∾

The classroom had emptied. The chairs were stacked neatly on top of the desks and the pencils were back in their pots. The light was starting to fade and the room was growing cold – the heating had clicked off and the old, stone building never did hold the heat for long at the end of the day. Rain rattled off the windows and the fluttering of the leaves outside cast shadows on the walls. Áine stood on her tiptoes, dusting off the blackboard of the day's work, ready to start on laying out work for the following day. She sang as she dusted – and already her thoughts turned to getting home, sitting in front of the range and enjoying a bowl of the stew she had prepared that morning.

She glanced at her watch. Lorcan would be by soon to pick her up. She didn't know why she had worried about their working together – things had run smoothly and she had the added bonus of him picking her up each day and driving her home. They would enjoy a brief chat about their day and then a kiss on the street before she got out of the car. As the afternoons had got darker, the kisses had become longer and she swore there were days when it was all she could think about – those precious moments alone with Lorcan. It made her feel giddy and elated and it was no wonder she sang as she dusted off the blackboard.

That night would be even nicer – Lorcan was coming for dinner. He did that at least once a week. His first meeting with her mother had gone so well that Rosaleen had told him he was welcome any time and he took her up on the offer. He would always bring a bouquet of flowers for Rosaleen which would make her act more than a little giddy herself and he would insist on clearing the table and washing the dishes when they were finished eating. Rosaleen had resisted at first, of course. She had chided Áine, telling her she should get up and do her bit and get that lovely friend of hers a cup of tea – but Lorcan had shushed her and charmed her and now, if he didn't make them all a cup of tea after dinner, he was likely to get some gentle ribbing as Rosaleen reminded him she took one sugar and just a drop of milk.

When she heard the door of her classroom open she turned, a smile on her face, ready to tell Lorcan that Rosaleen had baked an apple pie for dessert. She hadn't been expecting to see that Lorcan was not alone. The headmaster was beside him. Both men's faces were ashen and in that moment she was acutely aware that everything was changing.

Áine stood, the quiet of the room buzzing around her eyes, taking in the image before her, and she told herself that as soon as she spoke, as soon as they answered, everything would be different. She didn't know how, she didn't know why, but she could see by the way Lorcan started to walk across the classroom to her, his head shaking ever so gently, that something was very wrong. Mr Quinn, the headmaster, stood awkwardly – looking as if he would rather be anywhere else in the world than where he was. She was aware it was cold and she was shivering – a gentle shiver at first, which soon turned into something more violent as Lorcan grew closer. With each step she felt what was her life slip away. She raised her hand, willing him to stop. If he didn't reach her – if he didn't say anything – then it could be as if nothing was wrong just for another few moments. All she wanted was another few moments.

But he stepped ever closer – and she kept shivering.

"Is it my mother?" she asked, willing him to ask her what she was talking about. Willing him to tell her she was imagining the look of shock on his face. Willing the headmaster to shout "Goodnight then!" and leave them to get on with their plans. Stew, and pie for afters.

"Your mother is fine," Lorcan said.

A momentary flare of relief.

"But we need to go home now. She needs you."

She needs me, Áine thought. My mother needs me. We need to go home.

And Mr Quinn was shaking his head slowly, sombrely.

"Why does she need me?" Áine asked, trying to figure out if it was at all possible to freeze time, or to stop her ears from working, or to wake up from this dream. This didn't feel real, so it couldn't be real. She felt another bubble of relief rise up and threaten to burst out of her in a silly giggle – a nervous reaction she didn't know how to control.

"She needs you," Lorcan said again, his voice uncertain.

She saw Mr Quinn reach for her coat from the hook by the door.

"You're scaring me," she whispered.

"I'm sorry," he replied.

She realised he looked horrified, scared and out of his depth. Her feelings spiralled. She wanted to comfort him – but she wanted to know why.

"You have to tell me," she said, taking a deep breath to fight the urge to faint. "You have to tell me because I can't breathe."

He was reaching for her now and she realised her face was

wet and the shivering had been replaced by large, body-shaking shudders.

"I'm so sorry," he said as he pulled her into his arms. "I'm so, so sorry. It's Charlotte. She's gone. I'm so, so sorry."

The rhythmic back and forward, here and there, of the windshield wipers helped keep Áine grounded as they drove back to the house. She couldn't speak. She couldn't even allow herself to think too much. So she held on to what she could – the patter of the rain, the swish of the wipers, the hum of the engine.

Lorcan tried to speak a few times, mumbled a few words before he trailed off again. She didn't have the strength to talk to him. She was using all the strength she had to keep it together, to try and not simply stop to exist because her sister was gone. It was ridiculous. Absolutely ridiculous. Charlotte couldn't be dead. She was the most alive person she had ever known. She oozed vitality. She couldn't simply cease to exist. It wasn't possible.

And yet this is what she had been told, and what she was going home to try and accept. It was what she and her mother would talk about for days, for weeks, for months. She couldn't imagine anything else could ever be more momentous, that anything else could ever be more important. She wouldn't laugh again. Or smile again. As she drove she realised she would never be the same again and she cursed herself for not having perfect hindsight and enjoying the last few days of innocence more.

She didn't know how long they had been stopped and she hadn't noticed Lorcan get out of the car and yet he must have because she heard the car door open beside her and looked up to see him extend his hand to help her out. He looked uncomfortable, she thought, glancing at him. She felt momentarily sorry for him – thrust into the middle of a family crisis. He hadn't bargained for this – no one had bargained for this because these kinds of things didn't happen – they certainly didn't happen to her.

Stepping out of the car she felt the cold rain on her cheeks and she inhaled deeply.

"Let's get inside," Lorcan said, pulling his collar up and starting to walk towards the steps to the door.

She nodded. It couldn't be put off any more. It was as real as it would get.

Rosaleen stood in the middle of room, her eyes darting from place to place trying to find a truth that was more palatable than that which she had been told.

Aine was aware she was staring at her over the shoulder of Father Michael, summonsed to provide some spiritual comfort. Auntie Sheila was also there.

Áine looked at her mother and felt her heart sink further than she'd ever thought possible. Rosaleen was always strong – always. She had raised the girls amid the grief of losing her husband and, while Áine had been too young to remember the shock of that loss, she had always known her to be stoic, defiant even, in the face of any battles they had faced. "You keep looking forward," she would say. "We all have our crosses to carry and we just have to muster what grace we can while we carry them."

But now, there was a strange look in her mother's eyes – almost wild, feral, broken.

"We've called the doctor," Auntie Sheila whispered. "We think she might need a little something to settle her."

Áine nodded, thinking she could do with something to blank all this out herself.

"You should sit down," Father Michael said.

"Why?" Rosaleen barked back. "Will it bring her back? Will it make me feel better?"

"You've had a shock," the priest said, his voice calm and measured – this was not the first time he had comforted the bereaved.

Áine became aware that she was crying – that tears were flooding down her face and she couldn't stop them and watching her mother made them fall faster.

"We've had a shock," Rosaleen blustered to her daughter and Áine nodded, unable to find a single word of comfort. "We must sit down," she continued. "Go on, Áine, sit down and the shock will pass. We'll all feel better. We'll all feel calm and collected and set about drinking tea and accepting calls from well-meaning neighbours offering their condolences."

"Rose!" Sheila implored, one of a generation terrified of offending the clergy.

Father Michael didn't flinch. Áine was acutely aware that no one flinched – everyone was waiting to see what she would say or do, or what her mother would say or do.

"No, don't 'Rose' me," Rosaleen continued. "Did you not hear what that policeman said? Did you not?"

Áine wanted to say that no, she hadn't heard. She didn't know. She wanted to scream at her mother to be gentle, to share the news softly. She hadn't heard and she was afraid of what would come next – and of the images that would fill her mind. She was afraid to sit down, afraid her mother would launch at her, but she was afraid she would fall to the ground.

She reached for the chair back to steady herself as her mother shouted, "She drowned! My daughter drowned! My baby is dead. But sit down, it won't be so horrific. It won't be so real. It will be easier to deal with the fact that I won't ever see her again."

Rosaleen was sobbing now, her words distorted. Spit had flown from her mouth as she shouted and Áine stood and watched, afraid to move, images of her sister floating face down in a pool of water flooding her brain. Were her eyes open? Áine couldn't imagine those eyes dull and glassy, dead. She found herself sinking onto the chair. Auntie Sheila sat beside her and Áine felt the warm hands of her aunt on hers.

Rosaleen was in full flow now and Father Michael was

stepping up to the plate, doling out every platitude under the sun about God's plan and time being a great healer.

Rosaleen – a woman who bowed before the altar rails every Sunday and helped arrange the flowers on a Saturday – was shaking her head in fury. "God's plan? God's plan? To take my girl away? She's a mother, for God's sake. She has those children. God – who took away my husband – and now he takes her? Don't ever speak to me of God's plan!"

"I understand you are hurting right now," Father Michael said.

Áine tried to process what her mother was saying. Each word bringing a new wave of grief – how could her mother endure this? How could she endure this? And Jonathan and Emma? Oh God – and Jack. How was Jack? Was he there? Did he try to help her? Did the children see her? She felt a physical ache in her stomach.

"You might understand – but you don't feel it," Rosaleen raged on. "You don't know – don't tell me God is love and he will support me. God is a hateful, horrible spiteful creature and he can go to hell!"

Áine found herself unable to listen any more – so she stood up and without looking at anyone in the room she ran outside to stand in the rain to try and silence the screaming in her head.

She stood in the back garden, where they had spent so much time in the heat of the summer – where Charlotte had been so full of life, and she wept until her throat was raw, and her clothes soaked through.

It was only much, much later that it dawned on her that Lorcan had not followed her to comfort her and that he had gone home without saying goodbye.

The details from Italy were slow to come through. Painfully slow. It would have been easier if they had all come at once – like tearing off a plaster. But no, poor communications mixed with the fuzziness of tranquilisers to take the edge off grief and the exhaustion which came with trying to make sense of something which made no sense, meant that each day brought a fresh wave of grief.

Charlotte had indeed drowned – in the pool of the Italian villa she so loved. She had been outside on the terrace after dark when it was thought she had slipped or tripped and fallen into the water. She had bumped her head on the way into the water, they were told. She wouldn't have felt anything.

Jack had found her – he didn't know how long she had been in the water – but they were all grateful that neither of the children had found their mother's body.

And the children? The children were being cared for by friends while Jack tried to come to terms with everything. He hadn't spoken to either Rosaleen or Áine. Rosaleen called him a coward – her anger had not abated in the days which followed – but Áine could understand his fears. What could he say? How could he face them? She didn't want to face anyone. She wanted to lie in bed each day and look at photos from her childhood and pretend it was all a mistake. It was the only place she could escape the reality that everything had changed. As soon as she left her room she was greeted with mirrors covered with black cloths, the curtains were drawn and in the sitting room Rosaleen had set up a shrine to Charlotte. It made Áine feel sick to look at it – and to see her mother sitting there in front of it, in a daze, made her feel like she wanted to run away.

Charlotte wasn't coming home. That was established early on. There would be no real wake – no real funeral. She was buried close to the villa – close to her children and under her beloved sunshine. Rosaleen didn't have the strength to argue or the means to bring her daughter's remains home if she did. Father Michael had steadfastly tried to offer spiritual counsel and Rosaleen had repeatedly told him to go to hell. Even if

Charlotte was brought home she would not have a Christian burial. The God who killed her would have no place in laying her to rest as if that made some sort of amends for his actions, she had barked.

But instead she had set up her shrine – pictures, candles, a darkened room – a big pot of tea on the range and plate after plate of sandwiches for those who called round to shake their heads in disbelief and offer words of comfort.

Áine yearned to do something more. She yearned to see her sister. She yearned to talk to Jack to find out exactly what had happened. Her heart ached for her niece and nephew and she longed to talk to them – to offer them what comfort she could. She wanted to hug them and whisper to them over and over and over again how much their mother had loved them – and she wanted to tell them every last detail of Charlotte's life so that they would never forget her.

But instead all she could really do was lie on top of her bed and wish it was all so very different.

Chapter 18

∽ *Present Day* ∽

I wasn't sure how it happened. Even now part of me wondered had it happened at all? I was sitting in my car, outside my house, playing the scene over and over in my head again.

At some stage, while Jonathan had been telling how his mother had died – how she had been found lifeless, face down in their pool – and how his childhood had been torn to pieces, I had felt his hand on mine. I didn't even notice it at first. It had felt natural – while he talked – that he would reach out. I had reached out too – putting my free hand on top of his as I listened to the pain that hadn't eased over fifty years. He may well have been a grown man – and a successful, confident businessman at that – but there was, I saw, a great deal of pain in his eyes still. The kind of pain that doesn't go away. My heart had shifted when I realised he was showing me himself at his most vulnerable and it took every ounce of willpower I had not to reach out and touch his cheek, to caress his face, to feel the soft stubble on his chin … to look into his hazel eyes …

I hadn't pulled my hand away from his. He had pulled his

hand away from mine. Afterwards I didn't know how long we had sat there holding hands but I knew – or thought I knew – that it felt right. That in that moment I knew the real person behind Jonathan Hegarty's brash persona. The person who had been hurt as a child more than many of us had been hurt in our lifetimes – and the person who was doing everything in his power to stop himself from hurting now.

And, to my confusion, as I sat there in my car, I realised I had very much seen a Jonathan Hegarty who I wanted to kiss – and by the way he held my gaze before I left I had a notion that he wanted to kiss me too.

Indeed I was just thinking, again, of how his kiss could feel when my phone rang. In a way I was glad of the distraction – I didn't need to be losing myself in romantic thoughts. When I saw the person who was calling me, romance was the furthest thing from my mind.

"Matthew," I said as I answered.

"Ah good, good, you're there," he mumbled.

"You called my mobile phone, Matthew. Where else would I be? The whole point of the phone being that it is mobile?" I tried to keep the snippiness from my voice – to come across as just a little quirky instead. I failed.

"Okay," he breathed out. "It's like that, is it?"

"Like what? Matthew – you called me. What do you want? It has been a long day and I want a shower and something to eat and maybe some time relaxing."

"You could come here for dinner?" he asked, his voice tentative.

"And why would I do that?"

"Because I don't like how things ended last week, Georgina. It's not what I want."

"Oh," I said, "so you don't want to leave me? You don't want to see someone else? And you don't want our teenage daughters – who are trying to come to terms with it all – to meet her?"

He sighed again. I knew that what I had just said was exactly

172

what he wanted. He just wanted me to be okay with it too. I could visualise him getting frustrated – pinching the bridge of his nose in exasperation. Silly Georgie doesn't get it. Again.

"No … George. I just want it to be more amicable."

"I'm sure you do," I laughed.

"You can't be enjoying this any more than I am," he said.

"I'm pretty sure you are enjoying much more than me," I spat. "You're the one who is making all the calls here. You're the one living the life of a young single man. I'm the one picking up the pieces."

"Well, come over, Georgie. Let's talk. Tell me how I can help you pick up some pieces."

"Okay," I conceded, thinking that we needed to move forward in some way and at least now he was offering to listen. I looked at the clock on my dashboard. "I'll just check on the girls, get changed and come round."

"I look forward to it," he said and hung up.

"She's someone from school. A teaching assistant," he said as he speared some long-stem broccoli with his fork and ate it.

He spoke as if we were never married – as if it were the most natural thing in the world to talk to me about someone he was seeing. I imagined the broccoli choking him – just ever so slightly. Just enough to make him turn a little blue, maybe feel a little faint.

I nodded.

"I wasn't lying last week when I said I didn't know what I wanted – I didn't. And when Sam came over I told her that – I told her I was confused. That I had been with you forever – it was only natural I felt a loyalty to you. But … I can't lie, Georgie. Not to you. You deserve more. And, if I'm honest, Sam deserves more too."

I glanced down at the steak, untouched on my plate. It was such an awful shame it was going to go to waste.

"You said you wanted to start picking up pieces," I said.

"How are we doing that?"

"I need you to know, it was never about you. It was me entirely. I just grew up – we were so young."

"I grew up too, you know," I said. "I just didn't grow away from you."

I wanted to shout. I had imagined this scene being one where I threw a plate at his head, or beat his chest with my fists, or slapped him soundly around the face. But I think, in that moment, I had gone beyond that.

"It's too early for her to meet the girls. Much too early," I said. "And it won't be up to you to decide when they are ready for it. You turned their lives upside down too."

"I know," he said – and had the decency to look ashamed of himself. "I miss them so much."

The part of me that wanted to ask him if he missed me too was too worried about what the answer would be.

"You made your bed," I croaked.

"I did – and I'm sorry. If it's of any use. I am sorry. I thought we would be forever." And he reached out and touched my hand.

My mind flew back to earlier that day, when another hand held mine. When that other hand made me feel something good – something positive. It made me feel useful. It made me feel trusted. It made me feel like I was someone.

Matthew's hand didn't do that. In fact, it felt alien. With a strange realisation that made me feel lighter than I had in weeks I realised it had been a very long time since Matthew's hands had really made me feel anything remotely close to alive – to cherished, to wanted.

I slowly took my hand from his.

"I thought we would be forever too," I said softly. "But we just have to get on with it and pick up the pieces."

"Yes," he said, sadly. "Just pick up the pieces."

"Oh my!" Sinéad breathed down the phone when I told her

about Jonathan.

"Yes, I know. That's another fine mess I have got myself into." I was in bed, sipping a cup of warm milk to try and settle myself so that I had half a chance of getting some sleep.

"I'm not sure it's so much of a mess …" Sinéad said.

"Of course it is! Having any sort of feelings of any kind for Jonathan Hegarty is messy – no matter how you look at it. Combining that with the ongoing breakdown of my marriage."

"It's only messy if you let it be messy. The two aren't related, you know. You don't have feelings for Jonathan because your husband left you. And your husband didn't leave you because you have feelings for Jonathan."

"But I don't even know if they are feelings," I sighed. "It was a moment – a few moments. I felt sorry for him. Or fancied him. Or felt sorry and fancied him – in that moment. You've said it yourself, Sinéad. I've always been a sucker for a sad story."

"But his story's not that sad – yes, okay, he had tragedy in his life when he was small. And the situation with his aunt is pretty crappy – but, bigger picture. Successful businessman. Quite the handsome kind – if you go for the George Clooney look. Well liked, generally. Single. No strings."

"Well, there you go!" I said. "If he's such a catch why is he still single?"

"Because people get divorced sometimes, Georgie. Has he never mentioned the ex? Although from recollection it was a while ago now. All fairly amicable, from what I heard. Just one of those things where they grew apart."

"That's what Matthew said happened to us," I sighed. "Did we seem like we were growing apart?"

"I don't think I can answer that question without making you unhappy," Sinéad said.

"I think if you don't answer it, I'll be unhappy anyway."

She sighed. "If you two get back together you are not to

hold this against me and fall out with me for months, okay?"

"We're not getting back together," I said – and for once the words didn't feel odd in my mouth. My brain didn't scream at the thought. My heart didn't shatter. It ached – of course it ached because this was a very crappy thing indeed to happen. But it was the kind of ache that I knew would dull over time.

"I still want you to promise," she said.

"I promise."

"I think you started growing apart a long time ago. You just put up with a lot because you said that was how relationships were after so many years together. You said you couldn't expect fireworks all the time. But there should be the occasional sparkler. Or if you are lucky a great big Catherine Wheel every now and again. When was the last time you popped and fizzed?"

"Okay, I understand," I said, refusing to be drawn. Because if I was going to be honest about the last time I felt even the tiniest flicker or spark, it was that afternoon, in Áine's kitchen – when Jonathan's hand touched mine.

"I truly believe you will be happy again," Sinéad said. "I love you very much, my lovely friend. But stay in touch more, would you? I don't see you all weekend and all this carry-on happens? I live only up the street."

"I'll call tomorrow after work," I promised.

"Bring the girls. I'll make dinner. Give Cinder-Eve the night off cooking."

"You're a good friend to me."

"The best," she said, "Now finish your hot milk. Go to sleep and have sweet dreams."

"Night-night, sweetheart."

I hung up, finished my milk like a good girl and switched off the light.

That night I stretched my leg out, luxuriously, into what had been Matthew's side of the bed and enjoyed having more space to myself.

Chapter 19

Lorcan didn't come about so much in those early days. He said it was a time for family and that he didn't want to intrude. On the very rare occasion he did arrive, Áine couldn't help but notice that he looked deeply uncomfortable. He wouldn't take a seat and hovered close to the door as the neighbours sat about drinking tea. He would refuse a cup, saying he had work to do at home and he was only calling in to see how Áine was holding up. She wanted to find the strength to tell him that she would be doing so much better if he was there a bit more and if he was willing to hug her a bit tighter and reassure her that it would get easier. She wanted to tell him that grief wasn't catching and that, if he loved her as much as he had said he did, then this was the time to show it. But she didn't want to come across as needy or maybe it was that she simply didn't have the strength to be needy or to speak up for herself. Her needs felt silly. She felt selfish, lost and all at sea. So she watched him stand awkwardly, occasionally looking at his watch, before he made his excuses with a peck on her cheek, telling her that he would be thinking of her.

Rosaleen remained lost in her grief – even more lost than Áine. Auntie Sheila had told Áine she wasn't to worry so much, her mother was strong – but Áine knew that even the strongest of women could carry only so much. The loss of her husband had been tough enough – the loss of her daughter was unbearable.

Rosaleen rarely slept. Áine had to plead with her to go to bed – and yet her mother rarely listened, preferring to pull an old blanket around her shoulders and doze on the chair which had become her home.

And still there was little word from Italy. Jack's mother Olive visited – a messenger from her son. She sat, wringing her hands together, eyes red-rimmed, trying to explain why Jack wanted to keep Charlotte close to him and the children.

"He is heartbroken," she said, "I am so worried for him. I know, I know, that's no comfort to you – but Jack, he is grieving. He loved her so very much."

Rosaleen hadn't spoken and it had fallen to Áine to tell this poor broken woman in front of her that Charlotte had loved Jack too. The truth was Charlotte had fallen for Jack the moment she had laid eyes on him on a night out with her friends. Theirs had been a whirlwind romance – one which had left both Rosaleen and Áine dizzy with the speed of it. But neither of them could have denied how happy Charlotte was – Jack's larger-than-life personality offered her the perfect match for her own wanderlust. When he had announced he had secured work in Italy, it had been only natural that they would marry within a matter of weeks so that she could accompany him. They had a synergy that Áine had not seen in any other couple and when the children had come along – even though Charlotte had been convinced she never wanted to be a mother – their happiness seemed complete.

Áine remembered that first summer Charlotte had returned as a mother. She looked tired but blissfully happy as she nursed her newborn baby girl and Jack had been proud as a peacock showing off this chubby baby to anyone who would stop long enough to peek inside the pram.

"We've tried to persuade him to come home," Olive said. "We've told him he needs us now – that he can't raise those children on his own but he says he will. He says he will manage – but he doesn't sound as if he is managing. I wondered if maybe you would talk to him."

Rosaleen looked aghast. "And leave her? Out there? On her own? He buried her there – he can't leave her on her own. Charlotte never liked to be on her own – no, it simply won't do."

A red flush rose from underneath Olive's ivory blouse. "I understand this is difficult ..."

"You don't understand anything," Rosaleen said. "You have your son. He might be upset. He might be grieving but he is alive. And if you want me to call him, to beg him to come back, to leave my daughter who never came home, then I feel sorry for you."

Áine sat beside her mother and took her hand. "Mother, I don't think Olive is trying to upset you."

"Of course I'm not," Olive interjected.

"She's just worried about Jack – and the children," Áine said. "Jonathan and Emma must feel so lost."

Rosaleen just stared ahead and Áine realised her mother was lost herself and that she was unlikely to snap out of her grief any time soon.

"Perhaps I shouldn't have come," Olive said, lifting her handbag and making to stand up.

"Perhaps," Rosaleen said.

"I wanted you to know we loved her too," Olive said, her voice breaking. "She was like the daughter we never had. Jack was always no unsettled until he found her – and I'll always love her for that – for how settled she made him. She was an amazing young woman. But you must also know he wasn't responsible for what happened. You heard what the police said – it was a tragic accident."

Rosaleen didn't speak and Olive knew there was no point in continuing the conversation.

"I'll see you out," Áine said apologetically and she followed Olive into the hall. At the door she said, "I'm sorry about my mother. She can't see past her own pain at the moment."

"I can't imagine," Olive said.

"I think maybe you can. Please give her some time. This is tough on us all."

"Would you?" Olive said, taking Áine's hand. "Would you speak to him? He might listen to you, if your mother can't bring herself to. I know you care for those children. I know you want them to be safe and happy. I just want him to be safe too. You understand, don't you?"

Áine stood and looked at the desperation in the eyes of the older woman.

"Please, just think about it, Áine. Charlotte would want to know he is okay. She would want the children to be happy."

Áine bit her lip and felt the tears that she had so far managed to keep at bay form in her eyes.

"Just think about it?" Olive repeated.

"I'll think about it," she said, almost in a whisper, afraid that her mother would hear.

"I can't ask more," Olive said, offering an awkward hug which Áine pulled back from.

This was messier than she liked, she thought, as she closed the door and walked back into the sitting room where Rosaleen continued to stare into the embers of the fire.

"I'll put another shovel of coal on, Mother," she said. "I don't want you getting cold."

♥ Present Day ♥

"I'm a bit tired today," Áine said. "Must have spent too much time in the garden yesterday. I'm not as young as I used to be."

"Well, sure we can just take it easy today," I told her – but she seemed quieter and duller than yesterday – as if some of the colour had drained out of her world since I had left her sleeping so soundly the afternoon before.

"I dreamt of them last night," she whispered, over a cup of tea.

Her voice was so quiet it took me a moment to figure out what she had said. I sat down opposite her and waited for her to continue.

"I dreamt of Charlotte, and Lorcan, and my mother ... and Jack. I dreamt of them all – strange dreams where they were in and out of different rooms and I was trying to find them. I could hear their voices, see them sometimes even, but when I got close they were gone again or the voices would move and I couldn't touch them or get to them. They were so close to me."

"I would say those pictures dredged up a few memories," I said softly.

"They did," she said. "So many memories. Do you ever wonder if you made the right choices? Or wonder what would have happened if you had taken a different path?"

"All the time," I said. "Especially at the moment – I think all of us do."

"They say everything happens for a reason – but some things never appear to make sense no matter how hard you look at them."

"That's certainly true," I said.

"Charlotte shouldn't have died. But then if she hadn't ..." Áine shook her head.

I waited for her to say more, but she didn't.

She shook her head again. "Would you mind if I had a little nap today?" she said. "I really am very tired."

"Of course, Áine. I'll get you your blanket. We have the rest of the day ahead of us, sure – you do what you need to."

"You're very good to me," Áine said, as her eyes closed.

I felt at a loss in the house while she slept. I was so used, already, to her constant company and our chatter. I tidied – but there was not much to do, Maria having already been in that morning. I did some ironing, and made sure the fire was set for later. I filled in some paperwork for Brightly Care and still Áine slept. I hoped her dreams were less troubled than the night before – and that she found some peace.

And then, for the first time unafraid that he might be cross with me, I sent a quick text to Jonathan just to tell him that his aunt was a little unsettled that day – and had been dreaming of her family.

"I'll call over early," he replied – and to my continued surprise that made me smile.

My smile only faded when I heard Áine calling out in her sleep – some indistinct noise I couldn't decipher but the tone was clear. It was grief-stricken.

I knelt on the floor beside her, stroked her hand softly as she settled back to sleep – and I wondered did grief ever really pass?

Chapter 20

∽ 1964 ∾

"Be careful you don't get too attached," Lorcan had warned.

"I'm already attached," she bit back, her tone fiercer than she had intended. "We're talking about my niece and nephew."

"Who live in Italy – and who will go back to Italy."

"None of us know what will happen," Áine said as they sat once again in his car outside her house.

November had turned into December and Áine had managed, despite her mother's wishes, to talk to Jack and tell him that he should still come home for Christmas. She had told him things would be tough enough without having to deal with that burden all on his own.

"The children were expecting to come back then, anyway," she said softly, neither of them mentioning that Charlotte had been planning to come back too.

Jack had sounded different on the phone. There was no bravado, no confidence, just an air of defeat. He sounded tired and his grief made Áine's own sorrow feel keener.

But she had managed to get him to say yes, which had

pleased Olive but horrified Rosaleen and Lorcan. Rosaleen was firmly in the anger stage of her grief and she had shouted at Áine that she was mad to have even considered having the children visit for Christmas.

"We'll have to put up a tree, go through the motions for them. I don't want to go through the motions. Christmas and all it entails can go to hell and stay there!" she had shouted.

"Mother, it might do you good. Even if it seems impossible. We'll have a bit of her here with us this year."

"Excuse me for being selfish, but I'd like all of her here instead!" Rosaleen had shouted before stomping up the stairs and slamming the door to her bedroom.

Áine had been sure that Lorcan would understand and support her but he seemed put out at the very notion of the children coming.

"I thought we might have spent some time together over Christmas," he had said.

"There is no reason we can't. You know you are always welcome at our house," she had said even though he seemed to prefer sitting in his car outside in the drive these days.

He had looked pained. "I meant I thought we could have had some time together – you know, alone."

She was struck by the fact that he didn't understand just why she had to be there for her family now. Charlotte had not been long dead – she couldn't just be expected to carry on as if everything was how it had been before her sister's death. Especially when her mother was still in free fall and the prospect loomed of two bereaved children coming to spend Christmas with them.

"I'm sorry," she said, as softly as she could muster. "I know this is difficult but I promise we will have time for each other. It doesn't mean I care for you any less – I just have to support my mother. You have seen how distraught she is, Lorcan."

He sighed. "Of course. And you wonder why I don't like to visit? It's so oppressive. I don't mean to hurt you, but it's too much. Every conversation is about Charlotte. Her picture stares down from every wall and I'm afraid to open my mouth for fear of saying the wrong thing. We're allowed to move on, you know. You are allowed to be happy."

Áine said nothing, but she felt heart sink. It was easy for Lorcan to say it was okay to move on. What did he have to move on from? He had met Charlotte a handful of times. He didn't know her – not the real her. He wasn't grieving for her – if anything he was grieving for their fledgling relationship – one which she had hoped would continue once things settled down a bit. She feared, however, that it wasn't going to settle down quick enough for Lorcan's liking – and she couldn't help but feel bitterly disappointed in him.

He reached across and took her hand. "Áine Quigley, you know I love you, don't you? I just want to see you more. We should be having more fun at this stage in our relationship. I just want us to have fun."

She let him kiss her but she struggled to return his affection and, as she got out of the car and climbed the steps of her house, she started to realise that not only had she lost Charlotte but she had lost Lorcan as well.

It was cool and crisp the morning of December 20th. The windows of Áine's bedroom had frosted over and she breathed on the glass and polished it to see out as she got dressed. Shivering, she thought of how she wanted the house to appear as cosy and comforting as possible when Jack arrived with the children. Olive had promised to come over as well and Rosaleen had promised to keep a civil tongue in her head – at least in front of the children. She refused to get excited about it though whereas, whenever Áine thought of seeing her niece and nephew again, she felt a curious mixture of excitement and terror. They had been through so much – they would have changed – but they were still the young boy and girl who had run into the kitchen and snatched cookies from the cooling tray or begged for extra jam on their scones or who would sit with her in the garden as she read to them or they played together. They were still children and they still needed her.

But she feared how they would be, so she had gone out of her way to make things as welcoming as she could. She had prepared a bedroom for them to share, having agreed with Jack that they could stay for a few nights on their own while he stayed with his family.

She had bought new teddy bears which she had laid on their pillows and had also bought them new pyjamas, slippers and dressing gowns. She had hung stockings on the end of their beds and had set the fire in their room. She would light it before they went to bed and she would sit with them until they fell asleep.

Now she set about preparing the rest of the house. A tree, undressed, stood by the window in the living room with a box of lights and decorations on the floor. She wondered if the children would like to help her dress the tree – she'd give them the option anyway. She lit the fire, and moved through to the kitchen where she lit the stove and set about baking some of her niece and nephew's favourite treats. She lost herself in the simple acts of mixing and measuring, and closed her eyes to allow the aromas of the freshly baked cookies and fairy cakes to wash over her.

When everything was under control, she poured herself a cup of tea, wrapped her heavy woollen cardigan around her and stepped out the back door onto the steps where she had sat with Charlotte so many times.

Normally she hated the garden at this time of year – when all the spring and summer flowers were long dead and when the lush oranges and yellows of the autumn leaves had long blown away. But on this crisp morning, as the dewdrops, some frozen, twinkled on the frost-laden grass and a soft breeze shook the bare branches of the trees, she felt strangely at peace.

She could, if she closed her eyes, imagine Charlotte sitting there beside her – nudging her to share the gossip, telling her she needed to spend less time in the kitchen, begging her to come and visit them all in Italy. She swore, as she sat there, she could feel her sister's arms around her and she could hear her soft laugh.

"I'll look after them," she said to the empty garden. "Please don't worry. I promise you they will be okay. And I promise you that I will come and visit you, Charlotte. I will."

She was roused from her reverie by the ringing of the doorbell and she took a deep breath, feeling Charlotte was with her as she brushed down her skirt and headed to the door to welcome back the part of her family which was forever broken.

∽ *Present Day* ∽

"How is she now?" Jonathan asked as he walked into the kitchen.

I was preparing a simple dinner – potatoes and salmon – for Áine and she was sitting in the garden, soaking up the sun.

She had seemed only marginally less tired when she woke up but she hadn't been very talkative. It was such a change from the days before that I wondered if I had pushed her too far. Although I wasn't going to voice that to Jonathan. I didn't think I needed to anyway. He may well have been thinking the same thing.

"She's quiet – but she has been out in the garden for a while. She said she just wants some time alone."

He peeked out the window at her.

"I'm sure she would be more than happy to see you though. She's always happy to see you," I offered.

He smiled – a weak smile but one which made me blush anyway. "I never thought I would ever have to worry about her," he said. "She was always so strong."

"I think she still is – but we all have our moments."

"I suppose," he said, before pushing open the back door and walking out toward Áine.

Her face lit up instantly on seeing him and she stood up and pulled him into a hug. It was heart-warming to see them both together – and remarkable how her mood lifted.

She was smiling broadly when she came in for dinner. "Look who came to visit," she said, smiling. "As if he knew I needed to see him earlier today."

"He's a very good nephew to you," I said with a smile.

"I'm the best, aren't I, Auntie?" Jonathan said, smiling at me.

It was amazing, their bond – and how, when nothing else could fix her, he could.

"Mum is making us go and bake scones with an old woman," Sorcha announced with her usual level of teenage apathy over dinner that night with Sinéad, Peter and their daughter Aoibheann.

"I think it's a good idea," Eve said. "It could be fun."

I watched as Sorcha mimicked her sister, then contorted her face into an expression of disgust.

"Oh my God, Eve. Could you be any more of a lick-arse?" she announced, which caused Aoibheann – three years older than my girls – to snort in an undignified manner.

"Sorcha! Please!" I said. "Would you mind your language!"

"I've heard worse when Madam was that age," Sinéad said, which caused Aoibheann to throw her an equally disgusted look. "But nonetheless, Sorcha, if you could refrain from that kind of talk while here, that would be lovely."

Sorcha had the good grace to blush at being told off by Sinéad. She looked up to my very glamorous friend – and the pair had become close over the years, and even more so since Matthew had left.

"Áine's lovely," I said. "You don't even have to stay for

long, but it would be good to get to know her. I'll be working closely with her for a while and I think it would be nice for you to meet her."

"But old people are so uncool," Sorcha said. "We have nothing in common. I bet her house doesn't even have Wifi!"

I had to bite back a laugh at just how stricken she sounded at the thought of losing her access to Instagram for a whole hour.

"It'll be no bad thing to leave off the internet for a bit," I said. "Come on, Sorcha, I don't ask you to do much for me."

"Whatever," Sorcha said before continuing with her dinner and beginning a conversation with Aoibheann about the latest series of *The Voice*.

Eve reached over and gave my hand a little squeeze and I was pretty sure I saw Sorcha mouth 'lick-arse' out of the corner of her mouth again, but I chose to ignore it.

"I think you grasp any new opportunity when you get it, even if you're not sure at first if it's for you," Sinéad said – and, by the way she looked at me, I knew she was talking about more than the girls going to bake scones with Áine.

In fact, Sinéad had cornered me almost as soon as we had arrived for dinner earlier. She had dispatched the girls to Aoibheann's room and had sat me down opposite her at the kitchen island, with a coffee in hand, and told me to spill all.

"There's nothing to spill. Not more than I told you anyway. I saw him today. Áine was a little unsettled and he came over early to see her.

"Yeah, to see her," Sinéad mocked, laughing.

"It was to see her. I texted him and told him she was having an off day."

"So you invited him over?" Sinéad raised an eyebrow.

"Stop it!" I chided her, but I found myself smiling. "I won't deny it was nice to see him. Now that he has shown more than the standoffish, snobby side of himself, he's good company."

"Good-looking good company?"

"He's older than me – a lot."

"So's Harrison Ford – and you wouldn't say no," Sinéad teased.

"Look," I said, "it is what it is. I work for him. It's all very emotional. But yes, he is handsome. And I do like his company – but I like Áine's too. That's all it is."

But even as I spoke I knew that wasn't all it was. I had felt a flicker of something when Jonathan had visited that afternoon. When he had taken me aside to talk to me more about how his aunt had been, I had been aware that he stood a little closer than he had done before. I was acutely aware of the feel of his breath on my face as he talked, the fine downy hairs on his arms as he scratched his chin, the smell of his aftershave. I had been aware of how when he listened to my reply, he really listened. His face was set in deep concentration when I spoke – and when I smiled and told him I was sure the following day would be better – he had smiled back, the soft wrinkles of his eyes crinkling.

"We have to take the rough with the smooth," I told him.

"Well, you make things a little smoother," he said, touching my arm gently. "I'm sorry if I ever doubted you. You know she means so much to me. I just want to look after her the best I can."

"I think you already are," I said.

"If only it were that simple," he replied, sadly.

Chapter 21

∽ 1964 ∾

Áine didn't believe in ghosts. Not until she saw Jonathan, Emma and Jack standing at the doorway of the house in Templegrove looking like shadows of the people she had last seen.

It was a dull day but still it could not explain the greyness of their appearance – the dullness of their eyes and the look of apprehension on their faces. The children didn't scream in joy as they normally did when they arrived at their grandmother's house, and run down the hall to the kitchen to grab a cookie and pour a glass of milk that they would guzzle while imparting all their news and rubbing off creamy milky moustaches from their top lips. Jack didn't seem quite as large as life. He seemed small – older. He was unshaved and his shirt was wrinkled. Áine could tell it was more than just the wrinkles from a long journey. The shirt had probably been shown an iron once – but not in a while and not in the manner in which Charlotte would have made sure it was done.

Instinctively, although she had repeated to herself over

and over again that she should not, Áine looked over their heads. She expected still to see Charlotte, wrapped in her green coat, a vibrant red scarf wrapped around her neck, her red bobble hat perched on her blonde curls – like a Christmas tree without the lights. That was how Rosaleen described her last year in that get-up. "Wrap some paper chains around her and we won't need a real tree," she had laughed while the children had threatened to do just that – just as soon as they had finished making the chains on the living-room floor while singing Christmas carols.

There was no sign of her though – not even a hint of her on the frosty air. It felt so completely wrong. Even though Áine had known she was gone – she had grieved and wailed and sobbed – nothing had quite prepared her for the reality of not seeing her where she should be. Nothing prepared her for not hearing her sister shout "Let Christmas begin, we're here!" and for the noise of her and her family to fill the house entirely. She only thought she knew silence before – but this was silence on a whole new level. This was a silence where there should have been so much joy and so much love. This was the silence that came when it became, finally, for the first time completely clear that someone you loved was never, ever coming back. This was a silence that threatened, if it could, to deafen you.

Her heart was beating so fast, her mind racing, that all she could do was fall to her knees, open her arms and pull her niece and nephew into a hug and hold them as if she would never let them go. She felt their bodies, small and vulnerable, crush into her, their arms wrap around her neck, the tremble of their breathing as they tried, but failed to be brave.

"I'm so, so, so, so sorry, babies," she said. "I'm so sorry but I promise you that you will never be hurt again. Nothing will hurt you again. I promise," she sobbed as the ticking of the grandfather clock at the end of the hall beat out a lament.

"Cookies and milk!" a voice from the kitchen called, with

a strength that Áine had not been expecting. "And paper-chain-making later!"

Áine sat on the armchair opposite Jack who had yet to take his coat off. He was nursing a cup of tea but she didn't think he had taken even one sip though her own cup was half empty and had started to go cold.

She had never seen him look so vulnerable and, while there was a part of her that wanted to reach out to him and to comfort him – because there was no doubt he had loved her sister almost as much as she had – she couldn't bring herself to move.

"I know I messed up," he said.

She looked at him, wondering if he had expected her to reassure him that it was all okay and that he needn't worry himself. It would be kind to tell him so – but she couldn't. She couldn't say anything.

"I should have brought her home. I didn't think. I was just in shock … I just couldn't be away from her. I thought it was for the best. I wanted her near me – near us."

Áine nodded but still remained silent.

"I know you must hate me," he said, looking at the floor. "I know your mother … I know I have hurt her. I know I didn't let you say goodbye – but – I didn't know what to do. I was just in a daze. You don't understand what it was like. To find her – in the pool like that. To realise what had happened."

Áine shook her head. She wished she could close her ears as easily as she could close her eyes. She didn't want to hear what he was saying. She had thought about it so much – she didn't need to have any more detail, to find out any more. How she looked. Had she bled? Were there clouds of pink around her head from where it had struck the side of the pool? Did she look scared? Where her eyes open? Open but seeing nothing – ever again.

"And the children – they were in bits and I'm not the person who can explain things like that. I'm not the one who made it all better. That was Charlotte – she would have known what to say but I didn't. I didn't want to let her down, so I told myself I could manage and I could be in control." He laughed then – a pathetic, pained laugh which was as close to sobbing as any laugh could get. "I know I did it all wrong and if I could do it again I would do it differently. If I could do it again I would have made sure she hadn't had so much to drink, or that the doors had been locked or that the pool had been empty or that we had never left here to begin with."

Áine thought of all the things she would do differently if she could – she had regrets too – they followed her everywhere since she had heard the news – and still she couldn't bring herself to tell him she understood. All she could manage, without letting out her anger and her hurt, was to nod her head. She was sure if she kept nodding her neck would start to ache and that she must look demented – nodding and staring blankly.

"I know I will never be able to make it up to you, or the children, or myself for that matter for as long as I live and I know I have no right at all to ask for your help now – but I need your help, Áine. I really do."

His voice wavered and she saw him hastily brush away a tear – which was as foolish a folly as she had ever seen as another appeared to take its place straight away. He was, she realised, a broken man. Everything about him seemed disjointed and out of place. From how his clothes hung, wrinkled and twisted on his shrunken frame, to how his jaw jutted under the stubble that she would never have seen before. It was as if his body had folded over onto itself with the pain of the loss of her sister and she wondered if she looked the same. If she was all at right angles with herself – ragged edges that pushed everyone – even Lorcan – away.

"What?" she said. "What do you want, Jack?"

He dropped his head to his hands as he tried to catch his breath. Áine was aware of the ticking of the clock, the crackle of the fire and the way in which his breath caught in his chest.

"I'm admitting it," he said. "I'm admitting I have it all wrong. I can't do this. I can't look after the children. I am no good for them. Charlotte was the glue that kept us together. Without her we're nothing. I can't run the business and take the children to school, and host the meetings and soothe their nightmares and it is all starting to fall apart. The children are in so much pain."

Áine knew he wasn't lying. Their pain was evident when they walked into the house. Their pain was mirrored on her own face – she felt it every day.

"And I am just making it worse, Áine. I'm failing at everything and they deserve more. They deserve to be loved."

"You don't love them?" she bit out, the words startling her.

He shook his head. "No, you don't understand. I do love them – I love them so much but I'm no good for them. They need a mother. I can't be a mother. They need stability and I can't offer stability. Not now. I'm falling apart. But you … you and Rosaleen, you could offer them what I can't."

He was no longer trying to hide his tears and Áine was no longer trying to pretend to be indifferent to the situation.

"They have lost their mother, Jack," she said. "Are you really proposing they lose their father too?"

"Not forever – just until I can get on my feet. Get the business moved back here where we have people around us who can help us. Until we can look at each other without it hurting."

"I'm not sure it's ever going to stop hurting," Áine said. "We're grieving too."

"I know," he said. "But I know you and your mother. No matter what issues, no matter what problems, you get on with it. You treat the children as their mother would have. You bring fun to their lives. If anyone can make them smile again, it's you."

"They will be lost without you," Áine said, although if the truth was told she was sure that Jack was too broken to reach his children at the moment. They were all broken in their own way. But Áine knew there was something in what he was saying – and that having the children could help her mother heal.

"They are lost already," he said. "Áine, I wouldn't ask if I saw any other solution. If I could see any way of making this better on my own. I could get in nannies and tutors and do what I need to do, but they deserve more than employees. They need love – and it breaks me to say this, but I can't give them that at the moment. It's all I can do every day not to drink myself stupid to forget it all."

Something deep in Áine's stomach twisted. No matter angry she was at Jack, she could not watch his pain any more and she was sure her mother would love to have the children stay for a while. It would give her a lift – something to get out of bed for. She could do this – Charlotte would want her to do this, to put the children first. Whatever her sister had always said about not wanting children, she had been as natural a mother as Áine had ever seen.

"I have to speak to my mother about this," she said. "But yes, Jack, the children can stay. If it helps you get back on your feet – but don't forget, they need you. You are their father – and they need you more now than ever."

It was his turn to nod and, despite her better judgement, Áine found herself crossing the room and offering him an embrace. Hugging, they both wept for what they had lost.

The children didn't sleep in their room that night. They took the teddies of course but they slept instead curled around Áine while she lay awake wondering whether she had done the right thing by taking them on.

Rosaleen, hugely buoyed by the arrival of the children, had said it was a great idea. She had smiled – the first time Áine had seen her smile since Charlotte had died – and said it was the perfect solution and that she would never turn her back on family. She had hugged the children close to her as if she would never let them go and then, when they had begun to wriggle from her grasp, she had clapped her hands with glee.

"We'll have to go shopping for winter clothes," she said. "Won't that be nice? As soon as the shops open after Christmas we'll go and get you both sorted. It's a little colder here in January than it is in July. Oh and Áine, I'm sure you will be able to get the children places in the school – won't you? We'll have to arrange that?"

The children had looked stricken. Daddy was going away for a little, they were told, just to get himself organised and then he would be back and they would all be happier and settled and never be parted again. But they hadn't reckoned that "a little" would involve the need for a new wardrobe and a new school. A little, surely, would mean a few days – the Christmas break. A chance for their daddy to pull himself together and become a father to them again – and maybe play with them sometimes. Like he did before their mother died.

If Rosaleen had noticed that the children looked stricken she ignored it – but Áine felt her heart break for them. They must feel so confused. So when they left behind the beds she had made for them and instead climbed into her bed and wrapped their fragile bodies around hers she had let them and she had kissed them both on the top of their heads and told them the kisses came from their mamma – that Charlotte had sent them down to earth with the first flurry of snow that had fallen just that evening.

The children had jumped out of bed and run to the window to look out at the garden.

"The snow is coming down really heavy, Auntie Áine," Emma had squealed. "It must be Mamma sending us millions of kisses."

"It sure is," Áine had said before she was able to persuade

them to close over the thick curtains and climb under the blankets with her.

She vowed then that she would do whatever she could – whatever it took – to protect the children from any further hurt.

As the children settled in the living room the following day, sticking paper chains and watching the fire flicker in the grate, Áine slipped her feet into her boots and wrapped herself up in her good winter coat, hat, scarf and gloves and set off into the cold morning, the snow inches deep, to go and visit Lorcan.

They had promised they would go shopping for last-minute gifts that day – although that was before the snow fell and before the children had arrived and Jack dropped his bombshell.

Things were still fragile between them. They had tried many times to find that same sense of fun they had when they had first started courting. Charlotte liked Lorcan, Áine had reminded herself often. She would have wanted her to be happy so Áine had tried, so very hard, to be happy when she was with Lorcan. She couldn't be cross at him – she had changed. As he had pointed out, the start of a relationship should be the fun time – the careless, carefree falling in love she had dreamed of all her life. This was far from that – circumstances had changed their romance and, while he still told her loved her and promised to try to make things work, each time she saw him she felt him pull further and further away from her.

More than that, perhaps – as the weeks passed she cared less and felt her willingness to fight to hold on to something that wasn't working wane further.

She knew today would be the final straw. She knew that once Lorcan heard that she was now taking on the care for her niece and nephew that their relationship would be irreparable. She couldn't give him any definites. She couldn't tell him when Jack would be able to take care of the children again. All she knew was that her priority now was not holding on to something that was only limping along in the first place.

Yet still she felt a certain sadness as she trudged through the snow to his house. There was a time when she had been so certain he was the one – when they had shared those lovely moments together in the classroom, in his car, on the beach when she could see her life open up in front of her. The life she always dreamed of – a husband, a family – everything as it should be.

Knocking on his door, her face pink with the cold, she felt her heart sink as she waited for him. He smiled when he opened the door and ushered her in.

"You shouldn't have walked. I would have come to you."

"Your car wouldn't have made it up Creggan Hill, the snow is lying so thick. There is barely a being about," she said, as he helped her take off her scarf and coat.

He directed her to the living room where the fire was blazing.

"Let me get you a cup of tea to warm you up," Lorcan said as she settled on the couch.

"I'm fine, honestly," she said.

"Did the children arrive okay yesterday?" he asked, sitting down beside her.

"Yes, yes, they did," Áine said as she turned to look into his eyes. "And I need to talk to you about it." She took his hands.

"You're shivering," he said, rubbing her hands.

"Lorcan," Áine began and to her surprise she felt reluctant to tell him what she had to.

Surely she could say nothing – get over Christmas, have a kiss under the mistletoe, a kiss at midnight on New Year's Eve – swapping of presents and shared evenings with their families. He had promised to take her dancing, and the dress she planned on wearing, red satin, was hanging in her wardrobe. She could just say nothing and continue trying to fix things.

She looked up, into his eyes, and saw him look directly at her. He looked tired, she noted. It was hard to explain but there was no longer the same light in his eyes that there used to be when he looked at her.

"The children are staying," she said. "I don't know how long. But I imagine it won't be short term. Jack's not coping – he's not coping at all – and he asked us, he asked me, to look after the children until he can pull himself together again."

"And you agreed?"

Áine tried to ignore the vaguely accusatory tone in his voice. "What option did we have? The children need stability. They are lost, Lorcan. Totally lost. They need familiar faces and familiar surroundings. They need to be somewhere where they are not only being looked after but also loved. It's what Charlotte would have wanted."

Lorcan was still holding her hands, but not as tightly.

"I'm not going to ask you to understand," she said. "And I'm not going to make promises that it will all be okay if we just hang on another while and that we will eventually get time alone together like we need. I'm not going to ask you to wait for me either, Lorcan. I think we both need to move on."

There was a part of her, of course, that hoped he would fight for her but the bigger part of her was not one bit surprised when he nodded sadly and said, "Well, I suppose that's that then."

"I'm sorry," she said.

"I know," he replied as his hands slipped from hers. "We could have been so happy, Áine. We were happy. I would have given you a great life." His voice broke a little, but he coughed and settled himself. "You have your own life – you can't live Charlotte's for her."

"I should leave," Áine said, ignoring the thumping in her chest, and stood up.

"And go home again in that weather? At least let me try and drive you!"

She shook her head. It would be awkward – and more uncomfortable than walking home in still-wet clothes without having dried out or warmed up properly.

He brought her things to her without arguing and she slipped them on, then walked to the door, stopping only to apologise again before heading out where the snow was falling in fat, white clumps. She hoped there had been some truth in the story she had told the children last night – that the snowflakes were kisses from heaven – that Charlotte was somehow surrounding her with love and telling her everything would be okay.

❦ *Present Day* ❧

"I have to give it to you, girls," I laughed. "You definitely don't get your baking skills from your mother – these are lovely."

Eve beamed with pride and even Sorcha was smiling.

We were sitting at Áine's big dining table, enjoying their spoils of home-baked scones, clattered in real butter and some home-made jam.

They were delicious and the four of us, Áine included, had forgotten our manners and were talking through our mouthfuls, proud as punch of our achievement.

"You girls are naturals," Áine said. "It was a pleasure to have you here."

The afternoon had gone much better than I ever could have hoped. Sorcha had miraculously left her attitude behind and had behaved impeccably. She had even seemed to enjoy it.

"You are so much better than my Home Ec teacher! She makes cooking so boring!"

Áine had beamed back at her. "Well, I did love to teach – and I love to cook. It can be great fun – and therapeutic too."

"I'm always telling her that," Eve said, her nose perhaps a little out of joint that her sister was shining so brightly at scone-baking.

"And she should listen to you," Áine said. "Because you are a great cook, Miss Eve. Don't you have me and your mammy spoiled with lovely dinners?"

The two girls had been so caught up in their activities that the early evening had whizzed by – and Áine seemed to thrive on the company. When Jonathan arrived, just as the girls were packing up their remaining scones into a Tupperware container, Áine had rushed to show him what they had baked and beg him to try some.

"They're lovely. Even better than the ones we used to bake when you were little," she said with a smile.

"I don't think that's possible," Jonathan said. "Sure you said Emma and I were the best helpers you ever had. Don't tell me you've cheated on us now?"

Áine blushed and playfully slapped him on the arm. "Don't you try and make me feel guilty, young man! You know where you and your sister live in my heart! Now eat up that scone now."

"Yes, ma'am," he smiled and gratefully took a scone from Eve who had buttered it for him.

The girls smiled even more brightly when he gave us all the thumbs-up, his mouth still full of scone.

When he was finished eating he thanked us all.

"I'm assuming these two girls are your daughters?" he said.

"They are indeed," I said proudly. "My twins, Sorcha and Eve."

"They are lovely, like their mum," he said with a smile.

"They really are," Áine said. "We have had such a lovely day. Just perfect!"

As the girls got into the car, our goodbyes said, Jonathan called me back to the porch where he stood.

"Thank you," he said simply. "You are a breath of fresh

air, Georgina Casey – and I am glad you have swept into our lives."

"You're very welcome," I said.

"Your daughters are a credit to you and your husband," he said. "I hope he enjoys the scones as much as I did."

"Ah, he'll not get a chance to," I said. "He only sees the girls at the weekends and I can guarantee they won't last that long."

"You're separated?" he asked, his eyebrow raised in a way that raised my blood pressure.

"Yes," I replied, suddenly feeling tongue-tied.

"Well, that's very interesting," he smiled. "Goodnight, Georgina Casey."

I turned on my heel, walked back to the car and told myself not to read anything into this at all. Nothing at all.

Chapter 22

Christmas Eve arrived with a new flurry of snow. The children played the day away, until the sunset and Áine ushered them in from the garden and sat them in front of the fire to defrost. By six the children were bathed and dressed in their new nightwear, dressing gowns and slippers. They were drying their hair in front of the fire when Jack arrived. They were so excited about Christmas they had begged to get ready for bed extra early and were already desperate to climb the stairs.

"You've tired them out," Rosaleen said. "All that building snowmen and baking cookies and singing carols. It's no wonder they want to go to bed. I want to go to bed myself. In fact, I might just before your man arrives."

"Well, that might not be a bad thing," Áine said, her own head hurting with the exertion of the day. "You've done too much yourself today and a good night's sleep will leave you able to enjoy tomorrow."

"You're right, pet," Rosaleen said.

"I've lit the fire in your room. Take a book up. I'll bring you a cup of tea in a wee bit and build the fire up."

Rosaleen hauled herself up from her chair, the colder weather making her arthritis harder to bear. "That sounds perfect, love. I'll give the children a kiss and cuddle and head up. Are you sure you don't need me to help you play Santa?"

"I'll be fine, Mother, honest. You look done in."

Áine kissed her mother, finished tidying the kitchen and made sure the turkey for the following day's dinner was ready to go in the oven and then she heard the doorbell ring and made her way to the door.

The children jumped up. "It's Daddy!" they cheered, dashing down the hall as fast as their feet could carry them.

It was the most excited Áine had seen them all day. They almost tumbled her over as she reached for the door to pull it open, and Jack dropped to his knees as soon as he saw them to pull them into a huge cuddle. It would have been a picture-perfect image, Áine thought – had it not been for what was going on behind the smiles.

"We really missed you, Daddy," Emma lisped.

"Are we going with you now, Daddy?" Jonathan asked, his eyes wide.

"With Santa knowing to bring your presents here? Sure if you went with me, you'd miss out on them altogether, and then where would we be?" Jack said with forced breeziness. "I'm going to stay with Grandma and Grandpa, because I still have work to do – but I promise I will visit every day until it's time for me to go back to Italy. It's very boring in Italy at the moment, you know. You wouldn't have half as much fun back there as you do here with Auntie Áine and Granny."

Jonathan's lip wobbled a little and Áine's heart broke just a little at the sight of her nephew trying so hard to be brave.

"I don't really care about presents, Daddy, or if it's too boring at home," he said.

"I do," Emma piped up. "I care about presents a lot."

Jack laughed at his daughter's enthusiasm but pulled his son extra close to him, kissing the top of his head.

"Come in," Áine urged. "You'll all catch your death of cold. Come in and you can all have a proper hug by the fire."

Reluctantly the three of them pulled apart and Áine closed off the winter night and ushered them into the sitting room.

She followed them only as far as the door, where she allowed herself to stand and watch for only a minute. She felt as though she was intruding on something she shouldn't see – on the dynamics of a family unit in its own right that needed, more than anything, just to be together.

"I'll be in the kitchen if you need me," she said, amid the chatter of the children regaling their father with tales of all their crafty adventures with their Auntie Áine. "I've hot cocoa for the children before bed. I thought you might like to put them to bed when the time comes. They've been torturing me all day to let them go to bed, but I think they may have their second wind now that you are here."

"Thank you," Jack said sincerely. "Thank you, Áine – for all this."

She simply nodded and turned to go and sit by the range, with her book, a cup of tea and a slice of home-baked apple pie.

Once the children had gone to bed, relatively peacefully, calmed at the prospect that Jack promised he would come back the following day from his parents' house to see them after dinner, Operation Santa had begun.

Rosaleen had bought gifts for the children, which she had wrapped in festive paper. Áine had bought a few pieces as well – books, crayons and puzzles which she had filled their stockings with.

Jack brought in a few items from his car. "It's hard not to spoil them knowing what they have been through," he said, looking over his haul. "But it doesn't seem enough, does it?"

There was a doll and pram for Emma, a dolls' house and a host of colouring books, dresses and ribbons for her hair.

There was a set of Corgi cars for Jonathan along with a train set that Áine was sure would take up at least half of the playroom floor. There was enough chocolate to last the children through to Easter.

"I think they'll be over the moon," Áine said. "Are you sure you won't come in the morning? It might do your heart good?"

He shook his head, and rubbed his eyes. He looked so tired. "Do you know what Jonathan told me he had asked Santa for? He said he had asked if he could just please have his mamma back – and he promised if Santa brought that one thing he would never ask for anything ever again and that could be his best and only Christmas present for the rest of his life."

Áine sighed. "Oh God, Jack. How are we going to help them get over this?"

"I don't know," he said. "Charlotte would have known. She always had all the answers. She would have sat down, put her hands on her lap and announced that nothing was impossible and she would have had some way."

"And it would have been gloriously creative and bonkers and ..."

"Something neither of us can think of?"

Áine nodded. "I wouldn't mind if she told me how I could get over it too. And I tell you," she added with a wry smile, "if Santa could bring her back for me as well I promise I wouldn't ask for anything ever again either."

"God – this was not how it was supposed to go," Jack said. "We had our happy ever after, your sister and I. We had everything we wanted and more."

"Strange as it sounds, Jack," Áine said, "you can take comfort in the fact that you both lived your lives as fully as you could. She was so happy. I don't think I ever saw her unhappy when she was with you. Even when mother would give out to her about your carefree lifestyle, she would brush it off. She didn't ever doubt she was living her life the best she could, Jack. You shouldn't be so hard on yourself.."

"But if I had just woken up, just heard her ..."

"We could all play that 'if' game from now until forever but it's not likely to make a difference. I'm not saying it doesn't hurt – because it really, really hurts – but Santa's not bringing her back, Jack – no matter how many of us write him a letter and beg him to do so. So maybe the best thing we can do for the children – and for all of us – is to try and remember, over and over and over again, all the good things about her."

Jack sat back and smiled. "There were plenty of those. This may sound like salesman patter, but she was one of a kind – luminescent in every way. I'd like to say my business thrived because of my prowess, but it was, I think, largely down to the fact that most of the vineyard owners were that little bit in love with Charlotte. They always gave me their best prices – they called me one lucky man!"

"Well, you were that," Áine said, warmed at hearing just how much her sister had been loved. It was nice to know that love like that existed. It was nice to chat like this – to remember and to reminisce without recrimination and blame.

"You know what, Jack? I fancy a drink – would you like one? To fuel us for putting this train track together and building a dolls' house?

"You know, I think I really would."

Áine poured two drinks – a gin and lemon for her, a whiskey on the rocks for him and they set to work, companionably together.

When the sitting room had been transformed into a festive wonderland, Áine poured a second round of drinks and sat down on the hearthrug close to Jack, who was staring into the fire.

"We should clink these together – for Charlotte," Jack said, "who would have drunk us both under the table given half the chance."

Áine laughed and they clinked.

"God, I remember Mother being so horrified to find out Charlotte was drinking when she was just seventeen. She gave her a lecture on the dangers of alcoholism and made sure not a drop of the hard stuff passed through this house for two years at least. Charlotte used to tease her awfully, carrying in tall glasses of cold tea and telling Mother she was just having a wee drop before bed."

Jack laughed. "She had the wickedest sense of humour of anyone I have ever known. You know, she would come in to the poker nights at the villa and she could tell the dirtiest joke at the table."

"You don't need to tell me how wicked she could be," Áine laughed. "I grew up with her teasing me, pushing me, making me blush. I used to think she was just trying to make my life hell – but I think she was trying to make sure I didn't end up a dried-up old prune. She may well have failed on that one."

"The big romance?" Jack asked.

"Is no more," Áine said.

"I'm sorry to hear that," Jack said. "Truthfully, I am. I know Charlotte liked Lorcan. And yes, you are right. She wanted you to have the best of things – to be happy."

"I'm not unhappy," Áine said. "Apart from missing Charlotte."

He smiled. "I tell her I'm unhappy, that I can't imagine being happy ever again when I'm talking to her. I do that, you know – talk to her. You may think I'm mad – but I think it would be worse not to talk to her. I couldn't imagine that. I say to her that I just want to find some happiness again – but I don't know how I can."

"The children," Áine said. "When you saw them tonight – when they saw you. Those smiles – they were genuine. That was happiness, no matter how fleeting. I think if you could just grab onto those moments and hold them then they might become minutes, and then maybe hours, and then maybe days ..."

"You sound stronger than I do," he said, swishing the

whiskey around in his glass before taking a long slug.

Áine shook her head and she thought of whether or not she was strong. She didn't think she was – she was just coping. As her mother had coped before her.

"We'll all get there, in our way and in our own time," she said.

"And the children?" he asked, a glint of a tear in his eyes.

"They are welcome here until you do feel strong enough – but don't forget they need you. You saw that tonight."

"I did." He looked into the fire for a bit – the embers were fading now, the heat dimming. There was a hint of cold invading the room. As they had talked, put the toys together and shared their memories it had turned midnight. "It's Christmas," he said.

"So it is," Áine said.

"And Santa didn't bring her."

"No," Áine said, shaking her head. "But we've had a nice time talking about her – remembering her. I've enjoyed it, Jack."

"Me too," he said, wiping his eyes. "I mean that. But I'd best be off. I'm sure those children won't let you sleep too late in the morning."

"The spare room is made up – you just have to say."

"I've had one for the road," he said, shaking his head, "so the road is waiting for me." He stood up.

Together they walked to the hall where he took his coat and hat from the stand and wrapped up.

"Thank you, Áine, for your company, the drink and taking the time to listen. I'll be over tomorrow to see the children. I won't leave it too late – let them know I may bring an extra treat, and tell them I love them. We love them. We always have."

The opening of the door brought with it a fresh blast of icy cold air. It was snowing again – fat flakes again. It had its own kind of sound – snow. A buzz, a soft fuzzy whisper. In the light from the door, illuminating the pathway, it looked almost as if the stars were falling from the skies.

Or that kisses were indeed falling from heaven.

Áine watched as Jack walked towards his car and she realised she hadn't told him how the children believed that. He would like that story, she thought, so she called his name and walked towards him.

"She's here, you know," she said. "I tell the children she's here. When it snows. Close your eyes, put your hands out, Jack, and feel the snow."

Whether he thought she was crazy or not, he humoured her and tilted his head towards the sky. Áine did the same and let the cold flakes land and melt on her face and hands.

When she opened her eyes, she heard the door open on Jack's car. "I have to go," he said, his face turned to the car.

She stared as he climbed in.

"She's here," he said softly.

Closing the door, he drove off.

And when she climbed into bed that night, with the children at last sleeping soundly in their own rooms, she smiled instead of cried, and she whispered to the room and to Charlotte that she loved her very much.

Chapter 23

Only a week had passed when Sinéad arrived at my front door grinning from ear to ear and waving a piece of card at me. "Friday night. Glad rags. Me and you. No excuses," she said. She thrust the card into my hand and walked past me into the living room.

I looked down. It was a ticket to a charity dinner dance in the Everglades Hotel – a very fancy spot on the outskirts of town.

"*Northern People* bought a table, and Peter can't go. So you are my plus one."

"But surely there is someone else in the office you could take instead?"

"Well, of course there is – but I don't want to. You need a night out. When exactly was the last time you got your glad rags on for a night on the town?"

"Erm, when exactly was the last time I had glad rags?" I asked. "I have nothing suitable to wear to a black-tie event." Although, if I was being honest, the thought of dressing up did hold a certain appeal. It had been a very long time.

212

"You can go shopping. Or borrow something of mine. Don't sweat the details!"

"But the girls –"

"Will be with their daddy, because it's Friday night. Now I said no excuses, so no more excuses! I have a great girl coming over for hair and make-up."

"But I work until five thirty –"

"At six thirty. You'll be done by then. The make-up girl is going to come to your house, giving you time for a quick shower and a transformation. We'll be at the Everglades for seven forty-five – a little late, but just in time for dinner at eight. Please, please, please! You know you deserve this. You've been working so hard – and you need to bling yourself up a night to prove to yourself once and for all that Matthew Casey is an idiot."

"Well, when you put it like that …"

I watched as Sinéad's fist pumped the air.

"Good woman, yourself! It will be a great night – we'll have a blast. Why don't you come down to mine now and we'll see if I have anything you can borrow?"

It was Sorcha who told Áine of my big night out. The eldest of my twins had shocked me to the core by asking if she could go back with me to Áine's to help out. I had eyed her suspiciously and, yes, I had asked her what indiscretion she had committed that I was yet to find out about.

"Nothing!" she protested.

"So you are asking to go and see Áine, without trying to garner favour to get away with something you have yet to ask me about or tell me about?"

"You don't have to be so cynical, Mum," she said. "You wanted me to spend time with Áine, so I did. And I like her and now you're freaking out!"

"I'm not freaking out. I'm just mildly suspicious. Has the real Sorcha been abducted by aliens and replaced by a child I no longer recognise?"

"Mum, you are so not cool. Like, really not cool. I just think Áine's great. She has some terrific stories – and I think she's pretty kickass. Rocking that big house on her own – not a bother on her. I like her." She looked so sincere that I had to believe her – and I was determined not to look a gift horse in the mouth.

When she arrived at Áine's after school, Eve in tow, she brought a bunch of flowers she had bought in the local garage and even offered to make a pot of tea. Áine seemed more than delighted to see the twins, telling me it was nice to have a bit of a buzz around the house again with young people. I listened to their chat – the girls telling Áine what had happened in school that day with a freedom they never seemed to have with me – while I prepared dinner and did some of Áine's filing for her. I dipped in and out of the conversation and when I heard my name taken in vain I decided to listen in a little closer.

"She has borrowed a dress from her friend, Sinéad," I heard Sorcha say. "It makes her look brilliant. Not her usual mumsy self!"

I smiled – and then wondered was I right to smile. After all, while she'd said I looked brilliant in my dress she also said I normally looked mumsy.

"She hasn't been out in such a long time," I heard Eve say. "And I can't remember the last time she got really, really dressed up – she's getting her hair and make-up done and everything."

"Well, I have to make sure not to keep her late so she has plenty of time to get dolled up to the nines," Áine replied. "There's something so special about getting dressed up to go out dancing."

"Did you go to all the dances when you were younger?" Sorcha asked.

"Not as many as I should have," Áine said, "but I had

some memorable nights all the same. I'm sure I have some of my old dancing dresses upstairs in the back of a wardrobe somewhere. I'll ask your mum to help me dig them out sometime if you would like to see them?"

The girls squealed with delight at the thought – and as I tidied up and got ready to serve dinner I realised two things. The first was that I would really like to see those dresses myself – and the second was that my girls were bringing a whole new layer to reminiscence work with Áine, without even trying. I couldn't help but smile as I turned to put the plates on the dinner table and felt proud of my daughters – who were helping without even trying.

We were still in our little bubble of contentment when Jonathan arrived. He smiled at the sight and smiled even more when I plated him up some dinner. Since learning that he wasn't married and lived alone, I tried to make sure dinner went a little further so he could heat it up when he called over. Áine had let it slip that he often came straight from work and resorted to picking from the fridge rather than eating properly. He made a fuss at first, saying there was no need, but over the course of a few weeks he became grateful to have a hot meal there for him.

"I have an evening meeting later – and it's been a long day already. This is perfect, Georgina, thank you," he said.

"You work too hard," Áine told him.

"Not at all – sure what else would I be doing anyway? Don't worry, Auntie, I do take some time off from time to time. On Friday night I'm off out to a dinner dance – so I'm definitely not all work and no play."

It was precisely at that time that a piece of carrot decided to lodge itself in my throat. A swift near-death experience and a pat on the back from Eve later, I regained my breath just in time to hear Áine say, "Well, that's a coincidence, isn't it, Georgina? You are out on Friday night too."

Jonathan's eyebrow rose. "The Everglades?" he asked.

"Yes," I blushed. "My friend Sinéad is the editor at *Northern People* – she tagged me onto their table."

"Ah yes, *Northern People*. I've done business with them. I'm not sure I've met your friend though – remind me to buy you both a drink on Friday night."

"Oh, there's no need," I replied as my girls nudged each other with a distinct lack of subtlety.

"It's the least I can do," Jonathan said.

"Never refuse a drink from a handsome young man," Áine piped up. "You never know what it might lead to. Charlotte taught me that lesson."

My night out was turning into something much, much more than I had thought it would – and it was still two days away.

"If I was a younger woman and not fit for my bed at eight every evening I would get my dancing shoes on and come and join you myself," Áine said wistfully. "You grab the opportunities to dress up and have fun while you can. Life is not half as long as you may think it is – and you never know what's around the next corner."

That night, as I did my usual confiscation of electronic gadgets before kissing my daughters goodnight, Sorcha asked me for an extra hug.

"Do you like Jonathan?" she asked.

"He's a very decent man," I replied. "He looks after Áine very well."

"Mum, you know what I mean," she sighed.

"As I said, he's a very nice man."

"You deserve to be happy, Mum. Don't think Eve and I don't want you to be happy. We wouldn't mind if you saw someone."

"I don't think that's something you need to worry about," I told her, trying to force a little laughter into my voice.

"We know you and Dad aren't getting back together," she

said. "I think we are going to be okay with that."

"Sorcha Casey, I love you very, very much," I said, kissing her on the top of the head.

I left her room and held my breath until I reached the bottom of the stairs and could breathe out the sob I had been holding in.

Chapter 24

co 1965 ∽

Emma sat on the back stoop, looking out over the garden. The snow had started to melt – to bleed away into the ground and down the drain – and patches of muddy, flattened green were starting to appear.

Áine sat down by her niece and wrapped her arms around her. "Are you okay, sweet pea?"

"I wanted the snow to stay," Emma said, looking up at her aunt with huge brown eyes. "I don't like it melting. It makes me sad. If it doesn't snow any more, does that mean that Mamma isn't watching over us any more and sending us kisses?"

Áine shook her head and kissed Emma on the top of her head. "Of course not, sweet pea. Your mamma will always be watching over you and she will always love you. How could she not?"

"I think Daddy has stopped loving us," Emma said sadly. "Or not as much anyway, or he wouldn't leave us here."

"Are you not happy here, pet?"

"I am … I like it here. I do. You and Granny are lovely and

218

you read great stories and Granny gives great cuddles. But I miss Daddy."

"He comes and visits as much as he can. "He's just very busy at the moment but, believe me, he loves you very, very much. Granny and I are just helping him out a little – and we're enjoying having you here. And if you ever feel sad, or you need cuddles, or you need to cry, then you come to me, okay? Because you and Jonathan are my number-one priority now and I promise you I am never going to let you down."

Áine felt her heart swell as she pulled her niece into a cuddle, feeling her small body melt into her embrace and her face bury into her cardigan.

"I know it hurts now, baby girl, but I promise you that it will get better. You will always miss your mamma, and you will always love her – just like she will always love you. And me, and Granny and your daddy – we are all working hard to make things as nice for you as possible."

She felt her niece pull her a little closer.

"Will we sit here a little longer?" Áine asked.

"Yes, please," a small voice answered – and they sat, despite the cold, and watched the snow trickle away.

Áine couldn't deny it – her mother looked younger since the children had moved in. Even the stiffness in her limbs seemed to loosen and she didn't seem to reach for her medication as much. Rosaleen still liked to go to bed early but Áine had quickly realised she was smiling more than she had done in months. Just as the snow melted, and the flowers started to poke through again it was almost as if Rosaleen was coming back to life too.

She revelled in her new routine too – getting the children ready for school, helping them with their homework when they came home. She had started to love the new life in the kitchen each afternoon. She would walk in the door with the children and, as she prepared dinner, she would listen to them chat excitedly to their granny about their day.

The only fly in the ointment was the awkwardness in the staffroom when she ran into Lorcan – as she invariably did. They maintained a polite approach to each other, occasionally offering to make the other a cup of tea but it felt strained and Áine had taken to spending more time in her classroom on the pretext of marking work each lunchtime to avoid him. The children would wave at him though when they saw him – not quite understanding the delicacies of grown-up relationships. They just remembered him as the man who had bundled them into the back of his car the previous summer and taken them to run along the beach.

When Emma and Jonathan asked awkward questions about what had happened, Áine changed the subject quickly, distracting them with something infinitely more exciting than her deader-than-dead love life.

Besides, she knew now, as she embraced her new role in the family, that she just didn't have the time to devote to a fledgling relationship anyway and she used that justification to comfort her on the nights when she felt particularly alone and when she found herself, once again, sitting up in the kitchen on her own while everyone slept.

Lorcan had tried once to reignite their romance. He had called by her classroom one afternoon in February after the boys and girls had gone home for the day.

"I just wanted to see how you were doing?" he asked, standing awkwardly in the doorway. She gestured to him to come in – and he did, but he maintained a safe distance.

"We're doing okay," she replied. "It's not easy but we are getting into a routine and that seems to help."

"I didn't ask how you all were doing," he asked. "I asked how you were doing. You, Áine."

"Well, I'm doing okay – but I can't think of myself without thinking of them. Not now. They need me."

He looked crestfallen in that second and he sighed. "There

was a time, Áine, when I needed you and I liked to think that you needed me. And I hoped, despite everything we said at Christmas and everything you were dealing with, that the time would come when we might need each other again."

Áine looked at him sadly. There was a part of her that would always need him a little bit – that would always look back fondly at the few months they spent on the edge of something wonderful, but the rest of her knew – without a doubt – that what they had was gone. And it wasn't coming back. Life had changed too much. She wasn't the person Lorcan had started to fall in love with any more. She wasn't sure, all the time, who she was – but she knew that she wasn't her – the innocent girl who was ready to give the right man the world to the exclusion of everyone else. There was a five-year-old boy and an eight-year-old girl who needed her more than any man could. She would occasionally wonder what if – but she would never doubt her decision.

"I'm sorry, Lorcan. I'm really, really sorry," she said and stood up to walk towards him.

He put his hand up to stop her. "It's okay, Áine. I understand. I wish I didn't have to, but I understand. I won't trouble you again."

And he didn't.

Jack came each day. He hadn't gone back to Italy yet. He said, once he had left the house and all the memories it had, he was finding it harder and harder to motivate himself to go back. Then again he knew he had to – his business wouldn't run itself and while things were ticking over it was only a matter of time before his contacts lost patience with him.

"They only have so much sympathy," he said to Áine over a cup of tea. "And when I get back I'll have to hit the ground running. I suppose that will be good in some ways – I won't have time to think about things, but it means I also won't have time ..."

221

"To devote to the children," Áine finished.

He nodded sadly. "I finally feel as if they are settling a bit. I've seen them start to smile and laugh again – and they seem so at home. You and Rosaleen are giving them something I just can't at the moment."

Áine admitted there was part of her that was glad to hear it. It was a selfish part of her which had found so much joy over the previous month spending time with her niece and nephew. She would have missed them terribly if they went with their father even though she knew that they still needed him and he needed them.

"You know they will always have a home here, Jack," she said. "We've been loving having them here and they do seem settled. They are doing well in school – even making friends. Of course it is still tough."

"I'm not sure when it will get easier," he said sadly. "But it is a comfort to me to know that you are here for them."

"And their granny too," Áine said.

"Yes, of course. But it's you, Áine. You have a way with them. That creative spark. That softness that you have. It reminds me of Charlotte in a way. I'm good at talking the talk and putting bread on the table. I'm good at kicking a ball and reading to them but I fall short in other areas."

"It's the years in the classroom have honed my skills with children."

"No," he said, shaking his head. "It's more than that. You are a gentle soul, Áine. Charlotte used to say that about you – that you were a gentle soul – much softer than she was. She said you would have made a better mother than her – that you were more suited to the role than she ever could be."

Áine shook her head. Her Charlotte had always been a natural with her children even if they had not originally been in her plan. She loved them so deeply and was so good with them. Wild maybe at times. Rosaleen had not necessarily agreed with their bohemian lifestyle but there was no denying they were happy, healthy and clever children who, until the very worst had happened, had felt secure in their lives. That was the sign of a good mother.

"It's funny, she always said she would never have children," she said, "not until she was old and done with her travels. I remember when she first told us she was expecting though, she was so excited by it. Said she just had to go where life took her and life had not done her wrong so far ..."

"She was one of a kind," Jack said, sipping from the cup of tea. "And I think maybe you are too, Áine. I can't thank you enough for all you have done. Had you not been there for us – for me, I don't know how I would have managed. I'd been holding on by a thread."

"Maybe we all had been a wee bit," Áine said. "I think the children have saved us too. Truth be told, we weren't doing well either."

"And you are now?"

"We're doing better – and isn't that all we want just now?"

"It is," he said. "We have to start getting on with things. Never forget her, never stop missing her, but we need to move on – try and accept she isn't coming back. It doesn't even feel real saying that, does it?"

"No," Áine said, "but you are right."

"I'll talk to the children the next time I'm over. Float the idea to them of me going back to Italy on my own for a while – see how they feel. I would love it if you would help me tell them. Maybe we'll take them out for a bit – for an ice cream in Fiorentini's? Break it to them gently."

"I think that would be a good idea," Áine said, starting to tidy up the cups. "And I'll do what I can to help."

Jack stood as well, picking up the plate from the well-buttered toast they had shared and bringing it to the sink until they were standing side by side. Their hands brushed, just momentarily, and Áine turned to look at her brother-in-law.

"I appreciate it, Áine," he said. "I appreciate how much

you have done for us. How much you have done for me."

He held her gaze – for just a moment or two too long until she felt her heart quicken.

She turned herself away from him and quickly walked down the hall to get his coat. "It might still ice over tonight," she said. "You'd better be on your way."

"Yes, I'd better be gone," he agreed. Taking his coat from her, he put it on and wrapped his scarf around his neck. "I'll be in touch to talk about the children."

With that he was gone – and she was left, her back to the door, and her hand on her heart, her breathing heavy. Oh Áine, she chided herself, what are you getting yourself into? She was sure she had felt something and she knew by the way he had held her gaze that he had too. This man – her brother-in-law – someone who had always come across as brash, confident and larger than life. Someone the exact opposite of who she was. Someone who only three months before had buried the love of his life – her sister. Someone who, over the course of the last month had become someone she could confide in, who understood how much she missed Charlotte and who knew how lonely the long nights could be.

Chapter 25

୧ *Present Day* ୨

Áine had been true to her word that I could have a bit of extra time to get myself ready, and I had left Temple Muse before my normal finishing time. I made it home, where a lovely, very bubbly hair and make-up expert called Ciara was waiting to work on me. Sinéad was already there in all her finery and explained that Ciara was often called in to *Northern People* when they wanted to do extra-special photo-shoots. She had certainly worked her magic on Sinéad – transforming her from her usual well-presented professional office look to a vampy vintage glamour-puss ready for a night on the town. But, as I told her as she started tousling my hair and blow-drying it, Sinéad offered a much better canvas in the first place.

"Nonsense," Ciara said. "You have great bone structure, and your hair is so thick. There are women who would kill to have your looks as a starting point."

I giggled, bolstered by the compliments and the glass of Prosecco I had downed to give me some Dutch courage for the night that lay ahead. When I'd told Sinéad that Jonathan was going, she'd given me the kind of sneaky half-smile which told me that she already very much suspected that would be the case.

"I may have been aware of that when I offered you a seat at our table," she then admitted, grinning. "Sure why not make a little magic happen?"

"You are getting far ahead of yourself. You are all as bad as each other – you, the girls, even Áine was getting in on the act. She put £20 in an envelope and told me to treat myself to a drink – and not to say no if any handsome men asked me to dance."

Sinéad laughed. "I like the cut of her jib."

Ciara achieved what she had promised. She curled my hair into a soft, short fifties-style bob. She did my make-up so that I barely recognised my usual tired face in the mirror. My wrinkles were gone, my eyes were highlighted, my lips were delicately stained a very pale pink. I couldn't stop looking at myself in the mirror – and Sinéad almost had to pull me away to get me dressed. In a soft damson-coloured wrap-dress with a full skirt, and a pair of nude court heels I looked more elegant than I had in years. In fact, with the exception of my wedding day, I wasn't sure I had ever looked as elegant.

"Oh my!" Sinéad said, pulling me into a hug so she could take a selfie. "There is no way we look any way near forty! We are gorgeous and I am going to very much enjoy going out on the razz with you. It has been too long since we have partied anywhere other than at my kitchen table or your kitchen table."

"God, do you remember the days …" I started.

"Not that well," Sinéad laughed. "But sure we can start again tonight."

My earlier sense of confidence started to fade a little as we arrived at the hotel. Sensing my growing apprehension, it didn't take too long for Sinéad to present me with a glass of Prosecco – courtesy of *Northern People* – and introduce me to her fellow workers at the magazine who were already seated at our table and who had, it seemed, already started their own party. I was nervous of telling people what I did for a living – all these people who did glamorous jobs in the media, while I had been a stay-at-home mother for most of my life and now worked as a carer. I had very quickly learned people weren't all that interested in finding out about the caring profession. No one ever says, "Oh, I always wanted to do that" or "That sounds really exciting" when you tell them about your work as a carer. People tend to get a little strange about it – afraid almost that whatever you are caring for may be catching. Then again, I supposed old age was something that caught up with us all eventually – and people tended not to enjoy thinking about the days when they would become old and possibly infirm. But Sinéad's staff were kind and welcoming and many of them were three sheets to the wind. They welcomed me into their brood easily – and I had the genuine feeling they weren't just doing it to please their boss.

But no matter how welcoming they were, my mind was on someone else who might well have been in the room and I found myself looking around for him when I should have been trying to get into the full flow of a conversation. Someone Sinéad had been reminding me that I would see that night – in a social setting, away from the constraints, rules and accepted practices of a work environment. And I wouldn't be in my Brightly Care uniform – nor my gardening casuals. And he would be in a suit – a tuxedo at that. And perhaps seeing me would make him smile that special smile, the one that made the wrinkles around his eyes crinkle all the more, that he normally reserved for his aunt.

When I spotted him I felt myself flush at the feelings I was having. This was crazy. I could not really be contemplating this, could I? Finding another man attractive? It seemed preposterous. Here was me. Georgina Casey. Mother of two teenage daughters. Famous burner of dinners. Famous for being in denial about her age. Former child bride. Faithful wife. Here was me and I was sitting, looking like a better version of myself, sipping fizzy wine, mixing with business people and movers and shakers and contemplating crossing some sort of borderline with an older man whose aunt I cared for. I felt my pulse quicken and the room swim a little around me before I excused myself and headed for the ladies' room to try and catch my breath.

As I looked in the mirror, delighted to see that the great make-up job Ciara had done hid the flush on my face, I saw someone look back at me I didn't quite recognise. The girl I used to be. The girl who believed in taking chances, in following her gut, in believing in what her heart told her. The girl who so firmly believed that the universe brought people into your life for a reason – and the girl who had so recently learned from Áine that life can take you to places you never expected. And all of it can turn on the spin of a coin.

Once I had settled myself and vowed to drink no more until the end of the evening, I felt safe enough to return to the dinner table where things were becoming more raucous as the courses passed. There was still a charity auction to be held (I was determined to keep my hands down so as not to inadvertently bid on anything) and dancing to be done. I had been promised a whirl around the dancefloor by the partner of one of Sinéad's employees who said he loved "a bit of disco".

But, as I headed back to my seat, I found myself unexpectedly walking straight into Jonathan who subsequently told me he was on his way to the bar.

I was momentarily dumbstruck. There was no doubt about it, he looked exceptionally handsome in his suit. We stepped back from each other, mirroring each other's movements. We looked at each other, taking in the sight of each other out of our usual environment, and we both smiled at the same time.

"You look well," he said.

"You scrub up well yourself," I offered, not just the Prosecco I had consumed making me feel lightheaded.

"Why, thank you," he said. "To be honest, this isn't normally my scene."

"A mover and a shaker like you? I would have thought these kinds of events were staples in your social calendar?"

"Well, they are, but that doesn't mean I enjoy them all that much. Lots of false people wanting to network – just wanting to know what they can get out of you, or how you can help them. There aren't many real and lasting connections made at these kinds of things."

"No, I suppose not. I find it a bit scary," I confided. "I'm tempted to hide out here till the auction is done – afraid of my life of getting into debt and danger bidding on something by accident when I only meant to scratch my nose."

He laughed. "Well, I've given my secretary carte blanche to vote for something we don't need and won't use but will cost the appropriate amount of money, so how about I keep you company while you hide?"

I looked past him, where I could see Sinéad lost in mid-flow of raucous laughter with her friends, and nodded a quick okay.

"And as I was going to the bar anyway – can I buy you a drink?" Jonathan asked.

"Actually, I think I may have had enough," I said, but then, Dutch courage was a valuable resource at this time. "Then again, just a little one, as they say," I muttered. "Maybe a gin and tonic."

"Ice and lemon?"

"Of course," I smiled.

He gestured to a seat in front of the roaring fire in the lobby and told me he wouldn't be long and I used his brief trip to the bar to text Sinéad and let her know where I was. Just in case she would miss me. She replied with a series of smiley-faced emoticons which spoke volumes about her sobriety and also, in a rather disturbing way, her hopes for what the night would mean for me. Blushing, I stuffed my phone back in my clutch bag and looked up to see Jonathan approach with two gin and tonics.

"I thought I would join you," he said as he sat down opposite me. "I've had enough wine for one night."

"You can't beat a good gin and tonic, as long as it is made well," I said, sipping from the tall glass. "Ice first, then the gin, then a little squeeze of lemon, the tonic and a slice to finish it off."

"Sounds perfect," he said with a smile, sipping from his own drink and sitting back. "The barman may have left the squeeze of lemon out of these, but perhaps they will do?"

I sipped and nodded.

He drank then put his glass down. "Look, Georgina, I'm really glad to meet you tonight. I have been wanting to talk to you for a while – to thank you and –"

"It's my job," I butted in, embarrassed.

"We both know you have gone above and beyond your duties," he said. "I don't know how you put up with me when we first met. I know I can be insufferable at times. As I've said before, there are many people who are always trying to get something from me. And from my aunt. She is a wealthy woman, you know. When my father died, he left her, along with my sister and me, his business. I suppose I find it hard to trust people – and, with my aunt being so vulnerable, that made the issue of trust even more important. I know I was hard on you."

"I think it's understandable," I said.

He laughed. "I was an ass."

It was my turn to laugh. "Well, you were a bit. But as I said, understandable, and haven't we gone past that now?"

"I really hope we have," he said, looking straight at me.

"Look, Georgina, while we are spilling all here and now, I have to say I'm struggling at the moment and it's unlike me to be so troubled."

"Is it Áine? She's doing well these days, you know. I know we have the odd blip – but she seems happier overall."

He nodded. "Yes, she does. And I've no doubt that's down to you and how you care about her – but it's not about Áine. It's about you, Georgina."

I felt my stomach flip.

"I can't seem to get you out of my mind – and I know it's inappropriate. You look after my aunt. You work in her house, but if I'm being honest – and Áine tells me I should never, never ignore the chance to find some happiness, no matter how awkward it may be – I can't stop thinking about you."

I put my drink down abruptly – my hands were shaking so much I was afraid I might drop it.

He quickly reached across and took my hand. "Don't run away, Georgina."

"I wasn't," I muttered, looking back into his eyes – holding his gaze. "My hands … were …"

"Shaking?" he laughed, letting go of my hand and showing me the slight tremor in his own.

"If you want we can forget tonight ever happened, forget we ever had this conversation and I promise to be nothing other than professional and courteous when you are caring for Áine. But if you want, I could also cross those lines a little. Life's too short to wait for the perfect moment and, if I don't tell you that, already, you mean something to me I know I would regret it. I have to tell you that I look forward to seeing you every day – and when you smile, something in me which has been locked away for a long time smiles too."

He was so earnest, so honest, and yet he looked so vulnerable that I did the only thing I could in that moment – the thing I realised I had wanted to do for several weeks – I reached across and kissed him, as gently as I could. I could feel him respond, tenderly at first and then more deeply – and everything around us melted away until we were there in the moment, just two people who had been brought together in the strangest of ways.

But neither of us could stay in that moment for long – we were aware that we were in a public place, that no matter how personal this moment felt we were in a busy hotel lobby and Jonathan was high-profile enough to draw a few stares. At the same time, both of us knew that we were not done. Any doubt I had – any feeling that I was stepping out of my comfort zone – was gone. I was as comfortable as I could be, and as sure as I could be that this was meant to be.

When Jonathan pulled back, his eyes heavy, and suggested we get a room, I didn't need to think about it. I didn't need to question his motives – I knew them. I knew he felt just as I did. I nodded, and he asked again if I was sure.

I smiled, emboldened by the sense of passion in his kiss and the alcohol I had consumed, and said: "Jonathan, if you don't organise a room, I'll do it myself."

I had never been touched by anyone else, never caressed by anyone else. I had never been kissed by anyone else, undressed by anyone else or left utterly satisfied by anyone else but Matthew – and now I lay in the dark of this hotel room, feeling reborn. Although my body ached in a delicious way, and the blinking of the clock on the front of the television told me it was gone three, I was as far away from sleep as I could be. I was enthralled – wrapped up in this man who was holding me in a way I didn't think Matthew ever had. We talked, kissed, touched, made love, talked some more and the minutes and hours melted away. He had chipped away at the wall I had put up around myself – the feeling that I had done something wrong, that I had become unworthy of being admired, or desired or loved again.

When eventually we couldn't keep our eyes open any longer, as the sun started to peek through the dark curtains of our room, I whispered "Thank you" to his sleeping form and, as I drifted off myself, content in every way, I heard him whisper, "No – thank you," back to me.

Chapter 26

They say time is a great healer. Áine thought about that. She thought about it a lot. Spring had started to take hold and the garden had started to come back to life. It was strange to see the flowers start to bud and blossom, colours starting to fill in the dark, muddy patches which had lain so bare over the cold winter. It was odder still to feel that touch of warmth in the air, to be able to sit on the back stoop without her heavy coat pulled tight around her. Sometimes, when she closed her eyes, she could lift her head to the sky and feel the warmth of the sun burn through the remnants of the cool winter sky and caress her face with the promise of brighter days to come.

The world was coming to life again, she thought – and as she looked around the big house it was clear her family was coming to life again too. Slowly but nonetheless steadily.

There were fewer days when the sheer shock of the grief they all felt would floor them – and she felt she could talk to her mother now about the good times with Charlotte without risking Rosaleen taking to her bed to weep over the sheer injustice of it all.

In fact, Rosaleen would often gather the children round her and tell them stories of their mother – how naughty she could be as a child but how she always won everyone round with a flash of her blue eyes and a shake of her blonde curls. "She never stayed in the bad books for long," Rosaleen would laugh. "And you two, you've the look of her. You might just escape those bad books yourself."

Those times with the children gave Áine heart that her mother would survive this after all. Even when she was unwell – when she was crippled with her arthritis – the children would bring a smile to her face as soon as they ran in the door from school, eager to tell her of their latest adventures.

Their drawings and paintings were pinned on the walls.

Áine would listen out for the sound of Emma practising her scales on the piano in the dining room, sometimes coming in to sit beside her niece and join her in a duet.

Jonathan remained quieter. Áine couldn't hide her worry for him. She figured it must be tough for him in a house full of women – so far away from what he had always known as home. But he never said anything. If Áine asked him if he was okay he would reply that he was "Fine, thank you for asking" and set about playing with his toys or reading his books once again.

It had been two months since Jack had last visited – he had been true to his word for the first few months, visiting as often as he could and never going more than a month between seeing his children. But he had written this time – things were busy. The business needed him. He would do his best to get back to them as soon as he could and he loved his children more than anything.

With every letter that arrived Áine and Rosaleen felt a bittersweet mixture of hope and fear. At any time he could say he was ready to have his children back – and take them away, leaving the house too big and too quiet in their absence. But when he said he needed more time they were also not immune to the flash of disappointment across the children's faces – especially Jonathan's.

"Do you think he doesn't like it here?" Rosaleen asked one night, after the children were long settled.

"I think he does," Áine said. "But he's only a wee boy and wee boys want their daddy. It's hardly a surprise. It's easier for him when Jack comes to visit – it has been too long. Eight weeks is an eternity to a child."

"But when Jack comes there is always an upset when he goes again ... maybe it's better they don't see him so much?"

Áine could see, or at least understand, where her mother was coming from – the children were always unsettled and fretful when their father left. But still they needed to see him. They had lost their mother – she would not let their father slip away from them too.

She vowed to write to him the very next day and tell him that he needed to be there for the children, that although they might appear to be doing well they still needed to see him. She felt a strange need to see him herself, if she was honest. Although whenever that thought crossed her mind she tried her very best to push it to one side. She had to stay focused on the children. They needed her to stay in the here and now and she needed to stay that way herself. No good could come of any feelings towards Jack that weren't entirely related to him being the father of her niece and nephew and the widower of her sister.

It didn't matter that he was now someone she could confide in more and more – pouring out tales of her life to him in her letters, from the difficult children in the classroom, to long passages detailing simply how she had watched his own children sleep and how they no longer woke up crying in the night as frequently as they once had. She told him of the garden, the kitchen, of the books she was reading, the stories she was writing. And he wrote back, stories of Charlotte at first as he struggled to find his way in the world without her.

There was a comfort in their shared grief – and as the weeks progressed the comfort they found in each other turned into a strong friendship – one that made Áine look forward to the clatter of the letterbox in the hope there was a letter from him. He would tell her of Italy, of his business. They would discuss world affairs – the changing political landscapes, the change in social norms. He took her seriously and she learned from his approach to the world.

Deep inside, when she allowed herself to think about it, things were changing – and she wasn't sure she was able to stop her feelings from growing.

ᗍ *Present Day* ᗎ

I woke to hear the shower running. Lying back, I lifted my phone to see that it was gone nine. I glanced quickly across the room to the dressing-table mirror, delighted to see that my make-up – so expertly applied the night before – was still behaving itself, relatively speaking. I should, by rights, have woken up looking like a train wreck, but I didn't. My face was flushed, my hair messy, but if I wasn't very much mistaken there was a new glow to my face – a delicious post-sex glow.

I wrapped a dressing gown around me, hoping to avoid any awkwardness when Jonathan emerged from the bathroom although I didn't think I had ever felt so comfortable in my own skin. I tried to ignore the reality of us being in a hotel room and that check-out was looming – and the real world was waiting – a world in which Jonathan assured me he wanted to continue to build a relationship with me, if I was ready to.

He had asked me about my marriage, about what had happened, and I'd told him how I'd had to come to terms, pretty quickly, with it ending, and with the realisation that it had perhaps been over for a while.

He spoke briefly of his own marriage break-up – how he had fallen into a marriage because it felt like the right thing to do at the time. Another box ticked, he said. But it wasn't right. It was functional. They were more friends than lovers, until the pull of another lover became too much for his wife and she left in pursuit of her happy-ever-after.

"I always think you know true love," he had said. "It's the kind of love that still exists, still gives you that glow, even when you have known each other through every kind of good and bad time going. I always think there is just something more. Something that pulls you to that person. Something in the pit of your gut that just knows, that never questions, that never has to try and understand. And I think it can come when you least expect it."

He smiled when he came out of the bathroom, towel wrapped around his waist, hair wet. "Morning," he said, with a hint of shyness I found endearing. "I hope you don't mind – I ordered some breakfast for nine thirty."

"Thank you," I said, realising I was ravenous.

He started to dress and I had to force myself to look away.

As I sat down to eat, I couldn't help but smile myself. I knew this was more than just sex. I knew it was something more. I knew it with every part of me.

When he sat opposite me I smiled at him.

"That was a lovely evening," he said.

"It was."

"I would like to do it again sometime. Not necessarily a hotel room – fun as that was," he said with a cheeky smile. "But perhaps take you on a proper date. Dinner, the movies, the theatre – whatever you want."

"I'd like that, any of it," I said.

"Will you get cross with me if I call over to Áine's a little earlier some afternoons?"

"I'll get cross if you don't – but watch Áine doesn't get neglected," I laughed.

"I know, categorically, that now you are caring for her she won't be neglected," he said. "How long do you think it will be before she works out something has happened between us?"

"Oh God," I gasped. "Do you think she will know?"

Jonathan laughed – a gorgeous, deep laugh I was only just getting to know. "Georgina, you have been caring for my aunt for what, seven weeks now? I know she has dementia – but in some ways her mind is sharp as a pin and she will know. I could never keep anything from her – and she has been talking you up, you know. When you're not there. Telling me all about you."

I blushed. Áine was a crafty beggar! I'd have to have words with her.

"Oh God – really?" I asked, laughing.

"She fancies herself as a modern-day fairy godmother," he said. "She always has tried to make sure everyone else is happy. To her own detriment at times – but that's her personality – she would never change."

"And we wouldn't want her to," I said.

It wasn't lost on either of us that we couldn't, unfortunately, stop her changing.

I wasn't home ten minutes before Sinéad was banging on my door, her face bearing a bright smile which hid the hangover that she later told me was kicking her rear-end from one end of the street to another.

"Details," she said. "Quickly. Because I know your girls are back this afternoon and I know you won't want this conversation in front of them."

"I'm not sure there is much to tell," I said, smiling demurely.

"Oh my, the smirk on that face of yours! I would say there is plenty to tell. You disappeared pretty early. Where on earth did you go? And why on earth were you not in all morning?

And, come to mention it, why do you still seem to be wearing quite heavy make-up – very similar to what you wore last night?"

"We didn't go anywhere," I said, feeling a little wanton, but in a good way. "We stayed right there, in the hotel, all night."

"You did?" Sinéad was almost wetting herself with excitement at the very notion.

"We sure did."

"Well, flip me, lady! I have to say, you have some style. Was it great? Are you great? Are you okay?"

"It was lovely, and I'm good. Really good. Yes, it was a little strange – or different at least – but in a good way. Is it wrong that it doesn't feel wrong?"

"How would it be wrong?" Sinéad asked, her face a little more serious.

"If you had told me six months ago that Matthew would be gone, that I would have spent the night with someone else – that I would have feelings for someone –"

"You have feelings?" she asked. "You who insisted you didn't have feelings? You who insisted he was a pain in the arse? You have feelings?"

"I judged a book by its battered cover," I said. "The inside pages are nicer."

She sighed. "Look, my lovely friend, is it wrong that it all feels right? No, of course not. Life has a habit of taking mad turns every now and again. People come in and out of your life for reasons we don't really have to understand. Just go with your gut."

I looked at her. "Jesus, Sinéad, that's very philosophical of you and not at all your usual cynical self."

"Hangovers make me philosophical," she said, shrugging her shoulders. "And hungry – both for bacon sandwiches and for more gossip than 'it was lovely'. Lovely is not details. Lovely does not go any way far enough in telling me whether

Derry's most eligible divorcee is worthy of the title both in and out of the bedroom."

"I don't kiss and tell," I said, taking the frying pan out of the cupboard and starting to heat it.

"It's not the kissing I'm so interested in," Sinéad said. "It's the other stuff. All the other 'lovely' stuff."

I didn't see Jonathan again that weekend, but I did hear from him. He sent me text messages and once the girls were fast asleep he called me and we talked. When I went to bed myself, I felt giddy as a schoolgirl and looked forward so much to the following day when I knew I would see him at Áine's.

Indeed, when I arrived at Áine's the following day I spent a good ten minutes in the car making sure my make-up, minimal this time, obviously, was perfect and my hair was neat. I sprayed a little extra perfume – taking whatever measures I could to make the godawful Brightly Care uniform less of a focus. I had brought some bedding plants for Áine's garden, which I had picked up at the garden centre that morning. The day was bright – as May dawned – and I knew it would be the perfect day for working the garden together.

"Áine!" I called from the front door, smiling and wondering just how long it would take her to figure out 'something' had happened. Jonathan was sure she would know straight away – with just one look.

"I'm here!" she called from the kitchen and I followed her voice through to the hub of her home.

She was busying herself putting the kettle on the stove but, all around her, the cupboards were open, their contents emptied onto the table and workspaces.

"Good morning, Áine," I said. "Is everything okay?"

"I'm just making tea," she said, her voice a little shaky. "Just a cup of tea. Do you want a cup of tea?"

"I would love a cup of tea," I said softly. "Were you cleaning out your presses, Áine?"

She looked at the table, at the cupboards and looked confused. "I'm just making tea. Do you take milk? I can never remember who takes milk."

"Why don't you let me do it?" I said.

"Don't be so silly," she said, her voice stern. "I'm perfectly able to make a cup of tea."

"Do you want me to tidy the presses then?" I asked.

"Do you think I can nothing for myself?" she said, looking around the worktops. "All this fussing. Like I'm some silly little girl. I am perfectly capable of doing things myself."

She located the tea caddy and dropped two tea bags into the pot.

"I know you are, Áine – sure aren't you the most capable woman I know? But it is my job to help you."

She looked at me again – taking me in from head to foot and back again. Perhaps she would see something then. Perhaps this was where her sixth sense for gossip would kick in.

"Who said I needed help?" Áine asked.

"Jonathan," I replied, sensing that nothing about this was going how I thought it would.

She laughed, loudly, and for a moment I thought she had been winding me up the whole time. But then she looked at me again. "Jonathan is only a boy. Was it my mother? Did my mother think I needed help?"

"Áine," I said, "I'm Georgina. You remember me, don't you? And I help you here. Jonathan is a grown man now."

She looked at me, confused again. "Did you bring Emma with you? Where's Emma?"

"Emma is in England, remember? She lives there now with her family."

"I'm her family," Áine said, her voice raised a little more.

"Of course you are, but she is a grown woman now too."

"I don't understand. I don't believe you," she said, as the kettle hissed and whistled on the hob. "I don't know who you are."

242

"Áine," I said, trying to keep my voice calm, "I'm Georgina. I'm your friend. I'll pour us a cup of tea and we can talk. And, look, I've brought you some plants for your garden."

She looked at the plants I had brought in and walked to the table to examine them.

As I poured the tea, she planned where she would plant her flowers and the moments of confusion passed.

Later, when she was snoozing in front of the television I would tidy everything back into her cupboards and text Jonathan to tell him what had happened and ask if he could come a little earlier that day. It wasn't the flirtatious text I had planned on sending, but it was a reminder of what had brought us together and what, if we were to be together, we would have to face in the future.

Jonathan arrived just after four thirty and greeted me with a warm smile, despite his concerns. Áine had woken and seemed to be back to herself. She smiled when she saw him. "Ah Jonathan, you're here early today?"

"I am. I wanted to see if you were okay?"

She blushed. "I am. I think I might have been a bit confused earlier," she said, twisting the material of her skirt in her fingers.

She looked at me – and I wasn't sure if she was looking for confirmation that she had been confused or for me to tell her everything had been absolutely fine and she had nothing to worry about.

"You were a little confused, Áine," I said. "You know we have to expect these things."

"Maybe we'll take you to the doctor and see if you need a review of your medication," Jonathan said. "Don't worry."

"I'm scared," she told him, her voice low and quiet.

"I know," he told her. "I will be here for you. I promise."

"You won't let me get lost?" she whispered and I saw his head bow.

"I won't. I promise. But we're a long way from that. A long way. We'll get to the doctor's. We'll get more help."

"You won't let me down, Jonathan?" she said, looking frightened.

"Could you let us talk?" Jonathan asked and I nodded, and turned, leaving them to it, going to the kitchen. I looked out at the garden and wished with all my heart I could turn the clock back to when Áine felt safe, when Jonathan and Emma were under her roof, her mother was alive and her garden was thriving.

Chapter 27

⁀ 1965 ⁀

"Don't you get those clothes dirty! Emma! Jonathan! Do you hear me? I don't want your father thinking we are living in a pigpen here. Those are your good clothes, washed and pressed, and you want to look your very best for your daddy, don't you?"

Rosaleen was calling from the back step as the children ran about the garden and threatened to build a den in the bottom hedges. Ordinarily neither Rosaleen nor Áine would have minded. On several occasions Áine had joined in, brushing away the dirt and leaves to find them a special hidey-hole where they could sit and tell stories.

But not today – today Áine feared her mother would have a stroke if the children got so much as a smudge of dirt on their clothes. She may have maintained to the last that Jack Hegarty was no friend of hers but that didn't lessen her need to impress him or show that they had been more than capable of caring for his children. Rosaleen had directed Áine to have the house cleaned to within an inch of its life and to have a decent home-cooked dinner ready for his arrival. When Áine

245

had told her that a stew would do the trick and he could be grateful for it, Rosaleen had almost bitten her head off.

"No, we have to show him they are better off here than there! Haven't you noticed that they seem more settled now?"

Áine had thought of how both of them had ended up in her bed again the previous night and how they had been like two jumping beans all morning. 'Settled' was not necessarily the word she would use to describe them.

Then again she knew they were on edge, as the whole house was, because of Jack's imminent arrival.

"Do you think I've grown much?" Emma had asked that morning, stretching up on her tiptoes and reaching to the sky. "Do you think Daddy won't even know I'm his best big girl?"

"Or me, his best big boy?" Jonathan had said, as he stood in front of the mirror, puffing out his chest. "I have been eating all my vegetables to grow big and strong, haven't I, Auntie Áine? And running around as fast as I can. Do you think he will think I've got bigger and stronger?"

"You've both been great altogether and I'm sure your daddy will see how good you have been and he'll be delighted with you. Sure how could he not be?"

"Will you not even tell him about that time I was bold and sneaked a biscuit out of the jar?" Emma asked, eyes wide.

"It's our secret," Áine smiled, miming that she was zipping her lips shut.

"I hope he stays a while," Jonathan said. "I want to tell him all about school and my new friends and how good my reading is."

"I'm sure he will stay as long as he can. Now run on and play while Granny and I get the dinner on and the house ready. We all want to make a very good impression, don't we?"

The children had cheered and run on, clattering down the stairs like a herd of baby elephants while Áine stood and took stock of herself in front of the mirror. She brushed her hair back and fixed it with a ribbon. Nothing too fancy, mind – just a low ponytail. She pinched her cheeks to add colour and looked at the dress she was wearing. It was drab – more suited for the classroom than a beautiful spring day. She opened her wardrobe in despair, hoping something more colourful and less mumsy would jump out at her. In the end she opted for a pale tea dress, with a light floral pattern, which just about bordered on the fashionable. It was a far cry from the short skirts and bright colours some of the girls were starting to wear, but it was feminine and modest. As she smoothed the fabric down over her hips, she chided herself. No good could come of purposely making an effort just because Jack Hegarty was coming to town.

But there was no denying they had become closer. Their letters were being exchanged more frequently. He would enquire after her, and do his best to make her laugh with his witty way with words. She looked on him as a confidant of sorts. And, if the tone of his letters to her were to be believed, he looked at her in the same light. There was no word of romance, but she had started to see him differently. The layers of the confident man he was – the man who was showy and had to be the centre of attention at all times – had started to peel away. He was man who was in many ways very insecure – and who was struggling without Charlotte to keep him in line and to boost him when he felt down. He was a man who loved his children very much but had no faith in his ability to be a good father to them. He simply did not know how to cope and the only time he felt in any way in control of his life was at work. She understood, in a way. She had tried to focus on her work too, despite the awkwardness that still existed in the staffroom when she bumped into Lorcan.

She wasn't altogether frank with Jack about the children. She did her best to reassure him, to pretend that all was well, that they were coping well with their new surroundings, that they felt secure spending time with her and their granny, but she was well aware that she was not, and never could be, their mother. What she did tell him was that they needed him, Jack, dreadfully.

She felt a confusing mixture of emotions – from the feelings that she felt were appropriate and those which were sneaking in around the corners and waking her up at night. The excitement and the guilt made for a heady combination and, as she stood in front of the mirror, looking at an unfamiliar reflection of a woman who made an effort with her appearance, a part of her felt as giddy and light as the children did at the thought of Jack's arrival.

"Will he stay long, do you think?" Rosaleen asked as they sat in the kitchen later. "Here? Will he stay for a week maybe? The children need a good long stint with him." Almost as soon as the words were out of her mouth, Áine noticed a change in her mother's expression. "Or do you think he is ready now? Áine, tell me he isn't ready now to take them back?"

"I'm sure this is just a visit," Áine replied. "But for the sake of the children, I do hope it is a long one."

Their conversation was interrupted by the ringing of the doorbell and the same clatter of footsteps which had bounced down the stairs earlier bounced down the hall, accompanied by cries of "Daddy! It's Daddy!".

Áine felt her heart thump a little at the sound of his voice greeting the children.

"Well, I suppose we better go and let him see we're doing a good job," Rosaleen said. "Come on now, Áine, don't be making a show of us."

As they walked down the hall Jonathan was the first to turn his head.

"Did you see who is it, Auntie Áine? Did you see? It's my very own daddy." Jack had lifted him into his arms, and Jonathan had wrapped his own arms tight around his father's neck while Emma did her best to squeeze in and get her daddy to lift her too.

"So it is," Áine said, with a smile that was matched by that on Jack's face as he looked at her.

"What a tonic it is to see these children," he said, pulling them both closer. "What a wonderful, wonderful tonic!"

Áine found that she did not have the words to answer him. She just stood and stared while her mother launched into her own greeting.

"Sure of course they're a tonic. They are only the best children in all of Derry and they have been thriving here, haven't you, children? We should tell Daddy about how well you are doing at school."

"I want to show him my books," Jonathan said.

"And I want to show you my room, Daddy," Emma said.

"Sure your daddy has seen your room, pet," Rosaleen said. "Why not take him through and show him how good you are on the piano now. Áine has been teaching her, haven't you, Áine? She's very good with them, you know. Gives them that woman's touch that children need when they are so young."

"I'm sure she does," Jack said, pulling himself gently from his children's embrace and standing. "And I would certainly love to hear Miss Emma here play the piano and you, son, go and get me those books and we'll have a good look through them."

"And I'll bring tea, will I?" Rosaleen said. "And biscuits. Homemade, of course. Áine here had the children helping her in the kitchen this morning. She is a dab hand at the baking and the children loved every moment of it."

Áine felt herself blush furiously as Rosaleen rambled on as if the children were angels who never stepped out of line and she was some kind of divine creature who did nothing but guide them on the right path. She was sure Jack knew enough about his own children to know they were as capable of acting up as anyone else's and he didn't need the great act from on high to persuade him that they were better off left with their aunt and granny than ever setting foot in Italy again.

"Yes, Mother, why not go and get the tea? I'll come and

help you and the children can have a little time alone with their daddy who they haven't seen in a very long time."

Rosaleen smiled as Áine guided her to the door.

"Eleven weeks, Auntie Áine said. She showed me on the colander," Jonathan said. "Daddy, you've been away a long, long time."

Áine paused in the hall to hear Jack's response.

"I know, son," Jack said, choosing not to correct his son's mispronunciation. "I know and I'll make it up to you, I promise. I'm very sorry but I have been so busy."

"We missed you," Emma said.

"And I've missed you too, both of you, so very much."

Áine could hear the emotion thick in his voice. She followed her mother to the kitchen. She did not need to see any weakness in Jack Hegarty that would lead her to have any more inappropriate feelings for him.

"Let's let the children and their father be for a while," she said as she closed the kitchen door and set about setting a tray with cups and saucers.

"What do you make of that?" Rosaleen asked.

"What?"

"His reaction to the children. Do you think he means to take them back with him?"

Her mother's face was so stricken Áine felt for her. "Mother, you need to relax and what will be, will be."

"I couldn't lose them too," Rosaleen said, sitting down, kettle left to boil on the range.

"He is their father," Áine said softly.

"Still and all, I couldn't lose them as well," Rosaleen said.

"I know."

"I bet it isn't a patch on Italy," Áine said as she walked along the beach at the Donegal coast.

The children were running on ahead, dragging sticks across the sand, leaving a trail in their wake.

"Oh, I don't know. This has its own charms. There is something about Ireland that always pulls you back."

"But I'm sure Italy has the same appeal?" Áine smiled.

"Well, it is warmer," Jack said, laughing, and Áine pulled her cardigan a little tighter.

"The children seem very happy, Áine. I don't think I can thank you and your mother enough for all you have done for us. God only knows what state they would be in by now if they were left in my care."

"You cope with what you have to cope with," Áine said. "You would have managed in some way."

"But not this way. They seem happy and settled. They're acting like children again and not tiny adults trying to tiptoe their way through a world they don't understand. If they say you cope with what you have to cope with, I'm pretty sure I let them down badly in those early days. I could barely function myself – never mind teach piano lessons and read books and bake biscuits."

"In those early days I wasn't much better myself," Áine admitted. "Don't be too hard on yourself for grieving for Charlotte. It would be more worrying for all of us if you didn't drop a beat after she died and were able to go on as if nothing happened."

He shrugged his shoulders. "I suppose you're right. Charlotte would have come back to haunt me anyway. She always said if something were to happen to her she very much wanted me to fall to pieces for a bit out of sheer grief."

Áine laughed. "That sounds like Charlotte's strange logic alright."

"I know. She said it would prove to everyone how much we were in love. She said she would never be so magnanimous as to wish me not to cry and to move on with my life as if nothing had happened. She wanted the full works."

"She was one of a kind."

"She was." Jack smiled, dug his hands in his pockets and

walked on, listening to the calls of his children carried on the wind as they ran on ahead of them. "But, you know, she did want me to move on eventually. She made that clear as well. I wasn't to 'linger' in my grief. I wasn't to let it destroy me. 'Life is for living,' she said and while I had to be suitably destroyed for a while she said she would come back and kill me herself if I wasted what she couldn't have."

Áine didn't speak but looked ahead. The children were sitting on the sand, peeling off their shoes and socks and laughing at each other.

"Do you know what she said to me, Áine? She said she had grown up in a house where grief was ever present. That your mother had locked herself away from the world and not allowed herself a moment to live again after your father died. There was no greater tragedy, she said, than that. She would tell me that was why she embraced life so much – she felt as if she had to live for your mother too."

Áine felt tears well in her eyes. She tried not to think about her mother – and all those years sitting in that house, afraid to go anywhere, refusing so much as a weekend trip to Dublin or a day out at Portrush. "I'm happy as I am," her mother would say – but Áine could see that Rosaleen was not truly happy.

Áine glanced at Jack who was looking straight at her.

"Áine," he said, reaching out and gently brushing her hand, "she wanted you to live a little as well."

Áine found herself caught in his glance – lost in a moment where nothing existed but this man and her on this beach. She found herself caught on the horns of a dilemma, fighting the urge to feel the brush of his skin again against hers and the urge to run away from this moment – this conversation and all that it could mean.

A squeal of excitement, as the waves washed over the children's feet, brought her to her senses and she turned to see them smiling brightly at her.

"I think I'll go and dip my toes with the children," she mumbled and headed off down the beach, vowing not to look back.

Chapter 28

ↄ *Present Day* ↄ

I poured a glass of water and drank it quickly, trying to settle the unquiet feeling in the pit of my stomach. It wasn't long before Jonathan joined me in the kitchen. He looked worn out and I didn't hesitate in crossing the floor and pulling him into my arms. He held on tight as I tried to soothe him, telling him that it would be okay.

"She's getting worse," he whispered. "I know it."

"She has bad days. It's normal."

"But they are becoming more frequent," he said, pulling back and rubbing his eyes with the heels of his hands. "I can feel her slipping away. Yes, she comes back – but it takes longer, and less comes back. Less of the here and now – and she is getting so scared, scared and angry."

"We'll take her to the doctor's," I said, confidently. "It might just be that her medication needs to be tweaked."

He looked at me, put his hand to my cheek and pulled me into a kiss, the force of which took me by surprise. Everything was in that kiss – every ounce of pain he was feeling, every inch of hope he was clinging on to.

When he pulled away, both of us breathless, he said: "Georgina Casey, you remind me there is good in the world."

We both knew the doctor might not be able to do a lot. We both knew where we heading – but we both now knew that at least we were together.

He drew me over to the table and we sat down side by side.

"Would you care for her full-time?" he asked. "I'd pay, of course. But I'd feel more secure knowing you were here. She responds well to you – you have a way with her."

"Yes," I said, without hesitation. I would do anything I could to stop this wonderful woman from slipping away further.

"I should probably call Emma as well," he said. "Ask her to come back for a visit. It's been a while. She wouldn't want to have regrets."

"Áine will be here for a while," I soothed.

"Perhaps," he said. "But how much of her will be? Emma and Áine have, well, some unfinished business. It would be nice for them to sort out their differences."

I was surprised to learn they had differences – given Jonathan's devotion to his aunt and his assertion she had been like a mother to them after Charlotte died.

As if reading my mind he said, "After our mother died, Áine and my father . . . well, they fell in love. It was a huge scandal at the time – to my granny anyway. I don't remember much about that time – those early days. I was young – it just seemed to happen and I was happy to see my father happy. But it was different for Emma and my grandmother, especially Granny. She saw it as some sort of betrayal – and Emma worshipped the ground our granny walked on. They didn't see it like I did, even when it was clear how much they meant to each other. Jack and Áine. They made each other so happy – it wasn't conventional, but it was love. They held each other up for a long, long time. They were very happy."

I sat back, dumbstruck. Áine, who had brought me into her

confidence on so many things, had not told me about this love affair – the love affair which, it seemed, was the biggest of her life. She had been happy – she had found love after things with Lorcan hadn't worked out. I always assumed she had devoted so much of herself to Jonathan and Emma that she never had the time for love elsewhere. But she had, it seemed. Although they had never married. They didn't live together. Had it been the happy ending she had so deserved? It didn't seem like it.

❦ 1965 ❦

"They are asleep now – much as they tried to fight it," Jack said, standing in the doorway of the kitchen while Áine tidied up after supper.

"I think they're dreading your leaving tomorrow," Áine replied. She had seen the children try to hide their yawns and beg their daddy to tell one more story before they finally agreed to let him take them up to bed.

"I'm dreading it myself but it would be selfish of me to take them with me. You believe that, don't you? I know what I'm going back to – hard work from morning to night. It wouldn't be trips to the coast and days at the park. I'd have to get a nanny in – and no matter how good she was, she wouldn't be you. She could never love them how you love them. She could never offer them everything you are."

Áine blushed.

Rosaleen had, of course, been delighted at the news. Much as she had tried to hide her enthusiasm for fear of not comforting the children enough, she had been over the moon that they would stay under her roof.

"They have a home here always," she had told Jack. "Charlotte would have been happy to have them here with us. I know it. We'll care for them as well as she would."

Jack had expressed his gratitude while the children had sat, trying their very hardest to be brave but unable to hide their trembling lower lips.

"I will come back more," Jack said to Rosaleen, "I promise you that. And maybe you could come out for a visit in the summer holidays? I'm sure Áine here wouldn't object to travelling with you?"

The children had looked at Áine so hopefully she could not bring herself to tell them that she would prefer to keep her distance as much as possible. "That sounds like a plan," she said. She looked at Rosaleen. "Mammy might like a chance to go to Italy – to see where Charlotte is sleeping."

Rosaleen had put her hand to her mouth but shook her head. "No. There is no comfort in a grave," she said. "Charlotte is in my heart – and in these children. That's enough for me. And, my dear girl, I wouldn't be fit for that travelling nor that heat. You know me, I have lived here happily long enough. I'm happy for you to go on your adventures and come back to tell me all about it."

"Auntie Áine, please say you will go?" Emma had said.

"Yes, please say you will take us?" said Jonathan. "You'll love it. And I'll be able to pick up some of my toys that I didn't bring last time."

"Sure why don't we all have a think about it?" Áine said, knowing that she was well and truly sunk.

"It won't be long until they see me again," Jack said, breaking into her thoughts and bringing her right back into the moment – cleaning the kitchen with not another being near them.

"No, I don't suppose it will."

"And we must get organised for your trip. It will do you no harm to get some sunshine on your face."

"I get enough sunshine on my face here," Áine laughed. "In my own garden here."

"The sun is Italy shines warmer and brighter and there are plenty of lovely gardens too – although my garden isn't lovely.

It's a wasteland. It's fair to say your sister didn't share your talent nor do I."

"No, Charlotte never was interested in the garden, except to sit on the step and pull her skirt up to catch the sun on her thighs. Mother used to tell her she was indecent."

There was a silence then between them – only the ticking of the grandfather clock in the hall and the occasional creak of the floorboards to disturb the uncomfortable thoughts which were swirling around Áine's head.

"I suppose I had better go," Jack said eventually. "I have packing to do tonight if I want to get back in the morning to say goodbye to the children. I thought I might take them for an ice cream before I leave. Maybe you would join us? It would seem strange to do something without you – and besides you seem to have a calming influence on the children."

Áine was torn between wanting to tell him he was well able to manage his own children without her – and wanting to spend just an hour more with him before her life returned to its humdrum routine of work, home and little else.

"Yes, of course," she found herself saying. "But yes, you really should be off. It's getting late."

She sensed a reluctance in his demeanour but he turned to leave all the same, stopping briefly as he reached the front door. He opened his mouth as if to speak and she felt her stomach tighten with expectancy. Instead, however, she watched as he shook his head gently, gave her a soft smile and bade her goodnight.

It was later as she sat on the back step, the smell of the lavender from her herb garden filling the evening sky, that she allowed herself to close her eyes and imagine for just a moment what it would have been like if he had kissed her. Would it have made her a bad person? Was she betraying Charlotte? She didn't think so – she had never, ever found herself attracted to Jack in all the years he had been married to her sister. In fact, his gregarious personality had often grated on her – but she had seen a softer side to him in recent months and most definitely over the past week. She had seen him play with the children, feed their imagination with wild and wonderful stories, kiss better their bruises and make them laugh in a way that neither she nor her mother could ever dream of.

His manner was not the only thing she had noticed, of course. She had noticed the wrinkles by his eyes. She had noticed his tanned arms and strong hands. She had noticed the fullness of his lips and to her shame, as she sat on the back step, breathing in the lavender and nursing her cup of tea, she imagined what it would feel like to have those lips on hers. The thought was enough to make her gasp. She knew his touch would be softer than Lorcan's had been. She knew that his kiss would be sweeter. She knew, instinctively, that it would feel completely different – that she would feel completely different. But what would Charlotte say – if she could see? If she knew? What would her mother say? Would she take one of her turns and tell her she had let herself down? And the children – how would they react? What scared her most of all though was how she would feel herself – when all was said and done. Would she feel crushed with guilt – or would a world she never thought possible open up before her? Áine looked up to the sky. The night was clear and full of stars.

"Charlotte, I hope you understand," she whispered before going back inside, pouring the rest of her tea down the sink and heading to bed.

⚭ *Present Day* ⚭

Áine showed me a picture the next day. A picture she had of a younger version of herself with a handsome man, with familiar features I had seen echoed on his son's face. They were smiling at the camera and sitting close, shoulders touching.

"I don't talk about Jack but perhaps I should," she said. "But not everyone understood, so it was something we kept between us. It made it a little more exciting, I suppose," she smiled, but there was a sadness there. "It wasn't conventional – but it worked for us. And if you were to ask me if he was the love of my life, I would say yes. Did I feel strange about it? I did – I still do at times, and guilty. Charlotte loved him so much and he loved her. I wonder, when all this is said and done, will I see him again? Will he be with her in the next world? But he was worth it."

She was twisting her hands again, her memories starting to overwhelm her. I put the photo back into the box she had taken it from. "Life is too complicated sometimes, isn't it?"

Áine nodded. "It is, it sure is."

We made more tea, treated ourselves to a chocolate biscuit and sat opposite each other at the kitchen table.

"I'm sure I was going to clean these presses out one of these days," she said as she sipped from her cup.

Chapter 29

There were touches of Charlotte everywhere. Reminders of her. Photographs of her and the children on the sideboard, paintings she had done on the walls. Her potions and creams still sat on the vanity unit in the bathroom and a pair of her shoes still peeped out from under the settee. She was in every room – her spirit echoing across the tiled floors, down the halls and into the garden.

Áine had found it particularly hard to walk out onto the terrace. She knew this was where her sister had died – where all the energy which filled the other rooms in the house simply ceased to exist. She wondered where it had gone. Had it floated away into the sky, soaked into the ground, was it still buzzing around her now? She sat on one of the patio chairs and looked at the pool, which was now drained and looking sad in the baking sunshine.

"I'm going to fill it again," Jack said as he sat beside her. "I know Charlotte would be cross about that. I know she would think I was wasting a perfectly good resource and that the children should be allowed to run about and dive in when

261

they felt too hot, but it feels wrong. Just knowing she was there – not really knowing how long she was there."

"It must have been awful," Áine said. "Finding her. I'm sorry if I never said that. I'm sorry if I was too wrapped up in how I was feeling to say that."

"I don't think I would have registered it anyway," he said with a sad smile. "I was quite good at being wrapped up in how I was feeling too. But yes, it was awful. But at least it was me. At least it wasn't the children. I've found comfort in that, strange as it sounds."

It didn't sound strange at all – Áine knew she would do anything she could to protect those children. They were hurt and damaged enough – she could not imagine how much worse their pain would have been if they had witnessed their mother floating face down in the pool. A shiver ran through her as that image crossed her mind.

"There were many happy memories here too," Jack said. "I'm trying to remind myself of that. I'm trying not to remember just that one bad time. There were so many good times. Charlotte loved it here. I think she spent more time out here, basking in the sun, reading, playing with the children, drinking wine, than she did inside. She said she never felt more at home than she did out here. I try to remember that. To make myself come and sit here and understand just what drew her to this garden so much."

Áine shaded her eyes against the sun and looked around the terracotta terrace, letting the heat seep into her and enjoying the silence. "It's a wee bit of heaven on earth," she muttered.

Of course Áine had to have the full tour of the house, paying particular attention to the children's room. Both Jonathan and Emma had been beside themselves to be reunited with their own beds, their own toys and a wardrobe of summer clothes which would get little or no wear in a cold and drizzly Ireland.

"My favourite dress," Emma had trilled, slipping on a white broderie anglaise sundress and twirling around. "I'll need new sandals, Daddy. My feet have grown a whole size."

Jonathan was found, less noisy but nonetheless as happy, sitting on the floor of his room, his favourite books spilled out in front of him.

"Mammy used to read these to me but I don't remember the stories any more. I'm going to read them all again. Can you help me? And can I take them home with me – I mean, back to Ireland? Can I bring them back to Granny's?"

"Of course you can, pet," Áine said, sitting down cross-legged beside her nephew, "and if you want I can help you read some of them now."

"I've done a lot of reading practice in Ireland, Auntie Áine, I think I will be able to read some of these all by myself. If I get stuck on a big word though, I'll ask for your help."

"That's a very sensible approach, Jonathan," Áine said, ruffling his hair. He smiled up at her and turned his attention back to the books before him. "I've missed these," he said softly. "I do like being with you and Granny. But I like it here too – with my things."

"Oh, pet, I know. It's always nice to have our own things around us. We'll make an effort to take as much back as we can."

"Do you think Daddy will have us back here soon?" he asked, his eyes wide.

Áine took a deep breath. She knew it was better to be honest with him than to have him continue living with the hope that things could change imminently.

"I don't know for certain, pet, but no, I don't think that you'll be coming back here to live soon. Your daddy is a very busy man – and he loves you very, very much so he wants to make sure you are looked after the very best that you can be. He can't be here all the time – and I don't think he wants strangers minding you. I know it's tough, Jonathan, and that you need to be brave. But we, Granny and I, we love you and your sister very, very much and we will do everything we possibly can to make sure you are happy always. And Daddy has promised solemnly –"

"Crossed his heart and hoped to die?"

"Crossed his heart and hoped to die," Áine nodded, "that he will come and visit you all the time and you will come here for holidays all the time."

Jonathan nodded, and sniffed. "Auntie Áine, I think I want to read my books on my own for a little while now."

Áine kissed him on the head and stood up to leave the room. Her heart was so filled with love for her nephew in that moment that she realised she really, truly, never did want him to go back to live in Italy.

It was inevitable. Áine knew that. Each time Jack had visited they had grown a little closer and had started to relax with each other. They kept their distance while in Ireland – it was rare they would have time away from either the children or Rosaleen and, Áine supposed, each of them was fighting their own battle with their conscience. It was unspoken between them – but it was as obvious as if it were all they talked about. So as soon as Áine set foot on Italian soil she knew it was only a matter of time. When she walked around his house – the house he had shared with her sister – she was only more certain. She had told herself, when she sat on her back step at home looking at the stars each night, that she would find some peace there. She would know – she would feel Charlotte and she would know. It had comforted her to feel such calmness in that house. While Charlotte looked down from the walls at her, each picture was smiling. Her sister was the greatest believer in taking whatever you could from life whenever you could. Charlotte would have been delighted to see Áine here at her kitchen table, cooking at her range, drinking wine in the Tuscan sunset. Charlotte would have wanted her to be happy – and she would have wanted Jack to be happy.

They would have to be careful, she thought. They would have to be sensitive to the children, to Rosaleen. They would have to be sensitive to each other. Her heart beat a little faster at the thought that something so wonderful could come out of something so totally awful.

"They are asleep," Jack said, walking into the kitchen. "I think Jack was asleep before his head even hit the pillow."

"That will be all the excitement and all the travelling. It's been a long day."

"Don't feel you have to stay up to keep me company," he said, his eyes cast downwards.

Was it possible that Jack – he who had always shown so much bravado – was shy? Then again, she was aware her own hands were shaking a little.

"Well, let's enjoy this supper first. The travelling has made me hungry as much as anything."

"It smells good," he said.

"It's only an omelette," she said. "Don't get too excited."

"Anything I don't have to cook myself gets me excited," he laughed. "It doesn't come naturally to me. I'm much more of an eater than a cooker."

She served his omelette onto a plate and handed it to him. "Well, eat this then."

He put the plate down and reached for the wine bottle. "Shall I pour some more?"

She shook her head. "I fear if I drink any more I will be quite drunk," she giggled. "I'm definitely not used to drinking wine. It has gone to my head."

"Well, we can't have that," he said, sitting down at the table she had set for them and waiting for her to join him.

"I'm happy to see you here," he said. "It's nice to have some brightness about the place again. Even seeing the children here – seeing them smiling. It does my heart good."

Áine blushed, sat down and looked at him, feeling emboldened by the wine. "Are the children the only thing to do your heart good?"

He looked at her and reached across the table, tentatively, so very gently touching her hand. "No, of course not. I never thought …" he said, his voice breaking. "I never thought, nor even wanted to have feelings like this again. They say you only really get one love – and make no mistake, Áine, I loved your sister with every part of my heart. But yet I've found myself looking forward to each of your letters. I've found myself feeling elated at the thought of seeing you again and having you here … I wondered if I would feel it was wrong. But it doesn't. It feels right. It does feel right, doesn't it?"

Áine nodded, slipped out of her chair and stood in front of him. He wrapped his arms around her waist and pulled her to him, his head resting on her chest. Áine was aware he was shaking a little – just as she was aware that she was too. She tenderly touched his hair.

He looked up at her and got to his feet, lifting his hand to her cheek and tipping her face towards his. "Is it okay if I kiss you?" he asked, his breath soft on her face.

She couldn't answer, so she just nodded and closed her eyes as she felt his lips on hers.

His kiss was all she had thought it would be – tender and soft but determined too – as if kissing her was the only thing he wanted to do in the world. He kissed her in a way Lorcan never had. In a way no one ever had before and she felt the hurt and pain of the last year melt away.

She wasn't sure how long it was before they pulled apart, but when they did neither of them spoke for a time. There didn't seem a need. They just looked into each other's eyes in an unspoken moment of understanding that something had changed and things could not go back to how they had been.

There would be time for the conversations they needed to have later. There would be time to deal with the rest of the world later – just for now, in the kitchen, with nothing but the sound of the cicadas outside and the ticking of the clock on the wall, there was only time for them to enjoy letting go of loneliness.

∾ *Present Day* ∾

"Mammy, how's Áine? Did you take her to the doctor's?" Sorcha's face was filled with concern as we sat together and ate dinner that night. She had wanted to call over to Áine's after school and I had told her that we had an appointment – which had sent her into a spin I hadn't expected.

"She's fine, pet," I said. "As fine as she can be. We're going to try some new medication and we hope that will help her."

I didn't tell her that the doctor had been quite honest though – the new drugs, antidepressants to try and stem the confusion and upset – might not make a big difference. It was impossible to say. Alzheimer's, he reminded us, was degenerative and different in every person. If the antidepressants didn't help, we could try antipsychotics, the mention of which made Áine pale.

"I'm not crazy," she said, a look of defeat on her face.

"It's just the name for a group of drugs which may help," the doctor had offered. "Try not to get hung up on words."

"But it's getting worse?"

"Without a series of tests, it wouldn't be appropriate for me to make a comment at this stage," he said.

"But your opinion?" Áine asked.

He nodded slowly. "It does seem to be progressing. But again, try not to worry too much. For some patients this disease moves very slowly. In others, it can move in fits and starts – things can appear to worsen, but they can settle again."

"And for others, it's quicker?" she asked.

"There's no way to know how this will progress with you,

Áine," he said.

Jonathan was holding his aunt's hand, trying to reassure her as best he could. We talked through everything we were doing – we were doing it all right, we were told. No, there wasn't much else we could do. I could sense Jonathan's frustration at the doctor's words. That he wanted an easy fix. Or a hard fix. Or an expensive fix. As long as it was a fix.

We had left feeling a combination of confusing feelings – hope that the new drugs would help Áine on the days she felt more agitated, worried that they wouldn't stall the progression of the illness.

But I wouldn't tell the girls that. I would just tell them that we hoped she would feel better. They weren't fools though – they knew enough to know that ultimately, over time, Áine would become worse.

"Can I see her tomorrow?" Sorcha asked.

"I could bake some cupcakes tonight?" Eve offered.

"Yes, girls. I'm sure she would love to see you and that she would love the cupcakes."

They seemed happy with that and returned to eating their dinner.

Later, as I cleaned up, Eve sidled up beside me. "When I'm making cupcakes, should I make extra for Jonathan?" She had a cheeky smile on her face – one I couldn't help returning.

I swiped her gently with the tea towel. "If you want," I laughed.

"I'm glad he's making you happy," she said.

"Really?" I asked. "You don't mind that I'm seeing someone?"

"If you are asking does it feel a bit weird – yes, it does. And you can spare me the details," she said, pulling a face. "But if you're happy, really happy, that's all that matters. And you seem happy."

"We're taking it slowly," I assured her.

"I know, I know," she said, raising her hands. "And I know

you aren't trying to replace Dad. Or any of that nonsense we're supposed to understand and all. But all that aside, cupcakes? Yes?"

"That would be nice," I repeated – and despite the emotional nature of the day and the worry about Áine that wouldn't go away, I went to bed feeling positive about at least one aspect of my life.

Chapter 30

⌒ 1965 ⌒

When Áine woke the sun was streaming through the shutters on the windows. For a moment or two she wondered where she was – and what had brought her there. Memories – hazy and soft – flitted through her mind. The kisses in the moonlight, the talking into the small hours. She had no idea what time it was then – she only knew that there had been the slightest hint of light in the sky as she had gone to bed, reluctantly leaving Jack and slipping into the guest room. She should have fallen straight to sleep. She should have been so exhausted from the travelling, worn out from the heat and left woozy from the wine, but even as she put her head to her pillow she felt more awake and more alive than she had done in years.

She wasn't silly. She was well aware of the complications their situation would bring. Tongues would wag – there was no doubt about that. People would cast aspersions on her – and on Jack. Scandal was a great source of entertainment back at home.

At the forefront of everything were the children – who despite their outward appearance of being resilient and more settled were still reeling from their loss. Áine wondered if that would ever go away. She couldn't imagine it would. She still missed her father – or the notion of him anyway – and she had never even really known him. A child old enough to know and rely on the love of a parent could not easily move on from it. Their lives were also so diverse. She loved her work and her mother needed her. Jack had made no bones of the fact his work and his life was here in Italy.

But it was early days. It could be just the first flush of romance – one which would burn out quickly and in a few months she would be nursing a bruised heart and wondering what madness had come over her. Then again, every part of her body and her mind felt this was something different.

She had stared into the darkness of her room and listened to the sounds the house made around her until she could find no more answers and was fed up with questions and fell asleep. Now waking, she felt more at peace and she could not wipe the smile from her face. Maybe this is what Charlotte had meant all the time she had told her she should live a little – that there was a world outside of the four walls of the big house with Rosaleen at the kitchen table morning, noon and night.

She pulled her dressing gown around her and slipped her feet into her slippers – although there was no need for them, not like at home. The floor was warm under her feet as if the sun had been shining directly on it for hours. Before she left her room she had sense enough to brush her hair into a loose ponytail and pinch her cheeks to bring some colour to them. It was only then – when she felt she was looking halfway to respectable that she walked to the kitchen, following the noise of the children laughing uproariously with their father.

"Daddy is trying to flip pancakes," Emma spat out through her giggles as Áine walked into the room.

"He's not very good at it," Jonathan said, his face bright as a button with glee.

Áine looked at Jack who stood, shrugging, a smile on his face.

"We were hoping if we made enough noise you would get up and show us how it's done," he said. "I've already warned you that cooking is not my strong point. I should have stayed with toast, shouldn't I, children?"

Áine walked towards him, resisting the urge to kiss the smile that danced across his lips, and took the pan from him. "But if you had stayed with toast, then these lovely children of yours would not have had so much to laugh at."

"Laughing at their poor daddy, the cheek of it!" Jack said, shaking his fist in mock rage at them so that they laughed even louder.

As Áine set about making up a fresh bowl of batter, she marvelled at just how lovely it was to see the three of them laugh together – so loudly and without any reservations at all. This, she thought, as she stood there in a kitchen she had never cooked in before, in her dressing gown and slippers, listening to the laughter of her niece and nephew and this man – this man who was slowly but surely working his way into her heart – this was what happiness was. In that moment, she knew that more than she had ever known anything before.

⌒ *Present Day* ⌒

We fell into a pattern as spring moved towards summer. Áine remained relatively stable. There were days, when she was tired or it was too hot, when she would become more confused and at times more agitated. I would do my best to keep us all calm – tell her the heat made me grouchy as well, which it did.

June surprised us all by being both very warm and very dry. We – Áine, Jonathan and I – spent many hours in the garden which was now close to full bloom. My girls would call over at least twice a week, Sorcha having taken a liking to the piano in the dining room and Eve grateful to have someone to share cooking stories with.

Jonathan and Áine would talk freely about their past – about growing up in this big house and the mischief they respectively got up to. They talked about their summers in Italy – how Rosaleen still refused to join them and how Áine would cut her own break short, afraid of leaving her mother at home alone. She would talk about Jack – of the friendship they shared which had blossomed into something more – something which gave her a lot of comfort over the years.

Often I would just listen as they chatted – busying myself getting on with work around the house. And when Áine would take a rest, an afternoon nap or some time out in front of the television, Jonathan would come through to the kitchen and we would share our own quality time. I realised I had forgotten to laugh in the months before I met him – forgot about those deep belly laughs that made you fall head over heels in love with the person making you feel so joyous in the first place. But of course I was cautious of those 'in love' feelings. I held them close to me, only revealing how I was feeling in the intensity of the kisses we shared.

I felt younger too. I didn't worry so much about my age and whether or not I looked it. I felt confident and comfortable in my own skin – helped of course by ditching the Brightly Care uniform and turning up to work in summer dresses, or light linen trousers and soft cotton fitted T-shirts.

Sinéad noticed it – she said I had a glow about me. Being Sinéad, she of course said the glow was clearly the sign that I was being sexually fulfilled on a regular basis. But we didn't cross that line in Áine's house – no matter how strong the temptation became. Friday nights were ours though, when the girls went to their father's house. We both wanted to keep things low key for now – so when we went out for dinner, we chose quiet restaurants on the outskirts of town. Sometimes I would go to his house and sometimes he would come to visit me. The first night I was afraid of what he would make of my chaotic family home but, as he held me that night, as we talked again into the small hours, he told me how my house felt as though it was filled with love. It was, of course, even if I had forgotten that for a while after Matthew left.

The hazy days of June, which progressed into some blistering weeks in July, lulled us all into a false sense of security. We all believed in good things, happy endings and life being fair. The famous Emma even made plans to come home for a visit in August when she took a break from her work. Áine seemed greatly cheered at the news and she talked of a welcome-home dinner party, cooking all of her niece's favourite foods.

"The prodigal niece," Jonathan had teased – but even he had expressed excitement at the prospect of seeing his sister again. It had been a year since he had travelled to England to spend time with her. "Imagine us all being together under the one roof again?" he said and Áine had beamed.

"It will do my heart good," she said – and we all hoped that it would.

But as July neared its end, there was a change in Áine. To tell the truth, I think both Jonathan and I tried to ignore it, or minimise it.

"It's just a bad day," Jonathan said, when he visited towards the end of the month to find Áine more confused than usual. "She was out in the sun too long yesterday. We should have been more careful."

"I'll make sure she gets well hydrated today and it will do her no harm to spend a day resting," I told him. "Try not to worry."

Áine wasn't having it though. "I don't need to rest. I'll have plenty of time for resting when I'm dead and gone. There's the sun shining outside and you want me to stay in this house?"

"We all need to take it easy from time to time," I told her. "And you want to be in your best form possible for Emma coming to visit, don't you?"

She had looked at me and smiled. "Emma is coming?"

I ignored the sinking feeling in my stomach, that feeling that came when she forgot something big, something that had been almost the sole topic of conversation for the last few days.

"Yes," I said softly. "Emma is coming. In two weeks' time. We're going to have a big family dinner."

"Well, I'd better rest then," Áine said. "I don't want to be unwell when she gets here. She'll need me."

"She sure will," I said as Áine stood up and allowed me to guide her back to her bed.

She lay down, asked me to pull the curtains and then asked for a glass of water and some paracetamol. Once she had her tablets she drifted off and I was able to come back downstairs, call Jonathan and tell him she was settled.

"It was mention of Emma's visit that did it," I told him and he laughed.

"Poor Emma won't know what hit her. She'll be killed with kindness when she arrives. I must warn her Áine will be in full-on auntie mode."

"Do you think everything will be okay with them?" I asked, aware that Emma still carried a degree of hurt at her aunt's relationship with her father.

"I think so. I think the passing of time might have softened Emma a little – and, besides, I have her well warned. Áine doesn't need upset now and Emma is mature enough to realise the truth of their relationship."

"I hope so," I said.

"You will keep a really close eye on Áine today?" he asked.

"I promise," I answered. "And I'll keep you updated."

He thanked me and went back to work and I allowed myself to sit down with a cup of tea and relax.

I'm not sure how I didn't hear her on the stairs, or how I didn't hear the front door opening. But nonetheless the door was open when I left the kitchen half an hour later to go and check on her. The sight of the open door didn't overly alarm me at first. I figured I mustn't have closed it tightly when I arrived earlier and that the soft summer breeze had forced it open. I pushed it closed and went upstairs – and it was only when I saw that Áine's bedroom door was open, the door that I could very clearly remember closing, that I started to feel uneasy.

The uneasy feeling was replaced with full-blown panic when I saw that Áine was no longer in her bed – and yet I found myself temporarily frozen to the spot. It was as if my brain went into go-slow mood, trying to process what I could see and what it meant. The shock of adrenalin as I realised Áine must have left the house, and I didn't know when, or where she was headed, almost winded me. My head spinning, I turned and ran from the room, hoping that I was wrong. That she had simply gone to the bathroom, or that I would find her in the living room in front of the TV, or in the garden soaking up the sun we had blamed for her being out of sorts that day.

As I ran in and out of each room my hope faded and my anxiety grew. I grabbed my mobile and ran into the street. Perhaps she had only just wandered. Perhaps she would be there, in the street, and my panic would be over. I ran along the length of Temple Muse, I ran into the beautiful private gardens. I called her name with the panic normally reserved for frantic mothers hunting for wandering toddlers. With each shout of her name, my voice became higher – more strained, more panic-filled – and to my horror tears sprang to my eyes. I tried to blink them away to swipe the screen on my phone to call Jonathan. I won't lie – my heart was pounding at how he would react. Would he be angry with me? Would all his feelings for me mean nothing when pitted against his feelings for his aunt and the sickening reality that she had gone missing on my watch?

When his phone went directly to answerphone, I called his office number. Trying to keep my voice as calm and collected as possible I asked to speak to him, only for his secretary to tell me he was in a meeting and wasn't to be disturbed.

"I'm sorry but I really must insist that you get him for me," I said. "I'm his – his aunt's carer and it's about her. It's really quite urgent." As I said the words my voice began to shake and as I waited for him to come I felt all the contentedness of the last few months slide away.

"Georgina, what is it?" His voice was panicked.

"She's wandered off," I said. "I'm sorry, I don't know what happened. She was sleeping and then when I went to check she was gone, the door was open. I've checked the house, I've checked the street. I'm not sure what to do."

I could hear his sharp inhalation of breath. "Go to the house. Go there and wait in case she comes back. Check it again. Check every room, check the garden. Check it all. I'll drive around and look for her." He barked the instructions at me, and then the phone disconnected.

I stood in the middle of the beautiful gardens of Temple Muse – the gardens I had once longed to walk through – and I cried.

Pulling myself together, I returned to the house. I looked in every room – but half-heartedly. I knew she wasn't there. I could feel it. I thought of how I had sat down, allowed myself a break to drink some tea and how in that time she had slipped out. In her room, I noticed the clothes she had been wearing that morning were still draped over her chair. Her slippers were gone, her dressing gown too. My poor, lovely, proud and clever Áine was out there, wandering the streets in her nightclothes. Jonathan, the man I had allowed myself to start to fall in love with, was angry with me. I was angry with myself and I felt so completely paralysed by a sense of helplessness that I could hardly breathe. I couldn't go out and wander the streets in case she came back – so all I could do was wander from room to room and listen to the ticking of the blasted grandfather clock at the bottom of the hall and wait for Jonathan to call me and tell me he had found her, safe and sound. I don't consider myself religious but I prayed, and prayed hard, that she would show up, soon, and that all this would just be one of those blips that passed and that our lovely summer could resume.

Two hours had passed with no word from Jonathan when I saw a car pull up outside. Out of it stepped two uniformed police officers and I felt my body crease in half in preparation for the body blow that was about to come.

Chapter 31

∞ 1965 ∞

As much as the days were filled with fun, Áine found herself looking forward more and more to evenings when the air would cool just a little and the children, tired from their day's playing, would fall into a deep sleep. It was then that Áine felt truly alive – as Jack poured wine, they ate the home-baked bread and home-churned cheeses they had bought in the village earlier and spent hours getting to know each other. Áine had been shocked at how little she knew of her brother-in-law – but then Charlotte had no sooner fallen in love with him than they had disappeared off to a new life together. Áine had only seen him when he had his best salesman face on – trying to sell himself to Rosaleen as a good husband for her daughter or to Áine as the kind of man who would always provide for her beloved big sister. But the more she learned of him, the more Áine realised that those aspects of his personality were all bluff and bravado. Deep inside he was a man who was happy with the simpler things in life – who craved a family he could provide for and who was striving to make a positive impression on the father who had always told him he would amount to nothing. She had cried as he told her of his childhood – with a heartless father, heavy with his fists and light on emotion. His mother was too scared, or too selfish or too something to take any action when his father had rained down beating after beating on him – for supposed indiscretions he still didn't understand to this day. He had left home as soon as he could – worked his way up in the merchant navy and later worked his way through the ranks of the wine trade. But while he had found success in work, he had not found an ounce of love in his life until he met Charlotte.

"Does it make you feel awkward, when I talk about her?" he asked one evening, as they sat in the darkness, lit only by candles on the table on the terrace.

She looked at him. His eyes were searching her face – scared almost of her answer. It was almost as if he feared her saying yes, saying that she felt uncomfortable talking through all the memories of the woman he loved so much – even if she was Áine's sister.

Áine reached her hand out to his face, caressing his cheek – feeling the roughness of his evening stubble scrape against the softness of her skin. It was a sensation which she loved. "Jack, it would feel awkward if you didn't talk about her. I know you loved her. I know you probably still do – and I know she loved you so much. I could no more expect you to stop talking about her than I could expect you to stop breathing and still be okay."

"What I feel for you ..." he started.

"You don't have to put a name to it," Áine said, "not yet."

"But I do have to tell you," he said. "It's different. It's not more or less – it's different. I wanted you to know that. It's very special to me, Áine. I didn't think I ever could find happiness again but you are making me happy."

"You are making me happy too," she said softly, reaching across to kiss him.

As she pulled back she thought of how handsome he was,

and how vulnerable, and she wanted to do everything in her power to fix him back together again.

"How do you think the children will react?" he asked.

Áine shrugged. "I don't know but I think we should be careful. Let's not hurt them any more than they have already been hurt. We might be able to understand what is going on – but to them – they might not understand."

"I don't want to pretend not to have feelings for you," he said.

Áine thought how much she would love to be open with everyone about what they were feeling but still something held her back. "Then don't. Not now anyway. Not at night. Not when we have time together just the two of us. Let's figure out where we are going before we tell people."

He sighed. "I know you're right," he said. "It hurts me to say it, but you are right."

They fell into a routine of sorts. Once Áine and the children had returned to Ireland – Áine having to resist the urge to cling to him at the airport and tell him how she would miss him – Jack resumed visiting as often as work would allow. Between those visits he would write to the children and occasionally slip an extra envelope with a message just for her in it. When he did visit they would do all in their power to hide their attraction and the increasingly easy way they were with each other from Rosaleen and the children. They talked about the future, from time to time.

As more time passed they became more sure of each other and Áine would often imagine what it would be like to spend more time away from the dreary autumn and winter weather in Ireland and more time under the Tuscan sun. If she was honest, though, she spent more of her time dreaming simply of what it would be like to spend more time with Jack. Letters held their own comfort but they were not the same as the touch of a hand. She of course spent time with Jack and the children on their days out together but she had to make sure to give the children the time they needed on their own with their father. She also had to make sure not to slip up in their presence – not to reach for his hand or wrap her arm around his as they walked together. She had to be careful not to laugh too loudly or brightly at his jokes, or slip too big a portion on his dinner plate lest she be accused of playing favourites. She had to make sure never to straighten his tie or close her eyes in pleasure if he happened to brush too close to her. It wasn't easy and their routine wasn't perfect, not by a long shot, but it worked in its own way. They made it work because the more time Áine spent with Jack or thinking about Jack, the more she realised she never wanted to be without him.

But as the anniversary of Charlotte's death approached, Áine noticed her mother falling back into her old moods. She tried her best to maintain appearances in front of the children but, when the house was quiet at night, Áine could hear her crying in her bedroom. She had taken to carrying a picture of Charlotte with her from room to room, placing it in her eyeline at all times. She found it more difficult to get out of bed in the morning so there many occasions when it was Áine alone who got the children ready and out to school, telling them that Granny just needed a wee rest.

"Is she sad because of Mamma?" Emma asked. "Is it because Mamma is dead and not coming back?"

"Yes, pet, but you know it's okay to be sad sometimes. And she was Granny's baby. You know that, don't you? Whatever age you grow to be, you are always your mammy's baby."

"Except when your mammy is dead," Jonathan said, sadly. "Then you are no one's baby."

"You have your daddy, don't you? And me, and Granny. We all love you very, very much."

"But it isn't the same," Emma said. "Not the same as your very own mammy."

"No, nothing's the same as your very own mammy," Áine

said, feeling her heart sink, realising she had been inadvertently insensitive. The poor children – would they even remember their mother when they were older?

She wished she could take away their pain – but she never could – not fully. She could love them, and spoil them. She could raise them but she could never be Charlotte.

"Do you think she has forgotten us?" Emma asked, her voice solemn. "If heaven is as much fun as the most fun place in the world with everything you need to make you happy, then she might be too busy as an angel to remember us."

"No, your mammy looks down over you. She minds you and will always look out for you."

"I s'ppose so," Emma said, scraping her shoes along the ground as she walked. "I just wondered, if she is watching over us and looking after us so much, why is Granny still so sad? If she knows Mamma is close by?"

"I suppose she would like very much to give her a real cuddle," I said. "And it's sad that we can't."

"Granny told me as long as she lives she will never stop missing her," Emma said. "I went into her room last night. I know I shouldn't have. I know you tell us that when Granny goes to bed early to let her get her rest to help her old bones and all, but I could hear her crying and I was scared."

Jonathan listened wide-eyed – horrified that his granny would be crying in her bed.

"I just wanted to see if she was okay. I thought she might need her medicine or something. Sometimes I get a tummy ache when I'm in my bed and need some medicine. But she was really sad, Auntie Áine. She said she was crying because she missed my mammy and she felt all alone. She said she was scared we would all leave her one day and she would be alone in the big house by herself. I told her I wouldn't leave her because my mammy would have wanted me to take care of her. She was still sad, Auntie Áine, but she didn't seem quite as sad any more."

283

Claire Allan

"You're a good girl, Emma," Áine said, trying to fight the sinking feeling in her stomach. "But you know Granny will always be looked after." She knew her mother was grieving, and that she was particularly close to Emma, but she should have been more careful about what she said to her. Emma was just a child – she didn't needed to worry about her grandmother's fears about what the future would bring. "You're very good to watch out for her, pet."

"Would Mamma be proud of me?"

"Of course she would."

"And would Mamma be proud of me too?" Jonathan asked.

"Of course she would."

Jonathan looked at the ground and slowed down his step beside his aunt. She turned to see if he was okay and saw two fat tears run down his face.

"Jonathan, pet, what's the matter?" Áine asked, crouching in front of him.

"I'm not so much worried about Mamma forgetting us. I'm afraid of forgetting Mamma …" He broke into heaving sobs and Áine pulled him close into her arms.

"Oh pet, we will do everything we can to make sure you always remember her and remember how much she loved you."

"I used to be able to close my eyes and hear her voice," he said with a sniff. "I can't hear her voice any more. Sometimes I think it's her voice but it turns into you and Granny and not my mamma."

Áine felt her heart ache. There wasn't much she could say that would reassure him. She had to settle for making some cack-handed attempt at comforting him. "There was more to your mamma than her voice. You have to hold onto all the other bits and pieces as tight as you can. You know that?"

Jonathan nodded, sniffing and gulping back tears.

Áine felt a wretchedness come over her and she tried her best to shake it off.

284

"How about we go for ice cream after school?" she said.

"But it's winter time and we'll get a dose of cold," Emma said, though her eyes were bright at the prospect of such a special treat.

"Sure we will wrap up warm all the way home and sit in front of the fire as soon as we get there so the cold won't have time to catch us."

Though they were both still shaky and Jonathan seemed reluctant to move his hand from his aunt's, they both smiled brightly at her.

"I'd like that," Jonathan said.

"And maybe we could bring some ice cream home for Granny?" Emma said.

That night when the house was quiet, Áine was sitting in her usual spot in the kitchen marking her schoolbooks but her mind was not on her work at all. It had struck her that this time of year was bringing back painful memories for her mother and for the children. She wondered if, hundreds of miles from where she sat, it was bringing back painful memories for Jack. If it would change things. Grief does strange things to you, she told herself. Maybe, she thought, in the way that you think in the middle of the night when you are tired and emotional and feeling unsure of yourself – maybe Jack was thinking of his wife – and missing her voice and her touch. Maybe he was wishing, as hard as he could, for just one more day with her. She ran her fingers through her hair and tried her hardest to remember Charlotte's voice herself – but it wouldn't come to her either.

When Jack next came to visit, it was all she could do not to run to his arms before the children had the chance. She wanted to see the reassurances he had offered her in the written word before her – in his eyes, in the way he reached for her, in the way he kissed her. She wanted so much to know that they were doing the right thing and that they could make this work. They had kept their distance – they needed to bridge that gap now. But of course she couldn't reach for him. She had to smile and greet him in the reserved manner appropriate for a sister-in-law seeing her brother-in-law again, while the children rang rings around him in their usual high-spirited manner.

It was only much later, when the house was finally quiet that she had the chance to be close to him and she delighted in the fact that he reached for her before she had the chance to make the first move. He pulled her first into a kiss that told her just how much he had missed her, pushing his body against hers so that she could feel the weight of him on her. Before she had time to think, his hands were in her hair and her hands were in his, pulling his face closer to hers, kissing him as deeply as she could. They had barely spoken. She wasn't sure what she would say to him even if they did. She just knew that she needed him – she needed him to make her feel loved and needed in a way that no one else could. When she eventually pulled away from him, reluctantly, and just because she wanted to look him in the eyes, she whispered that she loved him and he answered that he loved her too. She watched him intently as he bent to kiss her again, his faced filled with a longing that she shared.

That's when she heard it. The squeak of the bottom stairs and, to her horror, the sound of footsteps running back up the stairs as if they had seen something they never wanted to. She froze in horror, pulling away from Jack. Instinctively she made to run up the stairs – to run after whoever had seen. But what if they hadn't? What if it was nothing to worry about? She turned back to Jack, who looked as stricken as she was. This was not how anyone was supposed to find out. This was not how it was supposed to be. Them losing the run of themselves, passionately kissing in the kitchen, making declarations of love. This was not how it was supposed to be and she didn't know, she had no clue at all how she should handle it. How could she even begin? Her heart sank to the pit of her stomach – all these efforts to be discreet – everything, for nothing. And now, of all times, when Rosaleen had become increasingly beside herself with grief at Charlotte's anniversary.

She returned to the kitchen.

"What should we do?" Jack said.

"You should go," she said. "I'll deal with it. I'll sort it out."

"No," he said firmly. "We're in this together. It's okay. We've done nothing wrong."

She stopped and looked at him. Suddenly afraid her legs would give out from under her, she sat down and wrung her hands. "I need to go upstairs. I need to know who it was. I need to explain. I need to let them know it's okay."

But, before she could gather enough strength to stand up again, the sound of footsteps coming down the stairs left her under no illusion. They had been seen. The secret was out and she would have to deal with whatever would come.

Chapter 32

ᴄᴏ Present Day ᴄᴏ

I sat in the stillness of my living room. It was still warm outside, but I couldn't stop myself from shaking, even as I sipped from a cup of tea which had already started to turn cold. I had texted Sinéad earlier and asked her to pick the girls up and bring them to hers for tea. She was the kind of friend who knew when to push me and when to back off and give me space. Thankfully she had just picked up the girls and promised to mind them till bedtime. Perhaps she thought I was off on a hot date – the thought brought forward a fresh flurry of tears. My head hurt and I took two paracetamol, glugging some cold tea to swallow them. I couldn't bring myself to eat anything, despite feeling my stomach rumble a little. I knew that if I tried to eat I would be sick – my stomach hadn't settled all afternoon. My phone sat silent beside me – nothing from Jonathan. Not that I expected to hear from him. He was busy dealing with matters in Temple Muse – matters that he had made very clear he didn't want me near.

Despite knowing, in my gut, that he would not call to my house that night, my heart still leapt a little when my doorbell rang just after eight. Taking a deep breath I stood up, straightened my clothes, and walked to the door. What I wasn't expecting to see when I opened it was Matthew – his mouth set in a firm line which let me know he wasn't happy about something.

"When were you going to tell me?" he asked as he stepped across the threshold.

He didn't say hello. He didn't ask if the girls were home. He just walked into the living room and waited for me to follow him.

"I'm not sure what you're talking about," I said.

"Oh please, Georgie. Please don't take me for a total eejit. Although, to be fair to you, you've been doing a pretty good job of that already, haven't you?"

"Matthew, I'm really not sure what you mean," I said, rubbing at my temples. My headache had not yet lifted and if anything it was on its way to getting a lot worse.

"You – and Jonathan 'high and mighty' Hegarty? A big romance in the making by all accounts."

I stared at him open-mouthed – not sure what to say. Not actually sure at that moment what there was to say.

"You looked very cosy out for dinner at the weekend apparently. Holding hands, sharing kisses. It was quite the date, I'm told."

"Matthew –" I began.

"Save it. You had the gall to act all pious when I started seeing someone else – telling me to be careful, to be sensitive to your feelings, to the girls. But you didn't see fit to take your own advice. I am assuming the girls know – or is he your sordid little secret?"

If I'd had an ounce of emotional energy left in my body I would have slapped him hard across the face – but I didn't. I felt empty. Completely void of the strength to fight back. "Matthew, not tonight, please," I said.

"Why? Have you a date? Is he on his way here now? You

289

who cried about how much you loved me and how much you didn't want our marriage to end? You didn't waste much time."

There was so much I wanted to say to him – so much that was running through my head.

"It wasn't like that," I said.

"It's never 'like that'," he sneered. "Do you know how humiliating it was to hear this from a third party? That my wife was seeing someone else?"

"Ex-wife," I whispered.

"What?"

"Your ex-wife, Matthew. I'm your ex-wife. You made that decision."

"But," he said, "you should have told me – you owed me that."

I slumped to the chair. "Matthew, I can't deal with this now. I just can't. I can't deal with you and your hurt feelings now. You walked away. You said I wasn't enough any more. You told me to move on."

"But I never expected you would," he muttered as he sat down beside me and took my hand. "I never thought it would really be over. No matter what I said."

I looked in his eyes, their sadness mirroring my own. There was a time when I wouldn't have hesitated to comfort him. When seeing that sadness would have been like a knife through my heart. There was a time when he was everything to me and then some. But everything had changed. And it couldn't change back.

"Well, it is," I said, standing up and moving away from. "And I'm sorry you're hurt – but we can't go back."

"But the girls … us … everything?"

"The girls will always be our girls. And us, maybe we'll be friends – but no, Matthew – everything has moved on. You moved on first – now let me."

When he left – which he did without saying another word

– I heard my phone beep and lifted it to see a message from Jonathan.

Áine is sleeping well now. Sorry for earlier. She gave me a scare. IT WASN'T YOUR FAULT. Am staying overnight. C U in the morning?

I curled up into a ball on my sofa and cried until my throat was raw.

As I had watched the police officers walk up the path earlier that day I had feared my legs would go from under me. What would they tell me? That she had walked out in front of a bus? That she had taken a bad fall? That she had collapsed?

It was only when I caught sight of her frail features peeking out from the back window of the police car that my heart started to settle.

"Is this the home of Áine Quigley?" a young police officer asked.

"It is," I replied. "She wandered off. She has dementia."

He looked at me with sympathy. "She was found in a distressed state at St. Claire's Primary School. Luckily there was a caretaker there who remembered her from her teaching days."

"We've been worried sick. Her nephew is out looking for her. I've been waiting here in case she came home."

He nodded at the car and a female officer helped Áine from the car and guided her up the path. She looked mortified.

"I know it can be difficult," the young officer said. "Does Mrs Quigley have a social worker? Perhaps there is more help you could get?"

I didn't want to tell him I was the 'more help'.

"Georgina," Áine sobbed, as she neared me. "I went to get Emma from school. But when I got there it was all closed. I don't understand . . ." Her face creased with fear and embarrassment. "Have I made a fool of myself again?"

"No, no, of course not," I said, guiding her through to the living room and sitting her down. The police officers were standing expectantly in the hall when I went back out to them.

"Thank you so much for returning her to us."

"You're welcome. My grandmother went this way," he said softly. "Take care of her. She's a nice lady."

"She is," I said, wishing them well as they left before grabbing my phone to call Jonathan and tell him she was okay. The relief in his voice was palpable and he told me he would be straight over. Áine was still distressed and I sat beside her, trying to soothe her.

"I'm in my nightclothes," she whispered. "What must people think? And poor Emma. Poor Emma will be waiting."

"Emma is in England," I said softly. "She will be here in two weeks. Remember?"

She nodded that she did, but I could see enough confusion on her face to know that she didn't know what to believe, or who to believe any more – so I simply held her to try and give her some sense of the here and now.

When Jonathan arrived he ran straight to her – and I moved aside. I couldn't read his face – not beyond the relief he felt at seeing his aunt.

"I'm so sorry," I said, after telling him where she was found. "Jonathan, I'm so, so sorry."

He looked at me – his face unreadable.

"You should go home," he said.

"I want to stay. I want to make sure she's okay. I'll put on a pot of tea."

"No, Georgina," he said firmly. "Go home. Just go home."

I knew there was no point in arguing – I was surplus to requirement and, face blazing with shame, I left.

I climbed into my car, drove home, closed the curtains and crawled into my bed for the afternoon. But I didn't sleep. Every scary possibility of what happened, what could have happened and what it all meant ran through my mind over and over again.

When Jonathan sent that text my mood changed – but still I felt conflicted. I felt relieved of course that Áine was okay. I felt grateful for his apology. But I felt like an outsider – someone who was not part of their inner circle. For all Jonathan's talk of how things were going between us, of how his feelings were growing, of how he trusted me, there was a clearly a part of him that didn't trust me. And I wondered if he ever would.

Still, I put on a brave face when the girls came home from Sinéad's – and told them I was going to bed early with a sore head rather than have them ask questions about why I looked dog-rough.

When Sinéad called to ask if everything was okay, I bluffed my way through our chat. Everything was just hunky dory, I said. I just felt as if I was coming down with something – and I would be fine. I didn't tell her about the day I'd had, or that Matthew had called around. I knew she would be knocking on my door in three seconds flat if I did – and I just needed to some peace and quiet.

I couldn't even bring myself to text back to Jonathan when he sent a second message an hour later, just to check if I had seen his first message and ask if I was okay. I switched my phone to silent – keen to avoid the rest of the world – and I went to sleep.

Chapter 33

∞ *1965* ∽

Áine watched as her mother walked into the kitchen, her face white – with fear? With rage? With disgust? Áine couldn't tell. She could see her mother try to find words – try to think of questions – try to make sense of things.

"I'm not sure what you saw." Jack's voice broke through the deafening, loaded silence.

"I didn't see anything," Rosaleen stuttered. "Your child – your daughter – on the other hand has just come running up into my bedroom half out of her wits. She told me her mammy was back – she told me her mammy was back because she saw her daddy kissing her mammy in the kitchen ..." Her voice shook the whole time she spoke. "I told her of course that her mammy couldn't be back and perhaps the wee pet was dreaming, but she told me again how she had seen her daddy kissing her mammy in the kitchen. She was adamant. She asked me was her mammy a ghost? She asked me were we being haunted? She's up there now, cowering, waiting for me to come back – and I thought," she looked from one of them to the other, "I thought when I came down here to check for

294

'ghosts' there wouldn't be a being about – and I could go back up and tell her that it was okay and that she should come in and sleep beside me ..." Her voice broke. "What I didn't expect to do was to come down here to find you two together. Tell me," she said, staring directly at Áine, "please tell me that Emma was seeing things. That nothing happened. Please tell me you were not dishonouring your sister – and her not a full year dead yet – by ..." She broke into sobs as she pointed at Jack.

And Áine swore she could feel any strength she had ever held in her legs seep out through her body. Feeling limp – feeling horrified and trapped – she slumped into a nearby chair while Jack stood – looking as horrified as she felt.

"It's not what you think," Áine muttered.

"Oh God!" Rosaleen wailed, grasping at her chest as if Áine's words had physically wounded her. "Oh God, you can't do this! You can't just step in where she stepped out."

"It's not like that," Jack said.

Áine felt shame overwhelm her. Was her mother right? Was it wrong?

"Well, what is it like, Jack? Let me ask you because this is what it looks like for me – that you two have no respect for my Charlotte. That you are carrying on – where her children can see you. That when people find out – and they will find out – they will think of you both in the same light as I think of you. That you are shameful! That she deserved better."

Áine had never seen such spite her mother's eyes before or heard such spite her voice.

"Look, Rosaleen, I know this is a difficult time –" Jack started.

"Apparently you don't." The spite had left her voice as quickly as it had started. "Apparently it's a more difficult time for some of us than others."

But Áine would have preferred the spite, she thought, over the grief, over the sadness, over the disappointment.

"Jack, I want you to leave this house now. If it weren't for the children, I wouldn't want to see sight of you again for as long as I live. Charlotte did everything for you – everything for both of you. She didn't deserve this. She didn't deserve any of this."

"Rosaleen, please let me explain … please …" Jack said.

"Don't 'Rosaleen' me. Don't ever say my name again."

"If I can just go and see Emma … just speak to her?"

"What and hurt her more? No, Jack – you get out now!"

Rosaleen's voice was getting louder and Jack, keen to not make a bad situation worse, looked at Áine and mouthed 'Sorry' before making to leave.

Áine wanted to beg him to stay. She wanted to say they could make Rosaleen understand – if she knew how much comfort they got from each other, and how much they genuinely loved each other, how they hadn't betrayed Charlotte, how they had fallen in love as they shared their grief for her … but she knew that Rosaleen was in no form for listening. She had been in no form for listening to anyone for weeks.

She nodded at him, tears sliding down her face, and she tried to hold herself together as he walked down the hall – as she heard Emma call out to him – and him answer only with the closing of the front door. Emma's call turned into a wail – one which Áine desperately wanted to copy. Rosaleen wasn't far from wailing either – and was rocking, her arms around her body, and sobbing as if her heart had broken all over again.

"I'll go to Emma," Áine said, standing up. "I'll go and talk to her. I'll calm her."

Rosaleen continued her keening as Áine stood up and wiped the tears from her eyes before making her way upstairs to talk to a very confused little girl who had believed, for just a few moments, that her mammy had come back to her – and who was trying to understand why her daddy had just walked out.

The wee girl was sitting on her granny's bed, her knees tucked in under her chin in her nightgown. Her eyes were red from crying and Áine thought she had never seen such a pitiful child in her life before.

Emma looked around at her aunt, rubbed at her eyes roughly and said: "Was that my mamma? I was sure I saw my mamma. Is she not really dead? Was she just hiding from us? Why would she do that?"

Áine crossed the room and took the child in her arms, aware that the truth was going to hurt her precious niece. She had never meant to hurt anyone. They had never meant to hurt anyone. They had tried to be so careful. Maybe if they had just avoided each other altogether ... but, when she thought of the comfort he gave her ...

"Sweetheart," Áine started. "Sweetheart, no, that wasn't your mammy. Your mammy is still gone, pet. She would never have left you unless she had absolutely no choice, pet. You must know she loved you more than anything in the whole world."

"But, I don't understand," Emma said, burrowing closer to her aunt. "I saw Daddy kissing someone. I know I did. It wasn't a dream. I know it."

Áine took a deep breath, trying to push her mother's reaction out of her mind. "That was me, darling. Your daddy was kissing me. I know you might be confused by that – but Daddy and I have become good friends."

"But Daddy loves Mamma," Emma said, pulling away and looking up at her aunt. "Why was he kissing you?"

"It's a grown-up thing, sweetheart," Áine said, feeling increasingly uncomfortable at the whole situation. Jack would know how to deal with it better. Jack would probably put it better.

"But you're not my mamma," Emma said, her confusion turning to anger.

Áine felt the words like a slap. "I know, sweetheart," she

answered. "I'm not your mamma. I know that."

"Why are you kissing my daddy then? That was Mamma's job. You can't take Mamma's job!" Emma's face was screwed up in anger now – but she was still crying, tears of a confused little girl coursing down her cheeks.

"Daddy and I … we have become good friends," Áine repeated, her cheeks blazing and tears pricking again at her eyes.

This was all turning nasty. The tender, genuine, real feelings she had shared with Jack. The feelings that he had offered her some sort of salvation and comfort at a time when she felt lost. It wasn't wrong. She hadn't been trying to step into Charlotte's shoes. She hadn't. But as she saw her mother arrive at the bedroom door, her face set like stone, and as she watched Emma get up and run over to her granny, run sobbing into her arms, she felt like she had just betrayed them all. What had felt so right now felt so wrong. It felt so sordid. She blushed to her core as she thought of just how passionately she had been returning Jack's kiss when Emma saw them. She thought of how much she wanted him and how she had come so close to losing her senses altogether and giving in to her desire for him. She couldn't speak – she was struggling to breathe. She wanted to tell her mother and her niece that she hadn't meant to hurt anyone, but she could see neither was ready or able to listen to her. She wanted to explain how slowly they had fallen in love. She had wanted to explain just how innocent it had all been. She wanted to tell them that she wasn't and never could try to be Charlotte. This was not about Charlotte.

Most of all perhaps she wanted to run after Jack – and get him to hold her, to kiss her on the top of her head, to wrap his strong arms around her and tell her that they had done the right thing and that this wasn't the end. Of all the losses she had endured in her life – this one, if that was what it was – would be one that she didn't know if she could recover from.

Not on top of everything else.

Feeling defeated, she walked past her mother and Emma without speaking. She knew whatever she said now would only make things worse – and, that aside, she couldn't trust herself to speak a word without breaking down.

Chapter 34

⁓ Present Day ⁓

For the first time since that horrible first day, I did not look forward to going to work in Áine's house. I didn't feel enthused. I didn't look forward to a day chatting with a woman I was fast considering a friend as well as a client. And I certainly wasn't looking forward to seeing her nephew. Perhaps it was churlish of me to feel stung – he had apologised. I knew he was stressed, and while I worked with Áine every day I knew I could never be as close to her, or hit as hard by the pain of her condition as he was. But yet, I did feel hurt. The reality that he was my boss and that he considered I had let him down, hit me sore.

I was tired still when I dressed and was grateful the girls were still sleeping. I wasn't in the mood for them to ask questions about why I was in bad form. The warm day felt more cloying than warming and when I reached Áine's I felt sick with nerves.

As I parked the car I saw Jonathan walk towards me. He looked worn out and a wave of sympathy washed over me.

"I'm sorry," he said as I stepped out of the car. "I tried to

300

call last night, I sent messages. I know I took it out on you. I shouldn't have told you to leave."

I looked at him, feeling tears pricking at my eyes again. "I didn't hear her leave," I said. "She was sleeping. She was sound out."

"I know. I understand," he said, reaching out to me, taking me into his arms.

I allowed myself to sink into his hug, knowing that we both needed the comfort.

"I was scared. I was so scared … when she gets worse … I need to talk to you, Georgina. I need to explain."

I looked at him, waiting for him to tell me what he needed to say.

He took a deep breath. "Come inside," he said, taking my hand and leading me in.

As we walked in I could hear Áine talking in the living room – to the TV no doubt.

"She's still unsettled today," Jonathan explained. "She's out of sorts. I've given her tablets, and some paracetamol because she complained of her head again. She had settled down … but …"

I popped my head in the door to say hello. I was surprised to find that Áine wasn't talking to the TV as I had expected, but instead rambling to herself. "Emma is coming," she whispered to no one in particular. "I've been planning for it. I have a bedroom ready for her and everything. Nice clean sheets. Towels. Her teddy bears. I couldn't find her teddy bears. Maybe I'll look again." She got to her feet.

"It's okay, Auntie Áine, I'll look for you if you want," Jonathan said, his voice resigned.

Áine turned to look at him and me, her expression startled. "You wouldn't know where to start," she said. "I know what I know. Come and see. Everything is ready."

I felt my heart sink and a quick glance at Jonathan showed that he was struggling with the pain of the situation. Áine stood and walked determinedly out of the room and up the stairs. All we could do was follow her to a bedroom at the back of the big house.

"This is the room we slept in when we were children," Jonathan said. "When we first came here."

Áine opened the door and walked in, and Jonathan and I followed her.

The room, as I feared, was cold and dark. Two bedframes stood, without mattresses let alone bedding. Boxes, sealed and dust-covered, stood against the wall.

Áine looked confused. Before she even spoke, I felt Jonathan squeeze my hand and I squeezed back, trying to will him strength.

"Oh, Auntie Áine," he said, letting go of my hand and moving towards her.

I expected Áine's usual reaction to times of confusion. I expected her to realise things were off kilter. I prepared myself for her to be upset. I prepared to try and help her find an anchor to combat her disorientation and to reassure her.

But she turned on me, her eyes flashing. "What did you do? Did you come up here and wreck it all? I had it ready. I had it all ready. Everything was perfect. Pyjamas and teddies and pictures of Charlotte and everything was ready. What did you do?"

"Auntie Áine," Jonathan tried to soothe her, stepping forward.

Áine looked at him as if she was seeing him for the first time. "Who are you? I don't know who you are. Why are you calling me 'Auntie Áine'? What have you both done?"

I watched as Jonathan moved towards his aunt and took her hands in his. She shrugged him away forcefully – for a small, old woman she was surprisingly strong – but, undeterred, he took her hands again.

"Auntie Áine, it's me, Jonathan. Let's just calm down."

"Do you think I'm mad?" she shouted back, freeing herself

from his grip and slapping him hard across the face. "You're not Jonathan. Jonathan is ten! He's coming here with Emma. I have the room ready. I have it all ready. I've tried to make it perfect because I know it will be hard for them without their mammy. I don't understand why you would say that! I don't understand what you have done."

"Please, Auntie Áine," Jonathan pleaded, the red welt on his face angry-looking.

"Stop calling me that!" she shouted, pushing him from her and looking around the room.

I stepped forward, feeling completely out of my depth and, if I was honest with myself, I was also scared of what she might do – and I hated myself for feeling that way.

"Áine, please. Let's just calm down. No one has done anything. I know this is scary – I know you are a little confused."

Áine looked at me, her anger passing as quickly as it had started, tears falling down her cheeks as she wrung her hands together. "I don't understand. I don't understand. I had it all ready. I had new pyjamas and teddies and pictures of Charlotte. I wanted it to be perfect. I don't understand what is happening. Why is that man telling me he is Jonathan? Who are you? I'm scared."

"Áine, do you know who I am?" I asked softly.

Áine looked at me intently as if trying to find some hint of familiarity in my face. "I don't know," she sobbed.

I took her hands. "You can trust me, Áine," I said. "No one is trying to trick you. I promise you. I know this seems scary but you are safe. Will we go downstairs for a cup of tea?"

Áine nodded. "But I don't want him," she whispered, nodding towards Jonathan. "I want my Jonathan. My sweet boy."

"Okay," I said, as I watched Jonathan, looking utterly defeated, step out of the way. "We won't do anything you don't want to. But how about we go and sit in the kitchen so you can look out at the garden? I'll make a cup of tea."

"I'm scared," Áine whispered.

"I know," I said as I ushered her downstairs, Jonathan following us.

"I don't know what's happening," she said. "Where's my mother? Why isn't she here? We need to have the house ready."

"It's okay," I soothed as I led her into the sitting room.

"Should we call a doctor?" Jonathan asked from where he stood, nervously, at the door.

"I think that might be a good idea," I said, not taking my eyes from Áine who was becoming visibly more distressed again. "The contact details are by the phone. Tell them she has had all her medication, but has seemed out of sorts for a few days – and now this. Tell them she's shaking and, if I'm not mistaken," I said, putting my hand to Áine's forehead, "she has a bit of a fever."

Jonathan nodded and headed to the hall.

I tried to get Áine to focus on me – to look in my eyes. "Áine, are you feeling okay?"

"I'm scared," she said.

"I know, but does anything hurt? Physically, do you feel unwell?"

But it was clear she was past reason – and my heart went out to her. She looked like a frightened child. I couldn't imagine what it must be like – to be so afraid of what was happening and yet have no idea why.

"The doctor is calling up. He will be here as soon as he can," Jonathan said from the doorway.

"Where is my mother?" Áine called, looking at him. "Where is she? I need her."

"She'll be here soon," I lied, not sure if it was the right thing to do or not, but I feared for the reaction she might have if I told her the truth. I wasn't sure she would able to understand the truth.

Jonathan didn't move from the doorway. Áine was keening

in the chair but more quietly now, as if she was channelling all her energy into keeping herself from collapsing under the weight of her confusion.

"I never expected this – not yet. Not for her to be so bad." He sounded so sad – so far removed from the confident and assured man I knew.

"This illness," I said, "it's awfully cruel."

He nodded and jumped as the doorbell rang, heralding the arrival of the doctor.

I hadn't expected Áine to end up in hospital – but when Dr Robbins arrived he was not "one bit happy" with Áine's condition. He confirmed she was indeed feverish and trying to get any sense out of her was proving impossible.

"I don't think it would do any harm to get her into hospital for a few tests," he said. "Sometimes another illness – a viral one or an infection – can play havoc with dementia patients. It could explain why she is so agitated and confused."

"So this isn't permanent?" Jonathan asked hopefully.

"Your aunt has dementia – by its very nature it's permanent. But this state now? Hopefully not. Although without tests, without treatment, it's hard to tell."

Jonathan looked almost as lost as his aunt as I drove us both to the hospital behind the ambulance. He didn't speak for most of the journey but I could tell his mind was racing.

"Let's just see how it goes when we get to the hospital," I said. "We'll not get ourselves into a real tizzy until they do their tests."

"I should call Emma," Jonathan said. "Ask her to bring forward her visit. It might help."

"It might," I said, with a degree of confidence I certainly didn't feel.

Jonathan took a deep breath to steady himself as we pulled into a parking space. "I don't think I'm ready for any of this," he said.

Then we got out and walked towards A&E.

Áine made a pitiful sight in the hospital bed. Her hair hung loosely around her face – I made a mental note to buy some dry shampoo and a soft brush to help tidy her up when she was fit. Áine would hate to see herself like this. She was asleep – still under sedation, the nurses said. Easier for everyone, they said. Let the antibiotics work, get her hydrated, let her rest. I didn't want to ask if it was just so that nurses wouldn't have to try and answer 101 questions they couldn't possibly know the answer to – or deal with the frantic cries of a distressed woman.

The ward was quiet and warm. Áine was wrapped in blankets. A jug of water sat by her bed even though she was clearly in no state to drink. Jonathan wasn't there. He had gone home for a shower and to rearrange his appointments for the days to come. I suspected he also just needed a breather. He had looked like a haunted man as the doctors fussed around Áine and tried to make her comfortable.

I sat on the high-backed chair by Áine's bed – and took her hand in mine. It was already blue with bruises from the cannula in her hand. I made a second mental note to bring over her nail polishes and hand creams and treat her to a manicure when she was back to herself.

If she was ever back to herself.

"Oh Áine," I said, "don't leave us yet. Jonathan needs you so much. I need you too."

A portly nurse arranging flowers on the windowsill looked at me and gave me a soft smile. "This one will be fine. I don't think she's going anywhere. A wee kidney infection. She'll be right as rain in a few days. That's the way with dementia patients. They might be weak in some areas, but they have the hearts of lions. They hold on for a long time."

"It's not her heart I'm worried about," I said. "I want all of her to hold on for as long as possible."

"Is she your mother, pet?"

"No ... no, she's my friend. My very dear friend."

The nurse bustled past me. "Don't expect miracles with dementia patients, love. They don't happen and, even when they do, they are only temporary. If you really care about your friend, you need to accept that in many ways she won't ever get better."

The nurse left the room and I looked at Áine's sleeping form. I couldn't be entirely sure I wasn't just imagining it – but there was a slight change in her expression. That stubborn look of determination I imagined she had worn when she decided to take Jonathan and Emma on as her own. Yes – there was the slightest, tiniest hint of a change in Áine which I took to mean 'Just you watch me'.

"You tell her, Áine," I whispered, wiping a tear away. "You tell her."

Chapter 35

⁓ Present Day ⁓

"We've reduced her sedation. She's still quite confused but that is natural with infections such as these. But as soon as the antibiotics really kick in and she is full hydrated again, she should be more herself. Hopefully she will become less confused." The nurse on evening duty was friendly and spoke in a soothing tone, looking at Áine the whole time she talked. "She's a lovely old woman. Is she your mother?"

We shook our heads in unison before Jonathan spoke. "No, no. She's my aunt and Georgina here is … a family friend. My aunt didn't have any children of her own. She never married."

The nurse looked at us, her face clouding with sadness. "Oh, that is sad. I'd say she was quite the looker in her day too. I wouldn't have thought she would have had a problem finding a husband."

The nurse was clearly fishing for Áine's life story.

"My aunt cared for my sister and me," Jonathan said, tenderly taking Áine's hand. "Our mother died, so she took on the role herself. I don't suppose she found the time for a

308

husband having the pair of us running around her feet. We were enough to keep anyone busy." He forced a laugh and the nurse smiled warmly at him.

"Well, it seems to me, if you spend so much time at her bedside now, she must have done a great job."

"She did," Jonathan said. "You'd never find a more loving creature."

At that Áine's eyes flickered open, slowly. She made to speak but coughed and reached for her throat.

"I think she wants a drink," the nurse said, pouring some fresh water and getting a straw.

"Here, I'll do it," Jonathan replied, gently helping his aunt to quench her thirst.

I watched them together – watched Áine's eyes light up at the sight of her nephew beside her. She tenderly lifted her hand to his cheek and stroked it softly.

"Jack," she whispered. "I wondered when you would come back."

☜ 1965 ☞

"I'm not sure where we go from here," Áine said, almost in a whisper.

She was sitting across from Jack in a small tea room in town. Her mother had watched her like a hawk since she had uncovered her relationship with Jack and it had taken almost a week before she had been able to see him alone. Rosaleen had made sure that they had no time together at all, just the two of them, when he came to the house to visit – and if he took the children out she made it exceptionally clear that Áine was not to go along with them. Áine had tried once to explain to her mother that her relationship with Jack was something they had never planned, that they only developed feelings for each other after Charlotte had died and that they had never betrayed her. But she hadn't felt strong enough to fight too hard – especially as Emma had become withdrawn and clung to her granny morning, noon and night. As for Jonathan, he just looked confused and had a look of sadness about him that broke her heart. It saddened Áine further to think that he had already endured so much change and heartache that he just silently adapted to whatever new drama came his way.

In that time she had craved Jack like she had never craved anything or anyone before. She had tried to find a way to see him – wondering if she could see him after school one day – but of course she needed to take the children home with her. In the end she had gone to work one day to have the school secretary tell her a young man had left her a letter. She recognised his handwriting immediately and smiled to herself when she saw that he wanted to meet her at Baptisti's on Saturday morning. She told Rosaleen she was nipping out to the library and ran out the door before her mother had the chance to question her further. Her heart had been in her mouth since – convinced they would be found out and her mother would have yet another reason to be disappointed in her.

But, wretched as she felt, when she saw him sitting there across that table in the tea room – those gorgeous familiar tired eyes – she had felt her heart lift. Sitting across from him, her fingertips touching his, she thought this really was the very definition of agony and ecstasy.

"Come with me," he said. "Come with me to Italy. Come with me and we can make it work."

She closed her eyes and breathed him in, letting the longing in his voice sink into her soul and warm her.

"I can't," she said. "The children? My mother? Emma is so angry."

Jack dropped his head to his hands. "She is. She hates me just now," he sighed. "She says I don't love her mamma any more. But we can make it work. We can. She will come round."

"It would kill my mother," Áine whispered, the reality of her words sinking in. "She has lost so much – if I went, if we went and took the children … it would kill her."

"You need to live your life," Jack said, but she could tell from the tone of his voice that he already knew his words were futile. He knew she was right – that Rosaleen could simply not endure another loss. Nor could she endure the perceived scandal of her daughter running off with her other daughter's widower. Áine had always been happy with her place in the world – but right now she felt utterly trapped. A tear slid down her face which she brushed away.

"Don't cry," Jack said softly, "please don't cry."

"But what do we do? We have hurt people already, Jack."

"We haven't done anything wrong. Whatever happens, remind yourself of that. We did nothing wrong. We never set out to hurt anyone."

"I can't hurt her any more," Áine said. "Her health isn't great as it is. Even before she found out about us, she was just about holding it together. Now, she's cracking around the edges."

"I can't lose you either," he whispered.

"Nor me you."

They sat in silence, listening to the chatter around them, the tinny sound of the radio and the sound of the rain hitting the windows.

"We can make it work," Jack said eventually. "Write to me still and I will write to you."

"I imagine my mother will be keeping a tighter grip on the post from now on."

"Well, I will write to you at the school, or to a post box, or whatever it takes to stay in touch. And, when I visit, we will find the time to be together in some way. And you come to Italy – in the summer. You put your foot down and you come with the children … and we … we will make it work."

She gripped his hand as tight as she could. She knew he was

311

travelling back the following day. He was set to visit the children later but she wouldn't have the chance to talk to him let alone hug him, or kiss him. Briefly she put her hand to his face and he kissed the palm of her hand. She would have left her hand there for a long time, she would have kissed him across the table, if she wasn't so scared she could make things worse.

"We'll do it," she whispered. "Whatever it takes."

"Whatever it takes," he whispered back.

He walked her home – or at least to the bottom of her street. Then he stood, aware of the daylight, of the neighbours, of the scandal that Rosaleen feared so much and he told her that she had fixed what he thought had been broken forever and that he was not prepared to let go.

❦ Present Day ❧

Emma was not what I expected. I had expected a harsh and cold exterior. I had heard how she had not visited her aunt in five years – not even when she had her diagnosis. I had heard of the child who been so hurt by her aunt's relationship with her father. I had heard that when she turned eighteen she could barely wait to leave the confines of Temple Muse and move to England where she had made a life for herself. I had heard that her relationship with her brother had been strained – perfunctory at best. That while they kept in touch, he would never describe their relationship as close. I had heard how she was coming to visit Áine now out of a sense of duty rather than a sense of affection – certainly not the same level of affection that Jonathan felt.

So I was surprised when Jonathan and I watched this grown woman, elegantly dressed in a soft linen suit, dissolve into mournful tears at the sight of her aunt in a hospital bed. While Áine still slept, this woman, who appeared at the door of the ward looking scared and sad, walked straight to her hospital bed and sat beside her, resting her head beside Aine's hand and telling her she loved her so very much, and she was sorry.

I felt awkward as I was intruding on a very personal family scene and I stood to leave, to just stand outside for a bit and let them have their moment – their chance to reunite. But Jonathan put his hand on mine, bidding me to stay seated.

"Auntie Áine!" Emma wept.

I watched as Áine's hand reached over her niece, patting her back, and her eyes opened and tried to take in the sight before her.

"My Emma? My sweet Emma, you've come home."

Emma reached out to her aunt, tears now flowing freely. "Oh Auntie Áine, I'm sorry. I should have been here sooner. I've been so hard on you."

"Hush now, pet," Áine said. "You're here. Everyone is here."

Jonathan and I left to get a coffee – to give Emma and Áine some time to talk. I sat at the long Formica table and shook a salt sachet, listening to the rattle of the fine grains as the contents moved about. Jonathan was in the queue, ordering two coffees and two chicken-salad sandwiches. For the first time in days he seemed more content – the arrival of Emma having eased his burden, I supposed. When Áine was out of hospital we would do something nice, I vowed. We would go out for a lovely dinner, maybe a night away in a hotel. Just the two of us – when Áine was well enough of course. I guessed he wouldn't want to leave her any time soon. But we would do something. I smiled at him as he walked towards me – my heart swelling with affection for him.

He sat down and I sipped from the coffee he had brought me.

"Do you know she's been asking for my father?" he said as I struggled to open the cardboard around my sandwich.

"Emma?"

"Áine," he said. "The nurse asked me this morning who he was. She's been asking when he is coming to visit. She got distressed when the nurse said she didn't know who Jack was."

I raised my eyebrow. "She is still confused – the antibiotics are only starting to kick in. Give her time. Think of how good the last few months have been."

"And how hard the last week or so has been," he said. "I asked the nurse how much she was likely to come round …"

"You know that's hard for them to tell," I said.

"I know, but I just wondered … you know, these nurses have a lot of experience. They've seen it all."

"And what did she say?"

He sipped from his coffee. "It was a mixed bag. She could get a little better – or she could stay where she is now. Or she could get worse. Well, ultimately, she will get worse."

"We have to take it one day at a time," I said softly. "You know she's a fighter."

He sat his coffee down and took a deep breath. "The thing is, Georgina, and this is what I wanted to talk to you about. Before everything. We don't have one day at a time. She doesn't want to fight forever …"

I looked at him, confused. His face was etched with worry again.

"What do you mean?" I asked him.

"She wants to go, George. Before it gets too bad. She made me promise, when she was diagnosed, I wouldn't let her go too far. She made me promise to help her."

I felt the air sucked from my chest. "Help her?" I asked – not sure if I wanted to hear the answer.

He leant towards me, checking first no one was within earshot, and whispered: "She wants me to help her end her life. Before she loses her dignity. How do I do that? How do I make that decision? I promised her – but how could I ever let her go?"

I didn't know what to say. He was confiding something huge to me. Something I could barely process. How do you get your head around something like that? How do you react when someone tells you something like that? Was I supposed to say I understood? Was I supposed to offer to help? Was I supposed to run screaming? Call the police?

"Oh Jonathan," I managed.

"I don't want to let her down, but I don't want to let her go," he said as my stomach turned at the thought of what we were discussing.

Chapter 36

"You look like hell," Sinéad said.

I shrugged my shoulders. "Gee, thanks," I teased.

"George, anyone would look like hell going through what you're going through. How were you supposed to react to that bombshell?"

"I don't know. I'm not sure what he expected. I felt for him. It's clear it's not something he wants to be a part of, but he feels he promised her."

We were sitting on Sinéad's sofa, drinking tea and fighting the urge for something stronger.

"Christ," Sinéad said, "that's serious stuff."

"It is. It's awful. He said the reason he hired me, the reason he had tried to lock the house up – all of it was to try and keep her well, to slow things down in the hope it wouldn't come to this."

"Is he going to do it?" Sinéad looked directly at me.

"I don't know, I don't think he knows. It's just ... so awful." I felt tears spring to my eyes. "It's so awful that she wants to give up."

Sinéad reached over and squeezed my hand. "Sweetheart, I know – I am not saying what she wants is right or wrong, but can you imagine facing that in your future? Knowing you'll lose your mind, your dignity, your ability to function for yourself? I have to say, I'd consider it if it were me."

"But she has so much love around her – she's so special!" I cried.

"I know that – and it's very clear how fond you've become of her. But that love – I don't want to sound harsh – but she won't even know that in a while. This disease is cruel, Georgina – it's horrible and it's unfair and it steals people from us. They're still there – still in their chairs and their beds but they are gone."

I curled my knees up to my chest and hugged them. "I'm not prepared for this. Not a bit – this wasn't in the plan."

"He may not do it?" Sinéad offered. "She could rally round. The doctors said. These things – there can be setbacks and then she could rally."

"In a way that's more of a worry," I said. "At the moment, she's not in any fit state to make a decision for herself, let alone swallow pills or whatever." I felt my stomach turn at the very thought. "But if she rallies ... Jonathan said this latest scare could be enough for her to ask him to help her now."

"He must be beside himself."

"He looked haunted," I said, thinking of how tired he had looked as we had sat in the cafeteria and how he had held me so tightly afterwards in the hall and had cried in my arms.

I wanted to make it all better for him – but I knew I couldn't.

∽ *1965* ∾

Rosaleen's anger remained. It simmered away in the background. Áine couldn't help but feel she had hurt her mother greatly and yet she couldn't let go of Jack, nor he of

317

her. When it felt as though it would get too much she would hear Charlotte's strong voice whisper in her ear that she deserved to be happy, that Jack deserved to be happy, and she knew that her sister wouldn't mind that they had found comfort in one another. Still it stung when Rosaleen would give her one of her stern looks to keep her in line, when she would question where she was going and who she was seeing. She was a grown woman who had made almost every decision in her adult life to support her mother and her family. But she didn't want to upset her mother further – so she played the good daughter.

At least most of the time. When Jack came to Ireland, she made sure she saw him. She would tell her mother she was going out with friends and she would dress up with lightness in her heart at the thought of seeing the man she had fallen in love with. When she was with him, she could truly be herself. She felt every ounce of hurt, every ounce of self-doubt, every pang that she wasn't good enough or worthy enough, slip away. She felt loved, cherished and needed – and it was worth the sneaking around and the keeping her joy to herself between visits.

When he was gone, she threw herself into caring for the children. Jonathan became her shadow – a little friend who kept her company each day after school, who played in the garden while she worked, who read to her at night to show her how clever he was and who would always tell her he loved her.

Emma remained more guarded – and that perhaps, more than her mother's distaste, was what hurt the most. Áine had to remind herself, time and time again, that Emma was a child, one struggling to deal with her loss, but her niece clung to her grandmother and, if Áine was honest, the child also quickly perfected her grandmother's stern look.

As the months passed Rosaleen's hurt remained, but Áine started to suspect her mother was now content or resigned at the very least to ignoring that which she couldn't see. However, as the next summer rolled around, Áine felt her heart lurch at the thought of telling her mother she would be travelling with the children to Italy.

"It's not much to ask for yourself," Jack had told her on his last visit. "And the children are too young to travel alone in any case."

"But she is still hurt," Áine had said, holding his hand over the Formica table in the steam-filled coffee shop.

He sighed, lifted her hands to his mouth and kissed them gently. "She will always be hurt. We will always be hurt. Charlotte's death broke a piece of all of us that nothing will ever fix. But I love you, and I know what it is to lose love. I don't want to lose it again – nor should you."

Áine had nodded and, emboldened, she had gone home and sat her mother down in the living room and told her she would, as she had the year before, travel with the children to Italy.

Rosaleen had dropped her head to her hands, before looking up again. "I can't dissuade you?"

"No, Mother. I promise you, as long as you live, I'll be here for you. I'll not leave you. I'll help you raise the children and do everything I can for them. I will never stop caring for you – and I promise you that I will be the best daughter I can be. But I need him, Mother. And this, these moments, are the only thing I ask for myself. If I'm honest, I will do this with or without your blessing, but I love you so much and I would very much prefer to have your blessing."

"I can't give that now," Rosaleen had said, and Áine's heart had sunk. "But I will try. For now, I'll tolerate it. I'll hold my tongue. But, my darling girl, please remember there are two children involved. Children who are confused and who will be grieving for their mother for a long time. Tread carefully."

"I will, Mother," Áine said. "I promise."

And so it began, the long-distance relationship Áine would

turn to throughout her life to keep her warm on cold winter nights in Temple Muse.

She would know that each summer she would arrive in the villa and, while it would have aged some more, and Jack would have aged some more, she was finally free to be the woman she always wanted to be. They would spend their days looking after the children – and their nights together on the terrace, drinking wine and laughing until the pull of the bedroom they now shared became too much.

When the children grew, and Áine visited on her own – a new stage of her life began. A stage where she felt reborn. They would travel through Italy, or fly to a neighbouring country for a few days and in those days and weeks she would feel complete.

But she kept her promise to her mother – and Jack understood. As they grew older, and more set in their ways, they felt comfortable with their separate lives and their frequent visits where the real world was put on hold and they could love each other without judgement.

And so it continued – until the day Áine received the phone call that changed everything. That Jack, now in his sixties, had passed away peacefully in his sleep. The shock of his loss winded her – and she started to allow herself to live a little in the past. When she closed her eyes each night she replayed the memories that had made her life the unique experience it was. And she promised Jack she would see him again, and Charlotte, and her mother and her father and all those who had shaped her.

Present Day

"When can we visit her, Mam?" Eve asked over breakfast.

"I'm sure in a few days," I told my daughters. "When she is a little stronger. She gets tired easily and the hospital want to make sure she gets her rest."

"She will be okay though?" Sorcha asked, her eyes wide with concern.

What was I to say? Yes? No? Maybe? Or well, until she feels strong enough to take her own life?

"Girls, you know that Áine is getting older and her condition is progressing," I said. "The best we can do is hope she rallies – but none of us know. Not even the doctors and the experts. She may live for years, or she may not." I felt sick at the thought that she could leave us sooner rather than later.

I noticed Sorcha – tough-as-boots Sorcha – was crying and I sat down beside her and put my arm around her.

"I'm scared, Mum," she said.

I did all I could do at that time – pulled her close to me and admitted that I was scared too.

Chapter 37

Present Day

I was asleep, lost in a strange dream, when I became aware of my doorbell ringing. Struggling to get my brain to focus, I sat up and, blinking, looked at the clock. It wasn't long after 6 a.m. Rubbing my eyes, I climbed out of bed and put on my dressing gown. I could hear the girls stirring in their rooms, a shout from Eve that someone was at the door.

I padded downstairs and opened the front door to see Jonathan standing there, soaked by the fresh morning rain. He looked broken. He wore a wrinkled T-shirt and jeans and needed a shave. His eyes were red from exhaustion and emotion.

He could not speak and he did not move. He just looked at me, a pleading look in his eyes, and I knew. I knew she was gone. The pain on his face was so raw, it could be the only explanation.

"Georgina," he stuttered and fell towards me, pulling me into his arms.

"Oh Jonathan," I managed.

At that I heard a creak on the stairs and turned to see the

two girls, faces pale, taking in the sight in front of them.

"Mam!" Eve croaked as Jonathan pulled himself from me and turned to hide his face.

"Girls," I said, my voice shaking, "can you go into the kitchen and put on the kettle?"

"But, Mam ..." Sorcha said, her voice shaking.

"Sweetheart, get your dressing gown on, and go and put on the kettle. I'll be in in a minute." I tried to keep my voice as soft as possible.

The truth was that I couldn't bring myself to say the words. I couldn't bring myself to say that it was Áine. And from what I could tell, what I could feel in the very pit of my stomach, Áine was gone. The fact that this might well have been what she wanted gave me no comfort. She didn't need to go. Not yet. Not so soon.

Reluctantly and falteringly Sorcha turned and took her sister's hand – a gesture I hadn't seen in many years. The pair went back upstairs to get their dressing gowns. They were good girls and I knew they would do as I asked. They would come back downstairs, and they would put the kettle on and that would at least buy me some time to find out what exactly had happened. As I saw them disappear from view, I turned and ushered Jonathan into the living room and onto the sofa where I sat down beside him and held his hand. We sat there in silence for a while – it may have been thirty seconds, it may have been ten minutes – time had become fluid and its distortion mirrored the thoughts and feelings spinning through my head.

"You don't need to say the words," I said softly, breaking the silence, as I watched this tall, confident, handsome man crumpled and folded with grief in front of me.

I didn't want to ask but I had to. I had to hear him say it even though I didn't know how I would react to his answer.

"Did you help her?" I asked softly.

He looked at me, his eyes red with tiredness and pain. A

Claire Allan

look of pure wretchedness on his face, he shook his head slowly.

"She was alone. She slipped away all on her own."

I stood in front of the sink and mirror in our downstairs bathroom and splashed cold water on my face. I had left Jonathan as I needed to go and tell the girls, reluctant to leave him but aware of my daughters and the distress they were in. I needed some fresh air, a moment to gather myself together. After everything, a massive stroke had taken Áine overnight. It hadn't been her illness. She hadn't declined in the way she had feared. She had gone – in her sleep it seemed. No pain, they had told Jonathan. She just slipped away. It was what she would have wanted, they said. Peaceful and calm. It happens sometimes, they said. It could explain the headaches she was having before, they said. The extra confusion. Yes, she did have a kidney infection too – that may have masked what else was going on, they said. Nothing they could have done, they said.

I had tried to comfort Jonathan – to assure him that her passing peacefully was a good thing. That he wouldn't have to carry the burden of being part of her death with him for the rest of his life. I had told him of the conversations I'd had with Áine where she talked of her wish to just slip away. But all he could see was that she had been alone. Peaceful or not, she had been alone and he couldn't help but ask himself the questions he could never know the answer to. Was she scared? Had she been aware she was slipping away?

And more than all that – he never got to say goodbye. None of us got to say goodbye and it seemed so terribly, terribly unfair. We didn't get to tell her how we loved her. And we did. I loved her – she had become so much more than a client to me. She had become my friend, my confidante, the person who had brought Jonathan into my life – and I knew I would miss her more than I could imagine now.

I wiped the tears from my face and pinched my cheeks. I took several deep breaths and offered a silent prayer up that Áine was indeed at peace and that we would all find some peace ourselves from that.

And then I went to face my girls, pulling them into the biggest hug I could – telling them that the old woman they had shared their summer months with had gone. My heart broke again as I heard them cry – knowing that nothing I could say or do in that moment could make it any better and that we all just had to work through this. It was as simple as that.

Sinéad had hugged me as I left off the girls to her house. Jonathan had waited in the car and, when I climbed back in beside him, I squeezed his hand tightly.

"Are you ready?" I asked.

"I'm not sure I will ever be ready, but I have to see her," he said.

I nodded. "I'll be right beside you, if you want me to be," I told him. "Will Emma be there too?"

"Yes," he said. "She's on her way there now."

I thought how hard this must be for Emma – who had only a few days ago arrived to see Áine, not thinking for a second this would be her last opportunity to talk to her.

"It's just us now," he said. "Everyone else is gone. Our mother, father, our grandmother and now Áine. Stupid, isn't it? To feel like an orphan, at my age. I should expect to be an orphan."

"I don't think there's an age limit on missing your family," I said. "And I know I'm not family, but I'm here for you, Jonathan. I don't intend on going anywhere – not unless you want me to."

He squeezed my hand tighter and turned to look at me. "Promise me you won't," he said. "Because, Georgina Casey, I have fallen deeply in love with you."

I reached over and kissed him gently – yes, I had fallen very much in love with him too.

Emma was there when we arrived. She ran to her brother and they embraced. "I can't believe it," she said. "I should have come sooner. I should have spent more time with her."

"She understood," he soothed. "And I don't think all the time in the world would have been enough."

"I wasn't really angry with her – I just fell into a habit," Emma sobbed. "I felt I would be letting Mamma down, and Granny down if I let her in totally. But I loved her. She was a mother to us."

Jonathan nodded. "We were so young," he said. "We were only children. You were only a child, Emma. You need to forgive yourself. She wouldn't want you to feel like this. She loved you very much."

I wondered, listening in, if he would take his own words to heart. If he would forgive himself for not being there when she passed.

Wiping her tears from her face, Emma looked up and pulled me into their hug. "Thank you for being there for her, Georgina," she said. "I know how much you meant to her. I know how you helped her."

And it was my turn to dissolve into tears. The three of us made quite the sight, standing there in the hospital corridor, hanging onto each other, feeling our loss intensely.

"Do you want to see her?" a nurse asked. "I can assure you she looks peaceful. There is nothing at all to indicate she was in any distress. She even took a cup of tea and some toast last night, chatted a little with the nurses on duty. She seemed happy."

We were grateful for this knowledge. That she seemed happy. All I ever wanted was for her to be happy. I closed my eyes and thought of her sitting in the garden, sipping from a cup of tea, smiling in the sunshine, talking to Jonathan or the girls, planting flowers, telling me about Jack, or Charlotte or her mother. And then I took a deep breath and followed Emma and Jonathan through to the hospital room where she was lying, as if sleeping, in her bed, her hands folded.

I let Jonathan and Emma step forward, keeping my distance, dreading the moment when I would say my goodbyes. I listened to them tell their aunt how they loved her – and thank her for all she had done. I heard Jonathan say he wished he had been with her, holding her hand, when she left and I watched as his sister put her arms around him to comfort him.

When it was my turn I could barely find my words. I just looked at this lovely woman and thought of the life she had lived. She had been one in a million.

"Oh, Áine," I wept. "I will miss you, my friend. You rest well – and say hello to Charlotte and Jack for me." I kissed her on the forehead and sat down beside her and held her hand. Jonathan and Emma sat with me and we shared our stories until a nurse very gently told us that it was time to take Áine's remains to the morgue.

We walked out together into the early morning sunshine – floored that the world was continuing on as normal all around us.

"We'll have to make the arrangements," Jonathan said.

"Shall we go back to the house and get started?" Emma asked.

"Yes," Jonathan nodded. "Although you might not be surprised to know she left instructions. She wanted her way."

"That was Áine, through and through," I said, smiling.

"Come with us," Jonathan said.

"Yes, please," Emma said, smiling softly. "I do believe Áine was not the only person very fond of you. My brother here, he needs you too."

He squeezed my hand. "I do," he said and I nodded.

The house at Temple Muse felt strange. It felt odd to know

that it would never again hear Áine's voice. That the kitchen would not be the hive of a home where she cooked, and ate and read. That the living room would not ring to the sound of her shouting at the TV.

"It's a nice morning," I said. "Why don't we go out to the garden?"

"I just have to get something," Jonathan said, "but yes, the garden seems the perfect place, doesn't it?"

I helped Emma make some tea and toast and we carried it out to the garden and sat looking around, marvelling at how it had been transformed over the past few months. It had given Áine so much joy.

"I think we spent more time out here than we did in the house," Emma said. "No matter the season. There was always something she would have us doing, or some game she would have us playing. I think we created a hundred different imaginary worlds out here – I'm quite sure if I looked hard enough I would find a few of the dolls from my doll's house still hiding in the bushes – or the 'magic woods' as we called them. Our childhood was magical – for all the pain and the grief of losing our mother and not seeing our father that much. She made it magical."

"She was so proud of you," I said. "Don't ever think she felt anything other than the strongest love for you."

Emma nodded, wiping away a tear and sipping from her tea, just as Jonathan walked out to us carrying a folder.

"All her arrangements," he said. "Everything planned. She was meticulous."

He joined us at the table and we opened the folder to see that, not only had Áine put arrangements in place with a local undertaker, she had paid for it all. She had chosen everything, from the floral arrangements (wild flowers from her garden) to the readings and music – and she would be cremated, her ashes scattered between here and her beloved Italy where Jack was laid to rest with Charlotte.

Among the formalities we found an envelope addressed to 'My Family'.

Nervously Emma opened it, as Jonathan held my hand, and she read from the letter inside.

Dear Jonathan and Emma,

I write this having learned that I have dementia. It seems so cruel – to know I may forget the times we have shared. The love, the joy, the pain, all of it that made us who we are.

When I was young I didn't want much in life – I wanted only to find a man who loved me and to raise a family. Your mother would tease me that I didn't want enough – that I lacked her adventurous streak.

But, my darling children, life has been an adventure – one we could never have predicted. I found love, with your darling father. A love that in no way replaced the love he felt for your mother but which gave us comfort, companionship and many happy times.

I may not have carried or given birth to my own children, but I hope you don't mind that a part of me considers you both mine. Certainly I could not be more proud of either of you – and as long as this mind of mine will allow me I will cherish the memories of the years we spent together. I could not have loved either of you more if I had borne you myself. I may not always have got things right – but, my darlings, my intentions were pure.

I don't know how life will be for us now. I don't know what I will put you through as these months and years pass. I am not afraid to admit, my darlings, that I am scared. I hope that I do not reach the stage where you consider me a burden. I hope that no matter how this disease ravages me, you

329

remember the person I was. I may slip away, but I am still me.
And the person I am will hold on to the love I have for you
all as long as I can, in this world and the next.

God bless my darlings,
All my love, always,
Áine
xxx

Epilogue

∽ *Present Day* ∾

It was Christmas afternoon and we had just finished dinner. It was lovely to see Temple Muse brought so much to life again. We sat in the dining room, which Jonathan had repainted a light and airy colour, and I smiled as I listened to the chat around the table. Eve and Sorcha had been in remarkably good form – helpful and delighted with the presents Jonathan had bought them. It was lovely to spend time with Emma too – to learn more about her life, to feel a part of Jonathan's family. It had been a wonderfully relaxed afternoon and soon the girls would leave to go and stay with their father for the evening (where they were expecting to be spoiled further) and Emma had made plans to go and visit some old friends.

Jonathan and I would have the night together and I couldn't wait. Perhaps I was too old to really enjoy sleepovers, but Jonathan made them so interesting. I smiled to myself at the thought of some quality alone-time with him. Our relationship was still in its first flush and it felt wonderful.

As we cleared the table, I heard a shout from the kitchen. "Mum, Jonathan, come quick!" Sorcha shouted.

We hurried to the kitchen where she and Eve were pointing excitedly out the window.

"It's snowing!" Sorcha shouted.

"I didn't think any snow was forecast for today," Emma said.

"Well, that is definitely snow falling," Jonathan said, taking my hand and leading me to the back door.

We went into the garden, followed by Emma and the girls and we stood marvelling at the flurry of snow that was falling softly on Áine's precious garden.

As the soft fat flakes drifted through the sky, landing and settling on the ground around us, we looked at each other. I was the first to smile although I could also feel tears pricking the backs of my eyes – and Jonathan and Emma followed.

"A message from heaven," Emma whispered.

"She's okay," Jonathan said. "She's happy."

I closed my eyes and let the snow settle on my face. "She's happy," I whispered. "And she's still with us. She always will be."

THE END

A note on this book

"No one understands dementia until it comes to their door," – those were the words spoken to me by Michael McIvor, at the time a support worker for the Alzheimer's Society in Foyle.

He was right, of course, but I already knew what it meant to have experience of Alzheimer's. For more than a decade my own grandmother has been fighting a battle with this cruellest of diseases.

I could list you the many things which hurt about Alzheimer's – the difficulties we have faced as a family. The sacrifices her children have made, and continue to make. Their pain – my father's pain – is rawer than mine can ever be.

I could tell you that it has been eight years since she knew who I was. I remember very vividly the first time she stared at me blankly. It was the day of my sister's wedding – a day of great celebration – and she asked me who I was. It also happened to be the exact same day my first novel was published and had soared into the top ten. She would have been so proud, had she known.

I could tell you, by the time my daughter was born six years ago, she was barely able to acknowledge that her latest great-grandchild had been put in her arms. She certainly didn't know the relationship they shared, or that my daughter's middle name was Anna – her own name.

But what has happened over the last ten years doesn't define my grandmother. I still remember the fiercely stern woman – the bad cop to my grandad's good cop – who could quiet us with a look. But her exterior was all bluff because it was Granny who would unlock the special biscuit cupboard and treat us to a chocolate digestive when we visited. It was Granny would slip 10p into our hands to buy sweets with. It was granny who made the hottest and strongest cup of tea known to man and Granny who loved my grandfather which such fierce love it winded me.

One of our last lucid conversations was just before I became a mother for the first time – when this devoutly religious woman pressed a prayer card into my hand to take into the labour ward with me. I'm not overly religious but I prayed through my labour using that card to give me strength – feeling the strength of generations past.

In telling Áine's story, I wanted to give a voice to people like my grandmother who led full and productive lives before Alzheimer's robbed them of what they should have had left.

I wanted to show that, along with their new status as a dementia patient, they are still themselves.

You don't understand dementia until it comes to your door – but I hope this book helps explain it a little.

If you enjoyed
Still You by Claire Allan,
why not try an exclusive chapter of a previous title
The First Time I Said Goodbye
also published by Poolbeg.

The First Time
I Said Goodbye

Claire Allan

Chapter 1

It wasn't that I didn't want to go. I did. I wanted to go with all my heart but I suppose in many ways I was a coward in the end. It was too much. There isn't a day that has passed where I haven't missed you.

* * *

Meadow Falls, Florida, USA, May 2010

It seemed only right that it was raining. It would have been wrong if it had been anything but. You can't bury someone on a sunny day. I couldn't have buried him on a day when the sun was splitting the stones and the sprinklers were dancing around the lawns and when the Southern Belles were out in force, fanning themselves and thinking about getting back to the wake for an iced tea on the porch. Black on a sunny day wouldn't have been at all comfortable. Not that the shift dress I wore was comfortable anyway. It was starchy, stiff, far removed from the comfortable clothes I usually slouched around in. "It suits you," my mother said when I walked into the church. She was already sitting in the front pew, her hands crossed, her gaze fixed firmly ahead, her eyes hidden behind her sunglasses. She glanced at me only briefly as she told me I looked nice, and I sat beside her and reached for her hand. Now was not the time to brush off her compliment – to tell her I was afraid the dress might choke me or split at the seams. She had enough worries without me adding to them. I stared ahead too, trying to fix my gaze on whatever she was looking at, and squeezed her hand. She didn't squeeze back, but she didn't shrug me off either.

We sat there, together, awaiting the big arrival. Waiting for my father to make his final journey into the church – neither of us being able to face walking in behind him, having people gawp at us in our grief, nudge each other at our tears, give us that pitying 'poor them' look. No, we had walked in separately, ahead of the congregation, and fixed our eyes forward, barely touching, and I tried not to breathe out. I heard the door of the church open, the footsteps of our fellow mourners, and I felt my mother breathe in – and as she exhaled there was a small shudder which revealed to me just how she was feeling. I squeezed her hand a little again as the music started to play – wanting to make it better for her – and wanting to make it better for myself, and I thanked God it was raining, because it would have been wrong to bury him on a sunny day.

It would have felt all out of sorts, as if the world was spinning off its axis, to have had the sun smiling on us when inside there was a small part of me screaming as if I was still six years old and the only person who could make it better was my daddy – the daddy who was never coming back.

* * *

Craig's arm slipped around my waist. I instinctively breathed in, away from him, and I tensed as I felt his hand take mine. He cuddled up closer to me, asking softly if I was awake. Yes. I was awake. I didn't answer. I didn't want to talk. I don't think I had actually slept. Maybe I had. I vaguely recalled Liam Neeson walking into our room at three in the morning, so probably it was fair to say I had drifted off. The rest of the time, however, I had just lain there, looking at the red light on the clock, watching the numbers slowly changing. My father had been gone four days. I wondered when I would stop thinking of it in terms of days, in terms of weeks, in terms of time passing, and just think of him as gone. Maybe I never would. Maybe now I just had another day to mark – another day to count from. It was one day since his funeral. One day since I had stood at his graveside and willed my heart not to shatter as they lowered him into the ground. I was a grown woman. I was thirty-seven. Now was not the time to scream for "Daddy". My mother had stood stoically. I'm not sure if she cried – she didn't sniff. I didn't notice a dabbing of eyes but I noticed her squeeze my hand a little tighter as we were invited forward to toss some soil into the grave on top of his casket. I hated that part. Even though I could feel the almost overpowering, claustrophobic warmth of Craig behind me, I had shuddered there in the clammy warmth of the graveyard. My mother had been led away by her friend Louisa, while I stood there and stared, entranced by the hole in the ground.

"We should go," Craig had said and I'd glanced up to see we were all but alone in the cemetery, the majority of mourners having clambered into their cars and the waiting limos to be ferried back to the golf club for lunch.

I was shivering in the rain – my neck cold as the drops slid down my back. They weren't cold. I knew they could not be and yet they felt like ice. I felt like ice.

"I don't want to leave him," I muttered.

"Then stay here as long as you need," he said softly and he let me stand there until I was shivering so hard that my teeth were chattering. I felt . . . I felt confused. Broken. Torn.

"We'll get you warm, we'll get you changed and then we'll go on to Green Acres," he said softly, leading me away, and in a haze of pain and grief I'm almost ashamed to admit that my only thought was that I didn't own a single other thing in black and I would look like an insensitive heel at my own father's wake.

I found the next most suitable thing I owned – a soft grey cashmere dress – and I quickly showered, put on some fresh make-up and tousled my short blonde hair, grateful I didn't have a look that required more work, before breathing deeply and telling Craig we were good to go again.

"You're doing well," he said. "You're getting through this."

I smiled – a weak, watery smile – gratefully clinging on to

whatever hint of reassurance I could find, regardless of where it came from.

"No choice but to keep on going," I said. "Time to go and mingle with the mourners, I suppose. To listen to them all tell me how he has gone to a better place, and isn't in pain any more and how he was a good man."

"He *was* a good man."

"I know. And I know folks mean well . . . but . . . you know . . ." I said, drifting off. Platitudes wouldn't make it better – no matter how well intentioned.

* * *

My mother had taken off her sunglasses by the time I arrived at Green Acres. She was sitting in a circle of friends, smiling and nodding. I was sure she was listening to the platitudes and being my mother – ever polite and afraid to offend – she was smiling at them. Part of me wanted to run over and tell her she didn't have to do that – but she would have killed me stone dead if I had made a scene. She would have glared at me, her lilting Irish accent which remained despite her many years away from home ringing in my ears: 'Don't you make a holy show of me or yourself, Annabel.' So I nodded in her general direction and set about fixing my own weak smile on and promising myself that I would not make a show of myself – not one bit. And I didn't. I behaved myself right until the very moment when the last guest went home and then I drank three glasses of wine straight, cried all over my mother who ended up soothing me as if she herself wasn't hurting, and had to have Craig tuck me into bed where I spent the following ten hours watching the clock flicker and change.

"We could go for a drive today," he said, in the half light. "Get out of here – clear our heads."

"I need to go and help my mom," I said. "I was pathetic yesterday. I need to be there for her."

"You've been at her side for weeks, Annabel. You need a

break. You will burn out – if you haven't already." His tone had veered from concerned to snippy.

My own mood changed just as quickly. "I've been at her side for weeks, so I can't just leave her now," I said, turning to face him. "He's gone. I can't just leave her in limbo now and clear off because the nasty business of the funeral is done with. She's spent her last few months caring for him. What in hell is she supposed to do now that she doesn't have that any more?"

Of course, I knew as I spoke that it was me that I was worried about – that without having to run to the hospital, pace the wards, feed my father softened food gently, hold his hand and read to him that I might be the one to fall apart. That I would have to finally accept this loss – and deal with everything else I had put on the back burner while I devoted my life to caring for the wonderful man who had always made me feel important.

My mother? Of course I worried about her too. She seemed calm – too calm – and that unnerved me. Then again everything unnerved me at the moment.

"She might want some space?" Craig offered and I shrugged his arm, which suddenly felt too heavy, away from me. "*We* might need some space from all this?"

"Not now, Craig," I said, sitting up and grabbing my robe from where I had thrown it on the floor.

He rolled back away from me. I knew without looking at him that he would be crestfallen – just as I knew I was pushing him away. But grief does funny things and I kind of wished it was socially acceptable to walk around wearing a T-shirt that said "*I'm grieving. Allow me to be a bit mad*" on it, because then I wouldn't have to try and make people understand. Surely they should know just how raw and horrible this felt? Surely they had all been there?

* * *

My mother sat on her bed, folding clothes and putting them into bin bags. T-shirts he barely wore, chinos that had become baggy and loose on him over the last few months.

"I'm packing them up," she said as I walked in, pushing her hair off her face and curling it behind her left ear.

"You don't have to do that now," I said.

"I know. But it has to be done sometime."

"But not now, Mom," I said. "You don't have to do it now."

"Annabel, pet, I know this is awful but I've been living with it for a long time. I knew this day would come. I was ready for it – sort of."

I didn't understand that, how she could be ready for it. Sure we had all known this wasn't going to end well but that didn't mean I didn't feel every shred of breath leave my body in the moment the breath had left his.

"I was there for him, Annabel. I was there and loyal and I loved him, right to the end. I always will love him but he's gone and, sweetheart, he's not coming back. So I need to move on."

She spoke so calmly that I felt the room swim a little. It was almost as if she were talking about paying the bills, or doing the grocery shopping. Something which might as well be done now. Not something that had ripped our lives apart. I rested my hand on the chair by her dressing table and looked at her again.

"I want to go home to Ireland," she said, folding his shirt – his checked shirt, the one he had worn when we went to the coast and walked along the beach. I had teased him for ogling the young, surgically modified women in their bikinis and he had told me he only had eyes for my mother. I looked at it: empty, folded, slipped into a bag. "And I'd love you to come with me."

I looked at her as if she were mad. She *was* mad. Maybe she needed the "*Grief makes you do funny things*" T as well?

"Don't look at me like that, Annabel," she said, lifting another shirt, folding it and placing it in the box marked for Goodwill.

Feeling churlish, I reached in past her and took it back out again, holding it tight in my arms, trying to get some hint of him back. All I could smell was her detergent and fabric softener – not a hint of coffee or musky aftershave. Not a hint of my dad.

"You want to go back to Ireland? And you want me to go with you?"

"It's not that hard to take in, is it?" my mother said, her face set in a way that let me know she was very much determined to go ahead with her plans – with or without me.

"But, Mom, you have a life here. I have a life here. I have the bakery. I have Craig. We have this house – your friends, your colleagues, your life." I was clutching at straws, of course. Straws of what I had, before. What I had before he was sick. When everything changed. What I really wanted to say of course was that I could not even begin to imagine how *she* could want to walk away from our home and our life, even though there was a part of me which wanted to walk away from my own life. I knew she was grieving but . . . I felt something constrict in my throat.

"Who said anything about walking away? I just want to visit. It's been a long time. I need to get away, don't you understand that? Everything has been on hold for so long . . . Everything has been so hard. Illness and death. Even this damn house – it doesn't smell like home any more. It smells of antiseptic and illness and the perfume of strangers come to pay their last respects. I just want to go home again. I'd love you to come with me – to see Ireland. Didn't we always talk about going? When you were small? Wouldn't it give us both a lift?"